TRACI E. HALL

Beauty's Curse

PRESS

Medallion Press, Inc.
Printed in USA

TRACI E. HALL

Beauty's Curse

DEDICATION:

For Greg, as always!

Published 2009 by Medallion Press, Inc.

The MEDALLION PRESS LOGO
is a registered trademark of Medallion Press, Inc.

Typeset in Adobe Garamond Pro
Printed in the United States of America

ISBN: 978-1-93-383656-0

10 9 8 7 6 5 4 3 2 1
First Edition

ACKNOWLEDGEMENTS:

This book couldn't have been written without Greg, Sheryl, Paul, Olga and the tiki bar. As usual, I need to thank Brighton and Destini for raising themselves while I write, and even bringing me Diet Cokes. My Babes! Thanks for helping me sort out plots, and Kerry, who listened when I whined. Trena, thanks for the last minute reads. It's been a tough two years, and I appreciate everyone for their generous and loving support. I am blessed!

Mushy stuff aside, I'd be nowhere without the internet. Research for this project has been immense. Wikipedia.com has been a great resource, as has catholicsaints.com, brittania.com, berkshirehistory.com and many others – thank you! Research books – King John, by W.L. Warren, Life in a Medieval Castle, Life in a Medieval Village, both by Frances and Joseph Gies. The Medieval Castle, by Philip Warner. The Medieval Warrior by Paul LaCroix, and Walter Clifford Meller.

This is a work of FICTION, although I've tried to stay true to historical facts. All mistakes are my own.

Chapter One

Montehue Manor
February 1193

"It's beautiful," Galiana Montehue whispered as she ran out into the winter-dead flower garden. The English countryside was blanketed in pure white; a new beginning. She stretched out her arms, twirling like a sprite, as the soft flakes of snow melted on her nose and cheeks. Air plumed from her mouth as she laughed aloud, spinning round until she was so dizzy she fell back into a drift of snow as soft as her feather mattress.

"Bless Mother, Father, Gram, and Ela. God speed them on their journey," she said, sticking her tongue out to catch the big, fluffy flakes as they fell from the gray sky. "Celestia and Nicholas, too, and the babe." For the tiniest of seconds, she regretted not being at her sister's side for the birth of her first child.

She'd sent a basket of Tia's favorite lotions and some

cream for the baby's skin, but Galiana hadn't wanted to go. Nay, she'd bartered for the chance to stay home and be the lady of the manor. Laughing again at the absurdity of it, her parents had not only agreed to let her take on the chore of running the household, but they'd added her twin brothers to her list of responsibilities. Of course, they'd also left eight seasoned Montehue knights, Bailiff Morton, and the live-in manor staff. They trusted her and weren't treating her like she was just a pretty face. And it had snowed the first snow of the year on the first morn after they were gone.

She sighed happily, thinking this to be an auspicious start to the day, as if the angels had come overnight and frosted the bare tree branches with crystals. She should paint it, she thought, sketching the scene in her mind.

Just last week she'd lit twenty scented candles to Saint Jude, who she'd adopted as her own since he championed hopeless causes, so that the path to a grand adventure would be made clear to her. "This has to mean something," she told the clouds above her.

"Talking to yourself again, Gali?" The voice that asked held a slight squeak that made her smile. A masculine voice, on the verge of becoming a man's.

"Ye've gone insane. One too many sliced cucumbers to the eye," a similar voice teased.

"Your gown is soaked. Come in before you catch your death," Ned, the older twin by five minutes, instructed as if his sister had truly gone around the bend.

2

"Have you been in the cherry wine?"

"With Gram and Ela both away, if you sicken, it will be old Dame Bertha to see to your compresses. She makes them too hot, and they burn. Come in. The hall is warm, and cook's made porridge with honey." Ed's tone was much more coaxing, and Galiana knew without looking at them that they would be standing, mirrored opposites, arms crossed in front of their chests like the men they would grow to be.

Just twelve, they were not men yet, although they would be soon enough, and Galiana felt the sudden urge to stop time. Squires for their brother-in-law, Nicholas Le Blanc, the twins had come home for the Christmas season. They had been underfoot for all of five days before Mother had one of her intuitions and the family was off across England to Celestia's aid. Poor Celestia.

"Were you two scoundrels following me?" Tilting her chin to the right, she glanced down her nose at them, even though she was lying back and they were standing over her. She'd practiced that look enough to know it had power.

Ned, a lock of blond hair falling over one blue eye, dropped his crossed arms to his sides. "Scoundrels? If Nicholas would permit us, we'd be off on crusade."

Ed, not to be outdone, lifted one arm high in the air. "For King Richard!"

Realizing her morning of joyous fantasy was shattered, Galiana struggled to her feet. Ned pulled her up and immediately dropped her hand. "Ye're soaked through," he said with a chastising shake of his head. "And chilled."

"What would Mam say?" Ed raised one blond brow.

Until now, she hadn't noticed the cold. "When did you two monkeys become so bossy? Hmm? Mother is not here, I will not sicken, and you could not go on crusade if Nicholas made you both knights tomorrow. King Richard has been captured by the German Emperor, and he's being held for ransom."

Ned's brows drew together, and he asked, "For certes? He is not dead, then? Father never believed it."

Galiana nodded. "Father Jonah just told me last night. If you two wouldn't have run off after evening prayers, you would have heard the whole story." Not that she could blame them. The older Father Jonah got, the less he seemed to remember. A simple sermon could take a very long time.

"We had to work on our shields," Ned said.

"I knew that sodding minstrel was lying!"

"Edward," Galiana gasped. "That is no way to speak." She turned, hiding an indulgent smile. "Even if it is true." The minstrel Eiredale was as infamous for his stories as he was for his singing. Desperate for entertainment, Galiana and her family ignored the fact that the bard was firmly in Prince John's pocket—and that he couldn't sing.

"My apologies," Ed said with a mock courtly bow.

"Is no one serious in this family?" Ned complained.

4

"At least you, Galiana, should understand the importance of this situation. If King Richard is being held for ransom, then surely the Old Queen Eleanor will pay it, and our king will finally come home. 'Tis better than going on crusade. We could be squires at court."

"Are ye calling me an imbecile? I knew that was important," Ed glared at his twin, with mutiny in his green eyes.

"I never called ye stupid, but if you feel that way . . ." Ned curled his fists.

"No fighting. Just because I'm in charge doesn't mean that you can get into trouble." Galiana held out her hand, absently watching a snowflake melt on her palm. "Has Bailiff Morton given you your chores yet today? Father said the stables will need cleaning and you both are to help. He doesn't want you getting lazy," she said with a straight face. The truth was, the twins had more energy than a litter of puppies, and shoveling out stalls was a good way to keep them from burning down the barn. Again.

"I still think Father should have left us in charge," Ned lifted his chin, as Galiana had done. "Look at you, out worrying in the snow. You are just a woman."

"Just a woman?" Galiana glared at her brother. "Have you been away so long that you don't remember I can thrash you?" She took a step so she was eye to eye with him. Another inch, and he'd be taller than she, Galiana realized with a pang.

"I was a lad. Besides, I let you win," Ned grinned fiendishly.

"Oh?" Galiana's first reaction was dismay that her brothers could be so shallow. Just a woman? They'd spent the past year with Celestia and Nicholas, so where had they gotten such an idea? Her second was to argue some sense into Ned's stubborn head. "You know perfectly well that in this family, women are not chattel. We are strong, warriors even."

Ed snickered, and it dawned on Galiana that she'd been teased. She bit her tongue instead of lashing them with it, since she'd been such an easy target. Brats.

"You two have quite a talent for knowing when I'm brooding." Most noble families sent their children away to be raised in other households; the girls went to the house of their betrothed, if it was possible. Her parents never saw the need, since their daughters could choose husbands for themselves. After Baron Peregrine's betrayal, her father had petitioned King Richard, now his direct liege, and received a written dispensation honoring the Montehue's unusual rights.

Ned put his arm around her shoulders. "You worry too much, and usually about marriage."

"You should let me and Ned pick your husband." Ed exchanged a devilish look with his twin.

"No," Galiana laughed. "I can imagine who you would choose, and it makes me shudder."

She'd been raised on stories of love, seeing her

parents' happy marriage and even Celestia had found wedded bliss. Was it any wonder there was a foolish part of her that wanted to feel love too? But she remained permanently disappointed.

For reasons she didn't understand, most men couldn't see past her beauty. She could endure only so many bad poems regarding her bright eyes and porcelain skin without vomiting.

Chivalry and courtly ideas were turning real men into girls.

"You're a grown woman now," Ed pointed out, getting to the very heart of Galiana's dilemma.

"You'll have to choose eventually. Or let Father; he would find you someone rich." Ned rubbed his hands together.

With her family's new status, they required more knights. And more knights cost more money, and taxes kept getting higher. By marrying a wealthy man, she could be a help to her family instead of a burden. Her only asset was her face. She'd been trained to be the ultimate lady, and all "ladies" were good for was making a prosperous marriage. It was time. She knew it, as did her parents, though they were too loving to toss her out to the village streets.

Like her mother, Galiana did not have any magical ability. Her grandmother, Evianne, had the gift, as did Celestia, and even Ela, the youngest at ten, could see auras.

The only assets she had were her talent with perfumes,

her skill at the lute, and white teeth. Which put her two steps above her father's prized mare. "What would you say if I told you I did not want to grow up?"

"It's too late," Ed laughed, and Ned slapped him on the back.

"Aye, I know." Unsettled, Galiana slowly danced in a circle around the garden, wondering if she would feel better putting her feelings to music. A snowflake drifted down, and then another. The hills in the distance were white and peaked like meringue. Which note would describe how the first winter snow covered the dreary past with a bright, unmarred finish? Maybe music was the wrong element. She stroked the air with an imaginary brush. She was a canvas unpainted. Or a stretch of linen unembroidered; an unwoven tapestry that, with the right care, would be discovered in all its glory come spring.

"Galiana, stop daydreaming, and come inside. We're freezing." Ed spoke, but both boys rubbed their arms and stomped their feet.

Pragmatic, Ned said, "I don't understand why you are so upset. Ye're a lady, and you can't go back to being a child."

The first snow was hope. And her brothers were ruining it.

"You're right." She bent down to scoop up a handful of snow with reddened, cold fingers. "I do not wish to spend my days in a convent. Nor do I wish to live with Aunt Nan in Wales. Nor to marry a complete boor.

Why should those be my only choices?"

"Lord Fendleton isn't a boor; he's got sheep." Ed looked to Ned, who confirmed the information.

She clasped the snow in her fist, watching it drip to the ground as she squeezed.

"And if you wed Baron Von Linsing, you could be a baroness; you're pretty enough for that. Right, Ned?"

"Prettier even. I saw a painting of a baroness once, and she had five chins and loads of gold chains and giant jewels."

"To hold up the chins," Ed said.

Galiana giggled. It was difficult to be irritated at the twins when they were bent on being amusing. She shivered, thinking her heart was as cold as the snow around her. What did it matter who she married, if she didn't care? "I don't want to marry, but I will."

"Lots of girls marry people they don't know." Ned covered his face with his hands for warmth.

"Our family is special." And the family was special—except for her. Even her mother had strong intuition. "I need to go to court."

"Can we come?" Ed stopped slapping at his arms and tucked his hands underneath his armpits.

"Father will never agree, for Mam doesn't approve of court."

"Ned, if it is a chance to get me off of their hands, they might do it. I cannot live here until I die of old age."

"We better leave tomorrow then," Ed joked.

"Hey," Galiana reached down and scooped up a handful of snow, then tossed it in Ed's face. It immediately shut him up, and he looked comical with snowflakes stuck to his lashes. "Be nice."

"This is war, Gali," Ed said, his green eyes bright.

Ned, caught between childhood and maturity, just stood there. Galiana grabbed another wad of fluffy snow and got him, too.

Then she ran as if the devil was after her.

Laughing, they raced behind trees and hedges, and for once the twins were not on the same side. It was every man for himself. A good shot, Galiana gave much better than she got. She was going to pay for this with chapped lips and the sniffles, but it was worth it. A hot scented bath, and lavender lotion for her skin—a warm brandy—and she'd be as good as new. Galiana was glad her mother was not here to stop the fun.

She lobbed a snowball that got Ed in the center of his chest. He brushed the remnants of snow from his soaking tunic, and Galiana's conscience urged her to go inside before they all ended up with the cough. Raising her hands, she laughed and said, "I surrender. Your hair looks brown; it's so wet. Come, let's go inside and have hot tea with honey."

"What happened to not wanting to grow up?" Ed demanded, his lips quivering.

"If we don't go in, none of us will," Galiana teased.

The boys exchanged one of their twin eye-contact

messages, and the next thing she knew they'd each grabbed up a fistful of snow and yelled together, "Charge! For God and King Richard!"

It took her a snowball to the nose to realize they meant a skirmish to the death. "I'm a lady," she protested with a yelp.

"You're just our sister," Ed shouted.

Her frozen toes made it hard to run, but she did. Ed cut off her route to the kitchen door, so she had no choice but to head for the trees. The snow, which moments ago had been falling in lazy drifts, now came down with a vengeance. She brushed back escaping wet tendrils of hair, while her long braids smacked against her back like a stinging lash.

Galiana pushed for the line of pine trees, glancing over her shoulder to see Ed facedown in the snow. Ned, laughing hysterically, was gaining on her.

Each step was like running upstream, until she reached the canopy of fir trees. They provided a natural covering that kept the inside of the forest remarkably free of all but a dusting of snow. Pine needles cushioned her soaking toes, and the dye from her silk embroidered slippers left a rainbow colored trail.

"Saint Jude, help me. Ned will find me for certes." Pausing, she listened for the sound of Ned or Ed, but the area around her was eerily silent. Not even a squirrel chittered.

She gulped, her breath coming faster and faster as

she realized how dark the inside of the forest was. How had she come so far inside without realizing it? Charcoal gray light filtered through the branches, and every ghost story her sister Celestia had ever told came to mind.

Of Welsh descent, Galiana believed in spirits. Knew as sure as she knew her own name that magic was real and that the world was more than what one could see.

A chill traced up her spine, and she shivered with premonition. But such was her luck that while she might be able to tell something was amiss, she couldn't say what it was. Nay, her gifts were music, poetry, and perfume. Useless, all of it.

She eyed a dark rock protruding from the snow-dusted earth beneath the trees and quickly dropped to her knees, scraping the would-be weapon free with her fingers. Galiana knew better than to come to the forest alone. What if both of her brothers had turned back? Spooked, she listened for them so hard that the loud snap of a branch cracking almost made her scream. Covering her mouth with her left hand, she grasped the sharp, pointed rock with her right. "Ed?" Her whisper sounded loud in the eerie quiet. "Ned?"

Without any supernatural gifts, she at least could hit the center of an archery circle every time. Scrambling behind a grouping of trees, Galiana's red hair was wet and brownish, helping her blend in with the tree trunks.

Someone on horseback was coming along the path. From the reverberating thud of hooves, she concluded it was more than one someone.

Whoever was traveling through the land behind Montehue Manor might just be lost. They were certain to have a good reason for being on the only back road leading to her home.

She'd been foolish to come here. Just a few days past, a woman had gone missing from the village. These were turbulent times, when even during the winter months men warred instead of rested. The ground beneath her soaked slippers shook as if a hundred horses galloped through the woods. Not that it was possible; a thin walking trail led through the trees toward the stream. There was not room for horses even two abreast, no matter how loud it sounded.

Her hand tightened on the rock as she hunched farther down behind the tree.

A soft robin's whistle drew her attention away from the direction of the hooves. How far away were they? Her teeth chattered with cold. Galiana berated herself. She certainly had acted a child today. If anything happened to the boys, it would be all her fault. The bird sang a louder note.

Not a robin. A blackbird? They usually didn't start cawing until spring. Her brothers had taught her more than she'd ever wanted to know about birdcalls.

"Ned?" Galiana whispered. "Ed?"

The whistle came again.

"Ned." Guilty relief washed over her as she realized

13

she wouldn't be alone. But danger still hovered in the air as the horses came closer. "Over here," she said. "There is room for us both."

Ned's wet head peeped from behind a large rock, a stone as big as a haystack. The hooves' rhythmic thumping made her heart race. They were coming closer. Faster. He wouldn't have time. She held up her hand, shaking her head and motioning for Ned to stay where he was.

Galiana dropped to her knees behind the brown trunk of the fir tree, closing her eyes as if that would make her invisible. She knew what could happen to a woman in the woods found by rogue groups of battle-hardened men. Sometimes the battered women came to the manor for aid, but more often than not, they hid their shame.

Please go away; please go away—to where? She lifted her head. The only place this tiny path led to was behind the manor. Either whoever was coming was bent on making mischief within the forest, or they'd made a wrong turn on their way to Scrappington.

Visitors would come through the front gate. High walls that could keep out an army did not yet surround Montehue Manor, at the very edge of the north quadrant of the village. With his station newly raised, her father had plans to hire more knights and build taller, thicker walls, but for now it was just the small group of men who guarded the boundaries.

That small group had been halved. Eight were providing her family safe travel to Falcon Keep, and eight had been left here to do their duty.

She pressed her hand to her chest, as if that would calm her rapidly beating heart. Crawling beneath the branches, she hugged the trunk, praying she was concealed from view. "Saint Agnes, if you help me now, I promise to marry and be a good, virtuous daughter." Hastily making the sign of the cross to end the prayer, she poked her head out to see.

Around the curve of the trail came the largest, blackest stallion she'd ever seen in her entire life. The eyes glowed red, and foamy spittle covered its lips, which were peeled back to bare yellowish teeth. She was shocked to find that such a stallion would even allow a rider, especially one as large and menacing as the one he carried. Covered from neck to toe in shiny dark mail, the knight held the reins loosely in one gloved hand while holding his sword hilt in the other. The blade pointed out as if the knight was after an enemy.

God help whoever was in his way.

She turned.

Ned's eyes were as wide and blue as bachelor buttons. Galiana could see he was stunned by the size and force of the knight bearing down on him as he stood frozen in the stallion's path. He held a branch in his hand as if to block the sword's deadly blow.

Without a thought, Galiana jumped from her hiding

place, getting a hoof-full of dirt in her hair as she followed the stallion. "Ned!" she screamed loudly, hoping to get his attention so that he would jump out of the way.

The stallion kept running, and Ned remained still. Before realizing what she was doing, she saw the rock she'd held so tightly in her hand sailing across the air with deadly accuracy.

It hit the only uncovered spot on the knight's body: the back of his head, directly behind his left ear.

The stallion raced on, not realizing that his master was falling backward. The clank of the sword dropping on a rock as it fell from the knight's fingers brought Ned around just in time to avoid being trampled. He leapt to the side, the horse's metal stirrups slicing across his shoulder as the stallion passed by.

The pounding hooves of more men on horses drowned Ned's scream of pain. Galiana knelt, mesmerized by the sight of blood flowing from beneath the knight's helmet. Then she was thrown to the ground, her arms wrenched behind her back.

"Bitch! What have ye done? If ye've killed him, I'll see ye hanged meself."

Rourke Wallis came to, roused from the oddest dream imaginable by the annoying sound of a lute. He had nothing against the stringed instrument usually, but his head ached and his leg hurt. In his sleep, it seemed he'd been searching the entire forest for a stable boy who'd tried to steal his pack.

The pack carried valuable papers, and if he didn't get it back, all would be lost. But then the dream changed, and the pack carried the Breath of Merlin, recently stolen from King William's treasury. Rourke's charmed life would not be worth half a pence if anybody knew he was sworn to find it and return it to Scotland.

Time was of the essence, and he urged his stallion faster, although as was the way of dreams, he couldn't go fast enough. Spotting his prey, a blond boy with huge eyes, he drew his sword when he heard from behind a feminine voice, as smoky and rich as a cask of Scottish whiskey. He'd turned to find her, but she was gone. Changed into a pine tree. Bloody damn it all. One minute things were clear, and the next all was shrouded in a mist so thick he couldn't find his arse in it.

Awake now, he realized he still couldn't see and it had nothing to do with the damnable mist. After attempting to lift his hands to rub the sleep from his eyes three times in a row, he concluded that his hands were tied. He was lying down on his back, bound and blind.

"Jamie," he bellowed with all his might. It came out as a croaking whine. The light strumming stopped, and that deep whiskey voice said, "Calm yourself, sir, before you cause more injuries."

"What happened?" Christ's bones, what had happened?

17

He couldn't complete his assignment if he was lying in bed like a whining sissy. He blinked again, and the scrape of his lashes against cloth only annoyed him further. "Why have you blindfolded me? Never mind; get it off."

"I——"

"Release me. I demand it." His blood surged as he quickly calculated the consequences of his captivity. He could be ransomed, unless whoever held him knew he was a master spy. Then nothing but torture and death loomed. "Bring me my knights, and get my hands bloody well untied."

He waited for his orders to be followed.

And waited.

The door slammed, and the scent of lemon and lavender lingered in the room. Rourke was alone.

His calf was on fire, and it felt like someone was sticking a hot poker in his eye. "Jamie! To me." He refused to give up. Knowing there was not one good reason—as if any reason would be good—he could be kidnapped and bound, he yelled until his voice was hoarse and his head pounded so hard he almost lost consciousness.

Finally, he heard muffled boot steps, then the creaking noise of leather hinges as a wooden door was opened. Boots . . . Jamie, coming down a set of wooden stairs. He strained his ears as if that would help him hear.

"Rourke, yer awake, man. We thought you dead."

"I feel dead. Untie me."

"You heard him, lass, untie him."

That smoky voice wavered, then said, "No."

Rourke gathered the last of his strength and yelled, "No?"

Spent, Rourke concentrated on her words, pinpointing each noise she made. Her footsteps were so light that if it weren't for the fact he was concentrating, which contributed, no doubt, to his damn headache, he never would have heard them. She walked like a lady. The press of her cool fingers against his forehead was an unexpected balm to his hot skin.

"I cannot untie his hands. He is a strong man."

Rourke puffed with pride, and even that hurt.

"But in pain, and more than likely stubborn. He'll not keep the bandages around his eyes. He may cause himself permanent damage."

His pride burst. Yes, he felt as if he'd been trampled, and, aye, he was stubborn. But no mere woman was going to tell him what to do.

"It's a risk I'll take."

There was a tiny voice inside his head that warned of disaster, but he didn't listen to it either.

"Mayhap."

"Do you understand, lass, who yer talking to?" Jamie's tone left no room for rebuttal, and, once again, Rourke found himself indebted to his foster brother.

Of dubious Scottish birth, both had been raised at

Eleanor's court. Told to learn and become rich, to over-come their bastard status and make men of themselves, men who could be both Scottish as well as English. Which had made sense until King Richard had sold King William Scotland for the price of a crusade.

Both knights had returned to Scotland to swear their loyalties to their newly reinstated king. Neither had been welcomed. To the public eye, they were hardly a step above mercenaries.

Rourke heard the hitch in the lady's voice before she said, "Nay, Sir Jamie, I do not know who this man is. You've barged into our home as if you have every right to be here—"

Jamie, never soft-spoken to begin with, broke in, "Ye tried to kill him."

"What?" Rourke struggled against his bonds, the back of his head thumping anew and competing with the pain at his temple.

She explained to Jamie in a rush, "You were in our forest, and he was about to run down my brother." Rourke heard the strain as she fought to remain calm. "I was but protecting my kin. That is not against any law."

"Ye'll hang, I'll see to it, if my man dies."

"I've no intention of dying," Rourke said, scenting the woman's fear in the air, stronger than her perfume. Confused, he clarified, "The blond boy, the stable lad who tried to steal from me? That's your brother?" Somehow he'd thought her noble, not a serving wench

20

or a tavern maid. Her speech was cultured.

"What? Nay. My brother stole nothing from you. And Ned is no stable boy; he's a squire for my older sister's husband, Lord Le Blanc, and heir in his own right, through my father, Lord Montehue. Poor Ned, injured by your stallion"—Rourke wondered if her brother's injury was the source of her underlying fear—"is locked in the upstairs chambers, along with our knights. I wish, nay, I demand that you release them."

"Not to worry, Rourke. They put up a fight, but until we know what happens with ye, locked up they'll stay. And lucky to have their heads."

"Brute."

If he wasn't at such a loss, Rourke might have laughed at the sheer indignation she'd poured into that one word. But he didn't understand what was going on, so he ordered, "Untie me. Take off these bandages."

She sighed. "Certainly, if you insist, I shall. But you are a fool. When you fell from your stallion, you hit your temple. The cut sliced downward, and you almost lost your left eye."

Rourke heard the knife slice through the cloth at his wrist. "Is that why my eyes are bandaged?"

She leaned over, and Rourke was bathed in the fresh mint of her warm breath as she stated, "I am not a healer. I did the best I could to clean the wound, which curves, like this," she traced the area lightly, "and ripped your lower lid. Your eye was filled with blood, so I rinsed and washed it with rosemary water until it stopped bleeding. You kept scratching at it, so you had to be bound. You could not control yourself."

Close to tearing the strips of cloth from around his eye, Rourke paused at the insult. "Wench."

She gasped. "I do not mean to be unkind. 'Tis that I fear if you strain your vision, or move about before the eye is healed, you may regret it for the rest of your days."

Hearing genuine empathy in her voice, Rourke decided not to have her killed. "Jamie, find me a real healer."

She stood abruptly, and he grabbed at her hand. He could tell she was a lady by the slenderness of her fingers, a musician by the light callous on her thumb. "Where are you going?"

"Release me." She tried to pull away, but he wouldn't free her.

"There are no other healers," Jamie said. "It seems that her entire family can heal but her, and she's the only one here."

"What about in the village we came from? Scrappington?"

"Sorry, Rourke, but this is the best there is."

He tugged at her hand. "Take off my blindfold."

She hesitated. "Fine." Leaning over him, she slowly peeled the cloth away. He expected to open his eyes and see. He opened his eyes and saw nothing.

"Jesu," Jamie said into the silence, "That was close."

Apprehension curled in his gut as the mattress dipped. She knelt on the side of the bed, and gently brought his fingertips to the wounded area around his left eye. Softly, he probed the stitched gash. "Ye did this with a rock? I don't believe it. My helmet fits over my head, and I had the visor down." He'd been after that boy, that thief.

"Aye. But the back of your head, betwixt the crown and nape, was bare."

"You were in such a rush, ye forgot to wear the mail," Jamie unnecessarily pointed out.

Rourke put his fingers over his right eye, which was not swollen nor hot. But he couldn't see, even though it was open. He knew better than to run to battle like an untrained squire. Dread settled in his stomach. "Impossible. You came from behind and threw a rock and just happened to knock me from my stallion as I was galloping past? You lie, lady!" he demanded, although he knew she spoke true, as the back of his head throbbed with each word from his mouth.

"Why would I?" Again, her voice was indignant, as if braining a man with a rock was acceptable, whilst lying was not. He imagined her, noble born, with straight, brown hair and thin, convent-ready lips. Throwing a rock?

Jamie said, "We were right there, Rourke, and saw you falling. She'd just thrown it."

"I am an accurate shot, my lord," she huffed.

"Obviously. That does not explain why I can't see."

23

Jamie asked, "At all?"

"Not a damn thing."

"You landed against some rocks when you fell, and your visor cut into your temple. It was an accident. Please tell your men to release my brother and my knights. We can make you welcome; you needn't treat us like you've got us under siege."

"They'll be released when I say so, lass. They never should have attacked us when we were coming in."

Her answer to Jamie was prim and curt. "You had me over the front of your horse, and Ned draped over another. What were my knights supposed to think?"

Rourke knew he should do something, but his head was now hurting all the way to his heels. Jamie could handle it.

Jamie was handling it. "And you, lass, will make certain that Rourke keeps his eye or else." Jamie pounded the wooden bedpost, and Rourke groaned as the mattress moved. He was not feeling well.

"He needs more medicine," she said. "The pain is returning."

"Ye'd best not be poisoning him."

Rourke's stomach heaved, and he grunted, knowing he'd never been this bad off in his life. He felt the sweat pop out over his forehead and lip, and his flesh grew hot. He supposed he could still serve his country with one eye, but it wouldn't be as easy. Downed, and not by a battle wound, but by a convent girl with good aim.

24

Ah, hell. Did she say her father was Lord Montehue? The rock had scrambled his brains. Loyal to the king, a strong warrior with a sizable income, properties, and a new title. Rourke had been sent to marry the man's daughter and stop a potential enemy in the event Prince John made a bid for the crown—by order of the prince.

Now he knew why Jamie had been dropping hints about "who" she was talking to—as in, Jamie hadn't given away Rourke's identity. Normally, he was not so daft. He supposed he owed the lady an introduction.

"I," he swallowed past the bile rising up his throat. "I am Rourke Wallis, and you are my prisoner until I say otherwise."

He heard her sharp intake of breath, then felt her cool hands as she pressed him back to the bed. "You are rude, as are your men. Why steal when something is freely offered?"

"You tried to kill me," Rourke said, eyes shut. "And almost succeeded." He knew it was not the whole truth, but he was in so much pain he could not unravel the knot truth could be. "You have my pack? Did the boy have it?"

"Don't know anything about a boy, but I've got it now, Rourke. Godfrey recovered it after the skirmish in the village; damn that Harold anyway. Ambushin' us. Never did like that sneaky bastard. Just rest, man, and heal." Jamie's voice roughened, as did his threats, "And, lass, ye'll be wishing you were dead along with him if he goes to meet his maker any time soon."

If he survived the fever, he was supposed to marry this woman he held under threat.

He wondered if she was the type of woman who could be swayed from anger with flowers. Once she found out the truth, he doubted she'd be happy. Since he was previously promised to another, he wouldn't be making anybody happy, besides Prince John. "What is your name?"

"Galiana."

"Pretty," he said.

She sniffed, and he sensed that flowers would not be enough to win her over.

The delirium from his fever drew him under, like a raging current in a spring-fattened river. "Galiana." He used the very last of his strength to demand, "Other than yourselves . . . no one . . . on pain of death . . . is to enter this room."

He had to protect his secrets.

Chapter Two

Galiana could not quite identify what she was feeling as she embroidered by candlelight, watching Rourke Wallis fight his fever. Fear for her brother. Fear for herself. She had no wish to die like some sacrificial Grecian virgin because this man had lost an eye.

Or worse.

Guilt? Definitely that. If she hadn't hit him with the rock, he would not have fallen. Aye, she thought crossly, accidentally stabbing her finger with the needle's point; but if she hadn't acted, then it would be Ned lying dead in the forest. Rourke's sword had been drawn to skewer whatever was in its path.

He tossed, and she sang softly to soothe him. His brow was furrowed, his dark brown hair damp with sweat. There was nothing more she could give him, so she kept vigil. When she'd lit her candles to Saint Jude, it hadn't occurred to her that this might be the answer she'd get. It was true, then. She tapped her lower lip thoughtfully with the pad of her injured finger. One had to be careful what one prayed for. Galiana had wanted change. Some small, harmless excitement that would let her feel important before she married the highest bidder.

Love was for the lucky few who stumbled over it.

The door opened with a crash, and Rourke's big, ginger-haired knight came barreling in without even a knock. Galiana let slip a small sigh of exasperation before setting her embroidery to the side. She'd been so agitated that she'd hoped the dip of the needle and thread through the fine silk would provide mindless soothing. Instead, her brain had been a jumble of thoughts, none worthy of the lady she'd been raised to be.

"How is he?"

Jamie glanced at Rourke, whose tall, bare body was covered with an ivory sheet up to the shoulders. Rourke's feet came to the edge of the mattress, and it had been difficult to decide what needed covering more. His feet? Or the broad expanse of Rourke's muscled shoulders?

For certes, that was not a ladylike thought.

Flustered, she looked away from Rourke and stared at Jamie. "He fights the fever."

"Need I remind you what will happen if he—"

"Nay," Galiana boldly cut him off, holding up one hand. "You needn't." She turned her back on the blustering knight, understanding that his constant barging in and out of the room stemmed from worry over a friend. "'Tis oft times worse before it gets better, or so Gram says."

"Who's Gram? And where can we find her? Do not tell me yer talking of that old crone in the hall, either. She'd like to poke Rourke's eye through."

Folding her fingers before her, Galiana admitted with a slight nod that watching Dame Bertha's palsied hands so close to Rourke's eye had been frightening. It had seemed natural to step forward and do the stitches herself. "Would you believe that I grow faint at the sight of blood?"

She glanced at the neat row of tiny black knots. Her skill with a needle had come in handy. She'd just had to pretend that she was working on an embroidery sampler and not a man's very handsome face.

Jamie scoffed, hand hovering over the knife hilt protruding from the leather scabbard at his waist. As if, Galiana thought, he could battle Rourke's fever himself. "Gram?" he prodded.

"The Lady Evianne, my grandmother. But she is with my sister; I told you that. North, then west, toward the Scottish border. Six days' ride, at the fastest pace. With the snow still falling the way it is, it would take longer to send someone, and by then—" Galiana shrugged.

"You said your sister is a healer, too."

Turning, she adjusted the trailing cloth of her head-dress around her shoulders. "Both of them are. 'Tis your misfortune that you have but my hands."

As if he could change circumstances by sheer force of will, Jamie held the knife out, the tip to her throat. "It will be your misfortune. Or your brother's?"

Thinking of Ned brought tears to her eyes that she couldn't blink away fast enough. Upstairs, her brother was under guard with the eight Montehue knights. Her family's vassals had all surrendered once Jamie had threatened to slice Ned's throat right at the door. Father Jonah was doing his best to clean the wound across Ned's chest; he couldn't be any better or worse than she. The family priest was the only one allowed to go back and forth from the solar to Celestia's dungeon-turned-sick room.

Galiana sent a swift blessing of thanks that her sister had the foresight to label everything, and that she'd kept a book filled with neat recipes for various illnesses.

After the good priest had shown Galiana where to find the supplies she'd need, he'd whispered to her that Ed had not been taken, and to claim but one brother. There'd been no time to question him, so she'd simply nodded. She was not a liar by nature. However, when it came to protecting her family, it seemed she could learn. She wiped at the cowardly tears, vowing to make them her last.

Galiana met Jamie's gaze directly, determination in every bone of her body. "If you harm one more hair on

Ned's head, I'll let this man die."

"Ye threaten me?"

Drawing on strength she didn't know she had, she lifted her chin—refusing to back down. "Nay. It is you who threaten me and mine. I have said I would give my all to this knight, even though he was out to harm my brother. And, yes, while it was my rock that knocked him from his beast of a stallion, it was his visor that cut into his temple."

"'Tis but a small difference, lass."

"Perhaps." Galiana felt her knees shake and was grateful for the thick velvet tunic she wore. "I am but saying, sir, that I will do my best. I am not"—Galiana paused, amazed at her own audacity—"going to be bullied into doing a better job because you keep pointing that at me."

Jamie lowered his weapon, and Galiana was unsure what his flashing amber eyes were saying. His lips were pressed tight together like a seam in a sleeve.

Tension broke as Rourke suddenly tossed back the sheet, baring his skin down to the hip. A fresh stain of burgundy blood flowered on the coverlet at his calf, and sweat beaded upon his brow and chest. Both eyes remained swollen shut, and Gali wondered what would happen to such a vital man if he could no longer be a knight in arms. She was reminded of their old hunting bitch, Daisy. Once she'd lost her back leg to a wild boar, she'd given up the will to live.

Rourke started speaking in a language Galiana didn't quite understand, hoarse and guttural, similar to her mother's native Welsh.

"What is he saying?" she asked Jamie, who had turned pale beneath his freckles.

"Nothing for you to hear, lass, nor repeat."

Shivering with a sense of foreboding, she said, "I should stitch that wound. When did it happen?" Peering closer at the gash, she gulped. "It must be done." Her stomach flopped even as she felt her trembling fingers still.

"Aye." Jamie tucked the knife away. "I'll hold his leg."

Galiana exhaled, swaying a little to the left.

Jamie grabbed her arm. "Ye really cannot stand the sight of blood?"

Shaking off his hand, she straightened. "Not especially, but I'll manage." Mint for me, she thought, walking to Celestia's shelves. To calm my belly. Now what for Rourke? she wondered, eyeing the rows and rows of dried herbs,

"Basil, marigold, and sage . . ." she read the labels aloud.

"For fever, aye—that is common enough that ye won't accidentally kill him."

"You, sir, are not helping." Galiana kept her back to the knight, gathering the ingredients.

Father Jonah called down the stairs, "Lady Galiana? Shall we call the leech? Poor Ned is out of his mind."

The leech? Montehues never used bloodletting unless there was a specific area needing to be released of infection. Even she knew that much. Calmly walking to the stairs, she looked up and into the priest's worried face. "I could go myself to the village," he suggested with a wink.

"Oh," she said.

Jamie shoved Galiana to the side and shouted upward, "Nay, not one person, priest or no, is leaving this manor."

Galiana glared at Jamie, then lifted one shoulder daintily. "Whatever you wish, sir. Father Jonah? Could you fetch me two eggs?"

"Where will he get those, lass?" Jamie asked menacingly.

As if she weren't the least bit scared, she answered, "The larder, of course."

Jamie waved the priest away. "Hurry back."

"You have no manners," Galiana accused, irritated enough to let him feel the weight of her temper.

"I need none. Ye have no clue as to how important that man over there is, and it is my sworn duty to see to it that he survives to fulfill his destiny."

"Who is he, then?"

She stared at him, daring him to answer. Needing to know, and knowing it would change her life once she did.

"A brother."

"Jamie, Jamie, man, to me." Rourke's voice lacked power as he called for his fellow knight.

Galiana took three large steps toward the injured man, but still Jamie reached Rourke first.

"Right here, Rourke, old Jamie's got your back."

"I hear ye, but I cannot see," Rourke said with great effort.

Galiana's heart fluttered as she watched Rourke's arm muscles straining against the linen ties in an effort to be free.

Jamie bowed his head, but kept his voice even. "Ye'll be fit, man, in no time at all. Sleep, would ye?"

"I think, Jamie, I must'a had too much ta drink." Rourke chuckled ruefully. "'Tis sick I feel, from my head to my arse."

Galiana put her knuckles to her lips at his language. This was no time for ladylike outrage. Not that she'd ever been outraged, but her mother had told her she should be. All ladies were.

Instead, Galiana had been fascinated by the slang of the villagers compared to the educated speech of the nobility. The traveling musicians and entertainers were a cross betwixt the two classes.

Jamie patted Rourke carefully on the shoulder, calming his friend with stories in that rough language they shared. Galiana gave them privacy, and gathered what she needed, careful to follow Celestia's written instructions to the letter.

Father Jonah delivered the two eggs. "Here ye are, my lady. How are you faring, here in the dungeon?"

His voice was kind, and Galiana felt the flush creep up her neck.

"'Tis not filled with the monsters I'd always thought," she smiled, taking the eggs from his outstretched hand. Cracking the first, she separated the yolk from the white and handed the dish of the clear liquid to the priest. "It will help Ned's wound heal and close. Spread it over the top, letting it dry. We must do this twice a day, according to the notes Celestia penned."

Father Jonah sighed heavily. "I am most proud of you, Gali," he said with a familiarity he hadn't broached since she'd turned fourteen and grown taller than he. "Your parents . . . they would be proud, too, seeing how you are overcoming your fears."

"I've not much choice," Galiana answered smartly to hide her pleasure that he'd noticed. Before this, Galiana refused to come down to the dungeon at all, certain it was filled with tortured souls. So far, she hadn't heard a single boo. She looked down at the dish she'd poured the egg into and sucked in a scared breath. "Oh! Oh, this is not good at all," she said with a shiver. "Look. Blood in the yolk."

"That's just an old superstition." Father Jonah said, calmly.

She gnawed her lower lip. "It's bad fortune, and danger."

Father Jonah took the dish away.

"'Tis nothing, my lady. Take this egg white for the

injured knight, and I will find another egg for Ned." He turned, then shook his head and whispered conspiratorially, "I almost forgot. Ed will be 'haunting' the manor, so if ye hear any strange sounds, act frightened, aye?"

Galiana watched the old man walk carefully up the stone steps. Acting frightened would not be much of a stretch, she thought. She sent a quick prayer to Saint Jude that Ed would not be found; then she took the tray of supplies, along with a freshly heated needle and black thread, and set everything on a small table near the cot, where Rourke lay muttering something unintelligible.

"What language is that he speaks? It's similar to my mother's language, but I can't make it out."

Jamie rose quickly. "Don't be listening in where ye should not be, lass, else you'll be minus those pretty ears."

Galiana huffed, refusing to give in to Jamie's bullying. I'll not think about the blood in the yoke. "It sounded like he said Merlin."

Jamie blew out an annoyed breath.

She sat down, setting the bandages and herbs around her and babbling on to stop her nerves. "Do you know the tales? Of a wizard so powerful he controlled the ancient kings? He lived on Iona, you know. I wish I could go there. I would ask for magic."

Hearing Jamie's audible gulp, she turned, the threaded needle in her hand. "Run this through that candle's flame, will you?" She picked up a damp, sage-scented cloth from a shallow bowl and wrung it out before gathering her courage

36

and peeling back the sheet to reveal the gash in Rourke's leg. "You cannot blame this injury on my family, sir. From whence did it come?"

"We were attacked by brigands on our way here."

"Mercenaries. Thugs." Galiana closed her eyes briefly. "The trouble seems to get worse as the years pass."

Jamie cocked his head. "With no king at the helm, ye mean?"

"Nay! I said nothing of the kind. My family is loyal to King Richard."

He handed her the needle and mumbled, "Pity."

Galiana paused before returning her gaze to Rourke's wound. "Excuse me?"

"I said, 'pretty.' Ye're a comely lass, ye ken?"

"Hmph."

"Why are ye not married already, with babes at yer feet?"

Point to flesh, press, pretend that this is a coarse piece of cloth, and not a man's skin. Her stomach rolled as blood came to the surface. Dark blood, with an unhealthy smell. Babes? "'Tis none of yer concern," she said shortly.

"I would know, too," Rourke said in his deep voice.

"Ah! Ha! Oh, sweet Brigid! Do not scare me like that." She swallowed, then picked the needle back up from where she'd dropped it on his leg. "Oh, no. No. I cannot pierce your flesh whilst you are awake!"

"Keep talking," Rourke instructed.

Galiana bit her lip, hating to see any creature suffer.

And at her own hands, it was unbearable. "I can't."

"Do it!" Jamie growled.

"Leave us, friend," Rourke said. "Your temper makes her hand shake worse, and I'd just as soon not bleed to death."

Jamie cursed, then stomped loudly up the stairs.

"Galiana, yes?" Rourke's throat was dry, and it irritated him to talk, but he could sense the lady's mounting frustration and knew she needed soothing before taking up the needle again.

"Aye."

"Tell me, then, why you have not married if you are as comely as Jamie says. Was he teasing you? Have ye two noses?"

She laughed softly. "He was but being kind, sir. And I have just one nose."

"'Tis large; it must be. Or have you a wart on your chin?"

Galiana made an odd sound before saying, "No. No wart. But if it is a beauty aid you seek, I could make it for you."

"Are ye calling me ugly?"

Her startled inhalation of breath made him smile, which in turn made his head ache like the devil. A groan escaped his lips despite his efforts.

"Since you're awake, I can give you the tisane I've made. For fever and pain."

"I could hear you and Jamie arguing."

"Your friend leaves no room for argument."

"I suppose that's so. It is a valiant quality in a knight."

He assumed she had no answer for that, as she said naught else. The sound of water being poured into a dish teased his ears, and he wished he could see. Damn, but his head ached, and now his leg throbbed as well, which could only mean infection. The bursting smells of sage and marigold filled his nose, and his throat closed against what he knew to be bitter medicine.

"Open your mouth, sir," Galiana said softly, yet in a way that left no room for denying her.

He did, and a saucer was placed against his lips. The sweet taste of honey surprised him, and he found he was able to swallow the bitter marigold without his throat closing around it.

"It will ease the ache. You've been fighting this fever, I will venture to say, since before you entered our forest."

"Your forest? All lands are the king's land."

He'd been attacked twice in the three-day ride from his keep to Montehue Manor. The first time, when he'd gotten cut on the calf, had been by bloody-thirsty mercenaries. He'd wondered if Lord Christien had been behind it. The second attack had come from Lord Harold. Brutal and sneaky, the attack was just like the man. Rourke had bested Harold with a blow to the chest, and the knight had wisely retreated.

Prince John was playing them all.

He heard her whisper something about patience and

virtues unrealized. "So what, Lord Rourke, were you doing in the king's forest with your sword drawn and your knights thundering so loudly you scared even the squirrels from the trees?"

Reaching to scratch his ear, his hands didn't get far, and he tugged against the restraints with frustration. "Why am I bound? You cut them before."

"I had to put them back; the eye is healing, and you keep wanting to touch it."

His strength was fading, and he lacked the will to argue. "You've had no news from the village outside your manor walls?"

"Your knights have locked my knights and my injured brother in the solar. The priest is not allowed to leave, and the only servants we have here are the ones who live in. The snow won't stop falling. How are we to get news?"

"That's right." Thank God, he thought, for that small favor. The agonizing pain in his head was relentless, and even though he fought against the oncoming tide of darkness, he knew it was no use.

"You are not going to tell me what you were doing in the forest? Fine then. How did you come to be at Montehue Manor? It's off the beaten path."

She was smart; he would grant her that. And relentless in her pursuit of the truth. "Protect me whilst I sleep, my lady." He kept his tone as light as he could, but he meant every word. "One day I will return the favor, upon my word."

"Protect you from what?"

He licked his dry lips, the throbbing in time with his heartbeat. Sluggish and heavy and agonizing. It was good his hands were tied, else he'd certainly pluck his eyes from his head. Anything to make the thumping stop.

"Lord Rourke? Oh, dear, protect you from what? I know only how to make perfumes and lotions."

"Not bad with a rock," he managed to mumble.

"Aye, I suppose that's true. Though before yesterday, I had no knowledge of it. An arrow, yes."

Rourke heard her rise, then felt a cool compress being laid over his forehead. Her fingers, soft and delicate, massaged the skin above his eyebrows, and the darkness receded just enough to warn her.

"Treachery," he whispered against the faint lemony scent of her neck as she leaned over him. "Beware."

"Treachery?" She sat back, wondering if she'd heard him correctly. It was hard enough to hear him when he spoke so low, but when he switched from French to English to Latin, and then to what she assumed to be some form of the Scottish tongue, it was challenging to say the very least. She'd been schooled in all but the latter, and it was close enough to Welsh in parts that she could make a guess. Although why he'd talk about Merlin escaped her, unless it was a story from his childhood that he liked and remembered.

Frankly, he did not seem the fairy tale sort of man.

With his tanned, rough skin, and the shadow of a beard covering his chin, and his dark, menacing brows, Galiana assumed he was a brooding, arrogant man used to getting his own way. He was gorgeous.

If he couldn't pick a language to charm his way, he'd call for his knights and battle for what he wanted. The idea thrilled her, and she clasped her hands together in her lap, perched on the edge of a low stool. It was time to finish the stitches in his calf, now that he'd lost consciousness. Cleaning the area again, she passed the needle through the candle's flame, doing it because her sister had written how important it was to heat the tip.

Galiana clasped his leg, his calf so muscled that she could not reach around it with her fingers. Rourke stirred against her, uneasy and no doubt in pain.

Picking a soft song that she'd learned long ago from one of the traveling minstrels, Galiana hummed softly in an attempt to soothe Rourke enough that she could finish stitching his wound. She tapped her finger against her lower lip, wondering if she should pluck the hairs on his leg so they didn't get caught, and mayhap worsen the infection.

It made sense.

And since no one was about to teach her, and she had no magic at all, she had to follow her instincts. By the time she finished, the area was plucked clean, and a neat row of black knots held the edges of the wound in place.

"I've never seen a finer job," Jamie said from behind her.

Pride flooded through her as she sat back and wiped her hands in a basin of violet-scented water. "Thank you," she answered, exhausted as the adrenaline she'd been living on faded.

"I'll sit with him, if ye'd like to get a morsel or two. I ordered yer bailiff to see to feeding my men and yours. He sure is a surly enough fellow."

"Surly?" Galiana rose and discreetly stretched her back muscles. "Perhaps he simply dislikes you."

Jamie laughed. "For a lady, you have a smart tongue."

She lifted the hem of her tunic and glided up the stairs. For a lady. What did he know? This lady was going to eat an entire chicken and a loaf of bread to go with it. And drink a full mug of ale, too. Galiana's stomach rumbled, and, once out of sight, she ran across the back hall to the kitchen. She slipped past Rourke's knights, who were eating at trestle tables in the great hall and flirting with the serving maids.

Cook, having done her part for the late meal, was snoring from her cot next to the fire. It was her job to keep the large pit burning at all times. Her two young helpers dozed nearby. Galiana grabbed a rosy red apple from a basket on the counter and then opened the walk-in pantry for something more substantial. A round of cheese, mayhap.

From out of the recesses of the kitchen pantry, a hand grabbed her elbow and yanked her deeper into the dark shadows. She opened her mouth to scream, certain she was going to be mauled by one of Rourke's knights.

"Shhhh, Gali, it's me, Ed."

She stopped kicking backward immediately and turned in his arms. "Did I hurt you," she asked in a whisper, running her hands over his face and shoulders. "Are you all right, Edward? Answer me."

He put his hand over her mouth. "Shh! They'll find me for certain if ye don't hush, Galiana. I hid in the forest and watched them bring you and Ned in . . . and that injured knight. Is it true you brained him? Who's the blustering giant who orders everyone about?"

Galiana peeled his hand from her face. "They don't know about you, then?"

"The servants aren't saying a word; neither are our men."

"Have you seen Ned? Father Jonah says he is fine— not a single stitch needed."

Ed grinned and rubbed his chest at the spot where his twin would now carry a scar. "Talking about it like he earned it in battle. He said he jumped in front of the horse to draw the knight's attention away from you. Did he do that? Did he?"

Nodding, Galiana brushed silly tears of happiness from her cheeks. "He was very brave."

"Lucky bas—, I mean, what a story, aye?"

"Is that envy in your voice, Ed? Your brother could have been killed!" Galiana's harsh whisper echoed around them in the stuffed pantry.

"Nay."

She heard the sound of his shoes shuffling against the hard-packed dirt floor.

"Okay, mayhap a little. If I was there, I could have tackled him from behind and then—"

"Hush, just hush." Galiana wrapped her arms around her waist, nauseated now instead of hungry. The thought of both her brothers injured, when she'd been in charge, made her stomach knot like a Celtic braid. "You, Ed, are very smart. You can take a letter to Mother and Father right away; do you hear me? Lord Rourke might have more men in the village; I don't know. Jamie, his 'brother,' doesn't do a lot of talking, except to threaten me."

Remembering what Rourke had said of treachery came to mind, so she added, "Trust no one. Stay off the main roads. Bring dry clothes. Sweet Mary Magdalene, was it really just this morning that I was filled with joy at the falling snow?"

Suddenly, Galiana realized Ed had been shaking her arm until she finally stopped rambling. "I'm not going anywhere, Galiana. The snow has not stopped, and we are snowed in just as surely as our enemy is."

His green eyes flashed in the shadows, and Galiana sighed. "What have you planned?"

Rourke sensed that he was not alone, but there was

no harm in it. It felt dark, safe. Like the deepest part of the night when secrets could be shared in whispers and sign language.

Quill to paper, paper to pack, and then it was time to travel. Horse's hooves wrapped in cloth, so as not to make a sound. If the sentry heard a thing, he'd have to be killed.

The last thing Rourke wanted was more blood on his hands. How much of the stain could his soul absorb before turning a rotted black? Serving two kings was ripping him asunder; serving a third would do it for certes.

The safe feeling gave way to night terrors that had been nipping at his heels like a rabid dog. There was an urgency bidding him to wake up, to get up. Merlin, magical wizard, a man with a long, scraggly, white beard. The stuff of lore and legend, yet he'd been haunting him. Dragons, claws, blood. So much blood. But there were still two lions he had to face before he could be free. He stretched his body; his hands were tied.

The atmosphere shifted, and he tensed, torn between the fogginess of sleep and the need to be aware. Cool liquid dripped on his leg. Quickly passing from cold to hot, it burned, and he smelled the stink of singed hair. "Be gone. What is the meaning of this?" He kicked out, relieved his legs were free at least, and yet his feet connected with nothing.

Ghosts.

An eerie laugh surrounded him, and more drops of liquid fire rained down on his bare skin. He struggled against the bonds that strapped him to the bed, angry at being tortured as he lay bound and injured. He'd foolishly thought he was safe. This could not be a figment of his imagination; the pain was sharp and fresh, and the stink of sulfur and wax wafted pungently beneath his nose. What need had Merlin of tricks? "Coward. Face me, if you dare."

A disembodied voice clucked like a chicken, then mocked, "Face me? Why, Sir Knight, ye have not any eyes left to see." The tone came from the left, and then the right. Rourke tilted his head from side to side. It seemed like someone was speaking through a tunnel, or a shell, mayhap. Or were they separate voices? He strained against the ropes.

"I have eyes, damn you." he tried to open them, concentrated with all his will, but the darkness remained. This was his worst nightmare, and he was trapped within it. "Jamie," he called out. "Galiana?"

"Nobody can hear you," whispered a devil to his left.

"You are locked deep in the bowels of the earth." The cruel voice to his right chuckled, but the chuckle turned into a gargling choke; then Rourke felt more drops of liquid fire hit his skin. He could not die; he had not yet made his peace with God. "Go back to hell, demons. I deny thee. Go to hell!"

The opening of a door seemed to suck the very air from the room. Footsteps raced down the stairs. Soft footsteps, a lady's slippers. He hated being so dependent upon every sense but sight.

God help him if he never regained his vision. All would truly be lost, and all of the suffering he'd caused or done in the name of royalty would be for naught.

"Sir Jamie! Awake, you—how dare you? Oh—drunk? Shame, shame."

Galiana, his lady protectress, lambasted his childhood friend and foster brother with five sharp, loud claps.

The swish of her dress as she walked announced her arrival at Rourke's bedside as surely as did her citrus perfume. "Lord Rourke, you were but having a bad dream."

Relieved to be awake and not stuck within the pit of his own mind, he joked, "'Tis hard to believe you are the same angel who sang my pain away. You sound like a fisherman's wife on the docks."

"I do not want to know what you know of that, sir. Your brother"—he imagined her gritting her teeth—"is dead to this world. Ale, and plenty of it, from the way his head is lolling to the side."

Rourke swallowed, his mouth dry. "A pint sounds fine, actually."

"Oh?"

He felt the weight of the mattress dip as she sat on the edge of the bed. He longed to reach out and touch her, to 'see' her without the aid of his eyes.

She scooted back, as if she'd read his thoughts.

"May I have some water, my lady, at least?"

"Aye," the back of her hand pressed against his forehead.

"The fever's gone, thanks be to all the saints."

"And you." He flexed his leg, and while sore, it seemed the infection was gone. His eyes were still covered, and he ached now to see the light. "How long was I sick?"

"Four days, altogether."

"Jesu," he breathed out with a whoosh. No wonder he'd felt like he was dying. He had been.

Galiana said in a brisk tone, "You are most fortunate to be with us still. I thought"—her voice cracked, and Rourke wondered at the emotion she was trying to hide—"I thought . . . Last night the fever finally broke, and the wound at your temple—" He felt the soft pad of her fingertips skim his face. "Never mind. All is well, without the details of it."

She sliced through the bonds that had saved him from scratching his own eyes out. Though the ties had been of cloth, the release of them felt like the removal of slave's shackles. "Let me help you sit up," she said, her breath sweet against him. His blood heated, but with a different kind of fever. Life.

"We can take the cloth off in a moment. I'll want to blow out the lamps and keep the light dim so you don't hurt your eyes."

"Thank you," he said, knowing it was hardly adequate.

"Drink this." She gave him refreshingly cool water, bringing the cup to his lips until he'd drained it. "More?"

He shook his head, wondering what she looked like, if her eyes were blue or brown, or if she was soft or angular.

She pushed pillows into shape behind him, and the sound of her punching them into submission made him smile. Her body brushed his, and he caught his breath. He owed her his life. That had to be the source of his response to her.

Grabbing one of the pillows and dropping it in his lap before he embarrassed them both he asked, "Why haven't you married, Lady Galiana?"

Pausing, he imagined her brushing light brown hair off of her face before she sighed. "Delirious for days, and this is the best question you have? Really." She sat down with an exaggerated slowness, and he was reminded that despite her hard work and unrelenting care, she was a lady. He enjoyed the feminine sound of her skirts, and the way she fiddled with the fabric. "'Tis a long story, and a boring one, but since you are so single-minded in your pursuit of it, I will tell you."

"You are not really ugly; I know it," he said. Even if she had two warts, he realized, she would have a special place in his dark heart.

"I am a great beauty actually, and it is the very bane of my existence."

Shocked into momentary silence, he responded to her comment with a dry "Sarcasm, my lady?"

She burst out laughing. "Aye." Galiana hesitated. "What are looks anyway? Everybody has a nose and eyes; they are tall or fat; they are bald or have hair. It is unfair that a woman must be judged on such things, when it is up to God. If I'd gotten to choose, I would have picked magic over a dimpled smile. But I did not, so it is a waste of precious breath complaining about it."

"Perhaps my brains are still scrambled," he made a show of tapping the right side of his head. "Did you say magic?"

"Aye. You don't believe in it, and that is fine for you. But I am of Welsh blood, and I know that there are ghosts lurking in every single corner."

The back of Rourke's neck prickled. He had seen magic firsthand. Men were more dangerous. "Well, at least now I know why you're not married. You are crazy."

"That is no way to talk to your betrothed, Rourke Wallis," a loud masculine voice boomed from somewhere above. Boots clomping down wooden steps made Rourke realize he really was in a dungeon, and his instincts whirled into gear as he recognized the voice of his most pragmatic knight, Godfrey Hughes. "When were you going to share the happy news, Rourke?"

More boot steps followed, and Rourke had to imagine his men, including young Will, his squire, as they filed into the room with military precision. Apprehension rose, but he kept his face void of expression.

Galiana stood. "Now is not the time for business, he's only just broke through the fever. And you are sorely mistaken. I am not promised to any man."

The realization that they'd gone through his pack without his permission, or Jamie's for that matter, gave him a sweating chill. But he'd been raised at Queen Eleanor's knee, and if there was one thing that he was damn good at it, it was intrigue. He could lie convincingly to his own mother. If he'd ever known the woman.

He reached out for Galiana. His hand brushed her hip, then the pointed tip of a long braid. He wanted to see her, to see for himself what color hair she had. He slipped the cloth from his eyes. Flashes burst before him, and he squinted. White-hot pain flashed through his head like a flaming spear, and then everything was dark.

Fisting his hands on the sheet, he swallowed hard. There was too much at stake. He had to play this off, or they were all dead.

Chapter Three

Galiana felt smothered by all of the very large, very angry, knights as they clambered into a space that was, despite all Celestia's cleaning, still a dungeon. Low wooden ceilings held herbs that were hung upside down to dry, and each time a knight's head brushed against a stalk, a sharp floral scent pervaded the room.

Which was better, by far, than the stench of leather, sweat, and male as Rourke's knights gathered in a semi-circle around the bed where he lay like an invalid, with only her between them.

He was an invalid, come to that. And he'd asked her for protection. Jamie snored loudly in the corner, completely useless at a time when she could use his brutish strength. She reached for the short dagger on the tray by the bed, the one she'd used to cut through the ties around Rourke's wrist.

They might be Rourke's men, but they looked to be on the edge of a revolt. Not unlike the rest of the country, she thought briefly. "Please, just go back up the stairs. Your lord requires rest."

One of the knights, the one with the letter in his hand, came closer, and Galiana remembered the bloody yolk in the egg dish. This knight was disaster in a huge chain mail package. He did not stop until they were practically nose to nose.

"It says here, my lady, that ye're to be married to Rourke Wallis. Your lands become Prince John's lands. The prince signed it himself. What say ye to that?"

She opted to keep her own counsel. She was not supposed to even know the curse words that were on the very tip of her tongue.

Galiana waved the short dagger in front of her, exuding false confidence. Or trying to. The knight had graying hair at his temples, and numerous nicks of battle scarred his hands and face, giving him a hardened appearance. Yet he lifted his hands up and stepped back two spaces as she said, "You, sir, are crowding me, and I do not care for it."

Rourke made an animal-type growl of warning from behind her, and she felt his angry impotence. She moved backward until her calves touched the mattress, then took a small sidestep, so that he could face his knights. Even though he could not see them, at least they could see him and understand the extent of the man's injuries.

"My most sincere apologies," the knight answered sarcastically, half-bowing so that now his nose was very close to the tip of her dagger, as if mocking her drawn weapon.

Galiana gripped the bone handle, thinking if he realized she'd learned to control her squeamishness in the past few days, he might not be so cocky.

"I am Godfrey Hughes, and this is Franz de Lacey." He introduced a smaller, darker man who looked like he should be a French aristocrat and not a knight earning a living for someone else. Arrogance bracketed his dark eyes, just as a full smile graced his red lips. Franz was the kind of man she turned down without even bothering to have her father read the marriage proposal.

Godfrey continued, "'Tis a pity it's taken us almost a week to meet with you, the lady of the manor. But I see why Jamie was so adamant to keep us away."

"Hiding such beauty is a crime, mademoiselle." Franz sent her a soulful gaze that left her cold.

"Ye're pretty, my lady," Will agreed.

"Aye, your hair is—"

"Remember yourselves, knights," Rourke warned.

Galiana lowered her dagger, even though danger hummed in the chamber. These were the exact type of men that had made her life so miserable in the past, expecting her to appreciate their unwanted attentions as they praised her for things like the shape of her chin.

"Jamie was acting on my orders," Rourke added in more of an edict than an explanation as to why the other knights had not seen her before. Other than a brief glimpse here and there, Jamie and Father Jonah had been excellent bodyguards, or jailers, depending on how one looked at it.

"Where's Jamie?" Will asked.

"She's worn him out," one of the knights in the back laughed. "Old Jamie's sleeping in the corner, a happy man."

The comment was in poor taste, and Galiana felt the insult burn in her belly. "How dare you say such a thing?"

From behind her, she heard Rourke knock over the table beside the bed. The loud clatter changed the tension as the man from the back shoved his way forward.

"Beg pardon." The man bowed low, his light brown hair flopping over one eye as he flirted with her. "Robert Marksman, at your service, my lady." He grabbed her left hand and pressed a kiss to her open palm.

Tempted to take her dagger and stick it in his eye, she yanked her hand down and made a show of wiping her palm on her skirt. There were rules of behavior for a reason. A noble society required people to rise above the crudeness that was everyday life. "You are rude, and your manners are appalling."

Obviously not impressed with her opinion, he moved closer, attempting to take the dagger from her hand, using his tall strength to cower her into submission. "Ye don't need that, my lady," he laughed crudely.

"I'll protect you."

Robert was filled with youthful arrogance, and Galiana doubted he would back down. Scared, she stopped trying to keep the dagger away from him, and instead tightened her grip and stabbed the tip of the blade into his hand.

He snatched it back, curling his fingers around the palm. "Why did you do that?" The wound dripped blood, and Galiana handed him a cloth, grateful that she wasn't a puddle of pottage on the floor.

"Because you are an uncouth idiot?" Franz suggested.

Galiana glared at the five knights. "Unless you all agree that this type of behavior is acceptable, I suggest someone teach this young man how to treat a lady." The men, knowing they'd crossed a line, retreated a few more steps.

Godfrey cuffed Robert, and Robert glared at Galiana before mumbling, "Apologies, my lady."

Not used to physical confrontations, Galiana's knees shook, and she wanted to sit down before she fell down. The look in Robert's eyes told her she'd best stay aware of him at all times.

Suddenly Rourke was standing behind her and lending her his physical strength. His hand dropped heavily to her shoulder, and she could sense how much it was costing him to be up from his bed. She'd never appreciated a man's presence so much.

He said in a very throaty, no-nonsense voice, "Robert, get out of here. You'll be pulling guard duty for the next sennight, and I'll be teaching you manners myself. Will, bring me my entire pack, and not just what Godfrey pilfered from it. Christ's bones, when I am able to wield a sword again, there will be retribution given for this."

"But, Rourke, we thought you dying." Godfrey shook the parchment in his hand, as if it were a reminder that he was the one who was supposed to be in control of the situation.

"So you decided to act like a group of rogues, insulting a lady in her own manor? Stealing from me, to whom you swore your sword?"

"Ye ordered her brother and her knights to be under locked guard. What were we supposed to think?"

Franz said, "Nothing was stolen, Rourke. But, mon ami, it appears odd that you were sent here to marry, and yet did not speak a word of it to us, your men."

Odd was an understatement, Galiana thought. Rourke's fingers curled around her shoulder so hard she knew it would leave a bruise, but she didn't cry out. It occurred to her that she was aiding her enemy. Her enemy, who looked like a Roman god come to life with the ivory sheet hastily twisted around his hips. She did not owe him anything.

But if she let Rourke fall, he would lose the respect of his men. And then they would be on her like a sharp-clawed falcon to its bloodied prey.

"I don't need your permission to marry where I

will," Rourke warned.

"The lady don't even know about it," Robert muttered.

"I am here on Prince John's order, as you saw. How can I trust you, now? You all swore loyalty to me, and if I fall, then Jamie is to lead." Galiana heard the faint strain in his tone as he said harshly, "If you can't do that—leave now. I need men, not bandits."

Robert hung his head, his jaw muscle tight.

Galiana noticed a hint of relief in Franz's charming voice. "Oui, now you are healed, and you can set things right. We thought we were gathering tax information, and we would begin the work."

"You thought to snoop." Rourke said.

"You would have done the same, if you were in our boots," Godfrey said.

"Never!" Rourke's yell startled her. "Now that I'm better, I'll be handling things differently."

Because it seemed like a good time, Galiana turned her head over her shoulder to tell Rourke, "My brother should be released, as should my knights." He'd taken off the bandage, and his eyes were open. For the first time, Galiana noticed the intriguing grayish gold color.

Rourke's breath tickled her ear as he stared straight ahead, "You may have your brother released, but your knights stay where they are. Franz, see to it that her brother is freed; get that old priest to help you. Free the bailiff, too; I'll want to go over the accounts for Prince John." Rourke oozed confidence and control, and she assumed he'd gained his sight back. "And, for God's sake, somebody wake up Jamie; his snoring is hurting my head."

The jest broke what was left of the tension. The knights needed a leader, and Rourke was it. "Leave that letter, Godfrey. Since the cat is out of the bag, we might as well discuss the details, eh, my sweet?" This time the squeeze he gave her shoulder was more of a caress, and it made her blush, as did the brush of his lips against her cheek.

He was insinuating that they had a much closer relationship than patient to healer, that she had agreed to marry him when both things were a lie. She opened her mouth to protest, but he angled his head and whispered softly, "Take the letter from him."

Godfrey stalked past her, giving Rourke an odd look as he held out the letter. "We have to talk, Rourke. Privately."

Disappointment washed over her as she realized the extent of the façade Rourke was putting on. Godfrey did not know that Rourke was blinded, and understanding that this would make her life potentially more difficult if he did, she again chose to help Rourke.

"Here. Let me take that." She plucked the letter from Will's fingers before he could protest, and put it in her apron pocket. "Now, I insist that you all go back upstairs. Surely Cook can get you something to eat, and you can take your ease by the fire. Tell me," she chattered, effectively separating Rourke from the men, herding the knights toward the stairs. "Has it stopped that infernal snowing?"

Franz answered with a wink, "Non, my lady. But we've cleared a trail from here to the stables. I offer my escort if you need a breath of fresh air."

"Thank you," Galiana answered, instinctively polite. "Have we enough food? Enough wood?" Without Bailiff Morton to take charge, it had been up to Galiana to delegate duties. Cook was self-sufficient. Jamie had allowed Galiana brief visits with Ned, who was not badly injured, praise Mary, and the Montehue knights. Bored with their captivity, she'd snuck them in a chessboard and some whittling tools after begging them to help her keep the peace.

She could only handle so much more. Galiana had a new appreciation for what it took to run a household. And one under an inside attack and locked away from the rest of the world due to a snowstorm, the likes of which no one alive could remember . . . She sighed and pushed a tendril of hair behind her ear.

Franz lightly touched her elbow, "Oui, we have enough of everything, even entertainment."

"How so?" Her pulse spiked. If traveling players could get through, for certes, someone, like Ed, could get out and get help before she ended up married—to a man who had her more confused than she'd ever been in her entire ordered life. Her prayer to Saint Jude for some kind of adventure had resulted in much more than she had expected. She should have been shocked and mortified at the things she'd done.

A woman alone—not counting Dame Bertha and the kitchen servants—in a manor filled with strange men. Nursing a man when she'd never even seen a grown one naked before. Perhaps, Galiana thought with an inward smile, she should practice fainting just so that she did not forget how. Although her mother always recommended finding a good chaise before falling into a swoon.

"—the round dances with the two maids and the old woman." Franz paused, gaining her wandering attention. "And then there's the haunting—candles being blown out, food disappearing, young Will's shirt was hung over the door," he chuckled. "How enchanting to have a ghost that gets on so well with the servants."

Galiana, skilled at hiding her expressions, thanks to her mother's teachings that a lady must always look interested no matter how boring the dialogue at hand, waved her hand dismissively and laughed. "Well," she said, shaking her head and wondering what she could say that wouldn't ruin whatever story Ed had concocted.

"The pranks are fine, my lady, but putting vinegar in the ale, though, that was cruel." He sent her a genuine smile. "It amuses me."

Did he think she was doing it? Galiana nodded at Franz as he walked up the stairs. He knew there was no ghost. For now, Edward was safe. She would have to get word to Father Jonah to get her brother to stop his tricks.

A ghost should never mess with a man's drink.

Robert, the last knight up the stairs, turned and smirked at her before slamming the door behind him. And locking it. Galiana shivered with trepidation. She had never liked the dungeon. Never. It was dark and confining. Then she remembered Celestia had installed a door leading outside from the sick room so her patients could have privacy. Although it was more than likely snowed in, eventually spring would come.

The thought enabled her to breathe through her panic.

Rourke asked, "Are they gone?"

Galiana turned, torn. Rourke's face was pale beneath his olive tones, and the stitches were stark against the reddened skin. She might send her very first patient into a relapse of fever if she beat him with, with—she looked around the room, growing angrier by the minute that he hadn't thought to mention the betrothal he must have known about from their very first meeting.

A silver candlestick.

Aye, that could do some damage.

"Do not be angry with me," Rourke demanded. Then he walked backward until he hit the edge of the bed and sat down heavily, his hands out to steady himself. Straightening his shoulders, he turned his face toward where she stood. She could see from his set expression that he would make no excuses.

Something else replaced her anger.

Her stomach plummeted, and Galiana dropped the

dagger she'd been clutching to the work counter with surprise. What she truly felt, and it did not matter that it was inappropriate and most unbecoming of a lady, was pride. Pride, that despite his injuries, he'd stood up for himself, and for her. Oh, Saint Agnes, what did that say about her moral character?

Since she was already doomed, she took a moment to study the sight of him, bare-chested with chiseled muscles that rivaled any sculpture she'd ever seen. His rich, dark brown hair was cut longer than what was currently fashionable and rested in waves on his shoulders. She dropped her gaze to the line of masculine hair that led below the sheet, a trail that her fingers wished to follow. Aye, she was going to go to hell, for this feeling had to be lust.

His was a beauty greater than her own, and she was certain he was aware of it, just as she was aware of hers. While she tried to be more than her looks, she sensed that he used his to gain whatever advantage he could.

"Why did you lie and insinuate that I welcomed your attentions?" She gathered the dishes and the tray Rourke had knocked over as he'd come to her aid.

"I was saving you from a group of bored knights bent on mischief. Is that so wrong?"

Put like that, she supposed not. "They are your knights. And they were after your blood." Remembering the letter she'd put in her apron pocket, she said, "I think we should talk about this."

"We don't need to talk," Rourke said, his mouth set in a stubborn line. "Prince John has ordered me to marry you. No discussion."

Putting the tray away, Galiana leaned against the center table and pulled the letter out, smoothing the wrinkles. If he would not tell her anything, then she would see for herself.

"What are you doing?"

"I am going to read the letter."

"You read?"

"Yes," Galiana rolled her eyes at the look on his face, just because she knew he couldn't see her do it. "English, French, Latin, and Welsh. My German is not as good as it should be."

"You could be a bloody priest. Give me that letter; it is private."

"Hmm, as private as keeping your reason for coming here? Because, as you said so romantically, our secret is out." She tapped her finger against her lower lip and asked, "I wonder what else is in here that needs to be known."

"If you read that—"

"What will you do?" She smiled, certain she finally had the upper hand—then squealed.

Jamie held his large knife to her back. "Fold it up— there's a good lass—and I can put the knife away. I owe you a debt of thanks for saving my man's life, but even that won't keep you alive if you read things you should not."

Her breath caught in her throat; then she carefully

folded the letter and shoved it to the center of the table. "There."

The pressure at her back disappeared, and she turned on her heel. "You have a lot of nerve, falling asleep when you were supposed to be standing guard."

Jamie's ruddy cheeks grew even ruddier. "'Tis true, the ale got the best of me. Lack of sleep, worry, and, er, did ye know that you have a ghost? It's been hard to sleep, what with all of the noise."

Rourke's skin chilled as the eerie voice from earlier, in what he was blaming on a drug-induced dream, seemed to echo in his ear. "There's no damn ghost," he rubbed the side of his face that wasn't sore, feeling the four days' worth of growth on his cheek. "I need a shave."

"You can't do that," Galiana said, as if he would attempt it.

"No." he smiled. "You can."

"Are ye daft?" Jamie asked. "You want to give the woman you've angered a sharp blade and tell her to put it at yer throat?" The sound of Jamie snorting with disbelief brought the first piece of normalcy to his day. He caused that sound from his foster brother at least thrice a week. He'd missed it.

"Do you have the letter, Jamie?"

"I do now," Jamie said.

"I am not going to shave you," Galiana primly announced. "And more importantly, I am not going to marry you. My family has a special dispensation from

King Richard himself. We, the Montehue's and all of our kin, cannot be forced into a marriage for political gain."

"Jesu." Jamie slammed his fist on the table, and Rourke heard the small sound that Galiana made in protest. "You can't have."

A royal dispensation? Christ. Rourke raked his hair back from his forehead. How to get around that? He supposed he could force the issue, wed her and not bed her, and get an annulment later. Galiana Montehue needn't know that he was already promised to another; he'd add that omission to the pile of others. Hell, if he could keep being a spy from Prince John, this little country-bred lady wouldn't be a problem. He was a gifted liar, after all.

"God's blood, I need my sight back." Rourke said aloud, as if that truth might go unheard if it remained only a thought in his head.

"It might not return," the lady said in clipped tones resonating with frustrated anger. "Ever." The sound of her tapping fingernails against the table was another sign. "It would serve you right."

"That's harsh," Rourke said, wondering if it could be true. Mayhap he was paying a steep price for something he wasn't sure he wanted. Power.

"It matters not at all, sight or none," she said with more heat. "I do not have to marry you, and I won't. You may stay here at the manor until the snow melts, and then you and your men need to be gone."

Rourke almost smiled, but he'd been cruel enough. She was vanquished, even if she did not know it. "Jamie. Go upstairs, find that dispensation."

"No!" He heard her tug on Jamie's clothes.

"Aye," his foster brother said, clomping his way up the stairs to the door. "Who the hell locked this door?" He pounded on it. "By God, open it, or I'll break it down," he shoved his shoulder against the wooden door, causing it to shake in its frame.

"No hurry, Jamie," Rourke spoke loudly, in the chance that one of his knights was on the other side, listening in. "Galiana and I have much to say to one another that does not require an audience, in celebration of our upcoming vows."

"There will be no vows," she said, clanking dishes together.

The door opened, but it was Father Jonah on the other side. "No need to break it down; 'twas one of your own who locked it. Patience, son."

"Patience? I'll give you until the count of ten to show me where the dispensation from King Richard is, else I'll cut off yer head."

The voices faded as the door shut.

"'Tis a good thing Father Jonah is deaf as can be. Why are you going on with this? I won't be coerced into marriage." He heard the determination in her tone and, coupled with how she'd handled herself earlier with Robert, that jackass, as well as her aim—he acknowledged she would be a worthy opponent. If his life were different, perhaps even a partner.

Sighing deeply, he said, "I can't leave until I can see. You wouldn't force me to travel in the snow while injured, would you?" Playing on her compassion, he rubbed the back of his head, which was hardly even sore. The only thing hindering him from success was his lack of sight. "I had it, although it was blurry, for a mere second or two. But now it is gone," he deliberately layered despair in every syllable.

Rourke heard her come around the table and felt regret for playing upon her sensibilities. But he had to have her. She'd be his cover. Robert, Franz, and Godfrey had been acting strange for the past month. At first he'd attributed it to lack of battle and boredom, but then he worried that Prince John had discovered he harbored a spy in his midst. Her hand lightly brushed his temple.

"It is time for more medicine."

"Nay, I do not need any more herbs. They are affecting my sleep, and I see demons. Dragons."

"The Breath of Merlin? It comes from a dragon?"

It took every emotion-masking skill Rourke had ever learned to not erupt at what she'd so innocently said. "Dragon's breath?"

She walked away, and he heard her busy herself with crockery. "No, no I am quite sure that you said Breath of Merlin, but it was in that rough Scots dialect, and mayhap I have the translation wrong."

He forced himself to laugh. "Whatever you've given me to sleep has brought on night terrors. Claws, blood."

"And lions. You were most vocal last eve. As you were conquering the fever."

Rourke's stomach clenched. A spy who wanted to keep his head attached to his shoulders never let a secret slip. Damn it. No way would his foster brother have allowed her to stay and hear all of that. "Where was Jamie, or was the sod already foxed by then?" His voice sounded light to his own ears, and he hoped she heard none of the stress he was trying so hard to smother. Christ, they could all be dead if he'd said the wrong thing.

"Nay, Jamie was getting some air, visiting with the other men upstairs a while. He's loyal to you. He barely ever left your side."

He didn't hear anything suspicious in her voice. Which, damn it, was all he had to go by. He heard regret that he'd been challenged by his knights in her tone, and, yes, he sensed she even felt some indignation on his behalf. Rourke's blood warmed, and he wished he could see her. A skilled spy required all of his senses. He had to read the way people held themselves, or their eyes, to get to the truth. Or past the lies.

"I heard your singing; 'tis a beautiful voice you have."

"Thank you," she answered stiffly.

"Why do you get so angry when you receive a compliment?" She had the confidence of a beautiful woman, and yet she'd said she was not. His men had been complimentary, but knights were trained to speak to noble ladies that way, even if a lady were uglier than a two-headed lizard.

"I don't want flowery words. I want . . . more."

Rourke laughed. "For most women, poetry is enough."

"Pah, I am not 'most women.' Do you know I can trace my ancestors back to Queen Boadicea, the Welsh Warrior who took on the Romans?"

Stifling the urge to mock her grandiose claim, he made a noncommittal noise in his throat.

"'Tis true," she insisted.

"Hmm. I thought that was a tale along the same lines as Merlin," he tried to jest, which he immediately regretted. He had to stay away from the topic of the mythical wizard.

"Well, it is not," she answered sharply. "But it is the reason that King Richard has granted our family the right to choose our mates."

"Ah," Rourke said, properly impressed by the way she'd neatly brought the conversation back around to what she'd wanted to talk about anyway.

"Our family is filled with great healers, and one daughter in each generation is supposed to be able to heal with Boadicea's magic flowing through her hands. Our generation got two. My older sister, Celestia. She's very petite and has one green eye, one blue."

Rourke frowned.

"And my younger sister, Ela, who looks like she's

71

supposed to. She can see auras. And I—I can play the lute and make perfume. Do you see how this is unfair? My grandmother can heal, and my mother—well, she cannot. But she's beautiful—so beautiful that my father fell in love with her when he was raiding the Welsh lands and he took her. Which is why she thinks that beauty should be enough. She doesn't understand that I want to be more. And when I try and explain it to her, she makes me learn another instrument, or bids me concoct another lotion."

"How many instruments do you have?" Rourke asked, remembering the light callous he'd felt on her thumb.

"Seven." She laughed softly. "I used to dream of cutting my hair and running away to join the traveling players. But then," her sigh was heavy, "I would think of never seeing my family again, and I just couldn't do it. They love me, and I love them. Oft times that emotion is more binding than chains. Have you ever been in love?"

"No." His answer was immediate. Being raised among the court by nursemaids and servant girls hadn't been horrible, and, thanks to his foster siblings, it hadn't even been that lonely. He'd always been quick to find the girl who would give him sweets in exchange for a smile, and as he got older, he learned to trade his smile for other things. Love was most often a commodity to be bargained over, and in those instances of true love, it was a weakness.

"I have never been in love either. Although I've seen it, and I believe in love's power, I have never fallen under its spell."

Intrigued, Rourke said, "You sound like a jaded court pet."

"I am not jaded, or spoiled. I, Lord Rourke, am a realist. Because I also believe that a marriage between two people with the same values can last, and perhaps affection can turn into love."

Her smoky tones made her a natural storyteller, and her subject matter made her even more compelling. "I'd wager you'd have been a popular minstrel, perhaps even in the king's court." Where someone as fresh as she would get trampled, until finding a protector, Rourke thought.

The sound of liquid being poured came between them, and then Galiana said, "Here, it's lemon and honey. Careful, though, 'tis hot."

He heard her sit across from him, and she took a sip.

"You didn't need magic to heal me. My leg is better."

Her cup clanked against the saucer, and he imagined her hurriedly setting it aside. "You could've died."

"But I didn't."

"Well," she paused, "it was only because I was able to follow my sister's directions. She kept a book of medicines. Although from what I have been reading, your inability to see most likely stems from the blow to the temple, not the cut so close to your eye. Or perhaps the blow to the back of your head."

It was the way she said it, so sorrowfully, that made

him reach out his hand. "I am sorry," she said. He was surprised when she joined her hand to his.

As soon as their fingers touched, he was hit with inspiration. He needed her, and she was bored with her life as a lady in the country. She went on about proposals of marriage for the beautiful people, and yet she was unwed. Galiana had to be one of those passively pretty girls who never called attention to themselves. No wonder she rebelled against a beautiful mother!

He could tell her just enough to win her assistance, and perhaps she would play along. Rourke could not tell her all of the truth—it would be a death sentence—but he could share enough information to get her on his side.

She said, "The only thing you can do is rest. And pray for your vision to return. Will you continue to hide it from your men?"

He rubbed his chin. Galiana's compassion was evident, and there was a good chance she would do as he asked.

The door swung open with such force that Rourke reached for his sword, which wasn't there. Damn.

"I've caught the treasonous little bugger. Found him scratching a letter to the bleeding King Philippe, asking for France's aid to bring King Richard back from Germany." Jamie's steps were heavy, and Rourke was able to hear the sound of scuffling feet. "He actually wrote, wrote—for the love of Christ, what were you thinking?—that Prince John is a usurper, with his eye on the throne. A coward who wants to steal England," Jamie spluttered. "Thank the sweet Lord that it stops there."

Chair legs scraped against the floor as Galiana rose. "Oh, Saint Vitus," Rourke heard her implore the patron saint of crazy people.

"Eh, Ned," she said, "What have you done?"

Rourke clenched his fists, furious that he couldn't see who else had come down the stairs. Squinting, he could make out a nondescript blur, which was at least better than grayish black nothing, but not bloody good enough.

Franz, with his cultured accent, said, "I went up to liberate the young man, and saw him writing this. He had your paper, Rourke. Your quill and ink all set out along his desk. What could I do?"

"Here, my lord. He had this, too, but I've put everything back where it was." Will dropped the pack with a thud to the floor next to Rourke's bed.

"How soon can ye ride? The boy will have to go to court and stand trial for crimes against the crown." The sound of Godfrey's ringed hand closing over the hilt of his sword made Rourke bow his head to hide his fury.

"Crown? Prince John doesn't have it yet," a young man sneered.

"Ned, Ned, oh, dear, shut your mouth." Galiana's voice rose as she spoke. "He's a boy, a child; he can't stand trial."

"I am not a child," Ned argued in a voice cracking between manhood and youth.

Rourke pulled the bag onto his lap, casually searching

in every single corner and pocket and seam. He ground his back teeth together in frustration. What he'd hidden was gone. Bloody hell.

This changed everything, and he had to think fast. If the person who stole the key understood what was in hand, it meant the end of Britain. Rourke had to get to court, immediately.

"Everyone needs to calm down," Rourke said, leaning back on one elbow as if he hadn't a care in the world. "Jamie, did you find the dispensation?"

"I've got it."

There was no way out of this situation. He would have to make the best of a bad bargain and hope that in the end the English crown was worth the price.

The problem was, he genuinely liked Galiana. She'd cared for him, despite the fact that he'd taken over her home and imprisoned her knights. She'd stood by him, even when he'd lied. A woman like that was worth her weight in gold. Mayhap he would make her a gift of that, when all of this was over. Any chance at their relationship remaining friendly was about to die.

"Franz, fetch the priest."

"I will not marry you," Galiana said, her light footsteps coming toward him. "Your knight has the dispensation in his hands, which is proof that you cannot force me."

If he'd had more time, if he had his sight, mayhap he wouldn't need to be so cruel. But he was out of options.

He needed an ally, and Galiana had already shown she had honor. A commodity he admired, since he had none himself. She loved her family. In order to gain her co-operation, her brother would have to go to the tower in London. He didn't have anyone else to trust.

He made his voice deliberate and cold. "Lady, you have no choices. Your brother has been caught in the act of writing defamatory remarks regarding our future king. He will stand trial." He heard the catch of her breath as she sought to control her emotions.

And felt like an ass. Colder, he commanded, "Jamie. The dispensation? Burn it. Where's that damn priest? We marry now, and leave for Windsor tomorrow."

Chapter Four

"How dare you threaten me? Or my brother? You have no rights here." Galiana's voice shook with anger. Her belly knotted with nerves as she was overcome by emotion. How could Rourke turn so hot and cold? She'd seen a glimmer of a heart, or mayhap she'd just been praying he had one.

"Me Lord Rourke has every right, lass." Jamie lifted the rolled dispensation bearing King Richard's seal with his left hand, and her brother with his right. The man was an ogre.

"Since when has brute strength ruled over common sense and chivalry?" Galiana felt the heat in her cheeks burn as she spouted the nonsensical question. Courtly manners meant nothing in the face of strength. Muscle was always the victor, and if she weren't a lady, she'd, well . . . Her gaze swept the work table, pausing at the small eating knife still on top of it.

"I don't believe ye're as innocent as that," Godfrey grumbled.

Galiana breathed in through her nose, wishing she could suck in a deep, bracing gulp of air instead of a dignified sip. Her fingers curled within the fabric of her skirts, and she edged closer to the table. "I don't particularly care what you think," she said with a jerk of her chin. Her mother would faint dead away if she heard her daughter talking in such a manner.

The thought bolstered her courage.

Ed, who Jamie and everyone else thought to be Ned, squirmed in Jamie's grasp, knocking his head back into the knight's chin.

"Argh, ye little bast—"

In the commotion, Galiana scooped up the knife and ran to her brother. She tried shoving him behind her, but he wouldn't stay. She had to be content with standing side by side. The two Montehues stood with their backs against the stone wall, her weapon out in front of them.

"You only have that wee little blade, lass?" Jamie's low voice taunted her. It was the sad truth that her hand trembled as she held the blade, but it was all that she had.

"You'll not take my brother to the tower. He's done nothing wrong—"

"Liar!" Robert said over the ringing sound of his sword being drawn from its sheath.

This time she went for that deep, courageous breath and refused to think about Mam—who wouldn't be pleased at this situation, no matter what.

Ed elbowed her, "Give me the knife, Gali."

"I think not. They'd skewer you for certes."

Her heart beat rapidly in her chest. She'd been given an easy job—lady of the manor had sounded so simple. How had everything gone so wrong?

"Galiana," Rourke called over the chaos in a voice as smooth as Cook's lemon custard. "You are right. We cannot force you against your will, and there's no need for Ned to go to the tower."

She lowered her arm, grateful that he, at least, was being reasonable. His face was turned toward her, and she realized he was listening for her. Calling herself an idiot for helping him at all, she cleared her throat. His eyes focused on where she was standing, and she had the impression he could really see her.

The man was a chameleon.

Her face warmed beneath his blind scrutiny. "You'll not burn the king's writ?"

Rourke's entreating expression slowly changed. Starting with the upward tilt of the left side of his full lips, closely followed by the right side of his mouth, resulting in a devilish grin that made her knees go weak.

Nay, the man was a demi-god, and she had the insane urge to write bad poetry. Galiana discovered a new-found sympathy for some of her admirers. She'd never been deliberately cruel in her rejections of them, and she'd never encouraged their attentions, but if they'd felt so strongly, so—

He coughed. "I am proposing a trade," he said with a dip of his forehead.

She would have agreed to anything that fell from his lips—if his knights hadn't laughed aloud, breaking the spell he'd bound her in.

"What is wrong with you?" Ed hissed.

Shaking her head, she lifted her useless weapon. Really, she thought with sudden clarity, who brings a cooking knife to a sword fight? "What trade?"

"We burn them both."

"What?"

Visions of poor Ed being burned at the stake had her preparing to attack. "Never!" Galiana waved the knife in front of her and her brother, as if that would keep the knights away. She risked a look at her enemies. Aside from Jamie, who was rubbing his chin and glaring at Ed, they looked bored.

"We burn the incriminating, treasonous, letter your brother wrote—after stealing the supplies—"

"Aye, little thief," Will agreed.

"What, and let the bugger off?" Robert kicked the table leg.

Galiana pressed her lips together, knowing she couldn't question 'Ned' until later. She hoped the real Ned had the good sense to hide until this farce was over.

"Bugger this," Ed said with false bravado.

"Shhh—that does not help." Galiana edged her brother closer to the back wall.

"As I was saying"—Rourke raised his voice—"we can burn the evidence of your brother's crime."

Nodding, Galiana started to lower the blade again.

"At the same time that we burn the dispensation. A fair exchange, don't you think?"

"No," Galiana spluttered. "I don't. My family is descended—"

"My lady, please stop putting off the inevitable. We see that the royal seal is on the dispensation," Godfrey said.

"King Richard's seal," Ed protested, scooting his head around her shoulder. "Ye can't burn it!"

Franz rubbed his short moustache. "Is a royal decree more important than a sealed royal document?"

Galiana noticed that each of the knights seemed to be pondering the question, as if they had a say in her future, too.

Was she the only one who did not?

Ridiculous!

And what game, exactly, was Rourke playing? She hadn't forgotten his whispers of treachery—had he been warning her he was the one who couldn't be trusted?

Nay, his warning had been too intense. The danger had to be from somewhere, or someone, else.

Godfrey, older than the rest of the knights and more seasoned at life, shrugged the issue away. "We're here on England's behalf—to tally the taxes owed for the crown and collect the difference."

"My father was recently raised in station and just gifted new land. He doesn't owe taxes until after the first harvest. This is but the first of February."

"We're in the middle of a blizzard," Ed cut in with sarcasm. "Or do ye tax on snowfall?"

"Watch your mouth, lad, else you'll be missing your tongue!" Jamie stepped forward, and Galiana slipped between the annoyed knight and her brother, who seemed unafraid—the fool.

Then again, she was in no position to judge, as she was holding a table knife against a room filled with war-hardened knights.

"Jamie, leave the boy be. The taxes were a cover to get into the manor so I could have the lady. My lady, what will you do? Save your brother from the tower because of his poisonous pen, by simply agreeing to burn the dispensation? Or sentence young Ned here to death by hanging for treason so you can be true to your family's trumped-up legacy?"

"'Tis not make-believe!" She responded to the taunt in Rourke's voice, infuriated. "What choice is that?"

"I wouldn't want you to try and annul the marriage, my lady, by screaming force."

"Just take her, Rourke, and be done with it," Robert smacked his sword against the floor.

"Robbie, you have much to learn about the ladies," Franz said with a sigh.

Godfrey humphed. "Aye, but he has a point. Wed her, bed her, and collect the rents. Prince John will be happy enough with that."

"And just how is our Rourke to have a happy household if he starts his years of wedded bliss with the bride unwillin'?" Jamie crossed his arms over his broad chest.

"Happens all the time." Robert snorted.

Galiana, quite irritated with the way the conversation was going, remembered she was trained to be a lady. Catching her brother's eye, she did as she'd been taught and fainted like a delicately wilting flower into Ed's waiting arms.

"Galiana?" Rourke heard her soft sigh, then his men rushing forward. Jamie, God bless him, said loudly, "She's fainted. Stand back; give her air."

"No wonder," Franz agreed. "The brave lady was a lioness protecting her cub," he said poetically.

The 'boy,' Ned, scoffed. "I'm her brother."

Rourke worried that perhaps the situation was too much for a lady of her standing, and hoped he hadn't pushed too far. Odd, though, since he'd gotten the idea the lady was made of sterner stuff. His life, and the lives of his men, depended on his character studies—but he wasn't himself now, was he?

He narrowed his eyes, feeling the tug at the side of

his face as the movement pulled at his stitches. For a mere blink in time, he saw shadowed images all bent over a blob of gray fabric.

Rourke fisted his hands in fury, and then relaxed his expression. He sensed someone staring at him, so he threw back his shoulders and ordered, "Bring her to the cot."

"She's fine," her brother said. "Don't touch her."

The entire family had control issues. Well, it was time they learned that he, Lord Rourke Wallis, was in charge. "Bring her to the cot, fetch the priest, and do it now!"

"She has to be conscious to say her part," Will snickered. Rourke decided extra lessons in knightly behavior would be added for the young squire. Not the prissy manners being touted at court, but polite behavior. For Robert, too.

"Why the priest?" Ned asked in a warbling voice.

Had he ever been so young? Poised on the brink of manhood, ready to do battle for what was right. Ha, Rourke thought as he pinched the bridge of his nose, *I was reared on lies and intrigue.* Battle with swords kept a man at his physical peak, while battle with the mind kept him sharp and alert.

It was his mind that would keep him out of the gallows today, and mayhap the innocent Galiana would forgive him at the end. He shouldn't care—she was a duty, nothing more. Except—except, damn it all, she'd been kind when he'd been vulnerable.

Jamie brushed by him. "I've got her here, although I'll not be part of a ceremony where the bride is snoring."

It was the tiniest intake of breath that alerted Rourke to the fact that the sweet, innocent lady might be faking. Relying on his senses was a part of what made him a successful spy—now, with his vision compromised, his hearing was more acute.

He turned, following Jamie's voice as his foster brother laid Galiana down on the mattress. Rourke could easily imagine a feminine form in his bed. She'd be faintly pretty, and soft. He didn't mind her sarcasm; it added the right amount of spice. The kind of woman a man could sate his hunger with. Squinting his eyes, hoping for a blurred shadow, he saw nothing.

A sharp pain pierced between his brows.

Jamie turned and put his hand on Rourke's shoulder. "I had a mangy dog once that looked better than you."

Rourke coughed to cover a curse. "I hope you slit its throat and put that mutt out of its misery."

"Feelin' bad, then?"

"Aye."

"Sit, here." Jamie casually pushed him down and Rourke sat, his arse miraculously hitting a stool.

His head throbbed. "The priest, Jamie. I want him to hold both documents until this matter is settled. I'd thought to leave for court tomorrow."

"Snow's kept us trapped in these past few days,

Rourke," Godfrey said. "But I'll look this afternoon. It would be nice if the skies would clear." Rourke was grateful for the older man's practicality.

"Will you bring the lady with us?" Franz's voice held a note of interest that brought Rourke's instincts to the fore. What if Franz was the other spy, the betrayer in their tight-knit group?

"The lady Galiana, you mean? Will I take my new wife to court?" Rourke turned his head toward the space where he could hear Galiana taking even breaths. He'd have to tell her that a person never breathed like that unless they were feigning sleep. "She'll obey me, whatever I command."

Her breath hitched, and he railed against Fate that he couldn't see her. He imagined her delicate fury would be intriguing to view. Was she blond, with fair skin, prone to blushes? Dark, with olive flesh that hinted of roses?

How long had it been since a woman had held a secret from him?

Jamie gave his shoulder a shove. "Rourke, my man, I'll send down the bailiff, and he can go over the monies. The priest can hold the letter that scrap of a lad penned."

"Don't forget the dispensation," Ned growled, and Rourke heard the boy's desire to protect his family in the undertone.

"Nobody's forgetting anything," Rourke assured him.

"Well, what are we doing, then?" Will asked.

Thinking quick, Rourke rubbed his temple wound.

"This pains me yet, but I'd be moved from the sick room to the master's chambers."

Again, he heard the barely perceptible change in Galiana as she tried to stay still.

"Of course," Godfrey said, "we should have had ye there already."

"Nay," Jamie clapped his large hand over Rourke's shoulder and squeezed. "This allowed more privacy, whilst the lady mended his broken crown, aye?"

While Rourke appreciated the sly innuendo that had his men chuckling, he detested the word crown. "My head aches, but I'll be ready to travel as soon as the weather permits. Has anyone been to the village since we've arrived?"

"No," Robert said. "We made a path to the barns and stables, but naught else."

Rourke dipped his head down, his hands to his temples, as a way to avoid making eye contact, or not making eye contact, with someone he couldn't see. He groaned for good measure.

"Out, now, all of ye," Jamie ordered. "Rourke, we'll get that chamber readied right away."

"I'll stay with my sister," Ned announced.

Rourke thought the lad might make a great knight, the way he took charge. He said, "You'll not, actually."

"You freed me!"

"Aye, from the solar. But I don't particularly trust you. Franz, keep Ned out of trouble, would you?"

"With pleasure," the French knight replied. Rourke knew if he could see the displaced nobleman, Franz would be stroking his beard, searching the boy for any sign of deceit.

Franz de Lacey was a master gambler, as well as a wicked swordsman, and he'd keep the boy from any further meddling where he didn't belong.

It would also tie the knight's hands, if he, by chance, happened to be the traitor in their circle.

Well aware of the dangers of court intrigue, Rourke didn't think he was the only one in the royal court's employ. But who served which king? That was the question that, if left unanswered, could lead to their deaths.

Christ's bones! All the players in this intrigue were in this room together now. Who had stolen King William's ring from his bag? His forehead throbbed with tension. Should he have Jamie lock the door, and demand a complete search of everyone?

But if he was wrong . . . What if the ring had fallen out of the pack? Or mayhap it had slipped from its pocket during the attack from Lord Harold. Then he'd be giving himself away. Icy tendrils of apprehension snaked around his shoulders.

It was possible, too, that whoever had stolen the token from King William might have already hidden it again—and then Rourke would have given up his advantage for naught. He stared as hard as he could, but nothing came into focus. What if his sight never returned?

Damn it to Hades. Real fear coiled in his gut—but just for a heartbeat.

He wouldn't be defeated. Not here, in this dungeon that smelled like lavender and lemon and sage. There was no pride in waving the flag of surrender.

Rourke banished any doubts regarding the success of his mission. He'd not failed yet, and even blind he could see more than most. It was who he was.

Another possibility, and the one that appealed to him most, was that whoever had taken the jewel didn't understand what they held.

The key to two thrones.

"Keep your hands to yourself," Ned said loudly. Then Rourke heard a squeal and imagined Franz was helping the impudent lad along. Scuffling up the stairs, Franz said conversationally, "If we are to be friends, then we shall speak to one another as friends, oui?"

The squealing persisted until Ned agreed. "Ye didn't have to pinch me ear off!"

Rourke allowed the brief hope that Franz, a man he respected, would not be his enemy—but he knew better than to trust anyone.

"You'll not force her, Rourke?" Godfrey asked from somewhere near the bottom of the stairs. Keeping one eye closed, the one that had stitches next to it, he lifted his head and set his mouth in a forbidding line.

"How dare ye ask that?" Jamie roared, taking two large steps away from Rourke's side.

"No offense meant, Jamie." Godfrey remained calm. "There is much at stake here, and the lady is a grand prize. Land aplenty, if a man were thinkin' to retire."

"Her father's lands," Rourke clarified. "Besides, I have no need of another man's property. And you already have a wife, and children, so don't think about the lady's assets." Then again, men did strange things for the good of their family.

Jamie's laugh sounded forced, and Rourke knew his foster brother was feeling the strain of this absurd situation. Jamie was the only one of his men privy to the fact that at least two other knights would be coming to claim the lady's hand. He had cause to be thankful for the snowstorm, as it surely had impeded their coming as he healed.

Rourke's head pounded with each booted step his knights took up the stairs.

Who had that cursed ring?

"I'll be back with the bailiff," Jamie announced from the top of the stairs, "and the priest."

Sighing, Rourke shifted on the seat and picked up the bag again. Deftly going through the pockets, he accepted that the ring was truly missing.

While his heart galloped like an unbroken stallion, his agile mind came up with a way to protect his secret. The ring, designed with silver filigree and old Scottish knots, had a unique stone, flat and polished to a milky blue shine, inlaid in the center. Though King William had worn it, as had many Scots rulers before him, it was not bulky nor overtly masculine.

It was obviously a ring of power, an antique. He'd say it was a family heirloom, and he'd brought it as a betrothal gift for Galiana. His pulse quickened as he planned how to explain the significance of the ring, while misdirecting its importance.

If any recalled King William wearing the ring, then he'd remind them that at one time, when Scotland's king had been without a crown, he'd worked for the man and the ring had been his pay. Then he'd remind them of his public, albeit staged, disgrace from Scotland's court.

It was plausible—and that was all Rourke needed to stay in the game.

With a lighter thought to the future, he turned his head toward the cot. An indistinct shape of drab color. "You can stop pretending that you're in a faint, my lady."

Galiana's breaths remained steady.

"'Tis just you and I now—there is no need for snoring."

She popped up from the mattress, the suddenness reminding him of a bird flushed from a bush. "What say you?" Her voice was a harsh, whiskey whisper. "Betwixt us two, there is naught but a farce. How dare you put me in a position like that? Wedded! For certes"— he heard the whoosh of air as she moved her hands like dervishes—"how am I to choose, if one of the choices rips me of my pride, whilst the other sends my brother to possible death? Oh!"

"Galiana, I have a plan, if you would but listen."

"Oh ho, so now you want to explain?"

"I've been ill, my lady, and hardly in a place where I could—"

"So you think to trap me with your pity?"

Her suppressed anger enticed him. Her strides were long as she marched around the sick room, her irritation so palpable the air crackled around her, the energy of it transferring to him like heat from a candle.

Perhaps, when he could see again, it wouldn't matter if she were just passably pretty. Her character would more than make up for any physical flaws.

No. What was he thinking? He couldn't stay married to the wren, although he'd remain faithful to her whilst they were wed. There were other plans for him, plans that placed him in a position of courtly power.

Knowing he was going to set her aside, the gentlemanly thing to do would be to avoid the marriage bed.

But, he acknowledged, she drew him to her. He would bed her often and well, he mused, rubbing his temples as she strode to and fro. He groaned again, with repressed lust.

He couldn't gain power with a country miss as his wife, not the power that he was being groomed for.

What a mess his life had become.

If only—no. This was what he'd been asked to do, and on bended knee before the Breath of Merlin and King William, he'd agreed.

"Stop walking so loudly," he complained.

She stopped, directly in front of him.

The citrus of her perfume invaded his nostrils, and he swallowed hard. He was a master spy, damn it all, and he could control his baser urges.

His manhood hardened at the thought of those baser urges, and Rourke leaned forward, his elbows on his knees, his nose accidentally brushing the fabric of her skirts.

She stepped back and cleared her throat. "Why didn't you tell your men you cannot see?"

"They grow restless here, and it seemed like the clearest way to avoid mischief. I'm a skilled knight, my lady, but I'm not at my best at the moment."

His best would be something grand; she knew it. Galiana stared down at the top of Rourke's head. He was studying the floor, bent at the waist, as if his stomach ached. By candlelight, his hair was burnished brown and lightly curled at the nape. His profile, the side that she hadn't mangled, was so beautiful it could have been carved in flesh-toned marble—she longed to paint his image, to try to capture the essence of him, for herself.

They couldn't marry!

He made her feel.

She'd already planned on sacrificing herself in marriage

to a man who would have no claim to her emotions. There was safety in knowing a layer of ice protected her heart. But Rourke stirred hope to life, heating her very blood. She'd feared she was too cold to love, and yet—she knew nothing of him. Nothing real. Dare she take a risk?

"If I agree to wed you, you'll not leave me here whilst you go to court."

He made an injured sound at the back of his throat, and compassion compelled her to put aside her anger—which was somewhat aimed toward herself anyway.

"Come, lie down." She tugged at his arm, which was muscled and immovable.

"I'm not ill, woman! Besides, I'll be moving to the master's chambers."

Her pulse leapt at the thought of him lying in her parents' bed. Her parents made no secret that they loved one another in all ways, and that bed knew it.

Her belly tingled.

"You'll be comfortable. There's a fireplace and a large bed with down comforters and a feather mattress."

"I don't plan on sleeping in there alone, my lady."

Galiana pressed her hand to her wildly beating heart.

"I can bring some extra blankets for Jamie," she pretended to misunderstand, letting her hand drop to her side.

He reached out so fast she shrieked. How had he known where her fingers were?

"We'll wed, as Prince John instructed. We'll go to court together, gaining the prince's blessing."

Oh, Saint Agnes, help me.

Knowing she was making what perhaps could be the biggest mistake of her young life, Galiana returned the pressure of his fingers with a light squeeze.

She'd wanted adventure, and Saint Jude had delivered. Inhaling deeply for courage, she drew on her family's legacy of warrior women.

"You needn't burn the dispensation, Rourke. I'll marry you. Of my own free will."

She exhaled in a very unladylike way, and her head grew as light as a falling snowflake. Black dots danced before her eyes. Had she really just been so daring? What would her parents say? Her heart fluttered behind her chest like a butterfly trapped in a jar.

"Oh, dear, I—"

"Breathe through your nose—hell, lean back, to me!"

Rourke's order penetrated the odd fog clouding Galiana's mind, and she managed to fall back into his outstretched arms. When she roused after what seemed like moments, her head was cushioned by the expanse of his bare, muscled chest. She nuzzled her cheek against his warmth.

"You make me feel," she whispered, acutely aware of the heat sizzling between them. But a simple linen sheet separated them, and his manhood jutted against the back of her thigh. Her insides melted, and she felt as languid as she had after a drink of her father's brandy.

"Do you do this often?"

The rumble of his chest beneath her cheek made her laugh. "This is the first time I've ever actually fainted."

He stroked the length of her hair, and she could have purred with contentment. It was so wonderful, this release of inhibition. What would it be like to love this man? Mayhap she could learn. Love couldn't be more difficult than learning the twelve stringed psaltery, nor as complicated as creating a skin softener for a lady's heels.

"We should talk"—Rourke's warm breath tickled her ear—"before the others come."

But it was too late.

The door slammed open, and Galiana jumped from Rourke's lap, her cheeks afire with shame for being in a compromising position and, she admitted to herself, awakening desire.

It was a good thing Rourke couldn't see her now.

"What goes on here?" Father Jonah came down the stairs, one hand on the wooden rail. "The master's chamber is being readied, and E—, uh, Ned, claims you're being forced to wed! I'll not have it, my lady."

Her hands trembled, so she put them together, as if in prayer. "Calm yourself, Father. I have agreed to wed Rourke Wallis." She couldn't believe how easily the words fell from her lips, as if they were meant to be. Her unthawing, romantic heart took wing, and she slid a glance toward Rourke.

His face was expressionless as he looked toward Father Jonah. The look chilled her, and she quickly returned her gaze to the priest, who had reached the bottom stair and held his hand out, palm up.

"What have you there, Father?" It looked to be a locket. Or a ring? The center stone sparked like blue tinder, and goose bumps prickled along her arms. She took a step toward the stone, her fingertips tingling. Father Jonah appeared unaware of the dancing flames crackling around the jewel.

Impossible. Galiana blinked, and the sparks were gone. She wanted that ring.

"I'll tell you, my lady, and then we can toss this charlatan to the goats."

Trepidation danced along her spine. Rourke remained silent, although the fine lines bracketing his mouth paled.

"See this? He can't marry you, my lady Galiana, for he is betrothed to another!"

"Is this true?" I should have known. Galiana cursed her gullibility.

Rourke shrugged. "I cannot see what the priest holds."

"A silver and blue ring." Her eyes itched with unshed tears. She'd been under a lot of strain; that's all. Rings didn't have dancing flames, and she did not believe in love. What she needed was a warm bath, her lavender and rose candles, and a cup of lemon tea. And mayhap a heated towel with rose oil upon her forehead, lest the worry bring wrinkles.

With a bark of scoffing laughter, Rourke said, "That's why the priest says I'm promised to another? Because he found the gift I was bringing to you?"

Startled, Gali realized her first instinct was to believe him and take the ring, but she carefully masked her emotions and replayed how he'd said the words—as if they were true, and yet she wasn't sure that they were.

Tilting her head to the side, she studied the man. He was too smooth.

"You're lying."

"My lady! I overheard one of his knights saying how Lord Rourke had been promised to another. That is why this wedding comes as a surprise to his men, too." Father Jonah shook his finger at Rourke.

"You eavesdrop and take those words as fact?" Rourke stood, anger evident in the furrow of his brow as he said coldly in her direction, "What difference does it make? I have been ordered by Prince John to marry you. You will marry me, or your brother goes to the tower."

He paused, but Galiana couldn't have spoken if she'd wanted to.

"This isn't a love match, my lady, so don't act the injured party. I promise you nothing of my heart. You'll never go hungry or be without clothing or a roof over your head. I don't believe in love."

The hope that had dared to blossom within her breast shriveled. Galiana lifted her chin. "Neither do I."

Chapter Five

"I'm ready, Jamie. Send the men in."

Rourke sat with his back to the fireplace. He and Jamie had placed the furniture strategically so that Rourke would be able to get up and walk around as if he could see.

He could feel Galiana's fury, hotter than the flames at his back. The roles in this game of chance had already been assigned, and he could only allow her anger to be an irritant—nothing more.

"This is foolish. We can't leave tomorrow. What if we get separated on the road? It would serve you right to get lost in a snowstorm. You could add chills and a cough to your current maladies. I'm no healer." He heard the mad whish of her chained girdle as she paced. "You could die, and then where would we all be? Prince

John will probably send another knight to take your place, and at least you are handso—" She stumbled over her word, and Rourke swore he could hear her grind her teeth. "Here. You are already here. This is ridiculous, and you risk too much."

Aye, she was quick of wit. He'd not told her that other men were on their way for her hand. But at least she understood that Prince John was serious in his quest to bind her family's loyalty to him.

"Great victory takes great risk." Jamie jumped to Rourke's defense. "Every knight knows that."

"Do I look like a warrior to you?"

Jamie choked. "Nay, lass, ye don't."

Rather than dwell on what Galiana did look like, Rourke emphasized, "The men won't know that I can't see—not if we stay with the plan. My sight will return. This is nothing more than an obstacle. If a tree falls in your path, you don't turn back, do you? No!" Rourke rubbed his hands together, remembering the queen's teachings with relish. "You cut the tree from the road and make firewood."

"Not only vanquishing the enemy, but gaining power from his demise," Jamie finished the lesson while Rourke chuckled.

"You both are demented," Galiana pronounced. "Tell me again why I'm aiding your cause?"

"Your rascal of a brother," Jamie said.

"Ned," Rourke agreed.

"Nay, you told me if I married you, he wouldn't have to go to the tower."

Rourke, knowing he was adding fuel to her fury, paused before explaining. "It's true. You agreed to marry me, and I agreed not to send your brother to the tower for treason—the defamatory letter he was writing, in exchange for the royal dispensation."

"Then my brother is in no danger," she said clearly. Rourke was impressed by the tight control she held over her voice, which was sensual and filled with promise even as she kept herself a hair's breadth away from yelling.

"Not exactly. You see, he'll still be coming to court with us, and possibly to the tower, depending on your behavior."

He heard her gasp of outrage but continued, "So that you do what you're told to do."

"On what grounds would he be admitted, if not for treason?"

She was smart, Rourke conceded, and single-minded. From his seat before the fire, he pronounced the death knell. "Theft. He pilfered my sack—gave my, well, your ring to the priest." He patted the spot beneath his tunic where the ring rested, safe on a leather thong.

"Saint Vitus help us, for you're insane." Galiana's voice finally rose, and he imagined that losing her decorum really pissed her off. He didn't bother hiding his grin.

"I'll go get the men," Jamie said before wisely leaving the room, the door slamming closed behind him.

It was no hardship to keep his grin in place as the delicate clicks of Galiana's footsteps stalked toward him. He wished he could see her, but everything was a grayish black. Since it wasn't complete darkness, he didn't complain.

Galiana stopped abruptly, then leaned over so her face was in front of his. Mint-scented words bathed his flesh as she spoke with enough charm to rival the queen. "You hold all the power. For now. Be warned, my lord, that if I see a chance to thwart you without harming myself or my kin, I will take it."

Amazed, amused, and aroused by her audacity, Rourke reached up, trapping her face between his hands. He brushed her cheekbones with the pads of his thumbs, then lowered her face down, as if for a kiss. But instead of pressing his mouth to hers, he brought her cheek to his. She sighed softly at the contact and didn't move away when he released her.

Galiana was sweet innocence, the exact opposite of the women who had raised him, in more ways than one, at court. He felt the pulse in her neck jump as her body reacted to his, and yet she remained still instead of giving in to virginal nerves. Intriguing.

"The first rule at court, my lady, is to never reveal your strategy. Keep your moves close to your"—her breath quickened—"breast. Else your enemy will pounce."

"I have no enemies." She lowered her voice to a sensuous whisper that had Rourke longing for the evening ahead. They'd be married, and he'd make sure no other man would take what belonged to him. Fair or no, the lady was a prize. He could learn her body with his fingertips. Who needed eyes in the dark?

"Except for you," she added softly.

"We needn't be at war, my lady," Rourke promised.

Galiana slowly pulled away from him, and he immediately missed her heat.

"We already are."

He heard the low jingles of the chains girdled around her waist, and he wondered what she wore. A bland tunic of semi-fine linen, in a demure brown or gray . . . His body tensed with need, and he didn't know if the lady he lusted after was fat or thin or plain or pretty. What's more, for the first time in his life—it didn't matter.

She was compassionate, brave, and adventurous. Reared to be a lady, but her nature cried out for more than the confines of sedate womanhood. He understood too well what it was like to be trapped by circumstances of birth.

"I don't know who you are," she told him.

He could be anybody. Whoever she wanted him to be. "It's complicated."

"Complicated." Her laughter seemed self-directed, and Rourke wondered why. "My parents will be back by the end of February, at the latest. We can announce the engagement then."

"Nay," Rourke tapped his fingers against the arm of the chair. "We'll have the priest marry us tonight."

Galiana made a strangled sound at the back of her throat. "Nay."

"It's for your own protection."

"How so?"

"My men are excellent knights, but we live in turbulent times."

"You don't trust your own men?" The fear she'd valiantly tamped down rose to the surface as she spoke, and Rourke wished he could explain more.

"It's complicated."

"I see." Her light footsteps were muffled as she paced the carpeted area of the floor. "So you've been ordered to marry me because Prince John wants control of my father and my father's knights—in case there is a war between the rightful king and those who want the throne?"

Rourke stopped tapping his fingers. "Caution, lady."

"What? I am but speculating as to why my future is to be laid in ruins at the whim of a prince."

"You've heard King Richard may be dead?"

"A vile rumor, my lord, as you must be aware."

His blood cooled. "What do you think has happened?"

She sniffed. "Queen Eleanor and William Marshall have taken great pains to send runners all over the country, defying the gossip with truth. Emperor Henry VI is holding King Richard for ransom. We are not so backwoods, my lord, that news doesn't reach us eventually. That vicious rumor was started by John, so that he could take advantage of our king's absence."

"Choose your words wisely, else your brother will not be the only Montehue in the tower." He forced his words to be harsh—for her sake.

"You threaten me?"

"I am warning you." His life was a game of chance, and now by knowing him, so was hers. She'd best learn to guard herself, lest she get hurt.

"Still, I would see Prince John before we wed, and put my case before him."

"What?" Rourke's gut tightened with immediate trepidation.

"He can't know about the royal dispensation; it will take but one meeting to explain."

"I can still burn the damn thing, and he need never know." Should he tell her now that in this particular game of chance, she'd lost three times over? Aye, it had been Prince John's wish that one of his vassals wed the Montehue daughter immediately. Prince John needed the Montehue warriors almost as much as he needed the Montehue coin. For what nefarious purpose? A chance to take the power for himself.

Rourke drummed his fingers atop his knee. Three of the prince's men had been given the challenge. Rourke had arrived first, gaining entrance, albeit unconsciously, to the manor, thereby claiming the lady. In what had been a typical Prince John move to catapult his men into action, things had become personal. He couldn't give Galiana up.

Lord Christien was an oaf—uneducated and crass. Lord Harold was crude and didn't believe in bathing. The sweet-scented Galiana would wither amongst his stench. Neither man had scruples—well, neither did he—but they were ruled by coin, whereas he was ruled by loyalty.

Besides, she provided the best cover for him on his mission. He would bring his grateful country bride to court, having saved her from the clutches of both Christien and Harold, very publicly cementing his loyalty to John.

"Excuse me?" Galiana's tone chided him for not paying attention. "You think there aren't copies of the dispensation?"

Outraged, Rourke rose to his feet. "You lie."

"I don't lie, and I dislike that you are so quick to malign my character."

He couldn't miss the haughtiness in her words, and he helplessly fisted his hands at his sides.

"Do not mistake us for country peasants, my lord, just because we are not at court. My father was recently given more land, but he'd held plenty before." Her voice was controlled. "All that changed is that he now swears fealty directly to the king. 'Tis true the manor has few knights in residence, but our resources are spread thin due to the newest acquisitions, and my parents' travel. We are educated, and we Montehues do not value deceit as an honorable asset."

He imagined her, with long, brown hair, and brown,

no, maybe blue, eyes. She would be determined to win his respect, aye, and she deserved it, no less. Could he take the maidenhead of a woman such as this, knowing he'd be setting her aside once this latest intrigue had passed?

Lust had no honor, and he knew he had to have her.

"You speak scornfully, my lady."

"You give me a headache, my lord, and that causes wrinkles."

She sighed, and then the click of the heels on her shoes told him she'd moved from the carpet to the wood floor around the edge of the room. He'd memorized the layout of the chamber—the large bed against the wall; if he walked five steps to the left, he'd be at the window. The fireplace to his back, and the door leading to the hall to the right. It was thirty steps from the fireplace to the wall the bed was on, and to the right of that was a small chair and writing table.

"You worry over wrinkles?" How old was she? She sounded too young to be worried about such things—but with women, one never knew.

Straining his ears, he heard her pick up something from the table and set it down again. A book? Bible verses, more like.

"I do my best not to frown, my lord, but you try my patience sorely. I'll have to rest for an hour or more with a lavender compress over my eyes."

He snorted. "Now you seem angry."

"I do not like wasting my time on napping, not

when there is much else to be done."

Rourke laughed. "Like what? We're snowed in, as you keep reminding me."

"I write my own music, and I embroider. I make perfumes and lotions."

Feminine frills. "You sang to me, while I was recovering." He remembered how much her soft voice had soothed him.

"Aye," she agreed dismissively. "I wish you would listen to me. I think it would be fair to take this case before the prince. I have no desire to marry you."

"You already agreed." Rourke clenched his jaw, then unclenched it. She was not the only one with an aching head. "What is wrong with marrying me? We've already established that neither of us believes in love." Women liked him; they wanted to marry him. Multiple women, from serving wenches to nuns, had proposed to him. What fault could this innocent girl see in him? "My blindness is temporary."

"Pah—I don't care about that. What do I get from the arrangement? I agreed, aye, but not to such a hasty tie! I want to wait. You should meet my parents first."

"We can't do that." Prince John would be at Windsor soon, and that's where he needed to be, as soon as humanly possible. King William's servant had sent the ring with a veiled message the same day the prince's man had arrived.

While King William didn't know, yet, that Prince John had demanded Rourke marry Galiana Montehue for the sole purpose of gaining warriors and a lord's support, the king was aware that Prince John was planning a royal take-over. The ring, a magical ring worn by Scots rulers since before there were kings, belonged to William and was the key to finding the stolen Breath of Merlin.

Then there was the matter of Galiana's other two suitors. Being blinded was damn inconvenient, and while the lady didn't know how much she needed his protection, she knew very well how much he needed hers. Rourke hated being at a disadvantage.

"I don't understand your hurry. My sister was rushed into marriage by our former liege—he was a rotten thief; the baron was." The sound of her hand slamming down on the wooden writing table startled him from his deep and worrisome thoughts. "Which is the reason we now owe direct fealty to King Richard—we were given the written dispensation so that such an instance couldn't happen again. And yet, here you are, demanding marriage."

"The ways of royalty are strange, but it isn't our place to question." Her sister's forced marriage explained much.

"Why are you so amenable to this fiasco?" From the way her voice carried, he knew she was facing him. "My dowry is adequate, but an obvious royal favorite such as yourself could climb higher."

Intelligent girl, for all her talk of lotions and perfumes. Rourke kept his expression sincere. "I owe my allegiance to England." True enough. "I have no family I need to please. My holdings are mine from victory."

Of sorts.

"You have nothing to lose, and a prince's gratitude to gain. Is that what you are saying?"

No—but he liked it. She had to think he was firmly ensconced in Prince John's royal camp. "A man must eventually choose sides."

"The correct side, else you might lose your head."

"You have the right of it, my lady." Rourke rubbed the back of his neck against a sudden chill.

There came a loud rap at the door, and it opened wide. Rourke carefully kept his gaze toward the sounds of his men as they filed inside. He greeted them with a gruff, "Stop shuffling your feet, Robbie, else you'll scuff the floors." Robert laughed, and Rourke was able to place him as standing next to the window.

Godfrey said, "Gray skies, my lord, and the snow's still fallin'." He was by the end of the bed. "It'll be bad tomorrow, and probably the next, too."

Franz spoke softly, "Mon ami, you still look like death."

"Thank you." Rourke heard him stand next to Galiana and say, "Good afternoon, mademoiselle." The man could charm the chemise off an old maid.

Galiana giggled softly and returned the greeting. The exchange annoyed him.

Jamie shut the door, saying, "Ned, boy, go sit on the edge of the bed there, where we can keep an eye on ye. Found him pilfering apples from cook in the kitchen, the wretch."

"He lives here." Galiana rushed to her brother's defense. "'Tis not stealing when you take from your own pantry, fool."

Something about Jamie always seemed to ruffle the lady's feathers. Rourke grinned. Jamie had that effect on a lot of people.

"Don't push; I'm going," Ned said. The lad's voice was changing and seemed a tad lower today. Or, Rourke chuckled, mayhap the boy was also put off by Jamie.

"My thanks, men, for coming. I have a few things I'd like to explain, as privately as possible."

"Then we should go, right Gali?" Ned's feet clomped forward.

"Sit down!" Jamie roared at the boy.

Gali? Rourke liked the sound of the pet name.

"There's nobody left in the manor to hear," Galiana said dryly. Franz laughed, and Rourke could tell they were standing close to one another. "Unless you don't trust Father Jonah? My good knights are all still locked in the solar."

"Your sarcasm is duly noted, my lady. I hope to rectify the situation, and since Godfrey predicts another few days of snow, I'd like to release your knights on a promise that there will be no treachery or retribution."

She scoffed. "You'd believe something I say?"

Rourke felt the sting of irritation. "You've agreed, Lady Galiana, to be my wife. What need of hostages have I?"

His world righted as she made a small growl of frustration. He was in charge, by God, and she'd best not forget it.

Rourke's calves brushed against the chair, and the fire warmed his back. He held his hands out, palms up, and turned his head from the window to the door, a relaxed smile on his face. This way it would appear he was looking at everybody without having to make eye contact—he hoped.

"I've decided not to have you all killed for going through my things." He paused for a heartbeat, wanting them to wonder if he was serious, before laughing. The relief in their tones as they joined in was evident. They all knew he was well within his rights to punish his men as he saw fit.

Godfrey spoke first. "Rourke, I swear we were just looking to do the job we were sent to do. To be of service to you."

Rourke hardened his voice so they'd not make the same mistake again. If he narrowed his eyes a bit, he could see an outline of a man—he thought it was Godfrey. "You go to Jamie for direction."

"And if I ever find out who put something in my ale, ye can count a beating coming," Jamie added.

His knights collectively denied any wrongdoing, although Ned grew fidgety. Could the boy be behind the ghostly games in the manor? Curious, Rourke set that puzzle aside for later.

"You all know we were sent here on behalf of our prince to tally the taxes. And because you went through my things, you know he sent me a private letter—" Rourke stopped speaking, listening carefully for anybody who might shuffle his feet or clear his throat, a clue as to who had deliberately betrayed him, but his men remained silent. "—ordering me to wed Galiana Montehue, and . . . fortify the holding." He knew the latter would confirm what Galiana had thought. "It worked out perfectly that Lord Montehue left in such a hurry—the manor was woefully unprepared. We won't make that same mistake."

Galiana's breaths were coming short and fast, and Rourke could but imagine that her fury might bring color to a wan face. Ladies liked their skin pale and avoided the sun when possible.

"Our father wasn't expecting a sneak attack, if that's what ye mean," Ned argued.

"A man should always be prepared for war," Rourke told the boy.

Enough was enough, Galiana thought. The guilt she felt for her part in this situation was overwhelming, but Rourke's imperious attitude was going to goad the real Ned into action. When and where had her brothers switched places? Thank the saints that Rourke couldn't see—she had a feeling he would note the minute differences and know he'd been had.

"War!" She fanned her face with her hand as if she were feeling quite dizzy. "This country needs peace, for mercy's sake."

She noticed Rourke's hesitation; then he dipped his head in her direction before continuing on with his lecture instead of going after her brother.

The idea to have the men brought to the chamber was brilliant, really, since it gave Jamie and Rourke a chance to set the stage. They were like traveling players, and both men seemed at ease with creating a scene.

Rourke was devastatingly handsome, even with the red cut at his temple. Galiana had been applying a mix of aloe and bees wax so the line would fade to practically nothing. It was the least she could do, and she counted her blessings daily that she hadn't killed him—first with the rock, and last with her feeble attempts at healing. She'd kept his wounds clean, and the rest had been pure Fate.

No, he would come out of the situation just as appealing as ever. He'd taken advantage of the private chamber and bathed, leaving his golden brown hair thick and slightly wavy as it dried. His shoulders were broad beneath the fine linen shirt and short fur mantle. Rourke's tunic and hose were also of quality, and she wondered what duties he performed for his prince to merit such finery.

The man was charming while being completely in

charge. His knights had no idea he couldn't see. If she didn't know herself, she'd not guess anything was out of place. She watched in awe as he paced before the fire, using his large hands to bring home a point.

Could she marry this man? He was beauty and strength melded into a whole. She bit her lip to stop her silly fantasies. Rourke Wallis was a liar. Aye, and he swore allegiance to Prince John; he'd all but admitted there might be some sort of coup planned.

Nobody had wanted to believe Prince John when he'd spread the news that King Richard was dead; the country had mourned its absent king. Constance of Brittany, wife of the dead Geoffrey Plantagenet, was mother to the possible young heir, Arthur. Rumor had it that her current husband had been chosen because he hadn't any political power, which had suited old Henry just fine. Not that Gali put much stock in scuttlebutt, but there was usually some small grain of truth amongst the stories.

"By the week's end, we'll travel for Windsor," Rourke said, and his men cheered, probably glad at the prospect of being on the move again.

She snuck a quick glance at Ned, but he was also intensely focused on Rourke. The man had an abundance of charisma. What kind of woman would he have chosen to marry, if he hadn't been ordered to marry her?

It took all of her willpower to keep her hands loosely at her sides instead of wrapping them around Rourke's neck.

He was handling the forced nuptials with more aplomb than she was, which galled. She was known for her beauty, her grace, and her charm, no matter the pressures.

Gali lifted her chin, careful to keep from frowning. She wore a sachet of rosehips and lemon zest on a woven silver chain around her neck, and she brought the scent to her nose for calm.

"Does that help?" Franz whispered into her ear. "You are too beautiful to be upset. Many ladies throw themselves at Rourke's feet, oui? He is dashing, handsome, and a court favorite."

"I don't care about such things." Her stomach hopped, and she folded her hands primly at her waist.

"You've never been to court; I asked the servants about you. Your parents have wisely kept you hidden away from lecherous eyes. I even heard all about your family's magical ability to heal. But you don't have that, do you?"

Galiana's belly coiled under the hushed onslaught of questions.

"Your sister was almost condemned for witchcraft, non?"

She jerked her elbow backward, the bony point landing unerringly in the knight's stomach, just hard enough to warn him he should step away. "Celestia is no witch, and I'll thank you to keep your allegations to yourself." She spoke softly, as if she hadn't a care in the world, as if she didn't want to punch the little nobleman in the nose.

"Is something the matter?" Rourke's commanding

voice brought a flush of heat to her cheeks that no scented sachet could fade.

"Non, my lord Rourke, I was but asking the lady if she was feeling well. She looked . . . faint."

Galiana almost called the man a weasel, but she refrained. Her mother would demand her finest manners. Since, like her mother, she had no magical skills, she could only hope being a lady would be enough to make her happy.

She doubted it.

"Galiana?" Rourke questioned.

"I'm fine, my lord. Pray continue? We are to brave the snowstorm and ride to Windsor, full force ahead."

Jamie choked on a chuckle.

"Can you be ready, my lady?" Rourke drawled, pinching the bridge of his nose.

Nerves ran the length of her spine, and she smiled at the knights, who were all staring at her. Casting a look at Rourke, she noticed him rub his temple and realized he needed to stop acting for a moment.

"Well, I suppose," she said, taking dainty steps toward the window so the men's gazes would follow her. She was quite practiced at captivating a room, even though she usually avoided doing so at all costs.

"I'll need at least five trunks for clothing, and one for my scents and lotions—they're quite popular, you know. I can make Prince John his own unique fragrance! All I have to do is caress a person's skin," she lightly tapped her finger against Godfrey's forearm, "and I can create a scent that magnifies their allure."

Galiana made sure the men were entranced, then giggled, lowering her eyes so her lashes demurely covered the flash of green. She remembered the lessons her mother had given her before pronouncing her a natural charmer. "For certes, 'tis warm in here. I'll have Cook make us some refreshments. Does anyone else"— she paused to moisten her lower lip—"need something to drink?"

Franz leapt toward her, clutching her fingers, "My lady, allow me to fetch you some wine."

"No, no, I think we should all go down to the hall." She'd not missed the leach of color from Rourke's face as she spoke. The men needed to leave before they noticed something was wrong and Rourke's lie was revealed. "I can play a song or two."

"I'll get your instrument, my lady," Will said. "What do you play?"

"Let me get it—I'm stronger than Will; I am." Robert shoved the squire aside.

Galiana calmly separated the men, grabbing Ned by the hand and pulling him from the bed. "My lute is not heavy at all, kind sir. We shall tell Cook to plan a feast. We'll celebrate—hmm—what have we to celebrate?" She urged the men toward the door.

"Your upcoming nuptials, mayhap?" Rourke's sarcasm couldn't be mistaken, but when she looked at him, he was sitting in the chair, his legs stretched casually out in front of him, one elbow resting on the arm of the chair, and his head propped up with his hand.

A man of leisure, or a man hiding pain? He was a mystery, and a terrific actor; she mustn't ever forget it. Besides, he still hadn't given her the ring that was supposedly just for her. The blue stone set in silver filigree piqued her curiosity, and she wondered for whom it had truly been meant.

A spurt of jealousy added more vinegar to her words than she intended as she said, "That's no cause for celebration, my lord. May we release my knights?"

"Aye." His voice was tired and it made her want to run her fingers through those golden brown curls cradling his head—ack. No, no.

"They'll not cause any harm, Rourke, so you needn't worry." Gali would see to it that her knights would stay safe.

"Jamie, make sure they take their share of the chores. We need to keep the paths to the stables free. We'll leave as soon as the skies clear."

Galiana decided that the man would give orders on his deathbed—and then she recalled that he had. Did he always get his way?

The white lines around his mouth reminded her that he was at the edge of his endurance. "Come," she sing-songed, "I don't suppose any of you play chess?"

She was at the threshold of the door before Rourke called her name.

"Galiana. Stay a moment," he said. "I have a question for you."

At her nod, Jamie directed the men out of the room so that she and Ned were alone with Rourke. "Yes?" Her fingers tightened around her brother's.

"We will wed tonight."

Chills raced across her skin. "That's hardly a question."

He said nothing, just scrubbed at his forehead as if he could pull the pain away. Galiana imagined reaching forward and softly pressing her fingers against his temples to massage the tension from his brow. Some barley water would do wonders, and mayhap a touch of valerian in his ale to help him sleep.

Rourke jerked his chin at the door. "Are we . . ."

Galiana looked behind her before realizing what he wanted. "Oh, we're alone—well, you, me, and Ned."

"I know you think you should take your cause and petition the prince. I can guarantee that your plea will fall on deaf ears."

"What?" Ned tugged his hand free of her grip. "Gali, you think Prince John doesn't know about the dispensation from King Richard?"

Galiana nodded, and Ned's eyes turned a crafty shade of blue as he said, "A king's word overrides that of a mere prince, aye?"

Rourke's jaw tensed. "'Tis not as simple as that. There are other . . . forces . . . at play." His shoulders slumped, but just for a moment before he straightened

121

them again. Compassion rose within her as she saw how valiantly he sought to hide his agony.

She reached out with trembling fingers, drawn to him in a way that seemed beyond her control. His hurt was hers, his courage against the odds inspiring. Yet she was unaccustomed to feeling anything so strong for anyone but her trusted family. She dropped her outstretched hand before she gave herself away.

"What's right is right," Ned practically shouted. "You're no better than Prince John, with his false accusations against the king—"

Gali stepped in front of her angry brother before Rourke decided to send him to the tower forever. As calmly as she could, she said, "You say Prince John is a friend of yours. Well, when King Richard returns, you will find your friend didn't do you any favors aligning your fate with mine. My family supports the rightful king, and my father just recently renewed allegiance through the queen mother, Eleanor."

"Galiana," Rourke growled.

Her belly curled with warmth at the sound, and her heart tripped. She breathed deep, absorbed at the way his grayish eyes turned molten gold as he stared at her.

Stared at her? God help her, but could he see her making a lovesick fool of herself?

She yanked on Ned's arm, signifying it was time to go.

"Wait!" Rourke ordered. "We will wed tonight— but my question is—will you hate me for it?"

Hate the man who was thawing her jaded heart? She supposed she should.

"Aye. I will."

Ned gave her an approving grin.

"It must be done. Tell that priest to prepare. And before he gives me reasons why it can't be done, tell him you will be sharing my bed this eve—married or no."

Galiana's mouth dropped open, and Ned shot forward like a rock from a sling. She barely had the strength to hold him back. She needn't have worried for the injured man. Rourke was up on his feet, his hand around Ned's neck, before she blinked.

"Don't try that again, boy."

"Argh!" Ned's face was red with anger.

"Release him," Galiana said smoothly, even though her nerves were jumping up and down in her throat. "I will tell Father Jonah that it will be marriage . . . or rape. That should help him favor the vows." Her stomach rocked with nausea and a wicked thrill of anticipation.

Calculating the good versus the bad, as if this dilemma were as easily solved as choosing between red paint or pink, she quickly decided to embrace the idea of marriage to this giant, handsome, arrogant man.

Rourke made her pulse pound faster. His smile curled her toes. He melted the frozen boundaries around her heart. Did wanting to feel his lips against hers make her wanton?

Probably.

Marriage to Rourke would mean an exciting life at court; she'd not be forced to marry a stranger, nor be some fat man's pretty ornamental wife. And so what if they didn't feel love? They'd just met, for pity's sake. Celestia and Nicholas had grown together in love; it wasn't impossible that such a miracle could happen for her.

Rourke released Ned, who gasped for air.

"There will be no rape," Rourke said, teeth gritted together.

"Ye're talking about my sister!"

"Hush, Ned, hush . . . I was but making a point; that's all." Galiana wrapped her arm around her brother's waist and drew him to her. He was shaking with rage. "Ned, darling, calm yourself now." She used her most soothing voice, but it didn't reach him.

Ned shoved away from her and darted toward the door. "Be strong, Galiana!"

"Come back, Ned!" She trailed after him, going as far as the hallway, but he was already gone. She patted at the worry lines between her brows, wishing there were some way to make it easier for him to understand. Life wasn't fair.

"He'll be a fine knight someday."

Galiana snorted, a definitely unladylike snort. It felt good, so she did it again. It was amazing how easy it was to be oneself when she wasn't being stared at and judged. Rourke couldn't see her, so she didn't have to guard her feelings. It was heaven.

"You doubt it?"

The nearness of Rourke's warm voice at her back startled her. How had he come so close? He was as quiet as a cat, no matter his large physique. "Nay. He just looked like he wanted to kill you now, and not wait for someday. He'll calm down." Until he found Ed, and then God help the rest of them when the boys concocted another plan.

The ghostly pranks had been amusing—to her and the Montehue household anyway—and the boys hadn't actually hurt anyone. Although she suspected the twins were behind the sleeping draught in Jamie's ale the night Rourke dreamed about Merlin's breath, or dragon's breath, whatever it was; she hadn't the courage to ask them outright.

"Will you be calm?"

She turned around to face her nemesis, running her gaze over his full mouth and his strong brow. She resisted the urge to brush back that stubborn fall of golden brown hair.

"I am not in the habit of throwing a temper tantrum, my lord." Galiana briefly pursed her lips. And then, since he couldn't see her anyway, she stuck out her tongue for good measure.

No wonder the boys misbehaved, she thought with a smile; it was rather fun.

His sigh was filled with exhaustion. "Thank you for distracting the men. My head seems ready to split in two."

Gali forced her hands to stay at her sides. She didn't understand why she felt the overwhelming need to touch Rourke. Her senses, heightened by years of training herself to see, hear, or taste beyond the ordinary, cried out to be near this man. It scared her. "I don't know what you are talking about."

"Five trunks of clothes is too many, I've been around enough women to know that. You will take but one trunk, possibly two, for all of your things. And you can't peddle wares at court as if you were peasant."

She sucked in an insulted breath. Been around enough women? "Peddle my wares? I beg your pardon, but my perfumes are highly sought after. They are gifts, Rourke, I want nothing in exchange once I make a scent." Galiana was tempted to poke him in the chest, another tricky way she could fool herself into touching him. She folded her hands together instead.

"I—"

She had to get away from him before she did something stupid, like throw herself at his finely formed feet. Galiana quickly assured herself that she would get back to normal, as soon as she could draw a breath of air that didn't have Rourke's masculine scent in it.

"Not that you would know anything about giving something freely, would you? You give, but with an ulterior motive in mind, thereby negating the gift. You will release my knights but only because you need them to clear paths free so you can leave here and get to court."

His face paled; the red of his cut, sharp against his skin. She thrust in; offensive.

"I feel sorry for you, Rourke Wallis. I think you have a colder heart than mine."

Chapter Six

He winced as she slammed the door behind her. Cold heart? If he had a heart, it would be cold, 'twas true—it was necessary for his survival. But his angel of mercy considered herself cold-hearted? If his head didn't ache so damn bad, he'd laugh.

How unusual for him to be overcome by lust for some prim, passingly pretty lord's daughter who played with perfumes.

She'd called his bluff, though, on his reasons for "giving," Rourke thought, chuckling as he made his way back to the chair by the fire. Six steps. There it was. He turned, lowered his hand until it touched the armrest, and sat.

A gift was a negotiation. Tit for tat. When was the last time he'd given something away for nothing? He scratched his chin, unable to come up with a single in-stance. Her talk of nobility, though—that stung.

A spy didn't have the luxury of being honorable, or honest. She was astounded that he would wed at the whim of a prince. Well, God help them if she ever found out what else he'd done for the royals in his life.

Or—his stomach rumbled with guilt—what he would do. Which was set the lady Galiana aside, with a king's blessing, to marry another. One who had a closer seat to the throne. Constance.

Constance of Brittany was engaging and eager for fun, but she never lost view of the throne; nor did she ever tire of envisioning her son ruling from it. So much would be put to rest if Richard would but name an heir, or impregnate Queen Berengaria, his wife.

Rourke reached beneath his tunic, pulling out the leather cord and the ring that Jamie had tied to it like a talisman. He rubbed the stone with the pad of his thumb, wondering if he was imagining the heat it gave. Not hot enough to burn, but steady, like banked embers.

Being raised at court, he had learned to forsake most of his inbred superstitions. He'd had no illusions left by the time he was seven—yet this ancient ring and the chip of stone called to his soul like a horn to the hounds.

Mayhap because the chip belonged to a larger gem. The Breath of Merlin. He'd seen it once, and it was as big as a man's head. One side was opaque, a milky white color striated with blue veins. The other side was as clear as a polished diamond—if they came that large, he thought with a grimace. He'd seen it when King William had privately made him swear his allegiance to Scotland's throne before publicly denouncing him and sending him to reside in Prince John's camp.

The power within the gem had terrified him.

Legend said that whoever held the stone held the power to be king—if the fates decreed. If a man gazed into the stone who had no right to kingship, he'd be blinded and go stark raving mad.

Passed between England and Scotland, lost to Henry I, promised back to Scotland by Richard, the gem had recently been stolen from King William's treasury.

From Prince John's confidence in rousing the unhappy barons and lords around England and France, King William surmised that the wily Plantagenet had it—and from the cryptic spoken words Rourke had gotten from the Scots messenger, the sacred, very secret, stone was hidden at Windsor.

Damn, he wished he could see! He dropped the ring beneath his mantle, needing the warmth of the fire against his suddenly chilled skin. What if his sight never returned? What good was a spy who couldn't see beyond the occasional shadow?

"The lady Galiana said you needed to rest."

Rourke jerked his head toward the voice of the man he trusted as he trusted no other human being alive. "So she sent you, Jamie?"

"Aye," his foster brother sounded uncomfortable. "She said I knew how to handle ye best."

"I don't need a nursemaid."

Rourke heard Jamie turn down the covers on the large bed. "Aye, and isn't that what I told her? Come on now. Just close yer eyes for a bit. She sent a powder to stop the ache in yer head, and she's sending that old Dame Bertha with a barley water compress."

Irritated at being so helpless, Rourke barked, "And now you're doing her bidding? Just remember where your loyalties lie."

Jamie went silent, and Rourke cursed, then apologized. The longer he was without his sight, the more of an arsewipe he became. "That pissed you off, and it should have. Give me the damn powder then."

He'd been put to bed like a child in need of a nap.

He wouldn't mind a nap, he thought as sleep descended, not if Galiana was naked next to him.

Tonight.

Galiana hurried from the solar, practically deaf from the cheers of her knights. Tired of their confinement, they would have agreed to mucking out stalls forever if it meant their freedom. She'd worn her best smile, charming them into believing she was happily marrying the man who was forcing her hand. Somehow this soothed

131

their fractured male egos into believing all was well.

"About time ye married." The bailiff scratched his hairy chin. "And while the circumstances were"—he colored with embarrassment—"not of yer own choosin', ye'll not be unhappy, will ye? But your father—he's like to lop me head off, once he returns from the lady Celestia's."

"No, he won't," Galiana assured the loyal man. "We both know there would have been fighting if Father was here. 'Twas for the better that my parents were gone when Rourke and his men arrived."

"We would have fought, my lady," the bailiff said in earnest. "But they had ye slung over the front of that Scottish heathen's horse, and Ned trussed up on another. We had no choice."

"I know, good sir. Please, feel no blame! If I hadn't gone to the forest," she paused, filled with remorse over her careless act of frivolity. It was only right that she pay the penance.

"Never mind that. Lord Rourke wanted in, and he'd have gotten in. He's the kind of man who gets his way, I'm thinkin'." The older man patted her arm.

Bailiff Morton was right. Either way, the end result would be her marriage to Lord Rourke Wallis. It had been ordered by a member of the royal house, and the Montehues were but vassals to the Plantagenet bloodline.

Her father might have demanded to see Prince John—but what would come of it? With King Richard being held for ransom, England's future was unstable. Aye, she told herself pragmatically, her father had sworn his fealty to King Richard through Queen Eleanor, but the wily woman had more than one son—and both wanted to wear the crown of England. Had her father's request for a written dispensation, stating that his daughters not be pawns in marriage, brought her name to the prince's attention?

Crowns and royal whims were for other people, she thought with a sigh of relief. She was to be married, she would have her adventure, and she'd prove herself more valuable to her new husband than the woman Rourke had originally intended to give the antique ring to.

He would come to care for her; she'd make it so. She thought, without conceit, of the men who had offered for her; for certes, she should be able to make the man she'd married give her his affection.

She was beautiful, and that mattered to some men. Rourke, as stunning as he was, was probably one of them. Galiana told herself she didn't need his entire heart. She understood that love was a rare and truly beautiful thing.

So why should she be miserable? Affection, respect, and—she blushed—the marriage bed held no fear for her. She had learned plenty from her mother and Celestia. A bit of pain at the beginning, which could be soothed with a numbing cream, and then—great pleasure. If, her mother said, it was done right.

Galiana adored the poems of chivalry and romantic

love (when they weren't directed at her) even though she wasn't naïve enough to believe in them. Her tummy flip-flopped like a ball rolling down the stairs. She was enough of a romantic to want the evening ahead to be perfect, and pragmatic enough to not expect much in the way of perfection.

The bailiff shuffled from one foot to the next, recalling her wandering attention.

Smiling, she said, "Would you please tell Cook to create a feast out of what is available? She said we were almost out of eggs, so I know she can't make a cake, but something nice. Roast chicken, or a stew of some sort. And some spiced blackberry wine?"

He nodded. "Your favorite. I'll be glad when the snow stops, and we can get to the village, my lady."

"I hope they've fared well. Tell the men to get along with Rourke's men and to keep Ed a secret. I have but one brother, remember?" And how to fix that little mess? Rourke would notice, eventually. She had no doubt of that.

"Aye," the bailiff chuckled. "And what of the resident ghost?"

"Ghost, mademoiselle?"

Franz had suddenly entered the hall to her left, taking Galiana by surprise. She squeaked, "Oh!"

"My apologies, mon cher, if I've startled you."

"No, no," she lied, smiling and bobbing her head in a nod. The Frenchman was a good-looking man, but she didn't quite trust him. It wasn't that he'd been inappropriate—

more that he was so . . . intense?

"I was but hoping I could accept your challenge?" His lips turned up in a practiced lilt that turned her cold with indifference.

She tipped her head to the side. "Hmm?"

"Chess?"

"Ah." She remembered. "It is my turn to apologize, good sir. I'm afraid I need to pack. I have nothing to wear to court."

"You will shine," Franz said, his dark eyes blazing with masculine appreciation.

"I will fade into the walls, I'm certain," she replied before turning back to the impatient bailiff. She'd not lead the knight into thinking his attentions were welcomed. "Bailiff Morton, ask our men to clear a path to my drying shed, if they can? I'll need to bring some herbs. Thank you."

She dismissed the bailiff and turned to Franz with a polite smile. "Excuse me," she said, brushing by him toward the stairs to her chamber.

She almost recoiled at the flash of anger in the Frenchman's eyes at having been so easily disregarded. Was he one of the men Rourke thought to protect her from?

"I'll see you tonight, mademoiselle."

Galiana peeked over her shoulder back at him, but didn't stop. "I'm honored that you will be there to witness the vows I'll share with Lord Rourke."

Facing forward again, she quickened her step, but

she still heard the man mutter, "Merde."

It probably hadn't been prudent to tweak his nose, but she had no interest in flirtations with anyone besides her husband-to-be. Rourke—gorgeous, fascinating Rourke—would consume her mind if she let him. At last, Galiana reached the safety of her room and closed the door behind her, her breaths coming more quickly as she remembered him sitting so confidently astride his black stallion, his powerful thighs— No.

This was not the time for her fanciful imagination to carry her away. Marriage. Court. Rourke would want a comely wife, one who wouldn't embarrass him with her country ways. Her options were limited. Rourke had been right about not needing five trunks of clothes. What she had would barely fill one.

Uncertain, she thought of what her mother might have tucked away—mayhap a dress or two she'd rarely worn that Galiana could make over into something fresh. "Oh," she said, her eyes itching with unshed tears. "Court. How am I to know what they wear?"

Galiana had never been anywhere as grand as that. The invitation for her father to swear fealty to King Richard via Queen Eleanor hadn't included the family, and, even so, her mother had said the ways of court were not the ways of their family, and she'd been grateful they hadn't all been forced to go.

Which didn't mean she and her mother weren't followers of current fashions. They bought patterns and studied what the traveling players wore—which was usually an inexpensive copy of what was fashionable.

She adored fabric; its textures and colors spoke to her tactile senses. Soft silks were gossamer wings against her flesh. Bright colors could lift her mood when even her brother's jests fell flat. Pastels helped her paint, and she proudly wore sturdy, brown linen when she gardened. Barefoot, if her mother wasn't watching. The feel of fresh earth between her toes helped her stay connected to what was solid.

When she sang, or painted, or played the lute, she transcended to another level of herself, a spiritual place where she could be free. When she blended her perfumes, her mind took flight, and it was as close to magic as she'd ever come. Some days it was tempting to live in that other world forever.

"I can sew," she said aloud, foraging through the trunk at the foot of her bed.

She had numerous simple white undergowns that were scalloped at the hem and neck. Gali gnawed her lower lip as she lifted a pale lavender tunic. She'd alter the longer sleeves to a three-quarter length, then add tippets that trailed so long they'd need to be knotted so as not to drag on the ground. Embroidery and gems would add decoration. Removable trims could change the look of a plain-colored tunic, and if she switched the buckles on her slippers to match, she'd be stylish in little time.

If Rourke thought she was leaving her cask of perfumes

and scents behind, he would need to think again. It might not be magic worthy of her great ancestor, but it was her one true talent, and it gave her joy. Peddling her wares, she thought indignantly. Just see if she made a scent for him . . .

His skin would smell like summer nights by the lake—she could too easily imagine burying her nose in the warm crook of his bare neck, or mayhap running her sensitive hands over his naked shoulders—"Ah," she moaned aloud. She was being felled by sensory overload.

A lady should never feel this way, but mayhap she wasn't a traditional lady.

The thought was oddly comforting.

Celestia had never cared about being a lady, not one golden arrow for following the rules of society, and now look—she was married to a handsome knight, and she was lady of her own keep. Gali said a quick prayer for Tia and the new babe before sitting back on her haunches in dismay.

Shoving a long braid over her shoulder, she accepted the sad fact that nothing new had appeared in her trunk since she'd last delved to the bottom. Her tunics and undergowns seemed to age before her eyes.

"The storage room!" Galiana leapt to her feet and headed for the small stone room that was but an overlarge closet. Her mother kept the expensive fabrics packed away with sweet-scented sachets inside cedar trunks.

When they were small girls, she and Celestia used to

play dress up on long, rainy afternoons. They'd always made Ela be the baby. Come to think of it, her youngest sister had always hated it.

She reached the door and stopped when she saw Dame Bertha leaving her parents' chamber, a stealthy look on her weathered face.

"Dame Bertha?"

"Aye?" The old lady looked up, squinted, and then walked the hall toward Galiana.

All she could think about was Rourke resting on the opposite side of that closed door. But, no, she had to control her ridiculous desire to see him. She'd but ask the old woman to help her search for fabric, or— she eyed the closed door—mayhap Dame Bertha would go through her mother's trunks with her? But instead of either of those questions, "How fare's Lord Rourke?" popped out of her mouth as soon as the woman was close enough to hear.

"Just fine, my lady. He's sleepin' deep. But he'll be right as rain"—she chuckled—"for the dinner and vows tonight, eh?"

Galiana gulped. "Good, good—"

"Yer not scared, are ye?" Dame Bertha reached out a shaking, wrinkled hand to pat Galiana on the arm.

"Scared? Of Rourke? Nay, I mean, why should I be? It—well . . ." Galiana could feel the blush start from her toes and end at her scalp. She might know about such things as the marriage bed, but talking about them—that was another matter entirely. Ladies didn't do that—she didn't think.

"I can help."

"Nay, nay," Galiana quickly interjected before she was on the receiving end of some archaic bedding advice. "I was actually hoping you could help me find some cloth. I'll need finer things for court."

Dame Bertha grinned. "Aye, that ye will! Well, now, yer mam has a green silk that sets off her eyes and would yours, too." She stepped back and summed up Galiana in a snap. "It should fit ye like a second skin! Mother Mary knows it's been a decade or more since she fit into it." The old woman cackled.

"Silk?" Galiana could practically feel the softness between her fingers.

"Your mam has a chest under her bed that holds some of her favorite pieces, but we'll need to be quiet, lest we wake Lord Rourke."

Galiana's heart skipped the tiniest bit faster. Rourke, sleeping in the big bed whilst she was in the same chamber. Her mouth dried. It was different, now that he wasn't ill or down with the fever. She'd been able to separate herself from the man as he lay injured. Guilt had trapped her senses, as had her fear of harming him further with her ineptness.

Now her nerves were in a jumble. Rourke was quite fully a vibrant man who stirred every heightened sense she had.

What would it be like once their lips finally met?

Would his lips be soft, as hers were? Or hard? Would he be forceful, or would he allow her to come to him?

"My lady?"

"Oh—yes, Dame Bertha, I'll be quiet. Under the bed, you say? I'll look, as quiet as a mouse, and then meet you back in my chamber. No sense both of us risking our necks."

The old woman nodded briskly at that. "Would ye care for a refreshment whilst we work?"

If she sent her to the kitchens, she wouldn't need to rush. "Yes," Gali replied, hoping her racing pulse wasn't evident in her voice. "I'd love a goblet of spiced wine, if you please?"

"Aye, my lady."

The old woman left, and Galiana paused, her hand hovering over the latch on the door of her parents' chamber. Dare she enter without invitation?

I miss you, Tia. You'd do what you wanted, and, oh, how I need to borrow your courage!

She loved her sisters dearly—they'd both inherited the legacy of Boadicea: her warrior-like courage, her beauty, and her healing magic. Even though there was supposed to be but one girl gifted in each generation, theirs had been gifted with two.

Galiana had gotten nothing.

Well, mayhap 'nothing' was not entirely true, she considered as she bit her lower lip. People said she was beautiful. Men wrote ridiculous sonnets in her honor, and her father received many offers for her hand in marriage—from rich barons to poor ministers. They all left her cold.

What was beauty without magic? Yes, she was tall like the legendary Boadicea, and she had the long, rippled, red hair of myth. Green eyes, full lips, porcelain skin.

It was an outer shell. She lacked the fire that true magic would bring. Gali searched for that power in every medium she could—painting, music, singing, cooking—the closest she got to self-fulfillment was when she created her perfumes. Then it was as if she could float on a cloud.

Magic equaled power. Beauty didn't grant power. Beauty was a pain in a girl's backside, truth be told. Her father had finally taught her how to shoot a bow and arrow so that stupid men would stop trying to kidnap her when she took her horse out on her daily rides, and then they'd forced her to accept an escort, too. Bothersome. Especially when she longed for freedom.

Her mother insisted she learn to be a lady and to have a lady's skills at running a home. Would Rourke appreciate her talents?

She'd gotten the impression that he traveled much, so mayhap a home-and-hearth style of woman was not the kind of wife he needed. Or—she gulped—would he think to dump her at his home and forget about her whilst he gallivanted around the world?

Reaching for the latch, she inhaled and then slowly

entered the room. Someone had covered the windows with thick curtains to block the waning afternoon sun, but enough light remained that Galiana could see.

She took note of the giant bed in the center of the room. Clasping the chains of her belt so they wouldn't jangle, Gali eyed the large sleeping form at the edge of the mattress. Rourke slept on his belly, and the fur cover had slipped from his shoulders down to rest at his hips.

Gali felt a small measure of relief to see that he wore his undershirt. If he'd been naked, she'd probably have run.

Or not, she thought with a delicious shiver.

She crept the fifteen steps across the room until she'd gone as far as she could. Galiana stole another peek at the sleeping Adonis who would be her husband, then dropped to her knees so she could reach beneath the bed.

Fingers outstretched, she couldn't feel anything. So she peeked beneath the frame, crawling forward and praying she wouldn't get caught. She breathed in a mote of dust, and it took all of her willpower to hold back the cough.

Her eyesight adjusted to the gloom beneath the bed, and she searched for the flat, rectangular chest that might be her salvation. Ah, she saw a burnished copper handle and tugged backward until, with a final pull, she freed the chest.

"What are you doing?"

Oh no. Like a thief caught in the act, she sat back on her heels, both hands still on the trunk. Her cheeks burned with humiliation as she bravely lifted her gaze.

Rourke's golden gray eyes were squinted, and Gali wondered what it was he could see. For certes, she was not at her best and, for the first time in her entire life, she wanted to be beautiful—for him.

"Galiana?"

"Aye," she acknowledged.

"What in the devil's name are you doing beneath my bed?"

"Well . . ." Her heart thundered before she remembered something he'd said to her. "It's, uh, complicated."

Leaning on his side, Rourke furrowed his brow.

"I see. Well, if it's games you want to play, my lady, then you didn't have to sneak around beneath the bed."

As quick as lightning in a summer storm, he reached over and unerringly grabbed her upper arms to pull her to him. She landed with an unladylike thud on his chest, and Galiana was so surprised she didn't even think to jump back off.

Instead, she reveled in sensual heaven. Rourke smelled better than she remembered, with his skin warmed from sleep. His cheeks remained lightly stubbled, and she reached out to brush the flesh with the tip of her index finger.

It was as if he were staring at her, even though she knew he couldn't see. His lashes were dark, with gold tinting at the tips, and the golden gray orbs of his eyes seemed to catch fire with an unearthly light the more she stared into them. Knowing she couldn't be seen, or judged, allowed her the freedom to enjoy this stolen moment.

His hands brushed up from her lower back, entangling in the curls of her hair until his fingers reached her neck. A low moan caught in the back of her throat as he deftly massaged the muscles along her nape.

Galiana closed her eyes in satisfaction. Then she opened them again; she didn't want to miss one nuance of Rourke's expression. He seemed to be enjoying the touch of her skin as much as she was.

He gently lowered her head until their mouths were a hair's breadth apart. This was the kiss he'd teased her with earlier, she thought, and her belly tightened with anticipation. There was no mistaking the hard jut of his penis at the apex of her thighs.

She pressed down, instinctively cradling his manhood, and he captured her lips while crushing her to him in a primal embrace.

"God's bones, you madden me," he whispered roughly.

This was power. Yet she was as helpless to it as he seemed to be. His lips were full, and his tongue teased the seam of her mouth. She didn't hesitate, and eagerly accepted his kiss. Their mouths warred, thrusting, then accepting, before starting all over again. His teeth nipped her lower lip, and the sensation spiraled to her woman's core. She shifted her body so that her thighs widened atop him, allowing him closer access to the part of her that throbbed with pleasure.

He turned, rolling atop her and pinning her to the mattress. Holding her wrists above her head with but one hand, he rained kisses along her forehead and the tip of her nose. Was this wrong, to want him like this?

They weren't married, but they would be.

But they weren't.

"What's wrong?"

"Nothing, my lord," she answered shyly. Her body thrummed with desire so loudly she wondered if he could hear it.

He dropped his forehead to hers, and she heard his breathing change as he fought to gain control. "You are the most responsive woman I've ever met, my lady." His hand slowly traveled up her waist until he paused below her breast. She stilled with anticipation. When he finally cupped her, she exhaled and pushed her aching nipple against his palm.

"Kiss me again, my lord," Galiana lifted her face to his, kissing whatever part of his skin she could reach.

"Nay," he growled low. "I'll not take you yet. This night will come soon enough. We must be wed."

Realizing Rourke was not going to finish what he had started made Galiana flush with embarrassment, and, after a second, she pushed him off of her. Every wonderful feeling she'd had faded until all that was left was the reality.

He was able to say no. She would not have done so.

Rourke was the champion in the play of power, and

Galiana found she didn't like it.

"Are you all right, Galiana? You are an innocent, and I shouldn't have taken advantage of your curiosity." He reached out, and even the brush of his fingers against her sensitized skin caused her to squirm.

"Don't apologize," she said as primly as a nun.

"Galiana." He scooted toward her, so she quickly hopped from the bed to stand on trembling legs—he needn't know how badly she still wanted him.

"I've just come for a cloak. I'll get it, and be going." She scrambled for the trunk handle. "You go back to sleep, Rourke. I'm sure you need your rest. My apologies for waking you. I'll see you downstairs," she babbled, controlling her new emotions as best she could.

"Galiana." Rourke's voice had returned to its lord-of-the-manor cadence, and she felt such resentment that she actually stopped to hear his directive.

"I will have you. Tonight."

Galiana fled the room, pulling the trunk behind her. Arrogant man! To think she'd enjoyed his touch so much that she would have given herself to him—marriage vows or not!

She was wanton.

A lady would never have responded to Rourke's kisses the way she had. She was ashamed. She'd been trained to be one thing: a lady her parents could be proud of—virtuous, beautiful, courteous, charming and capable of running a household. Tears smudged her vision as she dragged the trunk down the hall.

Her parents had trusted her, and look at what had happened!

Getting shackled in marriage to a stranger served her right. Her belly curled at the thought of being shackled to Rourke. He was a tempting punishment. For certes, Satan knew what he was doing when he dropped Rourke into her path.

She reached the door of her chamber and pushed it open. Dame Bertha hadn't come back from the kitchens, and yet Galiana didn't feel as if she was alone. Pulling the trunk inside, she called out for her brothers. "Boys?"

Mayhap they'd come to share a new plan of action to escape the manor, or "haunt" it. She peeked behind the heavy drapes over her window.

"Ed? Ned?"

Concern took the place of self-pity as she peered beneath the bed. Her trunk, already empty from her wild search for something to wear, remained open and barren.

Nobody was in her room. Chills broke out over arms, and she rubbed them as she walked to the window. "Stop frightening yourself, silly goose," she said aloud.

Tying the drapes back so that the fading natural light, magnified by the mountains of white snow, could penetrate her room, she looked out to see as far as she could see.

Was that a person at the tree line? She squinted, but then shook her head. It had to have been a trick of the mind. Dusk created its own mysteries. Add to that the falling snow in a storm that wouldn't quit, and what fool would be out in such weather?

It had been just a week ago that she'd welcomed the snow as a new beginning. A new year, with new resolutions. Ha.

The snow was suffocating. A trap. And she, the pampered lady of the manor, would be traveling in it with her younger brother and a band of warriors who were being led by a blind man.

Galiana sighed deeply. She saw the plumes of smoke coming from the village and hoped the people there were faring well. Surely they all knew what to do. If they could but make it to the manor, she'd let them in, but mayhap they were better off in their own homes, taking care of their families.

She'd ask the bailiff, on the odd chance that she should be performing some sort of miracle.

Miracles.

She pushed away from the window, and walked to the trunk that would, God willing, hold an answer to her prayer. It wasn't locked, which made it seem less like she was stealing from her mother. Galiana opened the lid and then sat back with a gasp.

Emerald green silk. Ruby red damask. White fur so

soft she had to bury her fingers in it before holding the stole to her cheek.

"You found the trunk, then?" Dame Bertha paused at the threshold of the open door.

"Aye. This is a treasure chest. See?" Galiana held up the green silk tunic that had been embroidered with polished emeralds. The style was classic, and it would need very little refurbishing.

"'Tis even more beautiful than I remembered."

Galiana floated across the room, so delighted with her finds. "And look! This red dress will but need some trim—the dark mink, mayhap? And, oh, what fortune! Silk undergowns."

"Ye've a talent with the needle, my lady," Dame Bertha encouraged. "Ye'll fit in right smart with those ladies at court. I brought yer wine and another candle."

"Thank you. Will you stay?"

"I've work to be done, my lady, but I'll be back in time to help you dress for dinner."

Engrossed with her creations, Galiana nodded absently, setting her wine on the table by her bed.

When Dame Bertha came back hours later, Galiana was on her second candle, and the gowns were laid out in various pieces as they awaited completion. "Oh my," the old woman said. "You've made quite a mess."

"Mess?" Her creative bubble burst, and Gali rubbed her lower back. "Never mind that. Have you seen the twins?"

"No." The woman pointed to the open chamber door. "No glimpse of our Ned." She winked conspiratorially. "And that old priest hasn't been to the hall yet either."

Her belly clenched as she asked, "Rourke?"

"Aye, he's at the head of the table, in your father's seat at the dais. He's callin' for ye—told me to tell ya to hurry, that ye're keepin' the men waiting. He's not letting Cook serve afore ye get there."

Anger kindled. "He assumes much."

Dame Bertha sucked in her lower lip. "He's a right good-lookin' man, my lady. Them's the kind that expect things to be given to 'em, and they get it, too," she laughed.

It wasn't fair. Galiana welcomed the rebellious thought, then nurtured it. Her chamber was cozy, with the candlelight dancing and the dark outside her window like a curtain. She didn't want to go down to the hall.

Why should Rourke always get his way? Because he was a man? A very, very handsome man? She remembered the embarrassment she'd felt when he'd rejected her and decided that, mayhap just this once, he wouldn't get his way. She would take back some of the power for herself.

"What are ye thinkin', my lady Galiana? 'Tis your brothers' faces I usually see wearing that mischievous look."

"Aye?" She grinned, then put her hand to her forehead. "I don't feel well, Dame Bertha, and I would appreciate it if you would send my regrets to the hall."

"Oh, no, ye don't." The old woman's eyes grew wide and round before crinkling back into the folds of wrinkles.

"Why not? We all know that I can't let my brother be taken to the tower, so I will marry Rourke—tomorrow, even. But why should he get to pull on the strings? I'm no puppet, and I'm tired of being made to dance."

Galiana dragged a basket from behind her trunk, pawing through the contents until she found a jar of white powder. "Perfect!" She held it out to show Dame Bertha. "With some expert application of this, I'll look wan and sick, a smudge of candle soot, and he'll think I'm dying."

"He can't see," the old lady tapped her foot against the floor, a smile creeping across her face. "So don't forget to groan, and we'll need to make this room much warmer, to effect a fever."

"That's the spirit, Dame Bertha," Galiana giggled, shaking the powder to her palm. "Rourke might not be able to see right now, but Jamie can. And that man has an eagle eye. We'll need to make this very good. You'll help me?"

"Of course, my lady."

It took a while before the two pronounced Galiana ready, and then Gali sent Dame Bertha down to the great hall with the news that Galiana was too ill to join the men for dinner. Too sick for her own wedding night.

Gali had instructed Dame Bertha to stay and sup, and then report back with Rourke's reaction.

The old lady wasn't to tell anyone, not even the twins, of their farce.

As she lay in bed, face powdered to a ghostly white with dark circles beneath her eyes, she congratulated herself on a job well done and a trick well played. Was it too much to have one little victory she could savor?

Nay. So why was guilt creeping around like an unwanted guest?

The joke could be taken as dishonest. Her duty bade her marry Rourke, and she would. The prince had demanded the wedding, and even though her family had a royal dispensation, her brother had committed an act of treason. Rourke would have been well within his rights to lock her brother in the barn until spring.

Instead, he'd offered her a bargain. More than fair, on his part, when she considered that he could have taken her by force—as some of his men had suggested.

Galiana blinked, wishing she weren't so susceptible to feeling bad.

Yes, he'd ordered the wedding immediately instead of waiting for her parents to return to the manor. He'd even refused to let her go before the prince to explain. Rourke said it was for her own protection, but she thought there was more to the tale than that.

Clutching the covers to her chin, she hoped she hadn't overplayed her hand.

Rourke just needed to be taught a lesson in patience; that's all she was doing. She counted to twenty. Thirty. Curse it! She threw the covers back and slid her feet to the ground. She could go down now and explain she was jesting.

But then he'd always know he had won.

One little victory. Her pride cried for it. Getting back into bed, she lectured herself on ladylike behavior. She drank her wine, waiting for someone to come and see how she fared. While she waited, she promised, starting tomorrow, she'd be the best wife a knight could ever ask for.

Chapter Seven

Rourke raised his head, listening to the moans surrounding him. The sound reminded him of a battlefield, and he wondered if he was dead. He couldn't see a blasted thing, his head ached, and his gut churned with fire.

"Jamie?" Rourke blinked and blinked, but nothing could clear the shadows from his line of sight. Was the room filled with smoke? Or was this his dream, where the Breath of Merlin came to swallow him in the name of the Holy Throne?

He gulped, his throat raw and rancid.

Turning his head to the side, he called again for his foster brother, and again, until he heard a familiar cursing.

Rourke crawled over bodies—men. His men? His hand scraped over the trimmed beard of Franz, but the man wouldn't wake, no matter how hard Rourke shook his shoulder. Next was either Robert or Godfrey; he could tell by the large shoulders. The man groaned when Rourke patted his cheeks.

Finally he made it to the giant body of his foster brother.

Jamie grunted when Rourke smacked him in the center of his huge chest.

"I'm here," Rourke said.

"Get off me bloody leg, would ye? Agh, damn, I've sicked meself, what in the hell?"

"That explains the stink. Where are we?"

Jamie sat up, then stood. "Can ye see?"

"It's dark." The memories were coming back. He'd been blinded: downed by a rock and a lady with good aim. He was to marry the wench, securing her family's knights and money—but then she'd gotten sick and couldn't come to dinner. They were to be married, and she'd stayed in her bed—away from the great hall.

As had her priest, and her brother.

"The bitch poisoned us," he said coldly.

"Ye don't know that."

"It looks that way."

"Ye can't see," Jamie pointed out. "Besides, she's a lady."

"You know as well as I that ladies can be treacherous—starting with Eve."

Jamie laughed; then Rourke flinched as a bright light hurt his eyes.

"Ye see that, then?" Jamie's voice held hope.

"Just the brilliance of it—it's fading already. A candle?"

"Aye," his foster brother said with a wealth of disappointment.

Rourke knew he would regain his sight. The alternative was failure, and he refused to consider it.

"God's bones, Rourke, it's a good thing ye can't see this. The men are all passed out on the floor, sick, most of 'em. What a mess."

"Are they dead?"

"No, poor bastards. If they feel like I do, they probably wish they were."

Feeling useless made him angry, and it took every last bit of willpower he had to keep his temper leashed. "She told me she'd get even, but this is ridiculous."

"Think it through, man. Why would she want ye dead?"

"Not dead, just sick. Are her own men here, too?"

"Aye. There's at least one in green and white curled under the table there. His head's in a bowl."

Rourke's shoulders tightened, and he set his jaw. Mayhap the lady was cold-hearted after all. To poison her own knights, too—just to get even? Was she that angry he'd set her aside? She'd agreed to the marriage, by God. He'd wanted their joining to be special.

An odd feeling of disappointment banked the lust she'd stirred when he'd kissed her in his chamber. Damn it to hell, she'd responded like a cat to his touch, and he'd almost bedded her before the pledge was taken.

It didn't make sense.

The men started to wake around him and retch, and he knew a deep fury that anyone, let alone someone he'd begun to care for, could be so deliberately cruel.

"Take me to her room, Jamie. Now. I would see for myself if she's feeling better." Galiana, with all her talk of honor. Rourke ground his back teeth together, wanting to storm up the stairs and drag the lady from her comfortable bed so she could see what she'd done with her trickery.

"Rourke," Jamie cautioned.

"Nay, don't argue—just lead the way, man."

Rourke stayed on Jamie's heels, his head thundering with pain.

Jamie pounded on the thick, wooden door of Galiana's chamber, demanding to be let in.

Each time Jamie's fist hit the door, a slice of white-hot light flashed across Rourke's vision, until Rourke ordered Jamie to stop pounding before his head fell off.

He shut his eyes tight, pressing his fingers down on the lids as if that would take away the searing fire.

Suddenly the door opened, and Rourke reflexively opened his eyes wide. He jumped back, seeing a shadowy white face, gaunt, with huge dark eyes and a pointed chin. "Death," he croaked.

The skeleton figure before him screeched with outrage, and the door was slammed in their faces.

Jamie's shoulders shook with suppressed laughter.

Rourke reached out and clapped his foster brother on the back of the neck. "You're laughing at me, Jamie?"

"Aye."

"I can see it. A little." Graying tones, in an indistinguishable shape, but he would know the silhouette of Jamie's broad shoulders and bushy hair anywhere.

"Ye can? Thanks be to God, Rourke. Yer blindness has been scarin' me."

Rourke glanced at the door.

"As much as she scared me?"

Jamie burst into loud chuckles, and Rourke, feeling foolish, joined in.

"If you two are not finished mocking me, would you please leave?" Galiana's whisper could barely be heard through the door. "'Tis impolite."

Rourke, buoyed by his newfound semi-sight, reached out and knocked against the door himself. She looked so pathetic he didn't even feel like strangling the wench anymore.

He'd thought—his hands tingled with the sensory memory of Galiana's curves and her long hair—she'd be a little bit pretty. For certes, it seemed she was not at her best. "Are you ill?" he called through the wood since she wasn't opening the door.

"Uh, just go away," she said in a tear-filled voice.

"Lass, the men downstairs are all sick—"

Her hesitation sparked Rourke's suspicion, and he cut off Jamie, shouting, "What kind of trick did you play?"

He hoped for a quick denial, but he didn't get one.

"Galiana?" Rourke shook the handle on the door until it rattled loose.

"I, I don't know what you're talking about—I'm ill!" she yelled.

Rourke's skills at outing a liar went to waste, since she did it so poorly. "Open this door, or I will kick it down."

He heard her sniffling tears, but it didn't stop his anger that she was denying him entry. "One . . . two . . . three . . ."

"Wait!"

Rourke found himself holding his breath, curious to see what apparition would open the door.

When it slowly creaked inward, Rourke impatiently pushed it farther. Jamie was at his back as they entered the dark chamber.

"You can see me?" Galiana said from within the confines of a large, hooded fur robe.

"Not wrapped in that, my lady," Rourke snorted with irritation. "Are you well?"

"Well," she sniffed, "I still have a slight ache at my throat," she produced a pitiful cough, "and my eyes are watering. You scared me, knocking at the door like that. Really, Rourke, you can see?"

"Shapes, features, no colors, but I'm not complaining. What are you up to, Galiana, that you are hiding yourself?" Rourke could be just as single-minded as she.

"I don't feel well, sir, so please—just stay back."

He could tell she was lying, and even though she

160

sounded pitiful, he didn't believe her. "Sick with regret, mayhap? Why did you do it?"

Her hands darted out of the robe, and she gathered the edges to wrap more tightly around her. "Do what?"

The bulky fur, while warm, didn't lend itself to giving away her figure, Rourke noticed. She seemed tall, but it could be the hood. Thanks be to their compromising positions the day before, he knew she was curvaceous— but the fur made her appear mammoth.

Was she planning on running out into the snow? It stunned him to think she'd rather take her chances in the snowstorm than marry him. Had he scared her away with his ardor? Nay, she'd been hot for his touch; his body remembered well.

"You poisoned us all," Rourke spat. "We should have assumed something was going on when neither you nor your brother came down to the hall. Not even your priest ate with the rest of us naïve buffoons. What were you hoping to do? Gain control of the manor? Escape into the middle of a snowstorm? Fool!"

The hood jerked back the smallest bit, and he got a glimpse of the woman's pale face. He couldn't see her ghostly features clearly, but he could tell she was concerned. It made him breathe easier to know that she was capable of remorse.

"The lads are sick," Jamie said. "What did ye give us all?"

Galiana shook her head, "I didn't do anything like that. I—my 'trick' was this." She wet the tip of her

161

finger and ran it down her face. Rourke didn't see a difference, but Jamie chuckled.

"Flour?"

"Cornstarch," Galiana said.

"Why?" Rourke demanded.

She bit her lip, and tears welled in her large, dark eyes. Maybe once she washed her face and stopped her bawling, she'd be prettier, Rourke conceded. He never should have pressed his suit yesterday; she was innocent, and it was his own fault if she was running scared.

He opened his mouth to apologize. He was the man, after all.

She hefted her chin and said, "I didn't want you to order me around."

Jamie snickered.

"So instead of following through with the wedding you agreed to, you feigned illness?" Rourke glared. Narrowing his eyes allowed him to reduce Galiana's three heads to just the one.

She nodded and wrung her hands. "I didn't poison anyone. I would never do that. I was going to teach you a lesson in patience . . . Oh, Saint Jude, I shouldn't have said that out loud."

Jamie dropped his chin, then turned on his heel. "I'll fetch the priest."

"I'm not getting married right now!" Galiana wailed at Jamie's back.

"Not for that," Rourke said, disgusted with the

circumstances and life in general. He wasn't used to women going so far to avoid his attentions. Well, she was a prim and proper young girl. What was he to expect? She'd probably been terrified at the thought of sharing his bed, although she hadn't seemed it when her tongue had battled with his in one of the most sensual kisses he'd ever known.

If he hadn't been so focused on regaining his sight, and control over his men, and, well, staying alive without being branded a spy—he would have sensed that the little flower needed coaxing.

"My lady," Rourke dipped at his waist, lowered his voice, looked up at her, and arched his left brow. "Forgive me. I owe you my life, and I've vowed to give you my protection."

Her large, spooky eyes widened. "You needn't do that. It makes you look ridiculous."

Offended, he stepped back. "Me? You're the one covered in dust!"

Galiana shrugged, but hugged the fur tighter to her body. "Do I really look so awful?"

Rourke took a deep breath and wondered if he should just marry the girl and leave her here. She wouldn't be able to hold her own at court; the vixens there would eat such an innocent waif alive.

He'd satisfy Prince John's demand, proving again his loyalty. The prince didn't need to see his bride. However, what reason would he have to go to court then, if not to show off his—he glanced at Galiana's hunched figure—"prize"?

Rubbing a hand over his face, he gave thanks that he could see—but not too clearly. His peers would understand that marriage for land and money was not for love or looks. He shifted his weight from one foot to the next, admitting ruefully that he'd assumed his wife, when he got one, would at least be comely.

His hands tingled again, and he could easily imagine the heft of her breast against his palm. Mayhap if he kept his eyes closed?

Her shoulders shook, and pity—for her—welled within him. "Don't cry, Gali. We need to find a cure for the men—something to make them feel better. I did not eat as much as the others, since I was waiting for you."

"Sorry," she mumbled into the hood of her cloak, which was once again covering her face.

"Don't be—it looks as if you saved me from the worst of the sickness. Who could have done it?"

Her eyes blazed at him from within the folds of fur, and he was struck as if by lightning. He stepped toward her, drawn to that gaze.

"First me, and now you are accusing my knights? They'd not risk being locked up again; I'm sure of it. Is my brother one of the sick?"

"Nay—although your knights are. Jamie said he didn't see young Ned."

She averted her face, and the primal connection was

164

gone. He shook his head to clear it. Her eyes had challenged him with an eerie power. Ancient. Goddess. He would have lain down before such a woman and offered her his soul.

"Then who?"

Yes, who? If not her men, then one of his? Perhaps he'd jumped to the wrong answer too fast. "Let's tally who's left on the floor."

"I can go to the sickroom; mayhap Celestia has a recipe that will calm a poison, but I think you must know the cause before the cure."

"Aye. I'll go with you, since I can't see well enough yet to wander about on my own."

She dipped her head, and Rourke saw he still had some ruffled feathers to smooth. Like a delicate sparrow hawk, she needed soothing.

"I'm sorry, my lady."

Galiana lifted a hand, which, thanks to his skewed vision, looked to have seven fingers upon it. "I'm grateful that you can see this little bit. Chances are great that you will recover—eventually. And I'll try to forget you thought so little of me that you'd accuse me of poisoning innocent people just to get even with you."

He couldn't miss the hurt in her words.

They reached the last stair, and Rourke heard the gasp come from within the confines of her hood. "The smell! Sweet Mary Magdalene, it reeks."

"This was the cause of my anger."

"Who would do something like this?" Galiana's controlled voice was tinged with deep anger.

"Your priest—that's who," Jamie yelled from across the hall. "He's gone. So is your thief of a brother. They took the dispensation, too. Left the ashes of the letter the boy wrote in a pile."

Galiana shoved the hood back from her face and walked ahead toward Jamie, her bearing as regal as that of any lady he'd ever seen. Her dark brown hair, in long twists and curls and braids, flew out behind her.

"You're certain that you knew nothing of this?" Rourke couldn't help the taunt at her back. She played her parts well, and he suddenly realized Galiana could be his equal—in all ways.

He didn't know what she looked like. He didn't know her.

God's bones, but she intrigued him.

"What gives you the right to place such accusations in this hall?" Galiana's knees shook with her temerity, and she grew amazed that the roof of the family manor didn't fall down upon her head.

Men were sprawled all over the floor, in varying degrees of distress. Her heart went out to them, and she stifled a groan when she almost tripped over Bailiff Morton.

"I wish Celestia were here!"

Forgetting Jamie for the moment, she bent down to shake the bailiff's shoulders. He awoke, his eyes bleary and crossed, and slowly looked around the great hall.

"My lady, are you all right? You're very pale. What's happened here?"

"I was hoping you could tell me," she answered wryly. "Everyone is ill. I'll check the kitchens."

"Not alone," Rourke said, suddenly next to her as she stood.

It was odd how comforting his great height was. Tall herself, she was usually nose to nose with most men. But not Rourke. "Are you afraid, my lord?" It was a poor attempt at a joke, and he didn't laugh.

"Afraid you might decide to run away from this foul deed, too."

She bristled. "Take care, else you might actually offend me."

Her bailiff stood on shaky legs. "I'll go, my lady."

"Sit, please, sir, before you fall. This will take a moment, no more." Galiana urged the man to a bench. Most of the men were sleeping still. She'd have to wake each one, but then what?

She was no healer, and her talent for making a lotion wouldn't help the men feel better, although—she discreetly tucked her nose in the fur of her robe to take a breath—her scented candles might create miracles.

Rourke stayed by her side as they walked across the

room, and Galiana wondered just how much he could see. Rather than running, she walked sedately so he wouldn't stumble. Her common sense urged her to fling open the doors so that fresh air could get inside. Cold was better than the stink of twenty sick people.

The smell grew stronger the closer they came to the kitchen. It was unfortunate that the kitchen wasn't in a separate building, she thought, but at least it was at the back of the manor. Cook had just roused, and the look of horror on her plump face as she noticed the disaster around her mirrored Rourke's. If they looked like that, then Galiana shuddered to think what emotion she was giving away.

"What in the devil happened here?" Tears streamed over Cook's round, red cheeks as she brushed food and dirt from her apron. "I've never fallen asleep at me duties, and they've"—she pointed incomprehensively at the two young kitchen helpers—"never been sick a day."

Galiana opened the back door to the cooking pit area. Thanks to the heat of the fires, the snow had melted in the center, leaving giant walls of white on the sides.

A gust of clean air rushed through the kitchen. Galiana was able to breathe and think.

"What did everybody eat last night?"

Cook's trembling hand gestured toward an assortment of large, black pots. "Pottage, with almonds and raisins, sticky buns, beef stew . . . spiced wine, ale. We was celebratin'!" She bobbed a quick curtsy toward

Rourke, then sputtered when she really looked at him.

Her cheeks flushed, and she giggled like a girl. "Yer weddin' feast."

Galiana rolled her eyes. Yes, Rourke was handsome, but really . . .

"Cook. Everyone who ate is sick. Is it possible there was something in the bread?"

Indignant, the cook shook her head. "Nay, I baked the bread meself."

Rourke scratched his chin. "Mushrooms?"

Galiana remembered how Celestia had been poisoned with an Amanita mushroom, and snapped her fingers. "I should have thought of that."

Cook shook her head. "I had to use what was in the pantry for the feast, since we can't get to the village."

Galiana sighed, then walked over to sniff the pots. She waved her hand beneath her nose, knowing she had to breathe deeply and identify what was in the pots— whether she wanted to or not.

She leaned over, closed her eyes, and inhaled.

"What are you doing?" Rourke's intrusive question broke her concentration.

"Smelling."

"God's blood, why?"

"I've trained my nose to separate scents. Usually for floral smells, but the premise is the same."

He crossed his arms over his chest, and her heart raced. That stubborn lock of hair fell forward, covering the stitches

169

on the side of his face. His eyes seemed clear—so clear he could be seeing inside her head. She quickly turned back toward the pot. The man was so good-looking it was simply unfair.

And he'd screamed when he'd seen her! She couldn't allow herself to think about that now.

Gali closed her eyes, taking a slower, deeper breath. Hops? Cabbage, almonds, raisins, cinnamon, beef, vinegar, pepper, sage—wait—was that—some sort of bark? And—"Oh no."

"What?" Rourke and Cook asked at the same time.

"Valerian—lots of it—in the spiced wine."

"A sedative." Rourke arched a brow.

"I don't use no valerian in me wine, me lady. And I know just to add a pinch when a body can't sleep or has a case of the nerves!"

Galiana nodded, her stomach in a tight ball as she pushed aside the memory of drinking spiced wine last eve. "I don't suppose you intentionally used buckthorn bark in your pottage?"

"No, no!"

Cook's eyes couldn't be any wider without falling out of her head, Gali thought with a shudder.

"What's buckthorn bark?" Rourke's expression was inscrutable, and it took all of her willpower to not squirm beneath it.

"People collect the bark from the alder trees in the summer. I helped Celestia a few times. So did my brotherssss—oh . . . the dungeon!" They wouldn't have!

"Dungeon?" Rourke dropped his arms to his sides.

"Sick room," Galiana explained, running from the kitchen. She picked up the front hem of her thick robe, kicked off her slippers, and ran in her bare feet, not caring in the least that her mother would be mortified. Across the great hall, to the door that led downstairs—Ed and Ned had gone with her and Celestia on that walk in the forest, and they knew that the bark acted as a purgative.

They liked their pranks, all Montehues liked a practical joke, but this—if they'd done it—was too far. What if they'd run away out of fear?

Why had Father Jonah gone with them?

It was too much to contemplate. She opened the door to a room she had hated in the past. It was dark, and Gali, even though she had no magical skills, just knew it was haunted with past ghosts.

"Why are you hesitating?" He'd stayed at her heels, though in her haste to find her brothers she'd forgotten he couldn't see well.

"I, uh," she patted her hand against her heart, not wanting to admit her fears. Why would he believe her, when she'd spent the past few days down in the dungeon with him?

"You're fast, for a lady." Rourke's eyes sparkled at her.

She opened the door all the way, knowing she'd never survive an onslaught of Rourke's charm. The stairs led down into an inky pit, and her toes curled against the floor. "I hate the dark."

"I've a candle, lass. Let me go down first." Jamie's voice came from behind her, and she whirled.

He looked at her face and winked. "Still looking pale, lass. I'd like to see if that rascal Ned is hiding down here. And from the way ye ran, so do you."

Rourke huffed, while Galiana buried her face in her hands. Rourke's foster brother had witnessed her running like a hoyden, then faking an illness, and now he'd called her on the true reason for braving the dungeon. "I don't like you, Jamie."

He chuckled and led the way down the stairs. Jamie quickly lit a ceramic bird-shaped lamp he'd grabbed from the hall and led the way down, lighting each candle sconce on the wall until the sick room was brightly lit.

"This is where you worked your magic, eh?" Rourke looked around, pausing at the cot.

"I don't do magic," Galiana sniffed. She eyed Celestia's work table and noted that her sister's book of herbal recipes was out, and open.

A telltale curl of bark lay next to it.

"They did it," she said. "Why? Stupid, stupid, oh—" Her knees trembled, and she welcomed the steadying hand Rourke placed beneath her elbow.

"Exactly. Why would Ned and the priest want to poison us all?" Rourke led her to the cot, and she sat on the edge to avoid fainting again.

Jamie said, "It's bloody convenient, lass, that ye

didn't come down to dinner."

"You really think I would condone this act? Nay, my reasons for feigning sickness were different. Why didn't they come to me before they left? I was in charge. My parents trusted me." Her eyes filled with warm tears as she recounted her failures.

"Ach, don't cry, now." Jamie sighed and looked away.

"I can't help it," Galiana's voice warbled, but it didn't matter. She fisted her hands in the fur of her thick robe. "Everyone treats me as if I haven't a brain in my head, and finally, finally, they give me a responsibility, and just see what happens . . . The entire manor is poisoned, I almost blinded Rourke, and I'm being forced into," she huffed, "m-m-marriage."

Rourke sat next to her on the cot and handed her a square of linen from a stack that Celestia kept on the table. "Here. Wipe your eyes, Gali, it looks like you have black streaks down your face."

Lovely, she thought. She was supposed to be this great beauty, and the one man who spoke to her heart thought she was Bruenhilda. "Why didn't they come to me? Oh, Saint Mary, please guide them to safety. You know they must think they killed everybody? Oh—" Fresh tears sprang from her eyes as Rourke put his arm around her shoulders.

"Is there something in this book that'll make everybody feel better?" Jamie patted at the pages.

Gali jumped to her feet. "Aye, there must be . . . something to soothe an aching belly." She should have thought of that instead of pitying herself.

"We can help ye, lass, but then"—Jamie exchanged a look with Rourke—"I'm going after that boy and the priest. They can't have got too far."

"I'll go with you," Rourke said firmly.

She'd told Ed to go to Celestia, and then she'd made a fuss over being forced to marry Rourke. Ned had been terribly upset. This was her fault again.

It was time to start acting responsible and stop lamenting what might have been. Galiana lifted her chin, refusing to consider that she'd soon be in the dungeon alone. It was different with Rourke here; even sick, he kept the ghosts at bay.

"Please, go now. If the snow is still falling, it could cover their tracks. What if they're lost? Hurry! I can handle everything here."

Jamie gave her a look of approval.

Rourke said, "We'll find them and bring them back—alive, Galiana."

If anybody could do it, it would be him, she thought as she watched them walk away. She wanted her brothers back at the manor fussing and kicking, and Father Jonah, too. But it would be better for everyone if the boys made it safely to Celestia's.

Rourke stepped outside, threw his head back, and stared at the gray skies. Well, everything was gray, but he didn't care. He took a cleansing breath of fresh, crisp air. "I hate to complain of a headache, since my sight seems to be returning. I hope the walk will clear it."

"Your gray vision, or your aching head? I wish to God I'd eaten as sparingly as you last eve. My gut still burns."

"Should we go back and see if there is something you can take to soothe it?"

"Nay, I'll be fine, now that I know I'm not dying."

"Not yet, anyway."

Jamie laughed, then pointed to the left. "They tried to cover their tracks. Do ye think the lady knew what was going on?"

Rourke stretched his back, accepting that Jamie would be leading the way, and content just to be mending. Galiana was a complex woman, a foreign language he desired to learn. Did he think she was capable of poisoning her own men? His gut said no.

"Well?" Jamie prodded, taking huge steps in the snow.

"Nay."

"Then why did the boy and the priest do it? And why did they take the dispensation? The lady had already agreed to marry you."

"Even though she didn't want to." Rourke set his jaw at the thought, quite clearly remembering her brother's anger. "Can you believe she thought to teach me a lesson?"

Jamie's loud laugh echoed around them. "Aye. Ye should have seen the look on your face when she opened the door!"

Rourke grinned. "She scared me, and I don't scare easily."

"Even in soot and flour, she wasn't that bad," Jamie teased.

"I like my ladies beautiful; you know that. This one is—" He paused, shaking the snowflake off his nose. "I don't even know what she is. Wrapped up like a Buddha in that fur coat, I could barely get my arm over her shoulder."

The belly laughs coming from Jamie urged Rourke to ask, "Well, at least tell me the color of her hair. Is it really as dull of a brown as I think?"

"Oh no, my man, ye'll have to judge your wife for yourself. One man's beauty is another man's hag," Jamie bellowed. "I think they're heading to the village. Let's cut across this way—"

One minute Jamie was in front of him talking, and the next, he was gone.

Rourke rubbed his eyes, wondering if it was a glitch in his vision, but then ran toward the large drift that all of Jamie had sunk in.

Reaching down until his fingers grabbed hair, Rourke pulled until he could grasp his foster brother's collar.

Nothing could happen to Jamie, by Christ. It was he and Jamie against the world—it always had been.

176

He yanked and pulled until, spluttering and red-faced, Jamie spat, "What in the hell was that?"

"Don't ask me," Rourke huffed, falling back in the snow. "You were leading the way."

Jamie exhaled, a plume of air coming from his mouth like smoke as he lay back, too. "I hope they made the village."

"Me too."

Rourke knew Galiana felt responsible for her brother and the priest. She'd yet to learn that people were responsible for their own choices in the world. Well, he'd not want to be the one to teach her.

"Should we turn around?" Jamie sat up and shook the snow from his head like a dog from a pond.

"We have to keep on."

"I know. I'll go a bit slower."

"Is it me, or is it getting darker?"

"Darker. And it's not even midday."

They plowed ahead until Rourke was sure his toes would never thaw. He'd lost feeling in his face a long time ago, and the frigid walk had made Jamie too tired to talk.

Everything was gray and cloudy, so he sniffed the air. "Is that smoke ahead?" Rourke blinked against the steadily falling flakes.

Jamie lifted his shaggy, wet head. "Christ, have mercy, I think it is."

"I'd run," Rourke said, "But I can't feel my legs."

They entered the village square and headed toward the first house. They knocked, and a wizened old woman with no teeth in her mouth cracked open the door.

She saw them, clucked her tongue, and invited them in. "What ye doin' out in this weather?"

It took Rourke a minute to thaw his mouth out enough to answer. "Looking for a boy, and the priest"— he inched toward the cheery fire—"Father Jonah."

"Oh, aye," the old lady crowed. "They was here, early this morning, they was."

Rourke's spirits lifted. The journey would be worth it, if he could bring Gali's brother back safe. And then he'd tan the boy's backside, but good, for all the mischief he'd caused. "Where are they now?"

"They left." She walked to the bubbling pot dangling from its hook over the fire. "Soup?"

"Please," Jamie said, rubbing his hands together.

He wouldn't allow the scent of barley and beef to tempt him from his questions. "Where, good lady, did they go?"

"That Ed—he wanted to go straight to France."

Rourke's gut dropped. "France?"

"Aye, we talked 'im out of it, though, at least 'til it stops snowin'!" She laughed, handing a bowl to Jamie.

"If they didn't go to France." Damn the boy. He planned to take the problem directly to King Philippe. He must not have realized King Philippe and Prince John were joined in treachery against Britain. "Where did they go?"

"Ach, to Wales was his second choice, but Father Jonah—he decided they should go to Falcon Keep."

"Where's that?" Rourke was getting impatient—which didn't warm his insides as well as did the soup Jamie was loudly enjoying.

"Dunno, me lord, but I gave 'em some soup, and Martha gave them some blankets, and off they went."

"On foot." Crazy fools.

"Nay, nay," the old woman shook her head. "Bartholomew lent 'em a mule, on account that the boys said their father would pay. Good mule, too. Your man there's finished. Would ye like some soup?"

Rourke, disappointed he'd have to travel back to the manor without Galiana's brother, nodded. He might as well have something warm in his belly before returning to the cold. "My thanks."

Had she said boys? Plural?

It wasn't in his nature to leave a stone unturned, and he heard Jamie's groan as his foster brother realized they weren't going directly back to the manor.

"Rourke, we'll never find them in the dark. And it's snowing again!"

"Stop whining, Jamie. Tell me, good woman, where does Bartholomew live?"

Chapter Eight

Galiana dropped the last of the filthy rags into the large, boiling pot of vinegar and tansy. She'd never been fond of the stone laundry area, but with the majority of the servants snowed in at the village, and the live-in servants all recovering from her brothers' prank, she had no choice but to do the wash herself.

She stretched her lower back, proud of the cloths already hanging on the drying lines in neat precision. The bailiff had helped her stoke the fire in the pit, and the laundry was filled with steam, which Gali knew would do wonders for her skin.

Patting her damp cheeks, she noticed how red and chapped her hands were, but stifled a squeal of dismay. Being a lady sometimes meant doing the things around the manor that nobody else could do—all whilst smiling and keeping a good temper, of course.

"'Tis a good thing you brats ran away, else I would surely drown you myself!" she muttered as she pushed the soaking rags around the large pot. The wooden handle had been worn smooth of splinters long ago, and Galiana's fingers fit easily into the worn grooves. "Aye, this would make an excellent stick to paddle you with."

Her words were false bravado. If she could see her brothers safe, she would do this penance and more.

It was her fault they were all in this mess.

Gali's arms ached and trembled, but she dare not think on it, lest she cry. Tears would do her no good, although she promised herself a nice breakdown in her evening bath.

"My lady?"

Wiping a sticky strand of hair from her forehead, Galiana turned at the sound of young Will's voice.

He stared at her until she cleared her throat. It seemed the squire had an infatuation with her, which was neither appropriate nor desired.

He flushed scarlet beneath her scrutiny. "My lady, I still cannot find Robbie—er, Sir Robert. He was at dinner last eve, but—" Will looked at the floor. "What if he went out in the snow? While sick?"

Galiana released the wooden paddle, letting it rest inside the boiling pot. "For fresh air, mayhap?" Worry settled across her shoulders, too.

"He would have been weak." Will didn't hide the

concern he felt for his fellow knight.

"Ned gone, and the priest. Now Robert?" A new thought came to Galiana as she tried to make the pieces fit. Rourke's warning of danger was never far from her thoughts, and she wondered if perhaps Robert was in the mix. What if her brothers had stumbled across someone else trying to poison the manor?

What if—she gulped with immediate terror—what if they were in danger? Not from the snow, but from a man? Sir Robert was a large knight; he could snap a boy's neck in two.

Galiana immediately untied her apron and headed for the hall, gesturing for Will to follow her.

He did.

There were times, like now, that Galiana wished for at least some sort of skewed intuition—even her mother had that—which was why the rest of her family had left for Falcon Keep. The lady Deirdre just 'knew' her oldest daughter needed her.

Gali concentrated and thought of her brothers with all her might, trying to see if she could reach down into her inner soul and connect with them. Were they safe? Tears filled her eyes, and she angrily brushed them away.

Worthless.

Her skills were nothing legendary. Celestia could heal just by laying her hands on a sick person. Her youngest sister could see auras and was promising to be an even greater beauty—although very, very tall.

She could match a scent with a personality. Hurray. She snorted derisively.

"My lady? Why are ye running?" Will asked, even though he was keeping step with her.

"What if Sir Robert is in a snow drift? He'd freeze afore I could save him! Lord Rourke will not be pleased to come home and find his knight missing. Aye, he will blame me, and I just cannot accept another fault today. We must find him; we must."

"Your fault, my lady? Never." He reached out to grab her arm, and Galiana swatted at his hand without ever slowing her pace.

"You are a comely young man, and a good squire to your lord. But you need to learn to not grab the ladies. Smile, be courteous, and they will come to you." She smiled at him to lessen the sting of her reprimand.

He tripped over his feet, but righted himself quickly. "But yer so beautiful, my lady, and I would fight fer you, I would, and honor you all my life."

Sighing, Galiana came to a halt. "I have no romantic interest in you. My apologies for speaking so plainly, as it is not my intent to cause you harm. Beauty is nothing. Character—that is what counts. Honor, integrity, loyalty—these are the things that will make you a great knight one day soon."

He nodded, and Gali could only hope he was listening.

"Lord Rourke is who you swear allegiance to, and he deserves your best; does he not?" She was tempted to tap her toe, she was so impatient, but she refrained. It was her duty to teach chivalry and manners, while respecting this young man's tender feelings. But, by the chastity of the Virgin, she was in no mood!

"Aye, my lady," Will mumbled to the floor.

"Good." Galiana brushed her hands together and said, "We needn't mention this to anybody else, my good squire. Renew your pledge to Lord Rourke, and we can forget this ever happened."

"Thank ye, my lady." Will clutched her hand.

She pulled it back, her head tilted. "What did I say to you about grabbing?"

"I wanted to kiss your fingers in thanks," he blustered.

"Ask, then." She kept her hand at her side. "Nicely. Use some of that charm your lord exudes."

Will exhaled, but then asked, "My lady, may I have the honor of your hand?"

"Put a friendly smile on your face," Galiana instructed. "You look like a hungry wolf instead of a charming young man."

Shuffling his feet, he did as told. "May I?" He bowed low, his palm up with his fingers outstretched.

Dipping her head, Galiana simpered and placed the tips of her fingers over his.

He brought them to his mouth for a kiss.

"Don't touch the skin with those mangy lips, boy," Sir Godfrey bellowed.

Will jumped back, his face red with mortification.

Galiana stepped forward, hoping she hadn't just made the situation worse for Will by embarrassing him in front of the older knight.

But Godfrey just rubbed his chin speculatively and suggested, "A lighter hand this time, Will, and the kiss needs to be just above the knuckles without landing. Took me years to master it," he added.

She smiled her appreciation for the older knight. "Shall we try again? Just once, since we need to locate Sir Robert."

Will made a significant improvement on the next try, and Sir Godfrey promised a few extra lessons in how to be a chivalrous knight.

"Can't find Robbie? I know I saw him this morning." Sir Godfrey led the way to the hall. "Once I was on me feet."

"You did?" Galiana breathed a sigh of relief. "So the chances of him being lost in the snow are slim."

"I was worried," Will admitted. "He was on duty to shovel to the stables, but he never did."

"He's probably sleepin' off the sick, boy"—Sir Godfrey clamped his hand down on Will's shoulder—"in private somewhere."

"Have you asked Sir Franz if he's seen him?" Galiana asked Will as they reached the open area of the great hall. The benches and the tables had all been cleaned and stacked to the side so that she could scrub the stone floor.

Dry, clean, fragrant rushes had been spread, and the windows had been flung open. The sick stench was not even a lingering aroma.

"Sir Franz"—Godfrey chuckled—"has been wooing that old dame for a bed."

"Franz and Dame Bertha?" Will choked. "Together?"

Galiana covered her mouth with her fingers to stop an indelicate snicker.

"Not like that," Godfrey cuffed Will's ear. "Fer sleepin'. That's why I'd wager Robert is off on some vacant pallet snorin' and—"

He broke off, realizing what he was saying. His dark brown eyes widened, and his cheeks got even ruddier. "My apologies," Godfrey bowed.

Will broke into loud laughter.

Galiana reasoned that the pedestal Will had been placing the older knight on had just crumbled beneath the weight of reality. "You are most likely correct, Sir Godfrey. I'll ask one of my men to look." She winked at Will, then noticed Dame Bertha slumped before the large fire.

"Excuse me, sirs," she said and went to see how the old woman fared.

The manor hall was clean, the kitchens sparkled, the laundry was almost finished, and she knew if she sat down now to join Dame Bertha for a rest, she might never get back on her feet.

"Ye look beat, my lady," the old woman said with a tired smile. She gestured to her embroidery hoop, which lay on the floor at her feet. "I thought ta do some mendin', but I couldn't keep me eyes open."

"You've worked hard today. Thank you." The cushion on the three-legged stool beckoned to her, but Galiana resisted the luxury.

"Me? Ye've done the work of five maids, and a few of the knights, as well."

Gali laughed softly, pleased that her efforts had been noticed. "Once everyone stopped puking, it was just a matter of cleaning up."

"What finally did the trick?"

"A decoction of mallow, licorice, and mint. I found the recipe on a scrap of vellum at the back of Celestia's book, praise be. For certes, our people missed my sister and my grandmother this day."

She'd also found a new recipe calling for clary that supposedly helped clear vision. Galiana was looking forward to sharing it with Rourke.

"Ye fared well, my lady. That is what they'll remember," the woman said kindly.

Galiana discreetly stretched her leg muscles as she stood enjoying the warmth of the flames in contrast with the gust of fresh winter air from the open windows. The combination was cozy, yet kept her from feeling closed in.

"Have you asked around? Does anybody remember

seeing"—she lowered her voice—"the twins?"

Dame Bertha shook her head. "Cook and her scullions said some of Lord Rourke's men were in the kitchens yesterday."

"Someone added valerian to the spiced blackberry wine—I'd made no secret I wanted some." Galiana reached back to rub the sore muscle at her nape. "Not enough to poison me, aye? But I slept sound, for certes."

The old woman's mouth thinned, and her knee trembled. "I brought it to ye. Ye don't think I did it, my lady?"

"Nay." Galiana said dismissively before peering at the woman, who had a sudden case of the jitters. "Did you?"

"Nay! Of course I would never do a thing like that, my lady, I've known ye since ye were a babe, fresh to the world."

Gali tilted her head to the side and opted for the cushion after all. Intuition wasn't needed to see Dame Bertha had a secret. "Well, you've obviously thought this through. Who do you think put the valerian in the spiced wine?"

Robert, Father Jonah, and both the boys—missing. Gali stared into the fire as if the answers were hidden amongst the dancing orange flames.

"I don't know, but Cook swore it was one of the big, dark knights of Lord Rourke's; she doesn't know their names, aye?"

"That would leave out Jamie, who has unmistakable ginger hair, and Franz, who can't be called 'large' on a

188

good day."

Dame Bertha leaned in and whispered, "I've got Sir Franz in me bed."

Galiana, grateful to all the saints that she'd been forewarned, was able to nod in serious contemplation instead of laughing at the poor woman. "Aye?" She managed with a straight face.

"He was askin' me all sorts of questions about ye, and I heard him talkin' to our knights and the bailiff, too. Even cozened that old priest, afore he took off."

A chill scattered across her shoulders, and she asked, "Questions about me?"

"Aye. I thought it was best if we knew where to find that one—he's a charmer, but as wily as a fox, to my mind."

"I agree. Good thinking, Dame Bertha. Uh"—Galiana tapped her finger against her knee—"what did he ask? And what, pray tell, did you share with him?"

The old woman's face paled. "He was sneaky, my lady. Just talkin' with me, about nothin' at all, and then he'd ask a question—like, did ye ever have a betrothed before? And"—she swallowed hard—"why ye ain't been married yet."

"Was it you who told him about Celestia? That she'd been forced to wed?" Her instincts about the Frenchman had been correct. He bore watching—but whose side was he on? Lord Rourke's? Or his own?

Dame Bertha exhaled with shame. "Aye. He caught me unawares, my lady."

"But you didn't tell him that Ned had a twin, did you?"

"No! None of us would give up the boys, even after what they did here."

Guilt on her family's behalf led her to get to her feet. "Thank you for telling me. I'll be wary. I just need to know one more thing. Did Cook, or the other servants, see"—she cleared her throat over the lump forming in it—"the boys add the bark to the stew?"

"No. But who else could it have been?"

Everyone in the manor, besides Rourke and his men, knew of the Montehues' love of jests. Rourke's knights had known she'd ordered the spiced blackberry wine. Well, to be fair, Ned had heard her order it, too. But why would he want her asleep? To keep her safe from her wedding night?

Her head throbbed at the direct center betwixt her eyes, and she quickly pressed her fingers against the spot. Stress brought wrinkles, and since she had no magic but only beauty to offer, she had to care about such things.

Although this day's work had been the hardest she'd ever done, it had been rewarding. Not magical, and not spiritual—but satisfying in its own way.

Galiana decided to have one more word with Cook, on the off chance that the woman, or her helpers, would remember who else had been in the kitchen.

Rourke fumed.

"If ye don't spew some of that fury, my friend, ye're like to melt all the snow in the fields. Which would cause a landslide, and we might not survive—and I, Rourke, have dreams of retiring someday."

"I'll vent my anger on the witch who deserves it!" His eyesight was murky still, but he welcomed a world in black and white and gray over a world he couldn't see at all. His vision matched his mood.

All her talk of honor and how her family didn't view deceit as an asset . . . She was the champion of lies. He stomped behind Jamie, careful to keep his strides the same.

"She was protecting her family; ye would do the same," Jamie pointed out.

"I thought I was being haunted. That night someone drugged your ale? But now I'd bet it was the two of those damnable boys playing one of their ill-gotten jests." He remembered his fear—a feeling he rarely admitted—as he'd thought his legs were being bitten by dragon's teeth. What had those rapscallions used? Hot oil? Liquid wax?

Some of his delusions had been due to fever and medicine, but the rest to those troublesome twins—he'd stake his life on it.

"Aye, those buggers will owe me once I catch up with 'em." Jamie stopped outside the outer gate to the manor. "Never mess with a man's drink, by God."

"Who's in the gatehouse?" Rourke squinted, but saw

a mass of gray. He'd never been to the front of the manor.

"Nobody."

"Why the hell isn't one of our men out here?"

"Too bleedin' cold, that's why," Jamie barked back. "We've been snowed in, Rourke, and unless ye've a sled and a pack of dogs, we are safe."

"Two boys and a priest just managed to leave, and if they can leave, then, Jamie, skilled knights can get in." Apprehension sat on his shoulder like a gyrfalcon, just waiting to tug the flesh from his dying bones.

He scrubbed at his forehead.

It would be time to tell Galiana a bit more of the truth, which was so fantastical as to be a story. Almost as silly as her claim to be descended from Boadicea. Who could trace their lineage so far? Aye, never mind the fact Boadicea was simply a legend, a symbol of a woman rising against the Romans and leading her people to victory; a temporary victory. Not real.

Jamie cursed fluently in three languages before settling back into the old Scots tongue he and Rourke favored so that their words would be secret. "I'll send Will, then Robert, to do a turn. But they can't stay more than an hour a shift, Rourke, else they'll fall into a sleep they'll never wake from."

"Give them an extra fur, then, but this manor and this woman need our protection. She'll not have the protection of my name, since the priest fled, and that makes her a viable prize."

"Bed her."

Aye, I'd like to do that, Rourke thought as he followed Jamie to the manor door. "I can't. Not now. It's the legal binding the prince wants. Her father's men, her father's coin—she doesn't need her maidenhead to be a bartering tool."

Jamie stopped and faced Rourke, shooting a hand out to grip Rourke by the upper arm. In an old Welsh dialect, he asked, "You're certain you want to marry her? You know you can ignore the prince, and wait to see if Constance will need a husband, just as you were doing with Lady Magdalene. King William wants the throne of England under his command—his pride demands retribution for that damn treaty he was forced to sign to save his people."

Rourke dipped his head, his mouth tight. "Prince John has ordered me to marry her."

"He placed a wager with three knights, to see who could get to the girl first! It is not just upon your shoulders," Jamie interjected.

"I want her," Rourke said coldly. "Why should I not have something I want? Every move I make is another man's will. She will be mine."

"Ye can't keep her," Jamie lowered his hand.

"I know," Rourke said, his breath a gust of white in the chilled air. "She'll not lose everything. I'll gift her with a home."

"Other than the small keep that we just left falling

down around our ears, your lands are in the wilds of Scotland. You think this prim miss will thrive there? Away from her precious family?" Jamie snorted with disgust. "They love one another enough to lie under oath, and to brave possible death in this damn weather! Those boys knew quite well that without the priest, the lady wouldn't wed you."

"So?" Rourke hefted his chin to glare at his foster brother's gray face.

"Think, man. She's a woman. Just a woman. And not the woman you are meant to marry. Let another man claim her as his prize to Prince John. Don't ruin everything we've worked for."

The door to the manor opened, and the Montehue bailiff called out to them. "Is all well? Did ye find the boysssss"—Rourke noticed the bailiff catch himself—"and the priest?"

He could see well enough to stomp toward the man in patterned livery, so he shoved his foster brother to the side and yelled, "Nay, good sir, all is not well. Bring me the lady of the manor—now!"

Rourke brushed past the bailiff, searching the room. He didn't know what the damn lady looked like without ghost-white paint and a fur robe, and it pissed him off even more.

"Galiana!" he bellowed, standing with his arms akimbo and his legs spread. He didn't care that the servants cowered, or that his knights immediately got to their feet. For that matter, Galiana's men stood, too.

He strode forward five large steps and yelled her name again. None dared to question him, but he felt the weight of their stares.

His shouting was rewarded by the patter of heels on the stone floor. Looking down and sniffing, he noticed that the manor was much improved over when he had left it that morning. Not a single foul smell remained.

"What, pray tell, is the problem here?" He assumed the tall woman who spoke was Galiana. "To shout like this is the lowest of manners," she chided before she rounded the corner and saw him.

"You speak of manners?" Rourke was itching for an argument. An explanation of why she thought she could lie, and yet think less of others for the same crime.

"Lord Rourke! You're soaked through, sir, let me order you a hot bath." She started to turn back toward the kitchen, but he called her name again.

She halted.

Her gown was large and shaped like a grain sack. He saw it as gray, but he supposed that was no fault of hers. Not even a plain braided girdle gave it shape. Her hair, a riot of dull brown waves that the small veil she wore did nothing to hide, needed a good combing. And her face still held traces of candle soot.

Either that, or she had a permanent birthmark between her eyes.

"You needn't marry her." Jamie's words teased his brain.

Her first words to him had held sincere concern for his well-being. When was the last time someone had cared like that? His world was filled with intrigue and danger. Hers was filled with perfumes.

"I don't want a bath, my lady." Rourke fought to hold on to his temper. "I want to know about your kin."

"Hmm?"

Her eyes, large and dark in a pale face with a pointed chin, gave nothing away.

"Ned?"

"You found him?" She ran forward three steps, hands out to him before she saw him shake his head.

"Nay. Jamie and I made our way to the village, my lady."

Her lower lip trembled.

"And imagine my surprise when I found out you have not one brother, but two. Twins, my lady?"

She swallowed, mute.

Her stoicism infuriated him. "Do you not think you could have mentioned this before we went tracking Ned in the snow? That mayhap there were three travelers, instead of two?"

He took a step forward, and she stayed put. Her courage against his anger stopped him from yelling further.

"You talk of honor. Of prizing honesty. Where is your honesty, my lady?"

One of the Montehue knights made a growl in his throat before asking, "My lady? I know ye told us to respect this knight, but he's not respecting you."

Galiana turned that pointy chin in the knight's direction and dipped her head in a regal manner. "Thank you. Lord Rourke is distraught and chilled. For certes, he meant no disrespect. No doubt the lord and I will finish this conversation over a meal and quite possibly without shouting." She turned back to him, and Rourke felt like a five-year-old being reprimanded for behaving badly.

"My lord? Should I have the bath sent to"—her words too smooth, giving away the buried fury she felt— "your chamber?"

She was no beauty, but it didn't matter. He wanted her with an intensity he'd never felt before.

Dame Bertha called from her perch by the fire, "What of the boys, then? And Father Jonah?"

Rourke rubbed his temple, careful to stay clear of the stitches. "Off to Falcon Keep, and the family there."

"On foot?" Galiana's question came out as a gasp.

"Nay. They bought a mule from a man in the village, and some supplies. I talked to the man, Bartholomew—"

"Good man," Dame Bertha said.

"And he told them which villages to stay at along the way. It was foolish."

Galiana bit her lower lip.

Rourke added, "He sold them furs and canvas, on credit, but they'll be fine."

"At least Father Jonah is with them," the bailiff said.

Shuffling his feet, Rourke said, "Actually, he isn't. The priest walked the boys halfway to the village, and then he went on his own. He wouldn't say where."

Bowing her head for a moment, Galiana looked back up and met his gaze. He was struck by a flash of verdant green, like an overgrown forest filled with bushes and ferns, but he blinked, and it was gone.

"And the dispensation?" Her hands twisted in her skirt.

"The priest took it with him."

Rourke waited for the prim lady to cry or fall into a faint, but she straightened her shoulders—by God, she was tall for a woman—and thanked him for the news.

Then she called to the boy carrying firewood to heat water for the lord's bath. "Will you need anything else, Lord Rourke? Sir Jamie?"

Jamie, damn him, said he'd take a bath. Then he added, "And, lass, ye did a fine job here."

Galiana smiled, actually smiled, at Jamie—who she'd said she despised—and Rourke thought the smile made her look pretty, despite the gray of her gown.

" 'Tis nerve of that man," Galiana complained to Dame Bertha as she climbed the stairs. "Yelling for me as if I was his, his"—she frowned—"squire or some such thing."

"It's the ways of man," Dame Bertha clucked as she huffed up the stairs behind Galiana.

"Father doesn't do it. Mam would skin him alive."

"That's why every man needs a good wife. Not that

ye need to worry about that now, eh?"

Galiana paused at the top of the stairs. "What do you mean?"

"No need for ye to marry in a rush, now that Father Jonah has run off with the dispensation."

"That's true," she realized, her stomach hopping with a flurry of tangled emotions. And was that a thread of disappointment?

Nay!

"If Prince John wants ye wed to the lord, here, then ye'll have to marry at court, now, won't ye?"

"I don't know . . ." Galiana pressed a hand to her tummy, not sure what to make of this change of events. "I could explain, as I wanted to, to Prince John, that our family has a writ, with King Richard's seal—but will he honor it? I don't have the blasted thing. Father Jonah has it. Now what am I supposed to do? I could rewrite the dispensation from memory and—."

"Stop dawdling, my lady," Dame Bertha said with a slight shove toward the chamber Rourke was in. "The lord's got a temper, and ye don't want it aimed at your head again."

"He deserves to be as shriveled as a prune," Galiana said with a shudder. "Are you certain you don't mind helping Sir Jamie with his bath?"

"Not at all, not at all." The old woman winked.

Galiana was left with no choice but to perform as lady of the manor and offer to scrub Rourke's back. How could she stay angry with him if he was naked as the day he was born?

Sharing an oath before God and Father Jonah would have given her the chance to explore these new feelings that Rourke aroused. No wedding; no wedding bed.

She swallowed, then opened the door with firm fingers. Galiana was the lady of the manor, and by all the saints, she could bathe a man without falling prey to her senses.

If the man were any besides Rourke Wallis, a man whose kisses melted her resistance, a man whose essence she yearned to inhale—aye, then mayhap she could do it.

Rourke's bare shoulders stuck out above the bathing tub, and his hair dripped with suds. His knees, covered in burnished gold hair, stuck out like wings of a bird, and her body hummed.

She turned on her heel to leave before she made a fool of herself.

Again.

"I need more hot water, and some mead."

Galiana paused at the threshold. Lady, lady, lady. She could practically hear her mother's chiding voice in her ear. They'd know as soon as her brother's reached Falcon Keep how far she'd failed.

"I'll go get it," she said.

Rourke wheeled around so fast that water splashed on the floor. "Galiana? What are you doing in here?"

Saint Agnes, help me! "I'm going to assist you with your bath."

"You're a maid!"

She hefted her chin. "Aye. But it is my duty, as lady, to help our guests with their baths. Dame Bertha is seeing to Jamie, and you know our staff is limited."

He leaned his head back against the tub, golden brown curls escaping over the edge. The texture of Rourke's hair was as fine as silk; her fingers remembered it quite well.

Clutching her skirt instead of Rourke, Galiana strode forward until she reached the edge of the tub. Eyes lowered to the floor, she asked, "My lord?"

"I, no—I'll finish myself," he spluttered.

"You've soap in your hair," Galiana pointed out, amused that he was as flustered as she. She reached for the pitcher of warm water on the low table before the fire. Next to a light repast lay a leather thong, the type a man might wear around his neck.

Her ring was attached to it, and her humor fled. Why would he not give this thing to her, when he'd made up such a story around it? What did it really mean?

Who was it truly for—what kind of woman would seep her way into this warrior's heart?

"Go," he ordered, discomfort instead of charm in his voice.

"Sit up; let me do this one thing, and then I'll leave you to your privacy."

"You think this funny, my lady?"

She heard the warning, and laughed with uncharacteristic defiance. "Aye."

He tipped his face up, and she sighed. How could she stay angry with him? Strong of brow, eyebrows framing beautiful eyes, and his nose—so noble—and his strong chin . . .

"Why do you stare? You've seen this face of mine before."

True. She was but memorizing it, feature by feature, so that if he didn't choose to marry her, she could have his image to dream by.

A dream Rourke was safer than the flesh-and-blood man, anyway.

"'Tis a good time to remove the stitches," she said. "Mayhap after I rinse your hair?" She pressed the pitcher to her chest so that it didn't spill.

"Fine," he growled. "Be quick."

"Would you lean back?"

"Nay. I'll dip my head forward, lest you see more of me than your innocent eyes need see."

Galiana gasped and forced her gaze away from his lap. Her belly recalled the feel of his manhood against her mound, and her fingers shook.

She poured the water carefully over his curls, using her fingers to wrest the knots free. Wanting to do this chore right, she took her time.

"Have done!" he demanded, and she noticed the strain of muscle across his bare shoulders. Thinking only to soothe, she caressed the length of skin, which immediately dotted with goose bumps, and Rourke exhaled so forcibly that the water before him rippled.

"You're cold!" Galiana jumped to her feet and ran to the towel hanging in front of the fire. She turned back, the warm cloth in her hands, to see him standing in all of his glorious flesh before her. Her eyes dropped to his groin before quickly rising back to his face.

Her cheeks were hot, so hot she thought she might expire.

"Hardly cold, my lady," Rourke said as he stepped from the tub. Water ran in trails down his skin to the rushes on the floor.

Galiana remained rooted by the fire, clutching his towel in front of her.

"I," she began, unable to find a single spot on which to rest her eyes. He was magnificent and much better endowed than the statues she'd seen from Roman times.

"The towel?"

"Oh!" She handed it to him, slayed by his slow smile as surely as if he'd stuck a knife betwixt her ribs. Once again, he was the victor in a game she didn't understand.

"Lady Galiana, forgive me for being blunt. But if you don't leave this room right now I will have you, on the floor, in the water, and I don't care who walks in."

For one tempting second, Galiana thought to rip her gown from her body and let him have his way.

But her mother's voice reverberated through her head—a lady would never do such a thing.

Chapter Nine

Rourke's gut clenched with unspent desire as he watched his tall, proper lady run from the chamber.

She obviously had no idea her plain, gray gown, when wet, showed through. And the place where she'd clutched the pitcher circled her pert nipple beautifully. He didn't need to see colors—nor clearly—to get felled by lust.

Jamie's words echoed around his head like bats in a belfry. He could ignore Prince John's order and let one of the other knights win the lady's hand.

Lord Christien, or worse, Lord Harold? Touching that long, brown hair, or kissing that soft, pliant, and eager mouth. Nay.

Priest be damned, he thought as he dried his body before the fire. How would he explain his actions to

King William? I'm sorry, my liege. I wanted her, and so I took her, and Scotland and England be damned, too!

Exhaling, he stalked over to the low table where a small plate of biscuits and sliced beef awaited. The ring winked at him from its leather binding—accusing?

What to do? What in God's name was he to do?

He needed a drink.

Rourke dressed, grateful he could see well enough to clothe himself. Hose, shirt, tunic, half boots. The entire time the image of the lady's nipple teased him until he was ready to howl like a kenneled hound. This was madness. He could forgive the lady for doing her best to protect her brothers. It was hardly her fault Prince John had made her the prize in a mad quest. Marrying off all the marriageable females to men he considered loyal, in a mad scheme to tie their families to him for when he made his bid for the throne.

Considering her prim and sheltered upbringing, Galiana was handling herself quite well. Remembering her ruse to teach him patience, he had to release the anger he'd been holding against her for her innocent lies.

God's bones, but she fired his blood—if he'd been coldhearted, as she'd accused, then she had melted him down to bright embers that would kindle at her touch.

He picked up the ring, knowing he should give it to her. He'd said it was hers, a betrothal gift. Would she give it back when he asked? He needed it. Britain needed it. Could he explain he would buy her a new one, once they were honestly wed? Something she could keep whence he set her aside.

She was intelligent, his plain miss. Galiana would jump ten moves ahead in her irrefutable logic and want to know why the ring was so important. She'd know that it had nothing to do with a woman. And if she noticed that the ring was more than just a piece of gemstone, what then?

Mayhap he could appeal to her intellect?

His study of human nature had taught him that women liked to be appreciated, and he'd be wise to treat her with respect. Flattery, also expected, but not overmuch—not for her. Galiana's looks, not her strong point as far as he could tell, would not garner many compliments, and she'd no doubt be suspicious if he was to overdo the meaningless flattery.

It irritated him that her looks should matter—when she was so much more than what Fate had given her. Small, dainty women abounded at court. He'd had his share of them. Lady Magdalene came to mind. Pretty, nay, beautiful, they tended to be shallow and concerned with gifts and posies.

He remembered Galiana's disdain when he'd told her not to peddle her wares at court—and grinned. Her feathers didn't ruffle easily, but he'd scored a victory there. For certes, she would be a popular one with her lotions and perfumes.

Rourke pressed his fingers above the neat row of

stitches along his temple. It was possible that she could be made into a favorite. Cloak and dagger mystery was his specialty, after all, and he could help her.

What would it get him? Would it protect her from the vicious gossips who might not see her for the woman she was?

He shouldn't care, bugger all.

His orders were clear.

His feelings weren't.

Since when did anybody give a royal god damn about Rourke Wallis's feelings, anyway?

A pounding on the heavy wooden door captured his attention. Not Galiana, with a knock like that. "Come in."

Jamie entered in a rush, his hair a rumpled, wet mess, his shirt untied at the neck and hanging off one shoulder.

Rourke crossed his arms in front of his chest. "Is something the matter?"

"Aye, Robert's gone missin'."

"Missing."

"That old woman dropped it in the conversation while she was scrubbin' the skin off me back with a wire comb, the old dog."

Worry over the man who'd been a member of his party for two years settled in his belly. "Was he sick, with the others?"

"She said they searched the manor, every room, and he's simply disappeared."

"Could he have followed the priest and the boys?"

Jamie shrugged his shirt up and tied the neck. "What, and when the boys went on to the village, he tracked the priest? He's a fine knight. He could have done—but it's too damn dark now to go after him, and the blasted snow hasn't stopped falling all day."

Rourke slipped the leather thong over his neck, careful to keep his hands away from the blue chip of stone as he tucked it beneath his tunic. "Tracks would be covered."

"I don't like this, Rourke."

"Nay, it doesn't bode well."

"Ye know we have someone in our group who is workin' fer Prince John, and possibly King Philippe,"

"And, more than likely, one of us is working on King Richard's behalf, as well. 'Tis left to you and me, Jamie."

"Yer not fit to go to court. Not yet."

"Why?" Rourke bristled at the implication.

Jamie pointed at Rourke's clothes with a snort. "Yer clothing is usually impeccable—yet ye've two different colored boots on."

"What?" Rourke looked down, but all he could see was the same shade: grayish brown.

"Ye'll not be able to go anywhere alone. Since ye can't wed the lady, that leaves me to be your constant companion, which will cause rumors."

"Ach, I'm no man's man, and everybody knows it." Rourke grimaced.

"And I am? Piss off! I'm sayin', with all the different

intrigues goin' on, that anything unusual had better have a damn obvious reason."

Rourke went to the trunk, where his clothes were folded, and lifted up another half boot for Jamie's perusal. "This?"

"Aye. Change the left one."

"What color am I wearing?" Rourke hadn't considered the challenge of dressing, but a wife, for certes, would be handy. Until his sight returned completely. It had to.

"One brown, one red. Nice choice, if ye're a court jester."

Rourke muttered a curse, then changed so that he was wearing two brown leather boots. "My tunic?"

"Black, and your hose are brown. Ye look right dashin' now, me lord," Jamie sneered.

"Hold your tongue, man. I'll wed the woman"—he held up one hand to forestall any argument—"as soon as we find a priest. And then—well, King William urges us to get to court."

"But our liege cannot know that ye'll be bringin' a wife. Not when he's expectin' ye to be free to wed another!"

"It's horse-tied I am, and what can I do? King William charged me with following Prince John's orders."

"As much as ye were able," Jamie scoffed. "Ye don't need to win the lady's hand. Let one of the other knights do it, and we can hurry to court without this woman in tow. She'll slow us down."

"Prince John wanted me to marry her. Why else would he have given me the edge? Perhaps it's his way of seeing which camp I'm in. He's forcing me to declare my loyalty. He trusts no one."

"Aye." Jamie scratched his smooth-shaven chin. "Being a snake in the grass makes a man suspicious."

Rourke laughed. "I can set Galiana aside, later."

"Ye want her in yer bed; just say it."

He paused. Jamie knew him better than any other man alive. "'Tis true. But I'd not ruin her reputation and leave her a whore, just to slake my desires. If I marry her, then set her aside, she'll have property to compensate for her lost maidenhead. Surely some man will marry her for that alone and give her babes and family."

Jamie broke out into loud laughter. "Ye've got it all worked out in yer head, eh?"

"What is so damn funny?"

"You. But I'll not ruin the jest by telling you the end of the joke before 'tis time."

"Arsewipe." Rourke knew no amount of bribery or boxing would make Jamie give up his secret. He also knew the omission wouldn't harm him—not overmuch.

"Yer over-complicating things, Rourke, thinking with your cock instead of yer brain."

"Do explain it to me, then, Jamie, in simple words." Rourke glared at his foster brother.

"Don't go to court; not yet. Take the lady back to yer keep. Wed her, bed her, and leave her there to adjust to wedded bliss—without ye. We go to court, make Prince John happy, woo the lovely lady Constance, and

210

find the damn Breath of Merlin afore King Richard loses his power forever, which, in turn, will make King William happy."

The air left Rourke's lungs in a whoosh. "Christ's blood, Jamie, that's brilliant. Why didn't I think of it?"

"Ye've been knocked about the head too many times?"

"Now who's the jester?"

"We can leave as soon as it stops snowing," Jamie planned.

"Just three days is all we need to reach home." Won in a game of chance, the keep didn't have much in the way of frills, but it was solid in its construction, and he was trying to bring the village back to life. His home would need a mistress, he realized with a grin. The idea had merit. He could keep Galiana to himself, and love her until he'd had his fill. Nobody at court would know who she was—which guarded her and protected him. He'd prove his loyalty to another quick-tempered Plantagenet, while appeasing his own Scottish liege.

"We leave in the morn." The ring gave a zinging hum against his chest as he contemplated riding pillion with Galiana.

"Yer bride to be is a lady, Rourke, not a warrior, nor a squire, to be facing the elements."

"What if Harold and Christien are on their way?"

"We're snowed in!"

"Her brothers, mere lads, and an ancient priest, and

possibly one of our own knights have managed to leave this manor." Rourke ticked the escapees off by folding a finger down for each on his right hand.

"She's a lass of quality, Rourke, and see that if ye see naught else."

"She's tough."

"She'll die, or lose her nose to frostbite."

Rourke stretched his neck from side to side. "That would be unfortunate," he said dryly. The last thing his tall, brown-haired lady needed was no nose above her pointy chin. "The hour it stops snowing," he conceded.

Jamie nodded.

"I'll marry the wench immediately—we're sure to have a priest around somewhere—and stay a fortnight with her before leaving for court. Mayhap Will"—no, not his squire—"or Godfrey, yes, Godfrey"—who was already married with bairns—"can stay with her."

"Will ye be able to set the lady aside?"

"Of course! She's gotten under my skin; that's all. It's happened before. And once I take my fill of her, I'll be fine."

Will she? He ignored his subconscious.

Jamie made a loud, doubtful noise from the back of his throat, which Rourke ignored, as well.

"Never mind all of this, Jamie. We've more important things to think about at the moment," Rourke stated.

"Aye. Robbie had to have left a trail."

"My fortune lately?" Rourke said. "It's bloody cold."

Galiana sat at the table on the dais and sipped at a goblet of mead. The manor was clean, and so was she. The bath she'd finally gotten had not soothed her spirit, though, despite the chamomile flowers she'd added. This was her home, and yet she was the only Montehue left in it.

She had lost all control of the manor.

Rourke, with his bossy ways, had easily included the Montehue knights when he'd delegated duties. Two men in the gatehouse at all times. Knights, his men and hers, posted at all the entry doors.

They'd seemed eager to accept direction. Even Rourke's. Well, what did she know about leading men? Rourke and Jamie had locked them in the solar. She'd told them, when they'd been released, that she would be marrying Lord Rourke Wallis. It was natural and right for them to follow his lead.

It irritated her to no end.

She tapped her fingers against the linen-covered tablecloth. Not one of them had even looked to her to make sure she was all right with their switch of allegiance. Sighing, she told herself to be mature. The family knights were used to answering to her father, not to her.

Galiana rued her mistakes as she waited for Rourke to join her for something to eat. Not that she was hungry, but

Cook was working extra hard to make up for the miserable meal of yesterday. Which, she'd made clear to everyone within yelling distance, had not been her fault.

Just who was at fault had yet to be confirmed. For certes, her brothers had run from the manor. But a knight in Rourke's pay was also missing. To be fair, even Father Jonah had to be suspect.

Cook, angry that someone had messed with her food, was searching for a scapegoat and, unfortunately, thanks be to the twins changing her salt and sugar when they were eight, the lads seemed the best fit.

The woman was careful not to call them awful names directly in front of her, but Galiana heard some colorful descriptions whilst just around the corner.

She sipped from her goblet and surveyed the hall. They'd pulled two tables and benches out from the wall so that people could eat. Normally there would be much more bustle, with knights playing chess, or servants cleaning, or the dogs snuffling around the floor for a treat—but this was no ordinary day.

The knights were off working at whatever chore Rourke had put them to, and most of the servants remained stranded in the village. The rest of them were busy with Cook. The dogs slept in their kennels.

Suddenly, the door opened, and Franz stomped inside with the red-cheeked bailiff.

Galiana rose to her feet, clutching her fur-lined cape tightly around her shoulders. The gust of wind made the fire flicker brightly for a moment, before it settled back down. If she were the type of girl to believe in portents—and she was—then she would have called that an evil omen.

Apprehension swirled in her belly as she noticed Rourke was not with the two men.

She lifted her chin toward Bailiff Morton. "How goes the search?"

Frost stuck to his trimmed mustache, and Franz rubbed his gloved hands together. He and the Montehue bailiff trod across the hall, leaving damp, snowy footprints along the way.

"We've fed the animals and searched the stables and the barn for Sir Robert," her bailiff said. "All of the horses are accounted for. Besides, the snow is piled too high to get out of the yard."

"Mademoiselle, Robert is not here. We've gone over every inch of the manor and most of the outbuildings, as well."

"I see." What would Rourke think of one of his men deserting him? And why would Robert have braved the snow and cold with neither food nor furs? "Did he take his things?"

Will entered the hall from the back, his face ruddy from cold. "His pack is still here, as is his stallion. His sword is gone, but a knight would never leave that behind."

Gali sensed his upset and so turned and sent a calming smile toward the worried squire. "You're concerned he went into the woods, mayhap too ill to realize what he was doing?"

"Nay," Will answered. "He's not impulsive like that. In truth, I don't know what to believe."

Godfrey and Jamie came in from the side door with two of her knights. "'Tis bad business," Godfrey mumbled. "Fer a place that's supposed to be closed up with snow, it's got more comings and goings than Thursday market."

Galiana rather agreed. "And yet nobody has left by horse. They've all gone by foot."

"And covered their tracks." The bailiff looked disgusted. "You've searched all the buildings?"

"Everything that was open, my lady," the bailiff answered. "The grainery is locked, as is your drying shed."

"Your knights tried to clear a path, as you asked, but the snow's too high to even open the door, lass," Jamie said. "Nobody's getting in or out of that."

"The shed has a window in the back, up high, for ventilation. You'd not be able to see the back from the manor, here." There was a sink, as well as tools and a little brazier for a fire. A man could survive if he could get inside. Galiana stepped down from the dais, realizing they didn't think her news anything to be excited about.

She sighed, keeping a simple expression on her face when she wanted to stomp her feet. Explaining in a slow, soothing tone, she said, "There is food and water both in the shed, as I spend much of my time there. Wood, for a small brazier, is also inside."

"Did you tell Robert this?" Rourke demanded from behind her. The man was as stealthy as a hunting cat. "Were you planning to meet him there?"

Galiana whirled around. "Nay, why would I have done so? But the shed is betwixt here and the forest—the snow wouldn't be as thick under the cover of trees, and it would be easier to travel. If a man had gotten caught between here and there, though, mayhap he could climb through the window of the shed and survive a few days from the cold. It is simply a thought, my lord."

Rourke's eyes flashed with golden temper. "Where is this shed?"

The bailiff led the way as Rourke called for shovels and men. Exasperated by his imperious ways, Galiana hurried to the kitchen to warn Cook that the food must wait—but when Lord Rourke called for it, it would need to be hot and plentiful.

The woman nodded and pursed her lips. "They still can't find that knight what is missin'? Which one was he again?"

"Tall"—Galiana placed her hand high above her own head—"and dark. He was kind of surly, and brawny."

"Aye, I think I had to shoo him from me kitchen, when he was lookin' fer the twins. One of 'em, anyway," she chuckled. "He found our Layla, instead."

"Yesterday?" Galiana leaned over to inhale the delicious aroma of thick bean soup with ham hocks and carrots. Robert had been in the kitchen.

"Aye, but we kept our mouths shut about the boys, didn't we?" Cook asked, and the scullions were quick to agree that they hadn't said anything about Ned and Ed being in the pantry.

"They were both hiding in the pantry when Sir Robert came looking for them, or Ned, rather?"

She remembered Ed finding her there, and she immediately went to the huge door and pulled it open. Her brothers didn't spill out like puppies from a crate, although there was a certain smell that brought her sensitive nose up.

Cook came in, too, directly on Galiana's heels.

"What's that stink? Has a jar of pickled beets been broken? Joey, get in here, boy—did ye do this, and not clean up after yerself?"

The younger serving boy blanched. "I ain't been in here all day, Cook"

"Well, who has?"

"I put a crock of butter by the front, Cook, but I never went ta the back," a girl said.

"Let me see, dear Cook," Galiana said in hopes of halting a dressing down for the entire kitchen crew. The woman's temper was infamous.

The pantry, kept cool but dry, was long and filled with stocked shelves. Sure enough, a jar of beets had been toppled. In fact, Galiana noticed in the dim light from the kitchen that quite a few things were missing.

"We've been robbed, my lady," Cook said indignantly.

"Mayhap someone was preparing for a journey? See what is missing, and that should tell us who took supplies and how long they planned on being gone."

"Ooh, that's smart, my lady." She glared at the two servants standing by the pantry door. "I'll do it meself, to make sure it gets done right."

"Thank you, Cook. Uh. Joey, is it?" Galiana walked out of the pantry and blinked in the brighter light. "Were you helping my brothers with their jokes?"

His young face paled until the only color left was the brown of his freckles.

"You won't get into trouble. I promise," Galiana said, bending over so they were eye to eye. "But I need to know what they were up to. Did they—" She lowered her voice to a whisper. "Did they mean to get everybody sick?"

"No, no, my lady, they didn't. They didn't!"

That made her feel a little bit better, at least. "But they were the ones to add the buckthorn to the stew?"

Joey exchanged a quick glance with a little girl standing next to him, whose brown eyes were as large as buttercups. "Neither of you will come to harm, if you tell me the truth."

Her soft tone encouraged the girl to say, "Master Ed put somethin' in the wine; that's all, my lady."

Saint Jude, her brothers had meant to poison her? Her stomach lurched as she remembered Celestia's open book of medicinal recipes. Everyone knew valerian helped people sleep, and Ned had been so very upset about her immediate marriage to Rourke. Had they deliberately sought to make her sleep through the ceremony?

Or had the potion been for Rourke?

"Ned told 'im just to put a little bit, my lady," Joey said as he dared to pat her arm.

She told herself to think about her brother's deeds later, and focus on getting answers. "So you say they didn't put anything in the stew?"

"No, my lady." The little girl looked ready to cry.

"Did you know my brothers were planning on leaving the manor?"

The two children shook their heads. Joey offered, "But they's always hungry, my lady, so it weren't no surprise to see 'em tote out extra food."

For certes, that was the truth. "What about Father Jonah? Did he come into the kitchen?"

The girl stuck her thumb in her mouth and stared at Joey, who seemed to be the one in charge of the talking. "Aye. He had words with Ned; he did."

"They were arguing?" Galiana wished she could rush the questions, but she was afraid to frighten her untapped fountain of information. She kept her smile open and her voice low. "What about?"

Joey shrugged and wouldn't meet her eyes.

"Please, Joey."

His face turned red behind the freckles. "Well, 'twas about you. Ned wanted to run Lord Rourke through with a sword afore ye suffered yer weddin' night, and Father— he says it'd be wrong."

Galiana stifled a gasp. The scene was getting clearer, and she could easily imagine her brothers talking Father Jonah into running away with the dispensation, after safely drugging her, so that she wouldn't have to get married against her will.

Her eyes filled with tears at their unnecessary but loving gesture. Father Jonah knew about Celestia's medicinal book of recipes, and he could have decided to gain them all time by making the manor inhabitants sick.

It wasn't her brothers. She smiled through her tears. But Father Jonah?

The girl sucked louder.

She had to be sure. "You didn't see who put the buckthorn in the stew?"

"Nay," Joey said, "else we wouldn't a been pukin', along with everybody else, aye?"

Good point, Galiana thought. "So what about Sir Robert?"

The girl took her thumb from her mouth so she could nibble her lower lip, and Joey blurted, "Him and Layla was kissin' in front of the pantry, and Ned come in the kitchen, see?"

Galiana didn't see, but she said, "Hmmm."

"Ed, he was inside already, and if he come out, then the knight'd see there was more than one of 'em."

"Oh, dear. Did Sir Robert catch them?" Had the

boys run so Ned wouldn't go to the tower?

"Huh-uh," Joey shook his head emphatically, jerking his thumb to the girl at his side. "I pinched Bertie"— Galiana looked at the little girl, whose big eyes now shimmered with excitement—"and she started bawlin', and then the knight left."

Bertie whispered, "Layla said he could see her later."

Galiana reminded herself to never underestimate children again. "I see. And where is Layla?"

"Sick, in her room," Joey said. "Too sick ta clean up the mess, aye, but not too sick to eat what we brought up to her, eh?"

Back to sucking her thumb, Bertie said nothing.

It seemed logical Layla should be the next person to talk to about Sir Robert's whereabouts.

Cook came from the pantry and cuffed Joey on the ear. "Get ta work, now, and earn yer keep. Both of ya."

Galiana opened her mouth to protest, but Joey ducked and ran to the spit, with Bertie on his heels. "Sorry, Cook," they said in unison.

"Never mind that," she said with a stern smile. "Now, my lady, we're missin' five links of sausage, three waterskins, and a bag of hard rolls. The beets must a been spilt when they was reachin' for the dried apples."

Galiana dropped her chin. "Ed and Ned love their sausage and dried apples."

"Don't I know it?" Cook shrugged. "They coulda cleaned their mess; that's all I'm sayin'. Or else asked me ta pack for 'em."

"You would have done that?"

Cook quickly looked away. "Well, not without tellin' ya, my lady."

Galiana laughed. "After they'd gotten a good start on me, I imagine."

"They're smart lads, and they'll be fine. It'll be an adventure to satisfy their boys' hearts, my lady, eh?"

"Just a week past, I longed for adventure, but now I've had my fill. Where is Layla's room? I'd like to visit her and see that she's feeling better."

"Lazy, that one, is all wrong with 'er, my lady."

"Still . . ."

"Above the laundry, my lady, with the rest of us."

"Thank you. And thank you, too, Cook, for looking out for my brothers."

"No thanks needed! I had a bunch of boys myself once."

"Where are they now?"

Cook snorted. "They turned into men, my lady."

Rourke climbed the slope of tightly packed snow behind Galiana's shed. Just as the lady had said, there was a window and, sure enough, it was broken.

A shirt waved from the top of the window like a banner on a tourney lance.

"Robert?" Rourke called as he reached the sill. Had his knight gotten lost in the storm? Had he been hoping for someone to rescue him? If Galiana was right, then it shouldn't be too late.

His gloves protected him from the shards of glass as he pulled himself up. "We've got you, man!"

Silence reverberated as the men behind him, holding torches and shovels, waited to hear Robert's voice.

It was dark outside; he knew that. Balancing carefully on his belly, Rourke realized it was just as dark inside the shed. He was living in a world of shadows, when they needed clarity. Mayhap it would have been better to send Jamie. He let his eyes adjust as well as they could, and made out the small brazier and a stack of wood. Flowery smells overwhelmed his nose.

"Robert?"

There was still no answer, and the relief Rourke had felt at seeing the shirt vanished like a melting snowflake.

Jamie pulled himself up the slope and peered inside. "Can't see a thing," he pronounced.

"You either? We'll have to go in."

"I'll go. You can lower me over."

"Nay, too dangerous. This will be the only time you'll hear me say this, but—"

"I'm stronger than ye? Everybody knows that," Jamie chuckled. "So you're over then?"

"Wait until I'm training again, and then I'll knock you arse over kettle. I can't see what's in there—looks like a bunch of weeds hanging upside down, and pots and such."

"What's this place again?"

Rourke slung a leg over the sill, brushing away the big chunks of glass. "Galiana works on her perfumes in here."

"It smells," Jamie said. "Gives me a bloody headache."

"Don't tell her that. She gets touchy about her works of art." Rourke slipped his other leg over and allowed Jamie to lever him down on the inside of the shed. Though the scents were even stronger inside, they reminded Rourke of spring.

He liked it.

"Ye'll have to jump now. Just let go. On three—"

Rourke dropped to the ground, his knees bent so that he didn't break a damn leg, on top of everything else. With his luck, he'd be stuck in here until the snow thawed.

"Why do ye do that? Hmm? I say three, that's when ye go—not before," Jamie complained.

"Stop whining." Rourke held out his hands, getting used to making out shadows in the dark. Shelves were stuffed with drying herbs or vials, and it looked like a wind had come through to scatter everything.

He looked down before he stepped ahead, not wanting to trip over anything. There was a large table in the center of the room. Lattice drying racks separated the rectangular room into many different partitions.

"Well?" Jamie called down.

"It's a mess in here," Rourke said. He stepped on something dried, and then a rush of crushed lavender captivated his unsuspecting senses. He choked, and peered behind the next partition.

He was grateful for the lavender, as it blocked the smell of blood.

"I found Robert," he shouted.

"Is he sick?"

"No, Jamie. He's dead."

Chapter Ten

Galiana's hand itched with the need to slap somebody—preferably the lying Layla. The impudent kitchen wench hadn't even bothered to hide the coin Sir Robert had given her, although her confession of what she'd done in exchange for the coin had taken longer, sapping the very last of Galiana's patience.

Layla didn't have so much as a sniffle—she'd been lying about being ill, as well as spinning tales about the money being a gift from her mother.

Once Galiana had managed to get the truth—that Sir Robert had paid Layla for putting the purgative in the stew—then it was another matter of listening to an entire litany of sins. For certes, Layla would no longer be a house servant for the Montehue family, Gali huffed as she searched for the bailiff.

The wench deserved time in the stocks!

But since they were all snowed in, Galiana would have to content herself with locking Layla in the small room above the kitchen. It was perfect: no window, and it could be locked from the outside only.

Layla's list of crimes had included pilfering bottles of good French wine, some of Galiana's old kerchiefs, and the lady Deirdre's ivory comb. It had not included why Sir Robert had wanted the inhabitants of the manor retching their guts out, and Layla wasn't the kind of girl to ask questions when there was gain in it for her.

Disgusted, Galiana was having difficulty remembering to take ladylike steps instead of stomping across the great hall. She spied the bailiff and was about to call his name when the front door of the manor burst open and Rourke, Jamie, and all of the knights not on duty spilled in.

Her first thought went to the floor. The floor she had cleaned three times already today would now once again be ruined by men's muddy, snow-caked boots.

Gali's next thought had more to do with how Rourke would react when he found out Robert was behind the poisoning. His warning of danger came back to her, and she couldn't help but think he wouldn't be very surprised.

Rourke exuded charm, but underneath it all, he trusted nobody.

Except Jamie. What would it be like to be the recipient of such trust? Her body warmed.

"Lady Galiana!" Rourke yelled as he strode across the soon-to-be sodden rushes. For all the care he gave the work she'd done, she may as well have let the dogs loose.

She sighed and arranged her face into what she hoped was a calm expression. A lady never allowed a harsh tone or a bitter look to betray her dissatisfaction.

"I'm here, my lord. You needn't shout."

"I'll bloody well shout. Are you not done with your lies? How else would Robert have known about the drying shed if not from your lying lips?"

Galiana stepped back as he fired questions at her like arrows. But she was annoyed enough to stop after two steps, then lift her chin and square her shoulders.

"I want that man brought up on charges."

Rourke came to a halt, his handsome face pale beneath his golden complexion. "What man?"

"Sir Robert," she said in a prim voice.

Jamie, ever Rourke's shadow, barked, "Answer him, lass! Did ye send Robbie to the shed on purpose?"

Galiana briefly lowered her lashes before she skewered Jamie with a gaze. "Nay, I did not. And furthermore, he will not be allowed one foot in this manor—not unless it is to be locked in the solar, as you did my knights, for absolutely no wrongdoing."

She trembled as she gave her order, but she would not back down from it.

"Impossible." Rourke carelessly brushed the droplets in his hair from the melted snow to the floor.

Gritting her teeth and smiling over the pain shooting through her jaw, she asked, "Why in Saint Mary's name not? Your man is guilty of poisoning the entire manor—well, with my kitchen wench's aid, but I will handle that issue. I demand he be punished."

"Methinks he's been punished enough, lass."

Galiana's temper slipped, and she rounded on Rourke's man. "If you think I will be satisfied with your knight feeling the effects of some cold weather, think again. My father will mete out a punishment suitable for the crime done to our people."

"Our men, meself included, sickened as well!" Jamie's shout echoed through the rafters.

"Lady Galiana—" Rourke, finally remembering his manners, spoke in a deceptively calm voice that simply spiked her own ire. "What Jamie is saying is that Robert has been murdered."

"Murdered?" She raised her hand to her mouth, sorry that she'd yelled. "Nay, that cannot be."

"And you were the one who suggested we look in the drying shed." Rourke nodded his head at her as if giving her permission to confess to the foul deed.

"Murder? Here at Montehue Manor? Ridiculous! That sort of thing simply doesn't happen. It can't happen," she explained as the room swayed around her. "My parents are away. I'm supposed to be in charge."

"I know all of that," Rourke said. "Now I want to know how my knight came to be missing his head."

"Missing his head?" Galiana envisioned her sacred space, the area where she created the best perfumes with flowers and oils, pestle and mortar. "In my shed?"

"Well, almost. Lass, we don't think ye did it; we just need to know how our Robert found the place," Jamie explained with uncharacteristic gentleness.

"I could never hurt someone." Black spots danced before her eyes.

"Of course ye couldn't—this was a man that did this to Robbie."

Rourke added, "Bloody mess. We'll need to shovel in through the front door. No way to get the body out the back."

Galiana gulped down the bile rising in her throat. Blood, violence. In her beautiful shed?

"It was Layla," she whispered. "Layla."

"Nay, a woman wouldn't have been strong enough for what was done." Rourke slashed his hand through the air.

"Bugger me," Jamie shouted as he leapt toward her.

Galiana heard Rourke exhale as he asked, "What? Again?" Then her head hit the stone floor of the great hall with a loud cracking noise, and nothing else mattered at all.

Rourke cradled Galiana's bleeding head as he lifted her up the stairs. He almost tripped over the lady's long, trailing sleeve decorated with tiny seed pearls before Jamie yanked it off with a rip of fabric.

"Thank you," Rourke said, leading the way to her bedchamber.

Dame Bertha was directly behind them, a basket of linens and bandages over her arm. "I've got the vinegar, me lord. That'll bring her 'round."

Jamie opened the door, then shook his head.

Rourke entered, the lady in his arms. He would have put her on the bed, but he couldn't find the damn thing. Veils and silks and furs were tossed about the room as if she were a fabric merchant.

"Not tidy, eh?" Jamie chuckled. "Ye don't need a housekeeper, Rourke, so wipe that look off yer face."

Dame Bertha set the basket down and immediately swept up an armful of cloth so that Rourke would have a place to lay Galiana down. His arms were tired, though he would never admit it.

"Ye should have let me carry her," Jamie chided.

"Step back," Rourke warned.

"Stubborn arse."

Dame Bertha snickered before pretending to be shocked. Rourke decided he liked that about her.

"Can you rouse her, good woman?"

The old lady smiled and nodded, seemingly happy to do his bidding. If only his lady would be so inclined . . .

Rourke took a linen square from the basket and gently lifted Galiana's head. He parted the hair until he found the dark line on her pale scalp that bled sluggishly.

He removed the circlet of braided twine and the veil of thin linen, revealing two thick braids wound in curls above her ears. The rest of her hair spilled loose down her back. He applied pressure to the cloth, absently noting that her hair, though boring in color, was soft as a kitten's fur.

The sharp, pungent scent of vinegar permeated the air, and Rourke lifted his head. Dame Bertha stood armed and ready with an uncorked jar, which she handed to him.

"Pass it under her nose, quick."

Rourke did as instructed and was satisfied to see Galiana's eyes scrunch together. For a woman who admittedly preferred beautiful smells, this would surely get her attention.

He did it again, just to see her squirm.

Her eyes popped open, and for the briefest time he thought he saw green fire, the exact brightness which could be found when burning fresh oak stumps.

The flame flickered out, and her eyes returned to their dull brown shade. He could have stared into those boring orbs for hours, waiting to see that mystical flash again.

She mesmerized him, this wren of a woman.

Her eyes closed again, and she burrowed her face into the crook of his arm, searching for protection.

He would give it.

It annoyed him that he was put at such a disadvantage.

He was not used to being drawn in by a female. He'd learned at Queen Eleanor's throne that women were not at all the weaker sex. Aye, most women were harmless. They bore their men babes and cared for the castle while their men were away in exchange for food and a roof over their delicate heads.

However, there were other women—Rourke squirmed as he remembered a specific few—who knew how to milk a man's secrets as expertly as a dairy maid did a cow.

And there was still another sort—the ones who could and would wear the breeches in the family, while hiding their brutish tendencies behind the title of lady.

But the rarest female of all—the one who wielded her feminine power with justice—that was the most dangerous woman on earth. She'd draw men to her like flies to honey and have them do her bidding, while they'd be grateful for the privilege of serving her.

He'd known only two women like that in his life, and both were royalty.

So how did Galiana remind him of those two?

She moaned softly, and his heart lurched.

God's wounds, she would be his undoing.

"Pass the vinegar again, me lord," Dame Bertha instructed.

"Nay," Rourke handed the jar back. "She'll be fine, in but a moment." How could he bother her, when she turned to him for comfort?

234

"Who is Layla?" Jamie asked.

"She works in the kitchen, newly hired from the village. She's a mite lazy, Cook's only complaint afore this, but Lady Galiana wanted to speak to her about Sir Robert."

"Where can we find her? I'll question her meself," Jamie said. "But she couldn't have been the one to, er, kill Robbie."

Rourke heard Jamie stumble over the brutality of the crime and realized he should have been more sympathetic to Galiana's tender ears. He'd thought to crack her polished veneer, but he'd gone too far.

Why did she affect him like this? She'd laugh if she heard he had a reputation as a charming ladies' man. All she'd heard from him was bullying orders and whining.

The old dame offered, "I'll take ye, sir. She's a room above the laundry, but my lady wanted her locked up until her parents return."

"What happened?" Rourke asked Dame Bertha.

"I don't know, me lord, just that me lady was very put out by the girl, and it was more than just poisonin' us all! We was looking fer the bailiff when you came in."

Confused, Rourke nodded at Jamie.

"I'll get to the bottom of the barrel, Rourke—ye can tend the lady, aye?" Jamie gave him an exaggerated wink.

"Watch your back, man," Rourke said as the two left the room. "This place is as treacherous as a battlefield."

"You brought the trouble," Galiana whispered.

Rourke looked down to see her frowning up at him.

235

He saw her realize she was snuggled next to him as he sat on the edge of her bed, and she immediately tried to sit up.

"Nay, be still," he ordered, angry that she was probably right. He had arrived at their idyllic home bringing trouble on his heels.

Though she had the aim of an archer, she couldn't have prevented trouble's entry into Montehue Manor.

She struggled, far from content to be trapped against his body. All he could think about was her lips beneath his, how her warm tongue had tasted, how her breasts had filled his large hands.

"Am I so repulsive to you that you risk making your head bleed anew?"

"What?"

Her brow was shaved free of hair to allow a smooth expanse of forehead beneath a circlet or wimple. It touched Rourke that his plain lady went to such troubles for beauty. It shocked him that he desired her without it.

He helped her sit, and she touched the linen square at the back of her head. "How did I do this?"

"You claim to never truly faint, and yet twice I've caught you."

"You caught me?" Her nostrils flared slightly. "I vaguely remember Jamie lunging for me, and let me tell you, that did nothing to calm my nerves."

Rourke laughed. "Aye, he's a big man, a Scots brigand through and through. But I'm faster."

"You always compete with one another?"

"Compete?" Rourke paused, thinking about the question. "We were raised together, royal bastards in Queen Eleanor's court."

"You share a sire?"

"I don't blame you for sounding doubtful." Rourke tucked the coverlet carefully around her waist and fluffed a pillow so she was comfortable. "I don't know who my parents are, and Jamie cannot claim a blood tie either, for all his fiery looks. Although there are rumors—but—" Rourke shrugged.

"How—" she lowered her voice, but emotion was evident in her tone just the same. "How can you not know your parents? Wouldn't the queen tell you if you asked?"

"Nay. We never wanted for attention. We were cared for, trained to be useful." He chuckled, but Galiana didn't join in his mirth, so he cleared his throat. "We could have been put to death. I prefer life."

She sighed, and her fingers smoothed the folded cover. "Aye, if you put it in that perspective, 'tis a good solution. Are there so many royal bastards, then?"

"A good crop of extras. Not just the king's get, but other indiscretions happen, and what is one more baby among many? No questions are asked, and there is safety in that for all involved."

It was the accepted way of the royal court, but he could tell Galiana remained unimpressed by the royal nursery.

"You never wonder if you look like a certain person? What if you were a—" She paused, and Rourke appreciated her attempt at delicacy.

"What if I shared blood with a king?" Rourke shrugged, though they were getting close to the heart of what drove him, and his liege. "It wouldn't matter. If the line was too close, then . . ." He jokingly sliced a hand across his neck. "The line would be erased."

She blanched, and her lips parted. Her breaths came in rapid succession, and he quickly apologized.

"I wasn't thinking, my lady." Rourke cursed himself for a fool, and lifted her hand to his lips. Her fingers were so soft that he absently rubbed the pad of his thumb over her hand. Her skin exuded a light and fresh floral scent that he was coming to recognize as belonging just to her. "Forgive me?" His voice dropped, and he searched her face. Would she accept his kiss?

She swallowed and leaned back against her pillows, making a small mew of distress as she jarred the bandage.

"I'm sorry," he said, stunned. She didn't want him. He didn't know what to do.

"My lord, I'm tired."

"You can't sleep after a head injury." Rourke vowed to keep her awake even if he had to walk her around the room.

"'Tis but a small bump," she protested.

He looked around her chamber and changed the subject to something safer than his ancestry. "Are you always so untidy? Clothes are everywhere."

238

She gasped, her eyes narrowed with outrage.

"Your shed was a mess, too—aside from the obvious. The shelves were stuffed with everything from dried flowers to ribbons."

"It is my space to create what I wish; it was not meant to be judged for cleanliness. I know where every last ribbon is," she said sharply. "Or at least I did, before . . ."

Rourke was left to find yet another thing they could talk about that wouldn't lead to shark-infested waters. "That doesn't explain all the clothes in here. Or will you blame the lack of a maid?"

Again that pointed chin lifted, and he watched with concealed amusement as she hid her curled fists beneath the covers. What did she think would happen if she let her true feelings be known?

He knew what it was like to constantly hide.

Mayhap that was why he got such wicked pleasure from catching her off guard.

"I was sewing, my lord. Gowns for court."

This time he was the one to have to mask his thoughts. "You were going to make gowns from this?" He reached over to the top of a trunk and pulled out a length of fabric. It felt rough and knotted, but he couldn't tell the color. His guess would be brown.

"You have something against wool, my lord?" Her sarcasm was lethal.

"Ladies at court do not wear wool. Silks, damasks, finest furs and linens—but wool? Pah."

"And what would they wear for a cloak, I wonder?" Pulling her hands from beneath the covers, she crossed her arms, and tapped one finger against her lower lip and pretended to be deep in thought.

"You said you were making gowns."

"I didn't realize you were an expert in ladies' fashions, my lord."

"From the looks of it, neither are you."

"You are giving me a headache," Galiana said. "When is Jamie returning? Yes, even his company is preferable to yours."

Rourke got to his feet. "He went to question Layla. Supposedly she knows something about what happened with Robert."

"She knows plenty, and she told me Sir Robert paid her—in fact, Layla even showed me the coin—to put the buckthorn bark into the stew."

"I don't believe it. Why should I trust a Montehue servant over the goodly reputation of my own knight?"

Galiana shoved back the covers and rose unsteadily to her feet. She looked up at him and pointed her finger to his chest. "I don't care what you believe, you arrogant man. What matters is that my brothers are innocent." She hesitated for a moment, and Rourke wondered what she was hiding. "Innocent," she continued, "and your knight, for reasons unknown to me, wanted the manor sick."

Rourke stared at her full lips, barely hearing the words from her mouth. He couldn't have her, not yet, but it was time to tell her she wasn't through with him.

"You aren't going to court, my lady."

She stilled, her expression giving none of her emotions away. Yet he sensed he may have hurt her.

"I have not been entirely honest with you."

She whirled away from him, her hair stinging his face. "This is news?"

Ah yes, Rourke thought, Galiana and her ideals of honor and chivalry. What a wagon full of lies. "Let me explain," he said, relying on his charm.

"You owe me nothing." She put her fingers to the wound on the back of her head, and she sniffed. "I believe this makes us even, my lord. A bump for a bump. I'll not count the stitches at your temple as my doing."

"Are you still bleeding?" Rourke's gut knotted at her dismissive tone.

"Nay, but I would not ask you for help even if I were. I want you to leave me alone. Now."

"I can't do that." He focused on the tall, straight line of her back—or tried to. It was obvious she was through with him. Yet he couldn't let her have the victory.

"You won't."

"You still need to pack—and lightly. Just the bare essentials of what you'll need to live day to day."

"You are not taking me to court, and you can't force a marriage without a priest." Her shoulders stiffened, and she seemed to get impossibly taller.

He reached out for her and turned her around.

241

Tipping up her pointed chin, he leaned over and stared directly into her eyes. Blurred, brown and gray shadows, even so close. "I know. We ride for my home. Three days from here, and God's teeth, my priest will say the vows in his undershirt."

Galiana forced her heart to repel the cruel stab of Rourke's rejection. He thought her a disaster, a woman unable to run a home, and one too countrified to bring to court. She thought he'd tell her Prince John couldn't possibly expect him to marry such a naïve and dull twit.

Then she heard the word vows, and her heart forgot all the pain. Her mouth met his halfway, and she boldly pressed her body against his. All that mattered was feeling his chest against her breasts, his mouth against her lips, his breath whispering in her ear. His hands, his wonderful hands, caressing her hips.

"Rourke," she whispered, nibbling his lower lip, not sure where to put her hands, only that she needed to touch every part of him she could. "Rourke?"

It seemed he understood her question, for he backed her up until the bed was at her thighs. She fell to the mattress, but within the safe circle of his arms.

His belt jabbed her, and she quickly unbuckled it and dropped it to the floor. He kissed her deeply, and his hands roamed over her shoulders, deftly removing her mantle. It landed on top of the belt.

Galiana embraced the cool rush of air against her skin as he untied the laces on her gown, dropping kisses against each exposed area of flesh along her collarbone.

She was hot to do the same to him.

He laved the column of her neck, and she tilted her head back to allow him access. His breath against the damp flesh gave her goose bumps. Her nipples tightened into peaks that begged for his mouth.

Slowly, he lowered her gown down her shoulders, trapping her arms to her sides. Her cleavage came into view, and Rourke kissed the virginal skin above her breasts. Galiana thought to consider that mayhap she shouldn't allow him such liberties, but Saint Mary Magdalene forgive her, she wanted to feel him on every inch of her body.

Her woman's mound throbbed, and she parted her legs so that his manhood, hidden behind his breeches, would fit against the ache.

Aye, she was an innocent, but she knew her own body well. Highly sensitive to nuance and touch, she'd learned to pleasure herself years ago. She knew just where she wanted Rourke's hands to be, and she squirmed until her breasts broke free of their linen confinement.

"Sweet Jesu," he swore before capturing one peak between his teeth, and the other in his hand.

The tension built, and Galiana closed her eyes to enjoy the swirling sensations Rourke was causing—but it wasn't enough. He was wearing entirely too many clothes, and she quickly untied the laces at his neck, unclasping his tunic. She reached down, trailing her fingers over the length of his waist, hip, and thigh, then lifted the tunic up and over Rourke's head.

She felt a physical loss when his mouth left her skin. "Your shirt, Rourke—take it off, too." Galiana sat up to help remove the rest of her clothes at the same time that she was helping him by kissing whatever she could reach.

It took a moment for reality to break through her fog of desire, but she realized that somehow her hair had gotten tangled in the leather thong around Rourke's neck, and he couldn't get his shirt all the way off, because she was connected to it.

"Wait," he ordered huskily.

"I don't think I have much choice, my lord," Galiana answered pertly. As desire ebbed to a manageable pace, she felt the chill in the room and the vulnerability of their position. "Hurry!"

Rourke's tug at her hair was none too gentle, but it remained stuck. "My knife," he growled.

"You are not cutting my hair," she said quickly, remembering how her sister had felt when her husband had accidentally lopped off a chunk. She should have been more sympathetic. Mayhap laughing hadn't been the best response, she thought with a shiver of regret.

"I thought I'd try the leather strip first, my lady, if you will reach down to my belt and get my blade?"

"You needn't be sarcastic," she sniffed, suddenly very conscious of her partial nudity. She covered her breasts with her forearm and gingerly leaned over to the side of the bed and the floor, to reach his belt.

"Why are you pulling me?"

"You have to lean with me, else you won't need a knife. You'll have taken my hair by the roots!" She refused to move her arm.

"You needn't be such a priss—I've already seen the goods."

"Oh!" Galiana's fingers reached the handle of the knife, but she reminded herself that she could be put to death for stabbing him through his heartless heart.

"Stay still," he ordered.

It made her want to scream. The knife cut through the thong with little effort, and her hair, all of it, was free. Galiana grabbed the closest thing she could, which just so happened to be Rourke's shirt, and tried to tug it over her head.

"You can't wear that," he said, taking it back.

In the struggle, the leather thong flew into the air, the dangling ring with it.

Galiana caught it squarely in her palm.

Silence passed as she and Rourke stared at one another. The ring pulsed with light between them.

"Do you see that?" she whispered in awe.

"Aye."

This ring, the one he should have given her, he wore

against his flesh. What did it mean? Who was it really for? It called to her.

Vulnerable, Galiana's heart was wide open, and the mystical energy she'd sensed before burst from the ring in thrilling color. Currents, like lightning, zoomed up her arm and through her entire system. It was like racing bareback on a fast stallion through an open meadow; it was as exhilarating as dancing barefoot in a thunderstorm; it was as powerful as Rourke's open-mouthed kisses.

Images played across her brain. Lush green forests, damp with life-giving rain. Mists of magic and secret power swirled across the ground like fallen clouds. She sensed the magnitude of what was to come—but when, when was this taking place? It felt old, and yet so important to what was happening now. She closed her eyes, unmindful of Rourke, or her partial nudity; if anything, it felt more natural.

Trained to give in to her senses, she easily gave herself over to the power in the ring. Transcended.

Magic.

Her fey soul had tapped into something ancient, and she eagerly followed where the images led. Through the forest, across a bubbling stream. She felt the cool water rush over her feet, but she laughed, as carefree as a fairy sprite.

She was being called forth from time to witness a sacred ceremony, and it was important that she remember the details. Bowing her head so her hair veiled the ring in the palm of her hand, she accepted the charge.

Galiana passed by a grove of trees: oak, solid and true. Yew and flowering ash. The ground beneath her feet thrummed with barely leashed power. A fire burned straight ahead, and she walked to it, as sedately as a lady entering a great hall.

Who would she see?

What would she see?

What ancient ceremony needed her current witness?

In her vision, she wore a loose gown of sheer gossamer, as opalescent as a soap bubble released to the air. Her feet were bare, and she wore her hair long and loose, with a crown of tiny rose buds. Ivy wreathed her wrists and ankles.

Am I a sprite? A nymph?

You are a witness, a masculine voice boomed through her head.

The fire parted in the center: flames to the left, and flames to the right. A cobblestone path cleared, and she knew she had to walk through. Fear, mortal fear, almost made her turn back.

But this was her chance to revel in the magic she'd always believed in, but could never touch. If it killed her, she would try.

Taking the first step was the hardest, because she feared the stones would burn her feet. Yet they were cool, and she walked ahead. When she reached the other side of the fire, she came to a clearing that was bathed in sun. Lions were everywhere. Some were napping; others were drinking from a clear pond. One, with a large mane of gold, padded toward her.

She was no longer afraid.

Galiana dipped her head and waited, and she wasn't surprised when the lion bowed before her.

A man materialized from nowhere, and yet Galiana sensed that he was everywhere, almost all the time. She didn't want to worry about such things now, but she put it to the back of her head to puzzle over later.

"Welcome to the beginning," the man said.

She swallowed and took another look around. "The beginning?"

"When the deal was struck between these isles and man."

"I don't understand."

"Nor do I expect you to." The man had to be older than ancient, yet his face was unlined and his blue eyes were bright with mirth. Galiana suspected that those eyes could fire with dangerous anger in the space of a heartbeat.

"You are called to witness the ceremony that made majestic warriors into kings," the lion suddenly roared. "They've forgotten honor. They've forgotten the old ways."

Before Galiana could respond, the scenery changed from beautiful and serene to dark and stormy. Gali sensed that she was no longer alone; that she stood with another one to witness. She couldn't turn around to see who it was.

The rain poured from the sky as if from a giant bucket. The talking lion, his mane stringy and limp, mutely carried a wiggling cub between his teeth as he stalked toward the tip of a granite and quartz slab. A man knelt in the mud, rain dumping over his dark hair. Lightning and thunder drowned out everything but the lion's roar of pain as he placed the cub before the man. The scene called to Galiana's compassion, and her tears mixed with the rain.

The man withdrew a bundle from beneath his cloak. Squirming, the cloth fell back, revealing a baby's crying face.

The cub lay down next to the baby, and the baby stopped crying. The rain spluttered to a stop.

A roll of thunder shook the rock, and the ground lifted as the man with the blue eyes raised his staff to the heavens. He spoke a language that invoked truly ancient gods, and goose bumps rose along Galiana's skin. He looked to where she stood and pointed his staff over the two young males, scorching them with blue flame.

They screamed—aye, even the young cub screamed—and it was a relief when the screaming finally stopped. The bodies lay still, but their ghostly souls hovered above them, unable to go toward heaven.

She shivered in the cold, terrified to blink.

Though she didn't understand much of what was said, she listened closely as the old wizard invoked powers of the cosmos that she'd always believed existed. It was her duty to witness this sacred ceremony and bring back a reminder to those who had forgotten. Whatever it meant.

Warriors and kings and the almighty lion. Scotland, England, and Wales. Three separate thrones, or one to be united?

A spike of lightning descended from the sky, and the bolt hit the place where the babe and the cub had lain.

They were gone, bodies and souls.

In their place was a quartz-like stone the size of a man's head, glowing with supernatural iridescent flames. In some spots, the stone was cloudy; in others, it was as clear as a raindrop.

"The Breath of Merlin!" She shouted aloud, not understanding what the words meant. The ring seemed to heat a hole into her palm. Exhausted, she tipped forward, protecting the ring with her body as she slept, dead to this world.

Chapter Eleven

"Are you awake?"

Galiana heard Rourke's panicked question and sought to open her eyes so that, whatever he was worrying about, he could stop.

"Her eyelids are moving," Jamie announced, and Galiana snickered. Or at least she thought she did.

"She needs to wake up, aye, and let go of that damned ring."

"Tell me again what happened, without all of the hocus pocus."

"She went into a trance. Jamie, I've never seen anything so terrifying in my life, and that includes the time we found that powerful old shrine to Mithras. Her eyes rolled back, and her hair poofed out like it was alive or possessed by the devil himself."

Once again, she was less than flattered by Rourke's description of her. To think, other men found her quite attractive . . .

"Has the ring ever bothered ye, Rourke?"

She heard the slightest hesitation before he answered, "Nay. It's just a ring, man. You?"

"Not a cursed thing. I've only held it a time or two, but I don't like fancy jewels, besides. Me warrior rings fit me best," Jamie said, and Galiana heard them clink. She knew some men collected weapons and such from their enemies and had rings made from the excess metal. She agreed Jamie would wear those best.

Galiana forced her eyes open. "I thought it was but a dream," she said, looking directly into Rourke's gray and golden orbs. She was oddly reminded of the lion as Rourke's longer curls fell forward around his strong, handsome face.

"What did you see?"

"Aye, lass, tell us. What happened?" Jamie urged.

"The ring!" Galiana sat up so fast Rourke fell off the edge of the bed. She held her palm out, and the jewel twinkled like a trapped, blue star.

"God's teeth!" Rourke exclaimed. "Doesn't it burn?"

"That's somethin' new," Jamie said drolly. "Is it cold?"

"'Tis warm." Galiana turned the ring this way, then that, to admire it from all sides. Set in silver filigree, the stone was hardly larger than her thumbnail, and yet it surely contained some of the sacred magic from the ceremony.

Rourke scooted closer.

"It's never done that before," Jamie said, taking a step back.

"I know," Rourke agreed.

She snuck a peek at Rourke and saw the longing on his face. She doubted he knew it was there, else he would hide it. "Would you care to hold it?"

"It's mine," Rourke growled.

As much as she would've liked to say nay, it was, unfortunately, the truth. She found herself loath to give it up. Rourke held out his hand.

She stalled. "What is the Breath of Merlin?"

"You don't know?" Rourke asked incredulously. "After that?"

"I know it is a rock—an important gem? But I don't know what it signifies. It was clear in the vision, but now—"

Jamie scolded, "'Tis none of your concern, lass, now give Rourke back the ring."

"He said it was a gift for me." She stared at Rourke until he flushed.

"You are an intelligent woman," he began. He was on his knees at the side of her bed, and his expression was so intent that she almost gave it to him—almost.

"I am highly educated, my lord." Didn't he know that in order to flatter her, he should be telling her she was beyond beautiful? That no star in the sky could compare to the sparkle of her eyes?

"I won't bore you with false flattery, or claims of eternal love—we both know there is no such thing. But I'm proposing a business decision betwixt us that would give us each what we want."

Jamie snorted, "Ach, man, ye've done it now."

The man was disgustingly blind. Galiana pursed her lips and tightened her palm around the ring so that Rourke couldn't even look on it. "How do you know what I want?"

He inched closer to her, covering her free hand with his. Blessed be, but his skin was warm, and it fired her senses in a way that would surely send her straight to Hades.

"My lady, I've studied human nature. It's why I'm a great warrior. I know you are the kind of woman who prides herself on creating beautiful things for the sake of pleasing yourself, and the fact that it pleases others is incidental."

That was true, she thought. "Go on."

"You also try to please your parents, breaking your spirit to conform into the lady they want—nay, expect—you to be."

His thumb traced circle patterns over the delicate flesh on the top of her hand. She could hardly think, but she agreed. "Aye, 'tis difficult."

"Wouldn't you like to be free? To choose your own destiny, even if it means breaking those bonds?"

"Nay, I would never disappoint my parents on purpose.

They've worked hard for me, and they love me. I'll be a good daughter and wed where it benefits them best. I am the daughter without magic, you see."

"You're marrying me, Galiana." Rourke pressed her hand to his lips, and she quickly pulled away before she made a fool of herself—again.

"I'm not going to be tucked away in your keep while you go to court."

"Ye told her that, Rourke? Bollocks."

"No, Jamie, I hadn't. Would you mind leaving me to sort my own affairs?"

Galiana heard the irritation in Rourke's voice. She glanced down to make certain she was clothed, and since her gown was in place and neatly tied, she flung back the covers and got to her feet. She grabbed a robe from the pile of clothes at the foot of her bed and regally tossed it over her shoulders.

"It is obvious to me that you meant this ring for another woman," she said before slipping it on her finger. The power magnified, and she stifled a gasp.

Rourke, openmouthed, jumped to his feet. "I was appealing to your intellect!"

"You, Rourke, are as dumb as a goat. Any man your age should know women like to be flattered with pretty compliments, not insulted with business propositions. I will not marry you. I am not your man; I am not one of your knights; I am a lady—the lady in residence here at Montehue Manor, where you have worn out your welcome. Not that you had ever asked in the first place."

Jamie punched Rourke's arm and hooted his laughter. "Ha. I knew your comeuppance would be worth seeing."

Galiana tossed her tangled hair over her shoulder and walked to the chamber door. She opened it, pointed her index finger with the ring shining from it toward the hall, and said, "Get out. Now."

Rourke protested. "My lady, I apologize if I inadvertently insulted you. The ring is—"

"Mine. For now, anyway. I have a feeling it is a small piece of a larger cloth. But since you won't give me answers, I will find them myself."

"Wait!" Jamie and Rourke cried in unison.

Galiana crossed her arms over her chest, as she'd seen Rourke do a thousand times. She tapped her foot for good measure. "I am through playing games. You either tell me what is going on—the truth, Rourke Wallis—or else you will never see this ring again."

She looked like a demon's spawn, with her finger pointing to the hall and banishment. Jamie stood outside the threshold, gesturing for Rourke to follow. Galiana's hair was Medusa-like, with wild tangles in maddening disarray. That damnable chin and those glaring eyes: how had he ever considered them boring or dull? She was ready to eat him alive.

He liked her better when she was a wildcat beneath him.

"The truth?" How could Jamie even think of retreat when the battle was just beginning?

"Has it been so long since you've told the truth that you've forgotten how?"

Rourke gritted his back teeth. "Nay, my lady, I was just wondering if you were strong enough to hear it. You seem to have this issue with fainting at the first sign of trouble."

"What? Oh!" Her mouth pursed, and she curled her hands into fists at her sides.

He laughed, grateful to regain the upper hand, even by foul means.

"I'll meet you downstairs, at the dais. We will discuss this properly. Hurry, because you've already tried my patience. I will want to know every last thing you saw whilst in that vision."

Her stance expressed her desire to rebel, but she'd been well-trained to hold her tongue—something he seemed to have forgotten.

"Mayhap you can dress appropriately? And do something with your hair, dearest lady, before the mice move in."

Rourke had one foot in the hall when the door slammed shut behind him, and he almost turned around to bang it back open.

Jamie grabbed his arm. "I don't understand what the deuce has gotten into ye, Rourke, but why do ye bait her so? We learned to talk sweet to get what we want, and yet ye go out of yer way to be an arse. Explain yer strategy, would ye?"

Exhaling like he'd just finished a skirmish where no knight was the clear victor yet each was bloodied, Rourke said, "I don't sodding know, and that's the sad truth. She just makes me"—he lifted a fist and shook it at the door—"crazy."

Jamie's eyes closed, and he clapped a large hand over Rourke's shoulder. "I was afraid of that."

"What?"

"Ye care for her."

"I don't either." God's bones, but when had that happened?

"Ye do. So whatever strategy yer not usin', we need to toss to the wolves. It's a new plan we need."

"I'd rather cut off my head."

"I can't stomach another one like that today. Ye'll need to be a man, Rourke, and live with the pain."

The two men made it downstairs to the hall, and Rourke immediately called to the bailiff. "We've packed your knight's body on ice, my lord," the competent bailiff said. "And Layla is locked in the room above the kitchen. She tried to escape, but I caught her, and I found this," the bailiff reached into his pocket and pulled out an enameled brooch in the shape of a shield. "She claimed it was the knight's and he'd given it to her. It seems too valuable for that, methinks, in addition to the coin."

Rourke accepted the miniature shield, thanking the bailiff, who walked away with a satisfied nod.

Jamie whispered, "Did Robert work in Brittany, Rourke?"

Pinching the bridge of his nose, Rourke thought back. "Jesu, mayhap. But then, Franz had lands near there, before losing them to Philippe, and Godfrey played the tournament circuit all over France. These devices are common enough."

"Robert is dead, Rourke. Murdered. Did he deserve it? Mayhap, if he paid the wench to poison the manor."

"But why? Did he have a prearranged meeting with someone from outside our group?"

The more he scratched the surface, the more questions rose to the fore.

He walked to the fire, where his knights were sitting with Dame Bertha. Godfrey and Will were engaged in a game of chess, and Franz was holding some gray yarn for the old woman. Hardly a violent scene.

"How is the lady Galiana?" Godfrey asked.

"Oui, how is she? Perhaps the mademoiselle needs more fresh air to stop her faints. Or richer blood."

"I can ask Cook to serve our lady liver and onions," Dame Bertha suggested.

Rourke was grateful he didn't faint. He detested liver and onions and would rather eat haggis with Jamie.

Will moved his rook, then asked, "Shall I read her some poetry? Or bring her sweets? Godfrey says a knight must remember to be kind and treat a lady like a delicate vessel."

Jamie snorted. "Godfrey, come now, the boy's bound to get his ears boxed."

Godfrey said, "Checkmate, young Will. And before ye listen to Jamie, ask him if he's married, aye?"

Will muttered, "Ye win again, Godfrey. Are ye married, Jamie?"

Rourke grabbed his foster brother by the back of the neck, reminding him to hold his tongue. "Lady Galiana is fine, and should be down shortly," he answered Franz to give Jamie time.

Releasing a pent up breath, Jamie said in his usual way, "I've no time for just one lass, Will, not when there's so many out there that want me." He pounded his chest.

Dame Bertha sent Jamie a wink before gathering her yarn and putting it inside her basket. "I'll let Cook know to start the biscuits."

"My thanks," Rourke said. "And a pitcher of ale while we wait, good woman?"

She simpered. "Aye, me lord."

"Now there's the charm I know you've got. Why don't ye use it on the lady ye need to?"

Rourke ignored the whispered question in favor of taking the seat Dame Bertha had vacated. "Men, listen up. As you know, our prince"—he met each man's eyes to assure them he was talking of Prince John—"has ordered me to wed Lady Galiana."

"I still don't know why it was a secret," Will complained.

"Because, as some of you know," he met Franz's intense gaze, "I was sort of promised to another, the lady Magdalene Laroix."

Godfrey nodded. "I'd heard rumors, but ye never said anything, so I didn't ask."

Franz whistled low under his breath while smoothing his goatee. "She's a beauty, and heiress to the border lands in Maine and Brittany."

"Loyal to Constance?" Godfrey asked, palming the wooden queen.

"Closest of friends," Rourke confirmed.

"Does the lady know, you know, about our lady?" Rourke admired Will for being loyal to the current lady, which was more than he could say for himself.

"Nay, nor does Lady Galiana know about Magdalene." Rourke stared into the fire as his men chuckled in sympathy. It was important to tell enough of the truth to sound believable, while directing the players where he needed them to go. It was no longer a question of if there was a betrayer in their midst, but who. Perhaps the person who had separated Robbie from his head thought the dead body would end the suspicion.

Robbie's brooch felt heavy in his pocket.

The mystery simply intensified the game.

"Well," Will said at last, "what are ye going to do?"

"I tried to tell the lady I'd keep her safe at my keep, but she refuses to go."

Jamie adjusted the belt around his tunic. "Fool told the lady she had to go, and couldn't go to court . . ."

Rourke glared at his foster brother.

Franz laughed and exchanged a look with Godfrey. "Seems young Will isn't the only one needing lessons in chivalry, oui?"

"When are ye goin' to marry her?" Godfrey asked. "Her reputation will be in tatters now, if ye don't. We've been here over a week, and her priest and her brothers have deserted her. People will think the worst."

"You are still going to marry her, aren't ye?" Will asked.

Franz tilted his head and waited for Rourke to speak.

Jamie sighed. "She says she won't marry him."

Lowering his head, Franz laughed some more. "Rourke, you have always had the luck of the angels— until now. What will Prince John say if you cannot marry one petite mademoiselle?"

"Petite? Franz, she's taller than you are. Besides, she doesn't want me."

"There is a first time for everything, and I am thanking God I was here to see you with egg on your face." Franz slapped his knee and grinned.

"She can marry me," Will said as he got to his feet. "Since she doesn't want you."

Rourke didn't appreciate the spurt of panic this announcement caused, and he was overly harsh as he ordered, "Sit down, Will. Chivalry need only go so far."

He heard a feminine gasp—and knew he was in serious trouble.

Jumping up so fast he knocked the stool over, Rourke faced the only woman he'd never been able to charm.

Angry and defensive was better than simply defensive, so he thrust his chest out and looked her up and down. "I see you found your comb."

She put her hand to her hair before realizing what she was doing, then dropped it to her side. "If you continue to insult me, I will return to my chamber."

Her hair was scraped back into a loose bun, revealing her unfortunate chin and bare forehead. She wore no wimple, probably because her head was sore from when she'd fallen. She wore a plain tunic in some undermined drab shade, with a grayish undergown. Rourke noticed she wasn't wearing the ring.

Smart girl. Why had it reacted like that for her, and not for him?

"You are marrying me." Even he knew he was being a prick, but hearing the rumble of his men behind him let him know he needed to change his ways.

"I am not," she insisted.

He shrugged. "There are other men."

"What?" Her smooth brow furrowed.

Jamie dropped his head forward until his chin hit his chest, but Rourke couldn't stop his tongue. "Aye, and they want you for the same reason I do—your land."

Her eyes widened, and her mouth dropped open.

"Prince John is a man who likes to get things accomplished, and he wants all of the unmarried, yet marriageable, ladies in England bound to men of his choice. It was a race, and I won. I will claim my prize. We leave in the morning. You may choose whether it be to court, or my home."

He paused, watching the array of emotions dance over her bold features. It was a bitter victory, but he would take what he could get.

"Ye'll be safer at my keep." He could tup her until neither of them could walk, and then mayhap his wits would return.

If she could be anybody it would be Boadicea, with her flaming sword and her quick wit. Aye, she'd cleave Rourke in two and leave a bloody trail as she dragged his limbs to the snow for pig fodder.

She concentrated on slowing her breath. Galiana would not faint again, not on Rourke's behalf. She'd been taught to be a lady, to maintain a civilized tone in extreme situations. This surpassed her mother's wildest imagination—and it could be wild—but she would handle it.

Drawing herself up to her full height—she'd not missed his remark about that either, the imbecile—she stepped forward until he backed up.

She'd learn to score these victories, else she'd never live with herself. Did women really fall all over themselves to do Rourke's bidding?

Dame Bertha announced, "I've set the pitcher of ale on the dais, me lord. Do ye need aught else?"

Galiana bit her lower lip in frustration as he smiled and waved at the old woman.

"My thanks," he called.

"Excuse me?" She tapped her toe. "I will go to court, and I will take my case before the prince. I'll not be some bit of meat to parcel out to the first man to claim me as a prize," she ground out, fury building within her.

"My lady," Rourke tried to interject.

"You've said your piece," she challenged. "I will go to court, and I will decide who my husband will be. Mayhap the other men know the value of truth and honor. How many men, besides you, are coming after me?"

"Two more, my lady. You need me to protect you."

"Two? Pah, I can handle two men, and you, without losing an eyelash." She glared at him before meeting each of his knight's gazes. With the exception of Jamie, they were innocent of the mad wager, she could tell.

"This goes too far, Rourke," Franz said. "Let us talk about it, and come up with a resolution that fits everybody's needs."

"I told ye, ye should have bedded her that first night, whilst the priest was here." Godfrey shook his head.

"What about chivalry?" Will demanded.

"Chivalry is fine, young Will," Galiana explained, "when men already have what they want."

"Galiana." Rourke reached out for her arm, but she withered him with a stare that had held off numerous men before him.

"I will thank you to keep your hands to yourself."

He looked like he was ready to suffer a fit. His handsome face was as red as an apple, and his jaw was clenched so tight she could see the muscle jump. He had to know she would not tolerate being treated like dirt.

And if he couldn't change, then she would marry another. She'd promised Saint Jude she'd wed suitably for her parents' sake, if she'd get just one adventure. Saint Jude, for certes, had delivered.

Rourke held land, which was good, but he was loyal to Prince John, which wasn't good. Her family had sworn to honor King Richard, and they would.

Unlike some of the local lords who switched allegiances with the tide, her father would remain true to his word. If she married Rourke, she chanced giving control of her land to Prince John. Could she do that to her family?

What if the other men were worse than Rourke?

The other men wouldn't be Rourke.

The thought cracked her chilling heart.

"We need to talk," he said.

If she stayed to listen to his words, she would cry. "I'll go pack. I'm assuming this was the secret you were keeping from me? That I was a prize, and you just happened to be the lucky winner? I'm sorry to say, Rourke, that your luck has run out."

She left him there and walked back to the stairs and up to her room before bursting into bitter tears.

Finally she'd met a man who made her feel something besides cold disdain, and he thought her hideous. At last she'd found magic—in the ring from the man she desired—and the cursed thing was for another woman. Love. She didn't believe in love.

A quick knock came to the door, and Dame Bertha stepped in carrying a tray of chilled wine, a goblet, and some bread and cheese. "How are ye farin'? Does yer head ache, my lady? I saw ye leave in a hurry, and then Lord Rourke asked me to bring ye some refreshment."

"Is it poisoned?"

Dame Bertha clucked her tongue. "What kind of question is that?"

"How can you not see what a horrible man he is?"

"He's just a man, one who blusters about whence he's confused."

Galiana accepted the goblet of wine, sniffing before she drank, just as a precaution. "Confused?"

"Aye, he's got feelin's for ye, and he doesn't know what to do about them."

"How do you know that?"

"I'm not the one that's blind, my lady," Dame Bertha chuckled.

"He orders me around like I'm his lackey," Galiana complained.

"And do ye do what he says? Nay."

"I combed my hair," Gali said, patting the loose bun.

"Aye, in the most unflattering style ye could."

"What?" She looked down at her slippers to avoid the old woman's gaze. "I don't know what you are talking about."

"Not a single piece of jewelry, not a touch of color to yer cheeks."

"He's rude."

"Has his sight returned, my lady?" the wily woman asked.

"Fine. I could have tried harder. But so could he."

"Aye. What is it that ye want?"

Rourke.

"I don't know." Galiana got up from her pout and started to help Dame Bertha fold the tunics and fabric strewn about her room. "He doesn't think I can do anything."

"So prove 'im wrong."

"What will Mam say, and my father? I would be marrying a man who supports the wrong Plantagenet."

"Don't know a thing about that. But, and this is an old lady talkin', if ye were married to a man in Prince John's employ, wouldn't ye be able to help out yer king? And mayhap yer family?"

"Saint Edward, the truth shall come to those who

seek it," Galiana recited from memory before laughing. "He thinks me a nobody? A country miss who won't fit in at court. Well. Mayhap that will be for the best. What an adventure to tell my children! I helped thwart a prince and save my family's honor. Aye, I do like the sound of that."

"My lady, never mind. 'Tis foolish, and I should have kept me tongue behind me teeth. Don't do it." Dame Bertha grabbed Galiana by the hand. "Ye can fool Lord Rourke into thinkin' ye plain, but he's not got his full sight. 'Tis not the same as going to court. Ye won't be able to hide what ye are."

"Mayhap." Galiana held her mother's green silk gown up next to her eyes. "Or perhaps it's time to be more of what I am instead of less."

Chapter Twelve

Galiana blew over the damp ink, wishing it would hurry and dry. She had no sand to shake over it, but when she'd decided to pen the missive to her parents, she'd not realized Rourke would be breathing down her neck to leave at day's break.

He was being a pain in her backside, for certes.

Finally, she'd locked the door to her chamber from the inside and pushed her large trunk in front of it for good measure.

She dropped the letter to the table, wishing she could explain to her parents in person.

Well, Mam, I was an idiot, and the boys and I had a snowball fight that somehow ended with the manor being taken over by our enemies. I'm being coerced into marriage, and I've finally touched magic, but it still isn't meant for me. The ring belongs to another. But I'll lie with Rourke, aye, and enjoy every last minute, because the lady you raised me to be just wants this man in her bed.

Strumpet.

The prim letter was safer.

Sighing, she looked over her chamber. It was as neat and tidy as if she'd never lived in it. With the exception of the trunk in front of her door, everything was in its place.

It made her skin itch to have everything so perfectly together. "My aloe cream." She snapped her fingers. "Now, where did I have it last?" Nothing smoothed patches of rough winter skin better than aloe.

And since Rourke was refusing to let her bring anything more than a small cask for her vials and oils, she decided she couldn't leave the manor without her lotion.

He banged on the door. "God's bones, Galiana, I will take this down by the hinges if you don't hurry up!"

"I suppose you are already packed?" She twirled a curl around her finger and watched it bounce into place as she sat on the edge of her made bed. "I'm not ready yet, sir, and that is that. You can't expect me to move to a new household without all of my things. My trinkets." She patted the magic ring, which was tied to a loop at her waist and tucked away against her hip so none could see it. She'd not wear it as a necklace, not when Rourke would think to look there for it.

"I'll buy you new trinkets; now get your bum out here," he growled.

She rolled her eyes, wondering if she'd left the cream in her knitting basket in the great hall. "You think me so easy to placate?"

"You have been far from easy," he muttered.

Galiana grinned behind the safety of the door, glancing around one last time. When—nay, if—she saw this room again, she would be a different woman.

She had but one cask for her perfumes and lotions, and two saddle bags for her clothes and shoes. One rolled blanket, one large purse for her jewels, and her lute; she couldn't leave without it.

All in all, she'd packed very little and tucked everything else away for her mother and her sister.

She'd not told them a proper good-bye when they'd left for Falcon Keep. She'd been glad to see them go. She sniffed. Mother Mary forgive her, she'd wanted an adventure—a chance to spread her wings and learn to fly.

Picking up the sheet of paper, she touched one finger to the ink. Almost dry. She waved it back and forth, wondering what tale her brothers would tell her poor parents. Rape and a takeover by Prince John's men? For certes, they'd come racing back from Falcon Keep with all the knights her father and Nicholas could summon— only to find she'd already flown the coop.

The letter explained as best as she could what had happened—about the imprisoned Layla, and Celestia's sickroom, the dead knight, and her own decision to marry Lord Rourke Wallis.

She took full responsibility.

"I'm coming in," Rourke yelled, and a large bang sounded against the door.

What was that? "A battering ram is hardly necessary," she chided, quickly rolling the letter into a tube and sealing it with wax from the candle on the table. She tied a ribbon around it and winced as the doorframe cracked.

Her father was going to be very angry about that.

Galiana had just stuck the letter in her tunic when Rourke managed to knock the door in, pushing back the giant trunk.

She waved the tips of her fingers at his scowling face. "I'm ready."

He looked around the room, noting the small stack of baggage she had by the wall, the neatly made bed and the tidied knickknacks. "By my lady, you try my patience sorely."

"As you do mine," Galiana said, slipping past him to the hall. "I've but to find my aloe cream, and say my good-byes."

To her surprise, Jamie, Franz, Will, and Godfrey, as well as a few of the Montehue knights, had all been witness to the exchange between her and Rourke. Galiana lifted her chin and swept past them all to the stairs without saying a word.

It was so quiet that her heels' clicking against the stone floor reverberated like nails in a coffin.

Until she reached the bottom of the stairs, when she

couldn't hold back a giggle.

Rourke's loud roar of outrage made up for the broken door.

Bailiff Morton came running, with Cook on his heels. "What's happening? Are we under attack?"

Cook brandished a cast-iron pan in one hand. "Get behind me, lady; I'll save ye from any brigands."

"Lord Rourke is the only rabble-rouser in the manor, Cook, though I thank you kindly for coming to my defense." She laughed.

The bailiff shook his head. "Take care that ye don't push him too far, my lady. A man has his pride."

"He's not cared one whit for my pride, now has he? Nay, I have been trampled down since—"

"Since ye felled him with a rock?" Bailiff Morton reminded her.

Galiana swallowed. It seemed she had drawn first blood.

"I just wanted to say good-bye." She changed the subject, giving Cook a hug. "Tell Joey and Bertie, too?"

"Godspeed, my lady," Cook said before heading back to the kitchen. Gali noted Cook's air of disappointment, evident in the dejected set of her shoulders, because she'd not gotten to brain someone with her pot.

"And would you please give my parents this?" She discreetly handed over the rolled and sealed letter to Bailiff Morton. "It explains that none of what happened was your fault."

"I should have stayed at your side, my lady." He shuffled his feet.

"How were you to know I snuck out the back? It was my impulsiveness that brought on this disaster."

"Lord Rourke was coming for you, my lady, whether ye hit him first or not. Destiny has a way of directing us."

"I suppose." Galiana watched the bailiff put the letter inside his vest. "I will miss you, and I thank you sincerely for all you've done." She leaned in to kiss the man's cheek and pretended not to notice his blush.

"It was me duty, my lady," he said, patting the letter. "Take care."

Galiana spied the basket of yarn by the fireplace and remembered her cream. Then she remembered sharing it with Dame Bertha, and decided to leave it there. The old woman was crying tears that disappeared into her wrinkles as soon as they leaked from her eyes.

Galiana reached forward and took the woman's hands in hers. "I'll miss you and all the kindnesses you've done for me. Be well," she said, blinking fast so she wouldn't join Dame Bertha in an emotional breakdown.

"Ye be happy now; 'tis yer nature, my lady."

As she looked around the great hall where she'd learned to curtsy, embroider, and faint, she had the oddest sensation that she wouldn't be back here for a very long time.

Rourke watched from the stairs as Galiana secretly passed something over to the bailiff. It was true that his sight was hardly clear, still dull and blurred, but the scent of ink had been strong in the lady's chamber. He hadn't stayed alive this long playing games of intrigue by not noticing things as simple as that.

Did she think to send a message to King Richard, warning him that Prince John was making his move?

He had to have the missive.

He waited until Galiana finished her last words to her servants before joining her at the front door. "My lady, Will is bringing your things down. I see you packed lightly, as I told you."

"It made sense, my lord. I was able to apply my"— she tapped the side of her head—"intellect."

She was lethal with her sarcasm.

Dressed for riding, Galiana wore a tight-fitting cap over the top of her head, and she'd attached a heavy veil tucked into her high-necked tunic. She looked protected rather than decorated.

Which was for the best, Rourke knew. Her face, without ornamentation, was heart-shaped, and pretty. Aye, even her pointed chin served her well.

"I hope you have a heavier cloak, with a hood? To cover your face and mouth," he pantomimed wrapping her head. "Before you take insult, 'tis for your own good. It will keep you warmer."

"To think I was worried you wouldn't have my best

interests at heart," she replied as she turned on her heel.

Her thick skirts, combined with her fur mantle and sturdy veil, made her look like a nun. Things would go easier for him if he thought of her as a daughter of the holy order, rather than recall the weight of her breast in his palm, or the warmth of her tongue as they dueled in lust.

Groaning, Rourke pulled his gloves from his cloak pocket and walked to the bailiff. It was child's play to misdirect the good man's attention and ease the letter from inside his vest. Rourke palmed the rolled missive and tucked it inside his glove as he put it on.

He'd read her treachery later. Mayhap he could threaten her with the tower, since her brother . . . brothers . . . were free.

"What's the plan, then? You shovel; then we follow on horseback, across all of England?"

Franz laughed aloud, not bothering to hide his merriment. "This journey will be one of my favorites; I can tell already, mademoiselle."

"If we don't freeze to death," Godfrey grumbled. He pulled his leather cap further down over his ears. "I'm cold, and we haven't left the manor. Me lady, did ye stuff yer boots with straw, like I suggested?"

"Aye," Galiana nodded. "My thanks. I added some to my gloves as well. Not comfortable, but I'd rather not lose an appendage to frostbite just because some people are stubborn."

Rourke gritted his teeth and exchanged a harried look with Jamie.

"Stubborn, or determined, my lady? I am doing my best to save you from certain disaster."

"You are the disaster which has befallen me, my lord!"

"There is no reasoning with you, Galiana. Your life could be at stake."

Disgruntled, Rourke led the way outside to where the horses were packed and waiting. The air plumed from their nostrils like mystical dragon smoke as their hot breath mixed with the cold, cold air.

"Refreshing," Rourke said, slapping his gloved hands together.

Galiana glided past him, allowing Franz to assist her to her horse. She'd chosen woolen breeches beneath her gown so she could ride astride, and the layers and layers of cloth on her body provided warmth, as well as a cushion for her rear end. Rourke approved. Contrary to what the lady thought, he didn't want her harmed in any way.

She settled herself on top of the mare, patting the horse's mane. Her voluminous skirts covered the horse's flanks. Lucky horse. In fact, once she put up her hood, Rourke thought she looked like a mound of blankets instead of a woman.

"I thought you were in a hurry, my lord." Her muffled voice prodded him from thoughts of lying with her in the cocoon of those same blankets.

"I thought I told you to keep the scarf over your mouth," he muttered as he mounted and led the way down the path toward the forest.

"Excuse me? Lord Rourke, are we not going the wrong direction? I need to go to the village and see how my people fare before I desert them."

"You aren't deserting them, and this is a shortcut. Once we reach the forest road, we can make better time."

"There are hills and valleys along the way. In clear weather, you are right: it would be the swiftest passage; but by trying to cross now, you'd risk a horse's leg. If we go to the village, we can use the road from there to the forest and not risk injury to horse or man."

She spoke as if she knew what she was talking about. He remembered Jamie falling into the snowdrift and knew she was right. It galled. Could he not be in charge of one cursed thing and have it go the way he wanted?

His men waited. He nodded. "Fine. To the village, but we are not stopping!"

According to Galiana, in good weather, or even rain, it took less than an hour to reach the village by foot. Now they were coming close to two hours, and they'd just come upon the village gates. The sight of smoke puffing from the houses was encouragement enough to draw them all forward. Rourke wondered if this was the bitterest cold ever to be had in England. It was even too cold to snow, which he hadn't thought was possible.

His teeth chattered, his toes were numb, and he hadn't heard a single peep from the lady in an hour.

He guided his stallion next to her mare. "Galiana? How are you?"

Would she answer? Was she going to give him the silent treatment for forcing her on this journey?

She pulled back her hood, and Rourke saw that she'd wrapped the scarf around her face so that only her eyes were visible. Even in this white, cold weather, he was overwhelmed with the sight of verdant green fields before she blinked and her eyes changed back to muddy brown.

Galiana slowly peeled the cloth away from her face, and he had the impression that she'd been quite cozy beneath all of her wraps.

"I'm fine. And you? Your lips are blue."

Rourke was sorry he'd asked. "We will be stopping in the village after all, mayhap to get some soup and stretch our legs. Hopefully a brewer will be open for business. You can see for yourself that your villagers are well kept." What else were the poor sods to do besides drink and visit? The fields were frozen.

He waited for her to say he was wrong and she'd been right about stopping, but she didn't. "I just wanted to let you know," he said.

"Thank you." She wrapped her face back in her scarf and returned the hood, leaving Rourke very unsettled. And shut out.

Had he made her so angry that she'd rather marry one of the other two men than accept his hand? Impossible! Women liked him.

If only she weren't so caught up in this ideal of honor and truth, he thought with a sigh. He moved his stallion back to the front of their small party, using the horse's large, strong legs to break through the snow. In some places, the snow reached the massive chest of the hard-working stallion. Jamie stayed at his side.

He'd been lying to women since he was old enough to understand that most of them preferred lies to harsh truth. What did it matter, if the lie caused no harm? And if it made a woman feel good about herself, then he really didn't see how it hurt. He never had an empty bed, unless he chose to sleep alone, and he learned the best secrets from his discreet partners.

Yes, it was shallow. He'd always understood that, and he'd chosen to be around women who knew that as well. With two exceptions—the queen, whom he flattered and who believed every word; and Constance, whom he flattered and lied to because his life depended on gaining her trust.

For the good of Scotland, and King William, and so, by default, all of the British Isles. Even Magdalene understood the game they played.

Galiana's words made him question his loyalty, something he couldn't afford to do, and still be a valuable spy.

He spurred his horse onward until he reached the edge of the village, where the outdoor bread ovens had melted the snow enough to make mud. He recognized the old woman who'd fed him and Jamie before, and raised his hand in greeting.

She curtsied back, staying close to the warm oven.

"Good day, my lord," she said, then added, "my lady."
Rourke turned to see that Galiana was right behind him,
emerged from her cocoon like a moth.

"Is Mary open, good woman?" Galiana called down.

"Aye," the old lady answered. "Chicken and dumplings today."

"Thank you," Galiana said, deftly directing her
horse through the village center.

They arrived before a house that looked like any of
the other houses, except for the noise coming from the
inside. Despite the cold, the windows were left open
and people sat upon the front porch. The piles of snow
climbed clear to the roof, and some of the village children
were sliding down after making their way to the top.

The noise shouted of life in winter's cool sleep.

"Lady Galiana?" A woman with puffy cheeks and a
toddler hanging on her leg came down the steps. "What
are ye doin' in the cold? Come inside, come inside. I'll
clear a table upstairs so that you and yer"—Rourke was
the recipient of a dubious look—"party can have some
privacy."

"Thank you, Mary. That would be appreciated."

"Hank! Jonny, Thomas, Matthew and Randolf," the
lady yelled in a shout that carried through the maze of
people and summoned the five men immediately. "Clear
the pink room upstairs for our lady, set a fresh fire, and
get"—she counted Rourke and his men—"five of the big
mugs out for these lads. They look cold, aye?"

"You are wonderful, Mary," Galiana gushed as she slid to the ground. Rourke had to give credit where it was due. Galiana rarely forgot her role as lady. So far as he knew, he and Jamie were the only ones to cause her upset.

"I'll bring yer mug, special meself," Mary said with a smile. "I know how ye like yer mead extra sweet. Now"—she led Galiana up the stairs, and Rourke and his men followed like sheep—"where are ye headed? Not after yer brothers, are ye?"

Rourke strained his ears, listening for the lady's reply. Would she call for help? Tell the formidable Mary to poison their ale so she could run off to her sister's keep?

"Court. It seems I've been invited to meet Prince John."

Mary halted abruptly and put her hand on Galiana's arm. "My lady?"

"No harm, Mary. I'm to be married."

Rourke felt the censure of Mary's stare and straightened his shoulders.

"But, my lady, the family has a dispensation . . . Surely not by force?"

Did everybody but the prince know about this bloody dispensation?

Not that Rourke was surprised by the pride in the villein's voice. In a smaller village such as this one, the peasants often considered themselves part of the manorial family—especially if the family, like the Montehues, so obviously cared about their welfare. The dispensation was a feather in their collective cap.

Galiana glanced back at Rourke as if he were an insignificant obstacle in her quest to court. How did she do it with a mere look in her eye? She didn't have eyebrows, and her mouth stayed in that same patient smile—yet the message was perfectly clear.

The lady would sooner marry a toad from a children's tale than marry Lord Rourke Wallis.

It stunned him so much he almost stepped back. Had he been so rotten?

For the first time in his entire life, Rourke called his outer appearance into question. Tall. Strong. He had a predilection for cleanliness. Did he have bad breath?

Nay, this was not about him; it was about her.

Wasn't it?

Never answering Mary's question, Galiana exclaimed over the tablecloth and the plate as if it were gold, and took her seat. Rourke sat opposite her so he could watch her like a hawk watched a fish.

Hungrily.

Mary and her helpers poured ale all around, except for Galiana, who drank her special mead. She met his gaze with a daring look as he hesitated to sip from his mug. The left side of her mouth barely lifted in a mocking smile, and it was as if she knew what he'd been thinking.

He lifted the mug and saluted her with it before draining it down and calling for another.

One of the five men placed a pitcher in the center of the table, and then another man put two steaming loaves of fresh bread at each end. Fragrant bowls of chicken and dumplings were brought before each of them, and then the peasants made to leave.

Mary got down one stair before turning around and asking, "So the messenger found ye, then, my lord?"

Rourke looked up, his spoon to his lips. "Eh?"

"The messenger. What was his name? Jonny? Thomas, ye gave 'im directions to the manor. What was his name?"

Thomas shrugged. "Never told me; just said as 'ow it was important."

Returning the spoon to the bowl without shouting took all of his willpower.

Jamie was not so inclined. He pounded his fist down on the table. "What in the devil's name are ye talkin' about? No messenger came, and one of me lord's knights was killed in the drying shed out behind the manor. What say ye now?"

Mary's eyes were round with fright. Rourke stood. "Calm yourself, Jamie. These good people didn't do the crime."

"He was like you." Thomas pointed to Jamie. "But his hair was blond. He wasn't as tall or"—he stretched his hands wide at the shoulders—"big. A fearsome warrior."

Jamie narrowed his eyes. "He specifically asked for Lord Rourke? Or was he lookin' fer the manor?"

"Excellent question," Rourke muttered. He tore the bread before him into tiny pieces.

Thomas looked to Mary, who looked to Jonny, who called down the stairs for Randolf.

Randolf arrived with another pitcher of ale, Matthew, and Hank.

Jamie and Mary quickly apprised them of the situation, and Hank scratched his chin. "He asked if there was any strangers at the manor."

Jonny interrupted, "The twins told Bart about the terrible knights capturing Galiana, and Bart told everybody 'bout how ye came searchin' for the boys with a red glint in yer eye."

Galiana's giggle was almost imperceptible, but he heard it.

"—so we said, aye, there were strangers. No offense, my lord." Hank shuffled worriedly from foot to foot.

"Blond hair?" Mary prodded.

Hank pursed his lips. "Methinks it was more brown."

"He had a limp," Randolf pronounced, coming round the tables to top off everyone's mug.

"A limp?" Rourke exchanged a glance with his men. They didn't know anybody with a pronounced limp. "Blond and a limp. That leaves out Lord Christien. Harold is dark and huge—there'd be no forgetting that."

"You just missed 'im, eh?" Mary's voice rose with suspicion.

Matthew rushed in, saying, "We offered him a room—he looked that beat—but he said he had business to take care of first. Aye, but then he never came back."

Rourke sighed. "He never came to the manor." Had Robert tried to defend the manor and been out-skilled? The near decapitation was cruel and seemed intently malicious overall. How he wanted to think the best of his knight—he'd fought side by side with Robert on more than one occasion—but what if Robert was working on his own agenda? What if somehow, as impossible as it seemed, he understood what the ring signified?

What if he'd arranged the assignation to relay information, and it had gone wrong or had already been intercepted by the enemy?

Too many questions, and now was not the time to ponder them without drawing attention to himself.

"Murder done at Montehue Manor, and with the lord away?" Jonny sucked his lower lip. "And yer leavin', my lady? What will the house do?"

Rourke saw Galiana swallow, the only sign she was disturbed by the question.

"Bailiff Morton is a competent man. He can handle the troubles at the manor until my family comes home."

Rourke could see that they all, Galiana included, thought she should be home to take care of business. "The lady does a great service in agreeing to be my wife. It is not her fault that she needs to leave the manor at this time. Prince John is desirous of meeting my new bride, and we"—he chuckled loudly—"would hate to disappoint a royal."

They all nodded as if they agreed, but not really.

Galiana toyed with the edge of her napkin before saying in a soothing voice, "My parents will be back before long, Mary. Would you please send some extra help to the manor as soon as you can? We've cleared a path, so that should help. Poor Cook is feeling very cooped up. This snow can't last forever, now can it?" She smiled invitingly, and everyone laughed in relief. Rourke admitted she had a bit of diplomatic skill.

"The bairns are havin' a time of it, all right, but me? I don't like diggin' out the firewood stacked against the house. Brrr," Thomas said as he left to serve the downstairs patrons.

Jonny, Matthew, Hank and Randolf followed on his heels, leaving Mary to ask, "Is there anything else to get ye?"

Rourke would have answered, but Mary only had eyes for Galiana.

"No, thank you, and our thanks to your staff for their attention."

Mary bobbed and disappeared down the stairs.

Jamie said, "The man looking for ye doesn't sound like Christien, and I swear ye knocked the fight out of Harold."

"He fell off his horse." Will snickered.

Rourke lifted his spoon and gestured to the men. "Eat, before it's too cold."

"I don't like it," Will complained.

"The soup?" Galiana asked in surprise.

"Nay, my lady, the danger. 'Tis there, but we don't know what, or who, it is. Poor Robbie, dead back at the manor, and us not knowing who his murderer is. I don't bloody like it at all."

"Will," Rourke reprimanded. "Watch your language. We don't talk of such things at a table with a lady present."

"This lady would hear more of this talk," Galiana said. "Actually, I have a few questions of my own, if I may?"

Rourke shook his head, but she ignored him and appealed to his men.

"Knights, just by being brave warriors, create enemies. Is this not so?"

Galiana made eye contact with each of his men, even Jamie, and they all answered, "Aye."

"So," she took a sip of her mead, inviting the men to drink as well. "A man, just by being born a man, could have an enemy who might want him . . . dead."

Again his men chorused their "ayes."

What was so special about her that she captured the attention of them all? Was it her expression? The wide expanse of her brow, or, never say it, the way she held that pointy chin?

She was tall, and bold of feature. Washed out, to his eye, and dull of color. She was very tightly controlled, but he doubted many saw beneath her charming and gracious exterior. He dunked a morsel of bread into his soup and popped it into his mouth.

"Did Robert have any specific enemies? Did he belong

to any factions that might not need him any longer? What of a lover, if not a wife?"

Rourke felt the weight of the enameled pin against his chest while Jamie choked on his soup.

Galiana turned her gaze on him and asked, "Who would know, if you left so fast and on a dare, to boot, that Sir Robert was with you, and coming to Montehue Manor? Assuming, of course, he had been intent on meeting with someone."

Nodding, Rourke agreed her questions had validity and answered, "My men and I were recuperating from a siege in Wales, and we were at my keep."

"Just served our meal," Godfrey recalled, "when the prince's man came."

"He wanted to talk to Rourke, alone," Will added. "So we all grabbed our food and went to the kitchens to eat."

"Oui. He wasn't one for idle chit chat, and he didn't stay with Rourke for long."

"Long enough to tell him he had to marry." Godfrey pointed his table knife at Galiana. "And tell him to collect the taxes whilst he's at it."

The lady dipped her head in acknowledgement. "And then?"

Rourke hurried to fill in the pieces of his own damn story before another of his men did. "He told me of the prince's wishes, and gave me the names of the other two men I would be competing against. Harold and Christien."

"Old rivals, I assume?"

"Yes. How did you know?"

"Prince John wanted you to marry me, so how better to ensure that you are the winner than to pit you against your bitter rivals? I may not agree with his politics, but what a brilliant strategist!"

Rourke snapped his jaw shut. "He played me." Me? Me. And I never saw it coming.

"Ach, man." Jamie pounded the table again.

Franz's laughter burned like salt on his wounded ego.

"So you heard who your rivals would be and immediately raced to win my fair hand and please your prince." She tapped her fingers against the table. "Why? What do you, Rourke Wallis, gain? Rumor"—she smiled sweetly—"has it that you were promised to another. And yet you leave your love behind to satisfy your prince."

"Prince John will be king someday," Will said.

Galiana gave a barely perceptible heft of her chin. "Geoffrey's son, Arthur, is next in line for the throne, if one follows the laws of heredity."

Rourke cleared his throat before the intelligent lady went too far. "King Richard needs to name his heir, especially considering this recent imprisonment."

"What if King Richard never comes back?" Will asked. "The emperor could decide to hang 'im or somethin'."

"We thought him dead once already this year," Godfrey agreed.

"Because Prince John falsely announced it to be so!"

Galiana's voice rose.

Franz studied his fingernails as he said, "If old Henry finishes Richard off, then the prince becomes a king, and we are all in good graces, non?"

"And what if the king comes home?" Galiana challenged. "And the prince is usurping the royal throne? What then?"

Godfrey pushed his bowl toward the middle of the table. "Then we hope the king is a forgiving man."

Chapter Thirteen

She'd broken bread with a bunch of idiots.

Once again, Rourke had managed to goad her into losing control of her temper. The fact that she'd been able to point out Prince John's strategy in getting him to be the winner of her hand made her feel a little better.

'Twas obvious Rourke didn't like game playing when he wasn't the victor. She had to wonder, however, why he'd seemed self-disparaging about getting bested by the prince. Even she understood royalty had to be devious in order to keep their thrones. Mayhap they were fed lies from the teat, and that was how they kept their heads.

It was no fault of Rourke's that he'd not guessed the prince's intent—even if it had been as plain as the nose on his handsome face—to her. The why behind the mad prince's request, however, remained a mystery.

The end of their meal had risen into a cacophony of argument, as each man had to say their piece on King Richard and his dubious return to England.

She shivered and wrapped her fur-lined cloak tighter around her body. The ground, smothered in white, with daggers of ice hanging from the trees, didn't look able to support the new taxes.

It was difficult on the people, but it was the king's right to raise money when he needed. And good British subjects couldn't leave their king languishing in some German prison, could they?

They had to come up with the ransom somehow.

Her family had sworn fealty to King Richard, and she would uphold the family honor.

Her horse neighed and slipped on the snow. Galiana's chilled fingers were numb inside the gloves, and she hoped she was holding the reins tightly. She honestly couldn't tell for certes.

She kept her eyes on the line of trees in the distance. It wouldn't be as cold once they reached the shelter of the forest, nor would the snow be piled as deep. The dark forest she and her siblings had told ghost stories in was now a beacon of safety.

Would Rourke recall his mad ride through the trees, when she'd thought he was going to slay her brother? She hated that Rourke was loyal to Prince John. Although for a brief second over their meal, she'd seen a flash of defiance cross Rourke's face. Why would a liege demand that a favored knight marry on a wager? Unless the prince had just cause to doubt the knight. Or was that more wishful thinking?

Why did men have to make things so much harder than they were? Opinions didn't matter to the absolute fact. King Richard was king of England.

While she agreed that an heir should be named as soon as royally possible, the throne wasn't up for grabs. King Richard's chancellor and Queen Eleanor were both in place to rule in his absence.

Mayhap it was something in the Plantagenet blood that made them want what they couldn't have.

Which made her think of wanting what she couldn't have—the ring, and the taste of magic it had given her. She'd been . . . cautious . . . of it, ever since the trance— but it called to her, like forbidden fruit.

Was the ring the Breath of Merlin, the thing that Rourke wouldn't explain?

It seemed Rourke had many secrets, and the more she brooded about them, the angrier she got. He had a secret woman in his life, someone he had dismissed as easily as an old boot once his liege had demanded it. And the ring and this Breath of Merlin business . . .

Rourke's talk of things he did for the royals in his life . . . He spoke of King William with respect. At least, she thought he did. Prince John didn't seem to hold the affection Scotland's king did. But hadn't King William turned Rourke, aye, and Jamie away?

The ring hummed against her hip bone, where she'd carefully sewn it to her skirt.

There was more going on than she was being shown.

She knew magic, and she knew sleight of hand; she would not be tricked or swayed from her course. If Rourke thought to deflect her thoughts so she'd do his bidding, he was wrong.

"My lady?" Godfrey called. "Are ye comin'?"

Galiana realized that while she'd been tearing apart Rourke's motivations, she'd fallen behind. Will plodded along to her left, asleep in his saddle. He'd looked so miserable that she'd offered him an extra blanket. Wanting to be a man, he hadn't accepted it.

He was frozen upright.

Nodding to Godfrey, she nudged her horse closer to Will's. Knowing she'd be sorry as soon as she did it, she lowered her scarf and pushed back her hood a bit so she could talk.

"Will? Will . . ." The intake of air to her lungs was frigid and stung.

He jerked awake, blinking. "Are we there?"

"Where?" Galiana exhaled. "We're traveling until we can't go any farther on the hope we'll find a town or village before we all die stuck to our horses like marble statues."

Will shook his head as a giant shiver overtook his body. "Lord Rourke will see us safe, my lady," he said grimly.

Wishing she had such blind faith in his lord's skills against Mother Nature, Galiana merely nodded. "You're certain you don't want a blanket?"

"A knight never complains."

"You weren't complaining," Galiana was quick to say. "I have too many, and I didn't want to stop to roll this extra into my pack." Using her numb fingers to untie the top cloak, she made a show of struggling with where to put it.

She felt Will's glance but pretended not to notice. "Saint Mary's tears, can I do nothing right?"

"Here, my lady. Let me help," Will said.

"My thanks," Galiana sighed, handing the cloak over. "Do you mind terribly holding it for me?"

Will wrapped the garment around his lap. "I don't mind at all, truth to tell."

She attempted a smile, which felt stuck to her teeth. "How long have you been Lord Rourke's squire?"

He pulled the front of his leather cap down. "Ten years?" He nodded. "Aye, that's right. We leave the nursery at seven to be fostered to worthy knights."

"Were you one of the ba—, orphans"—Galiana saved herself—"at court?"

Will grinned at her, having caught what she'd been about to say. "Aye, I'm one of Lord de Mortier's natural born. Me mam died birthin' me, and he died in battle, so Queen Eleanor took me in."

Galiana felt a spurt of gratitude for the queen on Will's, and Rourke's, behalf. And Jamie's and— "Are you all from Queen Eleanor's nursery?"

Will pursed his lips. "Uh, well, aye. Franz went to Normandy as a toddler, though Robbie served under a duke of Brittany, methinks. Godfrey trained as a squire with Lord St. Gerard, and Jamie and Rourke served for Lord Dumfries, afore Rourke was sent off ta Shaftesbury."

"He lived at the abbey?" Galiana thought that was unusual, since she didn't know of a castle there.

"No, no, he worked for Lord Lovell, in Wardorf. But Rourke talked about the abbess there, and how she taught him all she knew of courtly ways."

Since Rourke's manners were impeccable, when he wasn't ordering her about, Galiana thought the abbess had done a fine job. If the boys were fostered at the age of seven to serve as pages, then later became squires, how many homes had Rourke served in?

"Lord Rourke served the queen, too, but Godfrey says the best battle was when Rourke won the keep. The one he wanted to take ye to."

"He won his home? In battle?"

"Well, it was more of a wager."

Galiana repeated, "Wager. A bet?"

Will laughed, happy, it seemed, to get the reaction he wanted. "Aye, my lord is a master at games, and he won most fair."

"Did he make the family move out?"

"Nay, my lady, the keep was empty to begin with, a falling down bailey with naught much to recommend it.

Close to the Welsh border, aye, so the folks around the village scattered like rats rather than lose what they had to raiders."

"What did he do?" Galiana asked, fascinated at this glimpse into Rourke's past.

"He moved in, and soon the peasants returned— once he'd proved he could protect 'em." He smiled. "Then he hired those knights that could come, and then swore his fealty to the welfare of England."

Galiana thought that to be a rather nice way to avoid naming who Rourke swore to.

Rourke remained an enigma. "Did he ask for you specifically?"

"Nay, the queen, she has a soft spot in her heart, she says, fer Rourke, and she said I could do worse than to learn from him."

"I see. And you're happy?"

Will smirked at the feminine question. "Aye. I'm fed, and don't get beat, 'cept fer when I deserve it," he added earnestly.

Galiana realized this was excellent praise indeed.

The subject under discussion came cantering back toward her and Will, and Galiana cursed the flush of recognition her body gave.

Was it her burden to bear, this desire she felt for Rourke's lips against hers? It was doubtful he felt the same, when he loved another.

But then her gaze clashed with Rourke's across the

heads of their horses, and she was jolted into the vision she'd had of a lion's cub, a baby, and the old wizard. In the vision, she stood in the pouring rain with a man, her lover, at her side. The ring grew hot against her hip, and she reached for Rourke's hand.

Then, realizing what she was doing, she quickly dropped her own to her pommel.

"Why are you not leading the fray, my lord?" she quipped.

Rourke had missed her voice, even her sarcasm, not that he would let her know it.

"It is my duty to see why the two of you are flagging behind. Is your horse lame? Are you ill?"

He saw that Will had a cloak tucked around his lap and narrowed his eyes as he studied Galiana. The lack of visual acuity was annoying, almost as much of an irritant as the steady ache in his head.

Shadows blurred, and he'd had a moment or more of total blackness. The idea of being forever hindered in sight was beginning to scare him.

Rourke hadn't even told Jamie how bad it really was. There were moments when his world suddenly went dark, or the pain was so intense that he wanted to lop his own head off.

His stallion was well-trained to follow the lead horse.

It was safer to stay behind Jamie, but then Franz suggested Rourke spend some time with the lady Galiana—to woo her into submission. It seemed like a sound plan, so he listened for the sound of Gali's and Will's talking, and then directed his horse toward their voices.

Woo Galiana into submission, he thought with a sardonic chuckle. There was but one way he wanted her submissive and it involved them both being naked.

He cantered back, stopping so that they'd be forced to slow, too.

"Will, go see that Jamie has water," he ordered, wanting privacy.

"He'll make a good knight," Galiana said, smiling as she watched his squire go without question. "For certes, he holds you in high regard."

"So he should. I'm his lord, and 'tis by my sword he'll make a name, or nay."

"Arrogance is hardly a chivalric trait, and yet you wear it so proudly."

Rourke grunted, then positioned his horse to the lady's left side. "There is a point to this courtly business that goes too far from reason. You said it yourself—strength rules."

"Without chivalry, without honor, men misuse their strength for bullying."

"I cannot see anyone bullying you." Rourke wished that he could see her in truth, but gray spots dotted his vision.

"You've yet to tell me what the Breath of Merlin is."

"You change the subject?" He didn't like this one

either. She should change it again.

Rourke saw her shiver and moved his stallion closer to her horse. "Let's ride as we talk; you shouldn't have given Will your cloak. He must be tough."

"I didn't need it." She hefted her chin, daring him to notice her chills.

She was a shadowy blur, and yet her pride was as clear to him as a summer day.

"Why are you not wearing the ring? You took it. 'Tis important."

"Do you see the wizard, too?"

Rourke's stallion sidestepped in the snow, and his hands gripped the reins. "What wizard? Merlin? Have you seen him?"

"Merlin," she exhaled, the air so cold it plumed from between her lips. Rourke, for an instant of clarity, saw her mouth tipped in a mew of perfection before her face faded back into dull beige. He was getting delirious.

"I thought him a child's tale from ancient times. And yet—there's an ancient feel to the vision, a mystery."

"What?" He didn't understand and reached out for her arm, or what he hoped was her arm, beneath all of the cloaks and blankets. "Are you talking about the ring?"

He was surprised by the bite of jealousy he felt that the ring spoke to her, but it was quickly replaced by the realization that she would be the key to finding the stolen Breath of Merlin.

"The ring is the Breath of Merlin that you were talking

about in your sleep?" she asked, obviously proud to think she'd figured it out.

"Nay." He looked around, not that it helped. "Are we alone?"

She dipped her head. "Aye. Jamie and Will are leading, then Franz and Godfrey." She lowered her voice to a whisper, and he heard the concern in it for him.

It warmed him better than five cloaks could have done.

"The ring is not the Breath of Merlin, my lady. The Breath of Merlin—" He edged his horse closer to hers, close enough that their legs brushed. "'Tis a secret. I don't know why you can see what nobody else can."

"I don't either. But I think I am meant to see it—to witness; that's what they said."

"They who?" He needed more information—but at what price? What was he willing to give that might tempt the honorable lady?

"Never mind that. If it isn't the ring, then what is the Breath of Merlin?" She leaned over, so that the heat of her breath warmed his nose.

He was going to tell her. God's nails! He opened his mouth; only it was Godfrey's voice that rose above the chilled wind. "Riders! Comin' from the village toward us!"

"Get behind me, lady," Rourke ordered, his gloved hand immediately going to the sword at his hip. He grabbed the hilt and pulled it from the leather scabbard, point drawn.

"Rourke," Galiana hissed. "To your left."

He did as she said, wanting to protect her, but his gut wrenched as he realized that until the enemy was close enough for him to see, she had to protect him.

"Warriors," she said. "Three of them."

Jamie thundered next to him, his large war horse spraying snow in every direction.

"Looks like Lord Christien, damn him. Is he impervious to the weather? He had at least four days' hard riding." Jamie drew his sword and settled in his saddle.

"Aye, it took us three to reach the manor, but we made it before the snow fell so hard. Christien must have made a deal with the devil to travel through the storm."

"Who are you talking about?" Galiana asked, staying close to his right side. "Is this the man who was in the village yesterday? Could he have killed Robert?"

"Lord Christien is one of your other suitors, lass."

"Nay, the lady is mine," Rourke said, his chest tight.

"I will choose my own husband. I told you so, and I meant it."

"We needn't argue now," Rourke suggested. The grayish outline of riders and horses came into his line of sight. A banner bearing a dragon flew proudly from the rider's lance. The tall seat. The huge horse. Rourke knew for a certainty it was Lord Christien—a man he despised.

Another of the natural children Queen Eleanor had fostered before sending him out to the world, Christien had grown into an arsewipe with a nasty temper, a greedy nature, and a tendency toward raping his young maids. He was completely lacking in the honor Galiana so highly prized.

"He seems handsome enough," she said.

"He's wearing a helmet!" Jamie protested.

"His shoulders are wide, and his horse is huge," she added as if it mattered.

"I have a huge horse," Rourke said.

"Of course you do." She smiled.

"Do we charge?" Will piped from the back.

"Aye, or should we make a stand? Refuse him entry to the forest?" Godfrey's sword, also drawn, rested toward the ground.

All of his men were loyal to him, at least for now, and that was all he had to work with. Stay and fight? Or run, save the lady, and fight another day?

"He doesn't want to pass us, Godfrey. He wants the lady—by fair means or foul, if I know the bastard." Rourke inched his horse in front of Galiana's. "No matter what else happens, you are all charged with keeping the lady safe."

"Upon my soul, no harm shall come to you, mademoiselle," Franz said, coming to the other side of her.

"Excuse me"—she pulled her horse forward so the heads were all equal—"but Prince John said were three men who could marry me. I think 'tis only right that I meet this man, this knight who is hoping to win my hand."

Rourke gritted his teeth.

"My lady, this is not the kind of man who will appeal to your delicate nature," he tried to say.

"Pah, I am not a girl."

He watched her touch her hipbone, the third time she'd done so. Was she injured? Sore? No, it was as if she held a token of bravery— the ring.

Rourke would wager his horse that she had the ring in her skirt.

"Feeling lucky, my lady?" he asked, glancing pointedly at her hip.

Her pointed chin lifted, and then she drew her hood closer around her face, as if hiding her features.

Smart.

Suddenly an arrow landed at the ground between Rourke's horse's feet. His stallion reared, backing into Galiana's horse.

This was war. Christien obviously had no desire to talk. All he could think of was Robert and all of the blood, and what Christien might do to Galiana.

"To the trees!" he cried, turning Galiana's horse around and smacking its flanks. "Go, as fast as you dare!"

Damn it. Could they make the forest, where the horses would have better purchase?

Jamie and Will used their horses like plows and cleared the way as best they could, and yet Christien was gaining. Godfrey and Franz took the rear, and Rourke stayed right on Galiana's tail.

She was a bundle of blankets, but Rourke knew it

wouldn't matter what she looked like. Christien was after land and coin, and he had his nose so far up Prince John's ass he had a stench about him.

The man couldn't be trusted.

The trees were close, five horse lengths ahead of him. They had to make it.

Galiana bent low over her horse's head, and it occurred to him that she rode as if she'd raced before.

Where?

Why?

Her laughter as they broke through the first line of tall pine trees took him by surprise. She should be terrified, or at the least, cautious, but instead she galloped on as if it were a day of fun and frolic.

He grinned before remembering she needed to be careful.

"Galiana," he called so loudly that she lifted her head to turn and looked back at him. Her large dark eyes were eerie in the frame of her furred hood, "You'll marry me. As soon as we find a priest," he ordered.

"Ha!" She spurred forward, staying right on Will's heels. They reached the section of the forest trail that was barely wide enough across for one horse, but she didn't falter.

Rourke focused on Galiana and kept the pace.

"Ah!"

He heard Franz bellow with pain but didn't stop. There was no place to turn around, and no place to stand

and fight. He watched Galiana lift her head, and he knew she'd heard the sound of Franz's anguish as well.

She didn't stop.

She raced ahead, skinnying her horse past Will, risking, foolishly to Rourke's mind, her horse and Will's.

Then she overtook Jamie, yelling, "Follow close!" as she sped on.

Rourke felt useless as he lost sight of her and had to focus on Will's arse instead. But where there was a narrow trail, there suddenly was a low-hung dark cave, and his stallion reared up. Rourke banged his head against the rock ceiling. He thought fast enough to reach out from the cave and grab Franz's reins to pull his man in and to the back with Godfrey.

The sound of the horse's whinnying echoed in the dark, but Galiana didn't seem to care, as she alone urged her horse to the farthest back—where it was impossibly darker, at least to Rourke's eye.

"Come," she said, her face pale and ghost-like. "Follow me to the other side of the hill. It will take us closer to Scrappington."

Rourke hated feeling incompetent, and he detested having to rely on someone else to save him.

He didn't want to die, though—not today, not until he had tasted the sweetness of Galiana.

He pressed his knees into his nervous horse's barrel chest. "Come on, men, and duck."

The dark gave rise to all kinds of damning thoughts, but

Rourke stayed close to Galiana's horse's surefooted stride.

"You've been here before, my lady," Rourke stated.

"Aye."

"How is it that you, a lady born, would know of such a dark cave?"

"I've had to evade a suitor or two before," she said dryly. Rourke assumed her fright blocked her usual sarcastic tone.

"It is our good fortune, then. Where does this lead?"

This time she clearly jested, "The other side, my lord."

"Galiana, will you marry me?"

"We've no priest."

"We can handfast. 'Tis still common enough among the peasants."

"Now?" she squeaked, and Rourke thrilled over getting past her natural defenses.

"We could."

"I'll not marry you whilst we ride through a damp, spider-filled cave, Rourke. That is utterly ridiculous."

"We have the order from Prince John, and we can get the vows blessed later. We have but to say the words, and then we can celebrate with cakes and people later. My name will keep you safe."

"What words?"

"I, Rourke Wallis, take thee, Galiana Montehue, to be my wife." He held his breath and waited.

"Now you say it," he prodded.

"Nay," she said. "That is so old-fashioned."

"'Tis legally binding."

"We need to turn. Let me think." She halted, and Rourke barely made out a left tunnel and a right.

"This way."

"For certes?"

She shrugged. "If I'm wrong, we end up where we came in. If I'm right, we are on the other side."

Galiana paused, and Rourke watched as she calculated her choice.

"Left," she said. "Aye, left."

"Will ye say yer vow, my lady?" Will called from the back.

Galiana squealed. "What say you? Were you eavesdropping?"

"The sound carries, mademoiselle," Franz said apologetically.

"Oh!"

Rourke, frozen to the bone, practically blind and wet through, wanted nothing more than to drag Galiana, his prim and prudish lady, from her horse to his lap and kiss her senseless.

He followed her, as did his men, past each curve—straight out of the cave . . . and into Lord Christien's waiting crossbows!

Galiana struggled as the bastard tried to catch her and take her for himself.

Kicking and screeching, she yelled, "I take you, too, Rourke, I take you, too!"

Chapter Fourteen

"Let go of my wife," Rourke said, his sword hovering over Lord Christien's wrist.

"Yer wife?" Christien broke out laughing. "I don't think so."

"'Tis true!" Galiana said, the panic rising in her tone making Rourke even angrier.

"We were all witnesses, my lord, so take yer hands off our lady before I slice them off at the elbow," Godfrey said.

Franz and Jamie had their swords out, and even squire Will bore his knife with courageous intent. Rourke knew he couldn't falter, not now in the face of the enemy.

He narrowed his eyes until most of Christien's evil countenance came into partial focus. "How did you know where to find me?"

"You were but a means to an end," Christien said, trying to contain Galiana as she squirmed like an eel in a net. "I wanted this," he said, before doing something that caused Galiana to squeal, which in turn pissed Rourke off even more.

"She's fine, sturdy. She'll give me good sons, as well as her father's lands. Prince John promised me gold, as well."

Jackass. Rourke bowed his head, listening for the first opportune moment to wield his sword; nay, he thought, the small dagger at his waist would fly truer and faster.

"Defeated, Rourke? I told John's man ye didn't stand a chance against me, and I was right." He chuckled, turning toward his men, who laughed with him.

Hoping the arrogant knight wore no neck armor, Rourke fluidly snatched his knife from his leather belt and threw it where he imagined Christien's strong neck to be. He was rewarded with the sucking sound a blade makes when it pierces flesh; then he heard Galiana scream. Had he hit her?

Nay!

He squinted, praying for sight. Rourke was able to watch Galiana, a blob in gray, hop to the ground as Lord Christien slid lifelessly to the trampled snow of the forest floor.

"Saint Mary, Saint Paul, Saint Jude, oh, God's bones, he's dead. I heard the whish of the blade, and then he's dead," Galiana's voice sing-songed in hysteria.

"Come to me, my lady," he ordered through her nervous

litany. He held out his hand, and she took it at a run, easily vaulting to a sideways position in front of him on his horse.

"I'll not faint," she whispered, burying her cold face below his chin. "How'd you do that? You could have killed me."

He felt her tremble, so he rubbed her back. "Nay. I knew where he was. I listened"—he tapped the side of her head—"in here." Her hood had slipped, as had her kerchief and scarf. The lady's hair contained broken pieces of tree and a leaf or two.

She wouldn't be pleased, but it made him smile.

"Bollocks, but that was a damn fine throw," Jamie said, his voice so proud it was as if he'd done it himself.

"Aye," Will said in an awed hush. "Damn fine."

"That was a gamble I wouldn't have dared, mon ami. God surely was guiding your hand."

"Get yer lord, and be gone." Godfrey strutted his stallion before the two stunned knights. "And let it be known that Lord Rourke will not be givin' his lady up."

Rourke focused on holding Galiana close and asked in the lowest tone possible, "What are the two men doing?"

Galiana turned and wrapped her arms around his neck, shaking her shoulders as if she was crying. "They look angry, and uncertain. Young. Newly knighted, mayhap? They're bearing the same dragon banner as Lord Christien."

"Good," he said, patting her back. "I would have

saved you, even if you hadn't returned my vow." He laughed softly.

"'Tis a handfast, my lord, and so be advised that I can still set you aside if you displease me."

Done with her false sniffling, she jumped from his horse to the ground below, putting her hood back over her hair and covering her face once again.

"We can say the vows again and again, my lady." But he knew the one thing that would truly unite him and his brave lady, and it was going to happen tonight.

Galiana could hardly believe she'd been so bold. Telling him she could still set him aside. La, but what had she been thinking? She laughed to herself as she pulled herself up and over her horse. "I'm sorry, good sirs, for leading us straight to the enemy. I turned the wrong way."

"How did ye know the cave was there?" Will asked.

Thinking of the times she'd run away from other prospective suitors, she shrugged. "I grew up in this forest," she said. "But it's been years since I've ridden this way, and I forgot the turn." Riding had gotten to be a hassle that just wasn't worth it unless she had the family knights with her.

And they didn't appreciate riding across fields bareback into the wind. They always told her mother. Sweet Saint

Agnes, she was wed. She couldn't think about it.

"Now where?" Jamie asked, eyeing her speculatively.

"We follow this road, and it leads to the next village."

"Scrappington?"

"No, no. Bartle, a quarter-day ride from there. 'Tis not as big as Scrappington, but we should be able to find rooms there. My father said it took two days of riding to reach Windsor from there when he went over the summer."

"He swore fealty directly to the queen?" Jamie asked.

"Aye," Galiana said, the leftover adrenaline leaving her faintly nauseated. It had been a while since she'd been chased like a fox to ground. At first it had been exhilarating, but Lord Christien's hands had pinched her through her clothes, and she knew—just knew—she'd rather die than be married to such a brute.

"What did your father think of Eleanor of Aquitane?" Jamie's brogue deepened with the question, and Galiana recalled those green, lush forests in her vision.

She looked behind for Rourke, who was plodding toward them. She waited until his stallion could see her horse's tail. "Well, my father said she was regal and still beautiful."

"Nobody could be more beautiful than Queen Eleanor," Rourke said, joining the conversation.

Franz, hearing the comment, sniffed. "Not your usual charming self."

Galiana stiffened, but then acknowledged that Rourke hadn't ever actually seen her and that what he knew of her didn't always put her in the best light.

Jamie discreetly shook his head at the knights and verbally agreed that Queen Eleanor was a beauty. What was Rourke's man up to?

"I meant no disrespect to Galiana," Rourke said earnestly. "But Queen Eleanor has been the subject of love songs and poems; she remains the muse for courtly love."

Galiana felt jealousy mount in her breast for the royal woman who had so captured Rourke's fascination.

Jealousy was not a trait to be proud of, so she tried—she really did—to squash it like a spider.

Stifled by Jamie, none of the other men came to her defense. She was unused to being thought of as less than attractive. "For certes, I would never dare to compare myself to a queen," she answered with forced grace.

Will grinned.

"Your beauty"—Rourke attempted to justify his remarks—"is . . . unique. Your hair is . . . long," he said. Galiana shifted on her horse, wanting to turn around and leave Rourke to freeze. Mayhap he would come to his senses, and his sight, in spring.

"My lord, I don't think a dissertation of my, er, assets"—Galiana was grateful for the hood covering most of her flushed face—"is necessary. Especially not now, with your enemy not far enough away for my liking."

This remark immediately made all the men turn to the rear. She could have told them the way was clear, but she was happy to have their attention on something besides her face.

"Your enemy, too, my lady. One foe vanquished, and another at large." Rourke sat atop his stallion like the arrogant warrior he was. The man was a skilled knight, she thought begrudgingly, and he rarely let down his guard.

"Lord Harold? I suppose he is as evil as the man you just vanquished?" Galiana sniffed, not believing there could be two such knights.

"Not evil, no," Rourke smiled. "But a brute with no honor in battle. And he doesn't bathe."

Galiana wrinkled her nose. "Ew. Never?" She thought of the crevices where dirt could hide, and shuddered. "I suppose you are the best of the lot."

Franz's laughter rang through the trees. "Someday, Rourke and Galiana, you will look back at this day and laugh with me."

Lifting her chin rebelliously, Galiana said, "But it isn't funny now, good sir. Not even the tiniest bit."

They rode on, their horses more easily plodding forward since the snow was not as deep within the shelter of the forest. The thick stands of trees kept out most of the wind as well. Once the road widened, she rode in between Rourke and Jamie.

"I'm beginning to think I might actually live to see Windsor after all."

Jamie grunted, but Rourke picked up the thread of conversation. "You didn't think to trust me? I've proven myself fit."

Knowing he was keeping his disability from his men for a good reason (she thought of dead Robert), she loudly agreed. "You've healed nicely."

"You still have yet to take the stitches out," he reminded her.

"Tonight, when we stop." Her tummy curled as she thought of sharing a private chamber with the man she'd shouted vows with. Though they were not quite strangers, there was so much she didn't know about him. He said he had no family. Family. She hoped the letter she'd written for her parents would calm them so they wouldn't worry.

She could only imagine what kind of story her brothers would tell.

"What vexes you?" Rourke asked.

"How did you know I was upset?" she asked with surprise. "Unless you can add mind-reading to your list of skills."

"You're open to me, my lady. I can tell when your breathing changes, and by how you breathe, fast, or slow, what you are thinking—not specifics, for certes, but the emotion."

Galiana smiled, filled with a rush of self-consciousness. "How useful!"

"A jester's trick," he said modestly.

She glanced at him as he rode next to her, admiring his brow, his nose, his profile. "What other tricks do you know— besides being able to kill a man using your hearing alone?"

"I trained under King William, when he wasn't king." Rourke laughed. "He would tie a blindfold around my eyes and tell me that a true leader didn't need to see with his eyes, but needed to use his mind."

"Strange notion. Are all royals as crazy as that?" Galiana laughed.

"Not all of them," Rourke said, his voice deepening.

Was he thinking of the incomparable Queen Eleanor?

"It must have been an exciting time, growing up, for you. Moving around, meeting new people, learning new skills."

"Nay," he answered, his brow furrowing. "Lonely."

Galiana was afraid to break the fragile truth between them. She had the idea that Rourke didn't let this side of himself free very often. "You had Jamie."

Rourke looked over at his foster brother, who wasn't paying any obvious attention to their talk. Galiana never saw wariness in Rourke's eyes when he spoke of Jamie, and she knew that he trusted the brash Scot completely.

Was he foolish for doing so? Would Jamie betray Rourke to edge closer to Prince John? Galiana cleared her throat, hoping Rourke would answer her question.

He did. "We were together most of the time. Jamie always had brawn on his side. I was the brains," he said.

Jamie snorted, proving he'd been listening the whole time. "Ye were a runt, and if it weren't fer me, ye'd have starved."

"Pox on that! The girls loved me, even then. Betwixt us we ran the nursery, aye?"

"They loved me more often," Jamie laughed.

Galiana bit her lip so that she didn't laugh out loud at the ribald jest.

Even though it was funny.

"I think we're coming to the end of the forest," Galiana said, a mite sorry they couldn't continue the conversation. "The village is an hour ahead."

And it was the longest hour she'd spent in a while. Without the protection of the trees, the icy wind tore through her many cloaks. Her hood and scarves were no match for the freezing rain.

The horses slid in the slippery mess, icicles dangling from their manes and tails.

Galiana's nose ran, but froze, and she couldn't feel her face. Her fingers and toes were aching memories she knew would burn once life returned to them.

The sky was dark. The clouds were gray and turbulent.

She was miserable.

They were in an open field, and each man tried to shelter her from the chilly gusts, but there was no respite.

Finally, Jamie shouted against the wind, "There's lights ahead! It has to be the village."

"I don't bloody care if it's but a single one-room croft; we'll be sheltering in it," Rourke yelled back.

Galiana agreed wholeheartedly, but she didn't waste her precious breath on saying so.

When they arrived at the source of light, they smelled a fire going strong, and smoke rose from the cottage's roof. As Rourke had feared, it wasn't the village, but a single dwelling on the outskirts.

"Could be a sentry's home," Jamie said.

"Could be a leper," Rourke added.

"I don't care if it's the village witch," Galiana squeaked. "If they share their home, I'll be grateful."

"True," Rourke agreed, moving his stallion close to hers. "Jamie?"

Jamie dismounted and ran to the door. He pounded on the wood, calling out to explain they meant no harm.

The door cracked open, and a flurry of faces stacked from the bottom to the top. Galiana wondered how they all fit inside the cottage, and she knew there wouldn't be room for her and the men inside, not without putting the family outside. Which she wouldn't do.

Her spirits sank, but Jamie was busy discussing something with the face at the top, which belonged to the man of the house, it seemed.

The man wasn't without pity, and he gave Jamie a lighted torch, which Jamie shielded with his cloak, and gestured to go around the back of the cottage.

Even a barn was better than this, Galiana thought as her teeth chattered.

Will rode up and grabbed Jamie's horse's reins, and they all followed Jamie as he walked around the side. A large, three-sided outbuilding loomed in the dark shadows.

There would be room for them all to sit at the back and station the horses in the front to block the weather. They could have a fire, and, mayhap, she thought grimly, she could unthaw a little bit.

"Not the night I had in mind for us, Galiana," Rourke whispered huskily. Not due to desire but the ill weather, she was sure.

"We are safe; that is what matters," she said. She tried to move her legs, but they were frozen to the saddle. Galiana hated to play the weak and feminine role she despised, but in truth, she couldn't even wiggle her toes.

Rourke dismounted with ease, damn him. Jamie, Franz, Godfrey, and Will all quickly set about making the place as dry and draft-free as possible.

She felt tears begin at the corners of her eyes, but couldn't stop them from falling down her cheeks. At least they were warm, she thought with a sniffle.

"Galiana? My lady?"

Rourke came around the front of her horse, his hand trailing along the side of the animal until he touched the bulk of her sodden blankets. "Are you all right?"

"N-nay," she croaked. "I can't move."

"'Tis no wonder, my lady, since you are buried beneath one hundred pounds of wet fabric."

She appreciated his teasing voice as much as she appreciated him dragging the blankets off of her body. Will came, and Franz, and they immediately set the sodden mess over wooden posts and bales of hay to dry.

"There is no need to cry, my lady," Rourke said gently. "Come to me." He held out his arms so that all she had to do was tip to the side, and he caught her against his solid chest.

"You're wet," she sniffed.

"We all are," he agreed. "Let's sit by the measly little fire Jamie's got going."

Jamie muttered a curse Galiana would have loved to hear before setting a bale of hay close to the fire—but not so close it would catch sparks.

"Sit here, lass, and I'll get ye something to drink."

She assumed Rourke would set her down and leave her, but he sat and settled her on his lap. Galiana didn't mind at all as he talked nonsense in her ear. Her tears stopped, and Will handed her a piece of bread and some cold chicken. Jamie gave her the skin of ale, and she absorbed the knights' kindnesses.

The men talked low around the small fire, and she found their masculine voices safe. Her toes tingled, and the tips of her ears ached as feeling returned, but she didn't complain.

They were all together in this misery. Galiana felt her lids grow heavy and didn't fight the call of the dream keeper. She went quite willingly into sleep and dreamed of Merlin, blue fire, and lions.

"Want to put her down?" Jamie asked, gesturing to the pile of straw they'd laid for a pallet. "She needs to change from those wet clothes. Will hung some of her cloaks like a tent to allow for privacy. There's a few bales of hay." Jamie was not at all subtle about reminding his friend he had a duty yet to perform for the evening.

"Not yet," Rourke said, enjoying the weight of her in his arms. "I'll take first watch. Sleep, Jamie."

His foster brother looked Rourke straight in the eye, and Rourke had no problem reading the warning there.

He looked away. "Will, Godfrey, rest whilst you can. Tomorrow we'll ride through. The lady isn't safe out in the open." Rourke couldn't protect her on his own, not with his vision compromised. He'd made a mistake, mayhap, making them all leave in a storm.

"We'd be sore put to fight Lord Harold right now." Jamie tossed a piece of wood into the fire.

"I know."

His men thought him hale and perfectly healthy, and if he was acting strange, they blamed it on the lady. He needed Jamie, aye, and Galiana. How to protect his wife once they reached court?

Franz made an odd noise at the back of his throat, and Rourke remembered the man's yelp of pain during the chase through the forest.

"Franz? Where were you hit?"

The knight didn't answer at first, but then he grunted. "Shoulder. An arrow nicked me. 'Tis all."

"Let's have a look," Rourke said before remembering he could stare at the wound all night and not be able to help his man. "Jamie? My hands are full."

"Nice save," Jamie muttered before rising from the pallet he'd already lain down on. "I can clean it, Franz, but me stitches are not as neat as the lady's."

"I can wait 'til morn," Franz answered. "I prefer a gentle touch."

"Careful," Rourke growled, tightening his hold on his sleeping wife.

"No offense meant, my lord, non? But Jamie's more like to tear my arm off."

"I can stitch," Will said. "I've practiced on me lord's tunics."

"Aye, I'll take Will."

Jamie mumbled something about French sissies, and Rourke chuckled. Jamie sat next to him on the bale of hay. "No sense tryin' to sleep until Will's done operatin'. Don't cry too loud, Franz."

Franz retaliated with a string of French curses that everybody understood. Godfrey joined in with the jests, and Rourke felt a sense of camaraderie that had been missing from his life for a while.

Busy. He'd been so busy.

On behalf of King William, whose English wife had just borne a healthy baby girl, prompting the rush for action.

On behalf of Prince John, who didn't trust a soul alive, and thus kept him on a tight leash. John liked to drop tidbits of vital information, and then watch to see what those around him did with it.

Rourke thought back to Galiana's questions at the village and how she'd gone straight to the heart of Prince John, setting him up to win her hand. Why had Prince John wanted Rourke Wallis wed to Galiana Montehue? Was it specific to the lady? Or to Rourke? King Richard needed to be nudged into naming an heir—preferably Arthur of Brittany, whose mother, Constance, had been married to Geoffrey Plantagenet. Galiana had been right: Hereditary tradition said the crown of England should pass to the heir of Richard's older brother.

By right of might, especially if Prince John held the Breath of Merlin, the youngest brother, John Lackland, could win it all.

And then there was Eleanor, the queen who'd taught him subterfuge at her knee. Charm, manners, and deceit were rewarded with rich prizes of weapons, horses, and land.

She'd never told him who his mother was, although she'd hinted broadly that his heritage was royal. And that he could think of her sons as family.

Yet it was King William, above all, to whom he swore his allegiance.

Rourke glanced at Jamie, who was staring into the fire. The shadowy profile of his foster brother was dear to him, and he wondered if Jamie was thinking of the love he'd left behind in Scotland.

"Margaret?" His whispered question floated like an arrow to its mark.

Jamie sucked in a startled breath. "Aye. She's on me mind."

"Do you regret leaving her?"

"Nay. We were given orders, and what kind of knight tells his king to kiss his arse?"

Rourke snorted. "It was wise of you to hold your tongue."

Rubbing his hands together before holding them out to the fire's dancing flames, Jamie said, "She won't wait. I told her not to."

"She loves you."

"Love." Jamie stabbed his booted toe into the dirt. "We don't believe in that, remember?"

"I don't personally believe in it, no"—Rourke ignored the tickle of doubt in his belly—"but for you, mayhap a miracle will happen."

"What miracle would that be, man? Men and women disappoint one another; that's the straight truth of it."

Rourke would normally have agreed right away, but something caught his tongue. Galiana stirred against his chest, her palm rising to cover his heart. The damn thing beat faster.

"We were reared at court, and nothing is true there. Margaret is a woman who doesn't even know what a lie is. She's got"—he looked down at the peep of brown hair poking from beneath Galiana's hood—"honor."

"Aye," Jamie blew out a disgusted breath. "Another reason she's too good for me. She wanted me, ye ken? But I wouldn't lie with her. It was too important. What if I got her with child? I'll not donate my seed to another generation of court bastards. I couldn't leave her to bear the title of whore."

Stunned, Rourke felt his rationalization for bedding Galiana crumble. He'd been careful, true, to keep from spreading his get all over the breadth of Britain, but he'd never gotten to the heart of what drove him to caution.

Galiana was a lady, not a courtesan. Did he have the right to take her maidenhead, when he knew he would set her to the side as soon as his liege demanded it? He wanted her, and now, thanks to Jamie, he was forced to acknowledge that the taking would be dishonorable.

Being a spy didn't mean he could ruin an innocent woman's life.

She grew heavier in his arms, but still he didn't release her.

"What will ye do?" Jamie prodded the fire with another stick.

Rourke sighed, then leaned closer to Jamie's head and whispered, "I don't know. There's a chance King William will not ask me to wed Constance."

"His new babe is a girl. Not the male heir our liege was hoping for. That means he'll want ye closer to the throne."

"Aye." Rourke dropped his chin to the top of Galiana's head. "But do I want to be there?"

Jamie whipped his head around, and clasped Rourke by the shoulder. "Jesu, man, ye can't back out now. The king would kill ye, as would the prince. Ye've got to follow through on the plan. Too many sacrifices have been made."

"Sacrifices." What was one more? He'd lied, cheated, stolen—all for a chance to grab the prize for his king. He'd given up everything. Galiana's breath was steady, real against his face.

What if following through on this plan involved losing Galiana forever?

He and Jamie would be two worldly knights, bereft of the women they lo— Sweet Christ.

Rourke got up, with Galiana in his arms. His duty, which was wrong, warred with his desire for what he wanted. "This shouldn't take long."

"What are you doing?" Galiana's voice was a whiskey croak as Rourke lifted the hem of her damp skirts.

Rourke had never been so glad of the dark. "We must consummate the vows, lest Lord Harold take you. If something happens to me, then you'll get my property."

"The broken-down keep?"

"I have other land," Rourke said defensively.

"This doesn't feel good. I'm cold."

"It won't take long." Despite his dissatisfaction with the circumstances, his cock was ready for what must be done. The feel of soft skin against his fingers as he untied the ribbons at her waist stirred him, and he knew that wishing things were different wouldn't make them so.

"You're really going to—we're— I don't like this at all, Rourke. You promised me great pleasure."

He groaned. "My lady, the men are all on the other side of your cloak. The barn doesn't have a door, and if Lord Harold, or any other enemy that I may have at my back, decides to come in with their swords drawn, I can't be singing poetry to my shy bride."

His hand traveled up her chilled hip.

Then his fingers bumped into the ring, sewed into its pocket.

He could take it; she would never know.

But Rourke couldn't stomach stealing two things from her this night.

Her nipples were pointed with cold; he could see through her sheer chemise. His groin hardened. "Kiss me," he ordered. "How can I do this with your teeth chattering?"

"Wait," she said. "I need my bags."

"I brought them. We are back here on the premise of getting you into some dry clothes."

"Now that sounds lovely."

"You understand that we must do this?" If she could only absolve his guilt . . .

"Aye." She dug around the bottom of the pack. "But just because you are in a hurry doesn't mean that I

330

should suffer. I can do my duty, even though my body is far from ready, with this cream."

"Lotions—even now? I'll not go round smelling like a rose."

"It smells of honeysuckle, and if you want me to keep from screaming, you'll smell of it. I will help you put it on."

Rourke's penis throbbed, and he knew one touch of her dainty, ladylike hand on his manhood would make him explode. He grabbed the tiny jar from her hand.

"I'll do it."

"This is supposed to be fun, Rourke." She took the jar back, and kissed him. Her lips were warm, the only warm thing around them, and he clutched his hands to her upper arms. The chemise was soft, but her skin was softer.

"You need to put the cream on me, too," she whispered against his mouth. She lay back against the bale of hay as if it were a bower of flowers and this was their love nest, and not a stable.

The chemise fell to mid-thigh, and Rourke gulped. Her legs were shapely in his shadowed vision, and the dark patch of hair at her mound beckoned beneath the linen.

His mouth was dry, and his body trembled. He unlaced the front of his breeches, and yanked them down. She shook her head.

"Take them off, my lord."

His boots were out drying by the fire, so it was no big matter to do as she ordered. He swept his tunic over his head, and his shirt, until he stood before her, naked and proud.

"Are you ready?" she asked in a low voice.

He opened the jar of cream. "Aye."

The sound of Godfrey yelling as he stumbled over something startled them both, bringing them back to the reality of what needed to happen. Fast.

"I'm sorry, my lady. I will make this up to you."

She shivered and opened her arms.

A few minutes later it was over, and she was his wife, in all ways. It felt a hollow victory.

Chapter Fifteen

Rourke was avoiding her as if she were a leper.

Hadn't consummating their marriage vows been what he'd wanted? Far from the hot kisses of before, she thought with irritation. Thanks to the cream, she wasn't sore—not from that, anyway. Rourke should be treating her like a princess, and yet he was finding a multitude of things to do that didn't involve being next to her. She'd applied an extra touch of her lavender and lemon scent this morn just to make sure she wasn't repelling him with the smell of damp blankets.

Will was now her boon companion, while Jamie and Rourke rode ahead like the indomitable warriors they were.

This was their third day of riding, and she was worse than miserable; she was molding. The icy rain had crusted the top of the snow with a thick layer of ice, and they were able to plod along on top of it rather than break through the snow to make a trail.

She shivered, wet through all hundred layers, and chilled to the tips of her toes. Her lips were chapped, and the village they'd stopped at the night before had but one room to let and someone else had already rented it. They'd been given thin blankets and seats by the fire, and after paying extra coin, she'd gotten warmish water to bathe her face with.

Galiana couldn't even imagine looking worse than she must at this moment as she rode through the snow alongside the men. It would be her rotten luck that Rourke, who already thought her barely pretty, would gain his sight now and have all of his nightmares confirmed.

"Mademoiselle looks tired, non? Would you like to rest?

She was a hag. Looking over at Franz, who was rather white around the mouth and nose, she shook her head. "If I stop, I may not get back on." She attempted a lame smile.

He nodded and rode ahead, leaving her to her thoughts.

She passed the hours thinking of a hot bath, filled with crushed rose hips. She'd soak until her toes pruned, and then she'd generously apply chamomile lotion to her abused skin, and jasmine oil to her poor lips and fingers.

Windsor castle began to take on a mirage-like state in her head. Was that a stone turret she saw? Or a gate-house? The towns they came to were never London, but not one disappointment stopped her from hoping.

She kept Rourke in her line of sight, as if there were an invisible tether tying her fate to his. If he could ride with shoulders straight, so could she. He never slumped over, nor lost the reins. If only he would come back to talk to her, to ascertain her welfare, but nay. He sent Jamie to ask after her.

Galiana spent a lot of time dreaming of the wizard and the babes. No matter how many times she'd tried to get Rourke to explain the secret of the Breath of Merlin, something always came up, leaving her to her own vivid imagination.

She knew that the vision had taken place in the British Isles. The land was wild, untamed, and mountainous. Scotland, mayhap, at the dawn of man. It sounded right to her. Who was the lover she was with? Rourke's face was constant. Galiana touched the ring for luck, aye, and the hope that she'd travel back again. But the ring, while warm, was simply a ring and not a portal through time.

Her gifts were tactile; her nature, that of a dreamer. Was that why this ring affected her as it did? Not that it mattered—she'd finally been touched by magic, and it filled the empty crevice around her heart that had been longing for something more.

It was very similar to when she touched someone and knew what scent belonged to them alone. Like that, but bigger. More encompassing. It was as if she were

335

coming home.

Rourke had inadvertently given her exactly what she'd always wanted: magic. And he hadn't fallen prey to her beauty, when she'd been beautiful. She sniffed. He'd reached inside her frozen soul and made her feel.

Not always wonderful, 'twas true, but real. Rourke never put her on a pedestal and gifted her with pretty lies.

Mayhap he'd be forever impaired, and then he'd never know the truth of her trumped-up beauty. He might need her . . . but she immediately halted those ill thoughts. Rourke was a warrior; she surmised he was even more than that. He had to see clearly to survive.

It wasn't his fault her heart and body reacted to him the way they did. It was middlingly amusing that she wanted him and he was ignoring her.

His shout brought her from self-pity, and Will immediately perked up in his saddle. "'Tis Runnymede. At last. Not far now, my lady."

Not far was another quarter hour of riding before Godfrey rode back, a grin on his weather reddened face.

Chilled through, Galiana sat up as straight as she could without breaking her spine. She followed the line of Godfrey's pointed finger as he said, "Over there is Windsor. See the stone wall, and the gatehouses there?"

She nodded, noting that the castle seemed to be in a state of construction. New stone had replaced wooden palisades, and the round tower was being added to. "Is that"—she swallowed and thought of her brothers—"the tower?"

Will snickered. "Nay, me lady, that's a different tower."

"That's the Thames, aye?" Godfrey gestured toward the boats. "They'll need to fill their nets; I'm that starved."

Galiana laughed, delighted to actually be within walking distance to a hearth, thick pottage, spiced brandy—and a hot bath.

They passed through the outer gates with no problems. One of the knights recognized Rourke and Jamie and shouted out a "hello." By the time they'd ridden their exhausted horses to the moat, the drawbridge was already down, and across the way stood a lady's entourage, some knights and lords, and a flurry of dogs. A few armed archers watched from the battlements.

She was acutely aware they looked rough. With the exception of Rourke, who somehow repelled red cheeks and chapped lips, they could've been wanderers down on their luck.

Godfrey's dark stubble made him look dangerous and wise at the same time, yet he tugged nervously at his neck. Will's blond mustache underscored his youth. Jamie was daunting with his ginger red hair, a Scottish warrior fresh from the wild mountains.

And poor Franz. He'd fallen the farthest from his groomed visage. His face was pale beneath his normally olive complexion, his lips were pinched, and he had dark circles under his eyes.

Galiana was vain enough to wish for a comb and clean clothes, but cold enough to realize it didn't matter when compared to being warm again.

A messenger had obviously run before them, since they were greeted in welcome.

For Rourke, it was a very friendly welcome.

A lady with dark, chestnut hair flowing freely and without even a sheer silk veil for modesty's sake, glided down the large stone steps. Galiana watched as the woman brought her dainty hand to her mouth in a mew of surprised pleasure, her dark eyes widening with an unnamed emotion. "Rourke?"

Her voice was as rich as her embroidered tunic. Galiana wondered if this was the woman who had stolen Rourke's heart.

She should stay back and let Rourke greet his lady love. Mayhap they'd been separated for a long time, and he would appreciate this meeting.

The ring heated against her hip, and she clucked her teeth, pressing her knees against her horse's tired ribs.

"Nay, lady," Will said, trying to save her from making a royal mistake, no doubt.

Filled with, aye, jealousy, that horrible monster, she rode past Franz and Godfrey until she was directly behind Jamie, and almost close enough to touch Rourke's arm.

"Wait, lass. Ye know not what ye're doin'," Jamie hissed, blocking her horse with his.

So it happened that Galiana was forced to witness the lady, richly dressed and obviously in love with Rourke, run—with delicate, ladylike steps—to Rourke, her hands outstretched as tears of affection dripped down her rose-hued cheeks.

Galiana's stomach churned, and she hefted her chin.

"Who is she?" Galiana asked Jamie.

"Lady Magdalene Laroix."

She remembered that name. Had it been one that Rourke had mentioned in his fever? Nay, in the great hall. It was a good thing she was sitting on top of her horse, for her legs went weak, and she knew they wouldn't support her.

Her world was falling away beneath her, and she had nothing solid to hold onto. The ring couldn't give her love. And she wanted that more than she did its magic. Saint Agnes help her, she'd been a fool to think otherwise.

She curled her fingers into her horse's damp mane. What would Rourke do? Could he see well enough to play off his visual challenges to this, this . . . woman?

He cocked his head, his expression grim.

At the last minute, he held his hand out, and the lady caught it in his, her pretty mouth kissing the fingers of his filthy glove as if she didn't mind soiling her lips.

Galiana could hardly fault the woman for that, now could she?

She closed her eyes, her belly sick.

Franz whispered, "Mademoiselle, you will let another woman touch your man with such affection? Your husband?"

Jamie turned around and glared at the knight, but Will nodded at her with confusion. Godfrey stayed silent.

"My husband," she said softly.

She forced her way past Jamie, riding to Rourke's left side.

The lady stopped drooling over Rourke's poor glove and stepped back, her brow furrowed. "Who is this, my love?"

Galiana didn't wait for him to answer. "I am his wife."

Recognizing what the lovely Magdalene was going to do as she did it, Galiana quickly gestured for Will to dismount. The lady brought the back of her hand to her forehead, distress etched on her face. Staring at Rourke, she said, "I feel faint."

Galiana heard Rourke curse as the lady collapsed at his feet.

"You did that on purpose," Rourke said through clenched teeth. Galiana sniffed delicately, but he wasn't fooled. "Admit it."

"I'll admit nothing."

She dismounted, a mountain of blankets topped with a huge hood. Only her chin poked out to the cold.

"'Tis no wonder the lady fainted. You probably scared her to death."

"Oh!" Galiana clenched her hand to a fist. "I should leave you here alone."

"I'd be safer," he said dryly. "Jamie?"

"I'm here. I tried to stop her."

"There's no stopping the lady when she is bound for trouble; is that not so?" He spoke to the place where she'd been, but it was empty.

"I'm over here, my lord. Oh, aye, you can handle yourself just fine."

"What's going on?" Godfrey asked. "Does yer head ache, Rourke?"

Franz chuckled. "It should, but it's too hard."

Rourke turned toward Franz's voice and jerked his chin. "Piss off."

The castle's bailiff came toward Rourke. "My Lord Wallis! 'Tis good to see you again. I've readied your chamber, but I wasn't aware that your marital status had changed. Windsor is busy this winter, and all the apartments are filled." The man paused, then shrugged. "We've got you sharing your room with your knights. Mayhap your bride could sleep in the women's apartments? Else you can room in the city," the bailiff added hopefully.

"Nay," Rourke said quickly. "The lady will be fine. Could you have someone show her the way? My lady, I will see you at dinner."

He heard her splutter as a page unloaded the bags and cask from her horse. She had no choice but to behave, since they were surrounded by strangers. Rourke grabbed her hood as stomped past him, and she turned around. Emerald green hills and lush landscapes, of a promise made and a bargain struck.

He blinked, and she returned to dismal brown as she shrugged from his hold.

"Take care, lady," he said, wishing he could say more. He'd warn her to be wary of all ears—for they sat above vicious tongues. Beware feminine wiles—that a scorned woman was an enemy, no matter how sweet her smile—but there was no time, and no privacy.

"And you," she practically hissed.

"Mon ami, you've done it again. Made your lady spitting angry," Franz shook his head. "If I'd a lady like that—" He stopped when Jamie elbowed him, and Rourke thought Jamie was being kind to Galiana.

He also rushed to her defense. "I care not about the lady's looks, Franz. She is my wife"—for now—"and I'll not have anyone speak ill of her."

Franz stared at him, and Rourke got the feeling the man was rolling his eyes. But why?

Jamie said, "Will, thanks fer helping Lady Magdalene, but follow Lady Galiana now, and make certain she's comfortable. Then find me in the stables, lad, and help me with the horses."

Rourke should have remembered the fallen Magdalene, but his mind tended to focus on Galiana. He'd begged for her hand in marriage, so why should he be surprised she'd announced they were wed?

She didn't understand the art of subtlety, of keeping information locked away like treasure.

Looking in the direction of the chaos around

Magdalene, whom they were carrying up the stairs and back inside the castle, he wondered exactly how he was going to explain his wife to his lover.

Worse, he knew he'd have to explain things to Galiana.

Magdalene had been a stepping stone in his relationship to Constance. Constance ruled Brittany; well, she and her idiot of a husband did. Magdalene was Constance's best friend, and she lived in Maine, on Brittany's border—where she'd inherited property from her dead husband. The widow was lonely, great in bed, and provided plenty of information about Constance, speaking of her nonstop.

Information Rourke gladly used to further the cause of Scotland.

He'd made no promises to Magdalene, although he would have if she'd required them. Instead, he loved her well, gave her gifts, and became friendly with Constance.

Constance was a blond beauty, with golden curls and rosy lips. Her eyes were as blue as the cornflowers in spring, and her figure was petite and voluptuous. Her sexual appetites were known to the privileged few who could satisfy them.

King Richard had different tastes, else an alliance might have been forged betwixt the two.

What better way to keep all of England's power in one royal household?

Rourke never dwelled on the sexual choices the king made, although he pitied Berengaria. King Philippe was said to wander into either camp, but at least he made an attempt at marriage—proof being that his bride had died in childbirth.

The ways of royalty made no difference to him, although they all seemed to want the same thing—power.

What was power that people were willing to lie and steal for it? Personal honor—again his thoughts went to Galiana—were of no consequence when it came to getting the crown.

He saw that same driven focus in himself, and the taste was bitter.

Jamie kept at his side as they went to their room. "I'll stay with ye, man, else ye might make a mistake."

"Nay, I know this place like the back of my hand. As boys, we crawled over every stair, found every hidden passage. I'm safe here."

"Rourke, don't be stupid. Nobody is safe in court. And ye cannot see the enemy as clear as ye'd like."

Rourke puffed out his chest, insulted. Then he expelled a deep breath. "Aye, you're right. Mayhap we should let Godfrey and Will know I might need some help?"

"Ye don't trust Franz?"

"I don't think he killed Robert, no, but there is something he's hiding. I'd not like to give him a weapon against me."

"I'll watch him closely, too."

"Let's keep my shadowy sight betwixt us. My gut tells me we'll be finishing here soon. The Breath of

Merlin is somewhere in this castle, and who better to find it than us?"

"We need the ring."

Rourke sighed. "Nay. We need the lady, too."

Chapter Sixteen

Galiana felt like she was the poor country cousin coming to visit the city. Which she was, and she didn't like it. Not that she needed to be the center of attention, but being shuffled to the rear of the line galled.

She'd taken her status as a beautiful woman for granted, and she vowed not to do it anymore. So what if she liked being clean and sweet-smelling? If she enjoyed a smooth brow, and curling hair? It wasn't a sin to make the best of one's assets—but she was beginning to feel that mocking her God-gifted looks had been.

Her mother had tried to tell her that beauty had its own magic, but she'd scoffed—knowing the difference between real magic and illusions.

But hadn't Rourke commanded the attention of a gorgeous woman, who even knew how to faint properly?

That wasn't magic, she scowled. It was devious. And powerful.

What if he gained his sight this afternoon and saw what a pitiful creature he'd wed? She'd not be surprised if he set her aside to go back into the arms of the lovely Magdalene.

She followed the page through hallways and up stairs, entirely lost by the time they reached a chamber at the end of the hall. "Could I be any farther away from the great hall?"

The page opened the door, which wasn't even grand enough to have a lock, and shrugged. "'Tis all that's left, my lady," he said, his tone letting her know he didn't think much of her status compared to that of the rest of the members at the castle.

It was on the tip of her tongue to scold the impudent rascal, but then she took a deep breath and said graciously, "Thank you for showing me the way." He didn't look ready to change his attitude, and she couldn't throttle him, so—when sweet words weren't enough . . .

There was coin.

Galiana soon had the young boy racing back down the stairs for water, hot, and a towel. How well he got paid depended on how fast he did his duty.

While she waited, she looked around the chamber. The ceilings were bare of decoration, with the exception of some simple cornices, and the curtains over the glazed windows were a dull burgundy. The room had been designed to handle an overflow of guests. Poorer guests who wouldn't complain.

Four individual beds were in the room, with a chest at the foot of each, and a table with a pitcher and bowl for washing. There wasn't room for an armoire, so there were multiple hooks on each wall space next to the bed. It was designed for function, without privacy, Galiana noticed and squirmed.

How could she seduce her husband here?

It seemed two of the four beds were already occupied. Personal items were strewn on the top of the comforters, as if the other two boarders had suddenly been called away.

Galiana was left with the bed closest to the door, or the bed closest to the outer stone wall. One would be noisy, and the other drafty.

She chose the bed closest to the door so she could escape.

That settled, she set her cask on the bed and opened the lid. The canvas she'd wrapped round and round the cask had protected it from the elements, and her herbs and oils were safely tucked, unbroken, inside. The release of scent into the musty room was strong, but welcome.

Next she took the saddlebags filled with her clothes. Almost everything was damp, except for the green silk she'd wrapped so carefully in leather hides. Shaking the garment out, Gali was pleased it wasn't ruined. She'd have something beautiful to wear at the evening meal with the prince.

For surely he was here?

She laid out the fabric on the length of the bed to get rid of as many wrinkles as she could without a smoothing stone. Then Galiana quickly pulled out her other things, and, after dusting each with a scented powder, she folded and stacked all in the chest at the foot of the bed.

She'd deliberately chosen to keep her jewelry simple. "Less," her mother had said, "was often more."

Her brushes, her cosmetics, her shoes, and a clean tunic and dry linen undergown were set out and ready for her to change into as soon as that boy came back . . .

A knock sounded on the door, and Galiana pasted on a smile as she opened it. To her surprise, Franz stood unsteadily before her.

"Sir Franz—are you ill?"

Three days of riding together made him familiar, and she didn't hesitate to invite him in to sit on the edge of her bed—with the door open, of course.

"Non, mademoiselle, simply tired." He scrubbed his hand over his face.

"Have you a place to rest?"

"Aye, but I must find Will first. Have you seen him? He was supposed to have followed you here."

Galiana's nose scrunched. "He was spying on me?"

Franz appeared startled. "Non! For your own protection, my lady."

"Well, it would be easy to get lost here. It's a veritable maze."

Franz stood, swaying before righting himself. "I'll go the stables again, although neither Jamie nor Will was there."

Concerned, Galiana reached her hand out to rest her fingers on his sleeve. "You should sleep, Franz. It has been a difficult journey."

"And yet you look as fresh as a summer morn," he said with a flourish as he took her hand and lightly kissed her fingers.

"There is no need for chivalry when you look dead on your feet, good sir," she giggled. "Please, find your bed."

"If you need help touring the castle, I offer my services. I know it quite well."

"I appreciate that," she said, wondering if there was something else on his mind.

He nodded, then turned to leave just as the page returned with a huge bowl of water, and two towels. The page's eyes were wide at seeing a handsome knight in a lady's chamber, and Galiana knew her reputation was at stake.

"My thanks, good sir, for bringing me news of my husband. I will tell him of your dedication to me." She simpered and curtsied to Franz.

The French knight smiled speculatively. "You are a treasure, my lady. And quick of wit. Until later."

Galiana gladly paid the boy after he set the bowl down. It occurred to her that if Will could so easily get lost trying to follow them, then she had no hope of ever safely leaving this chamber.

But she didn't want to keep Franz from his sickbed.

"Tell me, boy—do you know Rourke Wallace?"

The page laughed. "Everybody knows Lord Rourke."

"I will pay you, if you can take me to him." Galiana paused. "He's a great warrior, then?"

This time the lad blushed. "Aye. But he's known more for his ways with the ladies," the boy said in an awed whisper. "Ye should know that, aye? Ye're beautiful . . . even covered with mud." Having reached the extent of his bravery, he turned and ran, calling, "I'll be back for ye!"

Galiana's belly coiled with uncertainty. She was at court, surrounded by women just as beautiful as she. Only they had experience swimming through the dark waters. How was she to know who had—she swallowed burning tears—been intimate with her husband? Or was it easier to speculate who hadn't been?

Angry, she bathed, then applied light color to her lips and cheeks. She brushed out her hair until it crackled and set a braided circlet of turquoise leather on top of a sheer ivory kerchief to cover some of her hair. Both colors accentuated the deep auburn waves.

Dressing in fresh clothes was a balm to her spirit, bolstering her flagging courage. She'd chosen a turquoise tunic with moderate tippet sleeves. Her undergown was serviceable linen with a scalloped hem, but her slippers were exquisitely embroidered with seed pearls and turquoise stones.

She added a bracelet of turquoise and pearl, and a dangling necklace of the same. A dab of her own lavender and lemon scent behind each ear, and she decided she was as ready as she could be.

The page arrived, as if by magic.

"Ye look lovely, my lady," he said, adoration in his youthful eyes. Her mother said boys were taught to give a lady their undying adoration, and it was up to the lady to teach the boy, usually a squire, how to behave in a chivalrous manner.

"Thank you," she said, accepting the compliment with a dip of her head. She held out a coin, and the page backed away.

"Nay, my lady. 'Tis my honor to lead you through the castle."

Galiana lifted her chin and smiled with approval. "Nicely done, young page. You will have no problem rising in rank with manners such as those."

He knew the castle well, and before she could assimilate which way to turn, she was standing before her husband's door, unaccountably nervous.

She knew he was sharing a room with his men, so it wouldn't be out of place for her to be in his apartments.

But wait . . . Once again, she was forgetting their shouted vows. She had every right to be here.

"My lady?"

Galiana looked down at the page. "You may go.

What is your name?"

"Gregor."

"I will ask for you again, Gregor. Thank you."

He grinned, showing a missing tooth in a bright smile, and left.

She had no choice but to knock and hope she wasn't interrupting a meeting between Rourke and his knights. How would she explain why she hadn't listened to his order to wait and meet in the hall over dinner?

Lifting her hand, she tapped lightly and the door immediately swung open.

She gasped.

"You weren't expecting anyone to answer, my lady?"

"How—"

"You were loud enough out there. Anybody could have heard you." Rourke gestured to the hall, which looked empty to her.

He pulled her inside the chamber.

If she'd thought her room to be bare, it was nothing compared to the starkness of Rourke's chamber.

"I thought they were bringing you to your regular apartment."

"They did," Rourke said, walking to the bench beneath the window.

"Oh." Did the man not value softness? Or color? He dressed like a man of means and taste, and yet this place—his private space—was barren and cold.

She shivered before joining him on the bench.

Galiana took his hands in hers.

"My lord . . ." she started to say.

He shook his head, his shaggy brown hair shining with gold in the late day sun. The neat row of black stitches along his eyelid gave her a good reason to have come.

"I but wanted to remove these," she said, reaching out to press her fingers against the bristled knots. Even now she couldn't imagine where she'd had the strength to sew such a delicate line against his eye. She'd been so careful to avoid marring his masculine beauty.

He tilted his head and smiled devilishly.

A thrill tumbled in her belly. He would be beautiful wearing an eye patch.

She pulled her sharp knife from the tiny little scabbard on her belt. "It won't hurt," she said, her fingers trembling.

"It will if you poke me in the eye."

"Oh!"

"I was jesting, my lady. Please, hack away. They itch."

"It won't scar," she said, breathing in the scent of him, the masculine combination of deepest night, strength, and temptation that never failed to heat her blood.

"You think I care about scars?" He sounded offended, and she verbally stepped back.

"Nay! Ah, well, mayhap. You are"—she swallowed and removed another stitch with her precise blade—"slightly handsome." Saint Vitus help her, he made her crazy with the fall of his hair around his angled face, his gray eyes that glimmered gold when he was angry, or aroused.

Her breathing hitched, and her breasts grew heavy with want.

"You find me handsome, Galiana?" His voice dropped seductively.

Only one stitch left, and then what excuse would she have to touch him? To mark him as belonging to her? Her body hummed with needing Rourke. Pleasure. His kisses had branded her. Their hasty wedding night in the cold barn had been disappointing. For certes, she knew there was more than that. While she understood why it had been so, she wanted a different memory of loving.

She yanked the last stitch and smoothed the sting with the pad of her thumb.

Then she boldly pulled his head down and pressed her lips to the tender new skin.

"Aye," she angled her mouth to fit his, reveling in the soft, yet firm, texture. "I find you handsome, husband," she said, reminding him that they could love without censure.

Their kiss, hot and lustful, weakened her with desire.

She'd race Rourke to the bed, she thought with a wicked laugh.

He pushed her back when she leaned in for another kiss.

"Nay." His voice was gruff. "I'll not take more from you than I already have."

Galiana's ardor cooled. "What say you?"

"I never should have consummated our vows."

Her chin lifted, and she straightened her spine.

"Why is that? You seek to set me aside? You've won your prize, and you've found it lacking?"

The visage of Lady Magdalene took over her mind. Delicate, a lady, and in love with Rourke.

But he didn't know how she felt . . . Ach, she couldn't tell him now. This hurt was bad enough.

"Lacking? Nay, never you, my lady. You are all things good in this world—too good for me," he said earnestly.

Hurt, Galiana rejected his words. "You and your lies. What do they get you?"

"Truth."

"What?" She didn't understand. She wanted him, he wanted her, and yet he still was not satisfied.

Rourke had to make her understand. Guilt, an emotion he wasn't familiar with, ate at his belly. He cared for her, which is why he never should have slept with her. He should have killed Harold as well as Christien, and then done battle with any man who dared get close enough to hurt her. He needed to explain his feelings. Instead, he said, "Let me tell you about the Breath of Merlin."

"So now you want to talk about that," she scoffed. He could see her blurred outline in the sunlight, but her loving and compassionate nature outshone the sun. His cold heart cracked open, and it hurt like hell. He owed her this much. At the very least.

"The Breath of Merlin is an ancient stone, the size of a man's head."

He sensed her stillness and knew he'd caught her attention.

"Man almost perished on the British Isles. There were all manner of beasts and monsters, dragons, and evil spirits who didn't want man to succeed. Legend says that the majestic lion, ruler of all, was losing power. The two leaders, men, and lion, came to Merlin to strike a deal. They each made some kind of a sacrifice."

Galiana's sudden inhale made him ask, "What?"

"Do you know what they sacrificed?" Her voice shook. "'Twas their babies—a cub and an infant, and there was a granite ledge, and a storm, and I witnessed this. The wizard said the truth had been forgotten, and it's my job to witness this thing done, and right the path."

The hair on the back of Rourke's neck prickled. "King William told me they sacrificed their firstborn males for a chance to blend their power together. But how could you see this?" He tried to fathom the courage it would take to stand before such magical power. He'd sworn his fealty to Scotland before the stone, when it had been swaddled in gold cloth, yet still it had terrified him.

He reached out for her hands, though he knew they shouldn't touch. True, he'd pushed her away, but his desire remained bright. She trustingly placed her fingertips in his outstretched palms.

"I had to see," she said. "Merlin said I was to somehow ensure that the power of the lion stayed in Britain. I got the feeling he was implying, 'beware of France.'"

Rourke felt the air leave his lungs in a whoosh of shock. "Sweet Jesu," he said. King William had the Breath of Merlin, and it had been stolen from him while he'd secretly been bargaining with King Philippe—who, in turn, had been making deals with Prince John—who, so his information went, had agreed to marry Philippe's sister, Alice, and give over part of England in exchange for control of Normandy.

The British kings weren't keeping their part of the ancient deal.

"Why you?" Releasing her hands, he rubbed the aching pain between his eyes.

"What does that mean?" she huffed. "I am not good enough to see these visions?"

"I meant no offense."

"I'm no great name? No seer? I've no magical bent?" She pushed away from him, hurt in every syllable.

"I meant that you have no—" He reached out and grabbed both her shoulders as if he were pulling her close for a hug. She strained against his hold until he whispered in her ear. "You have no ties to the throne."

She stilled, then sank back to the cushions. "I am not of royal blood, and I have no stake in whatever game you play." She crossed her arms, as if irritated. "Who are you? And don't tell me it's complicated."

He ignored her question. "Time is short. I must tell you what I know before the others return." Rourke inhaled before saying in a rush, "Whoever dares to look into the stone can see who would be king."

"So?"

She was obviously not impressed. He had to make her understand. "The stone has been stolen from Scotland's treasury. King Richard has been steadily losing power. Think about who has been gaining it." He kept his tone urgent and low, worried there might be listening ears, even though he'd had Jamie scan the room backward and forward.

Gali sniffed. "You think the stone is here," she whispered. "If it is, then Prince John stole it." Her voice rose. "Have him tell you where it is."

"Hush," Rourke said, pulling her to him so they were cheek to cheek. She was fierce in her loyalty to King Richard, and he admired that. He inhaled her unique scent. Lavender and lemon, a lady with spice.

She resisted his embrace, but relaxed when he didn't release her. If anyone walked in, they would see Rourke and Gali in love's hold.

He pitched his voice low. "He's not my prince. I'm a spy for King William."

Galiana's gasp was the only sign she gave that she'd heard him.

Rourke continued urgently, "I need your help to find the Breath of Merlin."

Galiana kept her cheek to his as she said, "A spy?" He waited for hysterics, but she chewed her lower lip and nodded. "I see now much that makes sense." She paused, then suggested, "Mayhap the prince has already looked into the stone . . ."

"Nay," Rourke said with certainty. "You see, whoever risks looking into the future risks permanent blindness. The man to see into the orb must be of royal blood and be a worthy contender for the throne. Prince John will take no chances until all of his plans are in place."

She tried to pull back, but Rourke held her close— because he liked the way she felt in his arms, not because he was worried she would betray him. "What does that mean? Do you know his plans?"

"'Tis gossip and not proven, but I heard that John actually paid Leopold of Austria to kill Richard, straight-away. But Henry, as emperor, found out, and demanded Richard for ransom."

"The prince is evil."

"King William says the bloodline is tainted with Norman blood. The Plantagenets made a bargain with their own devil and stole away what belonged in Scotland. It is why they are all slightly mad."

"I will help you," Galiana said. He was about to compliment her intellect, when she sighed.

"Tell me about Lady Magdalene. Why did she faint when she heard you were married?"

Pushed off center, as he often was around Galiana,

Rourke released Galiana's arms and leaned against the windowsill. Why was she thinking of that, and not the Breath of Merlin? Or the fact that he was a professed spy?

She sounded, he thought with a grin, like a jealous woman. "What?"

"You heard my question. Who is Lady Magdalene to you?" The outline of that pointy chin jumped as she stared out the window.

"The lady is but a friend."

"Do all your women friends faint at your feet—or was it the shock of finding you had a wife? Is my . . ."

He tried not to smile as she fought to calm her emotions.

"Is your ring meant for her?"

"Ahhh." Yes, that was jealousy in her voice. From what he'd learned of Galiana, she was not used to being out of control. He sought to ease her mood, though it was fun to tease her. "The ring was a prearranged signal from my king to proceed with our plan to come to Windsor." It was easier to tell her this truth than another lie about Magdalene.

She didn't follow the misdirection. The woman was single-minded and stubborn.

"The ring was not a betrothal gift at all?" Galiana asked in an unreasoning tone.

Realizing he was treading on dangerous ground, he answered, "Not until I had to come up with a reason for having it—when your brother stole it from my pack and gave it to your priest." He cleared his throat and looked

361

longingly toward the door. Where was Jamie, damn it?

"Your men were whispering about the surprise wedding. Which was doubly surprising since you had made promises to another." Galiana leaned in toward him. "Was that the lady Magdalene?"

She was like a court-appointed judge, the way she refused to lose sight of the question. Rourke shifted on the bench seat, wishing Jamie—hell, even the queen—would come in and save his arse.

He straightened his shoulders, wanting her respect. "In my line of work, my lady, a man can't always be as honest in one's relationships as you seem to think."

"No honor!" she exclaimed, throwing her hands up in the air. "No chivalry. No matter how charming you are, it is all a lie for you." Her disappointment was tangible between them.

"Your talk of chivalry galls me," he rebutted. "What is chivalry but layers and layers of manners to cover up the ugliness of our society? You believe that lie quite willingly, overlooking the death and dirt of the everyday. You use your lotions and sweet-smelling perfumes to cover the stench of unwashed flesh."

"I would never be party to lies!"

"Others do, and you create the means."

"Ridiculous," she sounded beyond offended now. Unfortunately, he knew what she would be like in the throws of delighted pleasure, the one place where she reveled in the give and take of power. Suddenly the air between them grew heavy, and he knew she was also re-membering their shared desire.

His groin throbbed.

He'd wager his sword that her short pants of breath were no longer caused by her temper. He flicked his tongue over his lower lip, and the intake of air between her lips was the sound he needed.

She desired him as much as he wanted her. Duty be damned.

Reaching forward, he grasped her head and brought her mouth, with her slightly parted lips, to his.

She flung her arms around his neck, and he lay back, welcoming the weight of her on top of him. She sprinkled his face with sweet kisses, while her hands un-erringly went to the hem of his untucked shirt. Lifting the fabric so that she could have access to his flesh, she followed the trail of her fingers with her lips. Sweet siren, he groaned, arching as her sharp teeth clamped over his nipple.

She licked the nub and moved to the other, repeat-ing the action and using her fingers to trail down the line of body hair to his breeches.

"You promised me," she said against his ear, "pleasure."

He was beyond remembering he was going to set her aside at his king's command. He couldn't be as strong as Jamie. Nay, he'd tell the king to piss off, by God. He had to have her. His penis strained against his breeches, aching for the touch, the soft caress of her hands.

She teased, knowing instinctively what brought him to the edge of reason. He would pay this debt for enternity, and gladly.

The door of the chamber swung open, and Rourke, forgetting where he was, thought to protect his lady but ended up dumping her to the floor.

"Fer Christ's sake, Rourke! Lock the bleedin' door if ye're rutt—oh, my lady. So sorry," Jamie exploded in a strangled voice.

Rourke pulled his shirt down and sat up on the bench, trying discreetly to find Galiana. His fingertips touched the top of her head, which was partly covered by a crooked circlet. He felt her shoulders shaking, and reached farther down. She had her face buried in her hands.

"Get out," Rourke ordered his foster brother.

"I have news."

"Give me a few minutes then. And don't let anyone else in," Rourke added in a softer tone.

The door shut gently.

"Come, my lady," Rourke urged, "sit up here. 'Tis my fault for getting carried away with you. You drive my passions, and I am not used to being without control."

She didn't budge.

"You can't hide there, you know. Jamie will be inside again."

"I'm humiliated," she said in a muffled tone.

"There is nothing to be embarrassed about," Rourke chuckled.

"Jamie thought you were having, uh, sex," she squeaked, "and it didn't matter with who, did it? I've heard you're a lady's man, but this—I won't accept such behavior, Rourke. I won't. We are married now."

He brushed his hand down the length of her hair. It felt so soft, and he imagined brown mink.

"Despite what you think, I would not dishonor you. I am no male prostitute plowing his way through the ranks of noblwomen everywhere." He snatched his hand back from her hair.

"But you are," she said, her voice thick with tears. "You sleep with women for information instead of coin. A service, for a price. Is that not what a prostitute does?"

Rourke's gut clenched, and he felt as if he'd been physically slapped.

"You speak of loyalty to the throne. But at what personal cost? When you die and stand before God, will He forgive each wrong because you were doing your duty?"

This so echoed his personal doubts that he reacted from the gut. "You are no saint, my lady, to cast stones. Leave me."

She didn't move, so Rourke pounded his fist against the wooden window frame.

"I told you to leave! Now. And don't come back until I say. When I want you, I will let you know."

Chapter Seventeen

"You don't think you were overly harsh with the lady?" Jamie said, regaining his footing after almost being knocked over as Galiana ran from the room.

"She throws me off balance." Rourke pursed his lips and cursed his aching head. The only time it didn't ache was when he was kissing Galiana.

Jamie shut the door, obviously deciding not to probe the tender subject. "I've a message from the king. It was for you, but I had to tell the messenger you were indisposed."

"King William?"

Jamie laughed. "Who else? Richard is not in the habit of writing, my friend."

"What does it say? I assume you read it, since I cannot." Rourke found himself teetering on the edge of self-pity.

"You're not going to like it."

Rourke felt a cool whirlwind begin at the base of his spine. "Tell me."

"He's not pleased that you wed the lady. In his letter, he says if by some miracle ye haven't consummated the marriage, to set her aside immediately."

Jamie waited for Rourke to announce a miracle, then spluttered obscenities when Rourke remained mum.

"You know I had to bind her to me."

"Nay, ye wanted her. You put us in positions where it was necessary. Admit it."

"What else did the letter say?" Rourke closed his eyes, wishing the sun's warmth were enough to take away the chill ebbing toward his soul.

"Ye'll have to set her aside, or kill her. The lady Constance is amenable to joining forces with ye."

Rourke pushed against the pulse in his temple as bile lurched from his gut. "Nay," he whispered.

"She'll set aside her idiot husband, and marry ye within the month."

"Why the rush?"

"'Tis rumored that John will make his move against Richard soon, and the lady wants her son's position secured."

"She should marry John then."

"Aye, if John weren't promised to Alice, ye ken? It's easier being a bastard these days."

"We've got to find that stone and return it to Scotland." Rourke widened his eyes, furious that all he saw was gray and dull outlines. Enough to keep him from bumping into the walls, but hardly enough to smoothly plan an extraction from a fortified, enemy, castle.

"Did she give ye the ring?"

This time it was Rourke who buried his face in his hands. "I didn't even ask her for it."

"Bollocks!"

"Send Will after her. Mayhap she'll give it to him," Rourke said, knowing the life he'd dared to hope for had been nipped in the bud. He couldn't kill Galiana.

He'd have to set her aside after all, which would be the death of him.

His entire body pounded with an ache that could only be eased in Galiana's embrace.

"Will never met me at the stables, the bugger. I put the horses away meself and almost missed the messenger. The king's around, I think. Close enough to watch what ye do for himself."

Rourke shuddered. "Will never met you? That's odd, man. We need to find him."

"Bloody lot of help ye'll be," Jamie snorted.

Franz knocked once and entered the room. Rourke was hit with a scent, lavender and lemon, over something else. "You've seen the lady Galiana?"

"Oui, and what a welcome to you, too."

"Is she all right?"

"She was when I saw her earlier in her room. Nasty little chamber overlooking the back courtyard."

Filled with unreasonable jealousy, Rourke gritted

his teeth. "Why were you in her room?"

"Relax, mon ami, I was but searching for Will. The lad disappeared, and I needed my bags."

Now goose bumps chased the chills in his veins. "You were looking for Will, as was Jamie? And neither of you could find him." He thought of Robert, of the smell of blood mixed with perfume. He pulled the enameled device from where he'd pinned it inside his tunic. Betrayal.

Franz said, "Where did ye get that, Rourke?"

"It was Robert's."

"He served Brittany? I never knew that," the Frenchman said.

"It was before he swore his sword to me," Rourke said with a shrug, noting the interest in Franz's tone.

"We'll go look for Will again," Jamie announced. "He's probably in the kitchens, stealing a bite from the maids."

"For certes, he's a handsome lad—mayhap he's stealing more than that, eh?"

Franz's chuckle didn't ease Rourke's apprehension.

"Are you joining us, Rourke?"

Careful to keep his gaze toward the window, Rourke answered curtly, "Nay. I've errands of another nature to do."

Jamie shuffled Franz out of the chamber.

Will was missing. Where was Godfrey?

Rourke couldn't keep track of his own men. How on God's earth was he supposed to find the magical stone? He was useless.

Galiana realized she'd taken a wrong turn when she found herself in a lavishly decorated hall. Two servants in neatly pressed clothing went from chamber to chamber to see if they were needed.

Most guests said no. Just as Galiana was gathering the courage to ask for help, one guest answered the door using a lovely voice that Galiana immediately recognized as belonging to Lady Magdalene Laroix. Her fingers clenched, and the ring she'd tucked beneath her tunic burned.

She stepped back against the wall, shielded by a marble statue and a large fern.

"I need refreshments," the lady snapped. "Ale and meat will be adequate."

The servant quickly agreed and rushed to the lady's bidding. Galiana knew the right thing—the honorable thing—would be to follow the servant down the stairs and find her own chamber.

She stayed hidden.

Once the hallway was clear, Galiana idled toward Magdalene's chamber door. While finely constructed, the rooms had an echo that allowed Galiana to hear from the outside.

No wonder Rourke hadn't wanted to speak freely.

He was a spy. She was not a spy.

So what did she think she was doing?

Her pulse raced as she pressed her ear to the wall, sweeping her gaze up and down the hall so she wouldn't be caught. Magdalene's cultured tones grew harsh and guttural as she berated whomever she was with.

"You bring me this news and demand payment? Where is Robert?"

A man's voice, low and unrecognizable, mumbled something that made the lady screech with outrage.

"You lie," she said. "You killed him?"

A mumble.

"Then who?"

Galiana jumped back as the door to the chamber opened, although the lady had her back to the hall. Shaking, praying to all the saints that she wouldn't be caught, Galiana held her breath.

"You can leave, if you think to threaten me. I'll not have it and neither will Constance."

"My lady, you misunderstand," the man's voice, while muffled, was clearer. "I am protecting your reputation, for a small fee."

"Blackmail." Magdalene slammed the door closed, and Galiana darted down the hall to the first set of stairs she could find. Intrigue was around every corner, and she was ill-equipped to deal with the challenge.

How did Rourke manage it?

Ending up in the courtyard by the kitchens was a relief, and she searched the bustling servants for her only friend in this castle. Gregor. It was like trying to find a blond needle in a haystack.

Pages, squires, kitchen scullions, and cooks all had chores to do, especially this close to the dinner hour. Racing back and forth, they didn't stop to ask her what she needed, although quite a few almost told her to move out of their way before realizing she was a lady of rank.

Galiana passed a boar on a spit and smiled at the young girl whose job it was to turn the crank at an even pace. Remembering Bertie and Joey and her brothers made her eyes well with sadness. Would she ever see them again?

She shrieked as a beefy hand landed on her shoulder. "Lass, what brings ye here?"

She whirled, grateful to see Jamie and, behind him, Franz. She looked beyond them, but Rourke wasn't there. "I'm lost," she said, a tear spilling from her eye.

Franz immediately offered assistance, but Jamie elbowed the knight aside. "Ye'll be fine. Have ye seen Will?"

Galiana shook her head. Should she tell them of overhearing Magdalene's argument? The two men would probably laugh at her, and tell her that lover's spats were common at court. It hadn't sounded like the two were lovers, though. Indeed, it seemed as if the man was a stranger to Magdalene, and whatever he'd come to tell her had been important enough for her to grant the man audience.

In private.

Because she was being blackmailed. The man's voice teased at her trained ear. She knew it; she just couldn't place it.

"Godfrey's not turned up yet either," Franz said in an effort to explain Jamie's gruff question.

"I can ask around, if you tell me where to look. I can't even find my own chamber, though, so I don't know that I'll be much help."

Jamie shook his head. "We'll get ye back to your room. The last thing we need is another person lost."

"My lady?" Galiana looked down as the young girl at the spit pointed toward the back of the brick bread oven. "He wants ya," she said with a bob of her little head.

She looked over and saw her page waving at her from the corner.

"Gregor," she sighed with relief. "My page," she explained to Jamie and Franz. "Don't worry about me now—find Will and Godfrey. And"—her stomach tensed—"will you save me a seat with you all at dinner?"

"But of course!" Franz bowed low, and Galiana was disturbed by the pinch of white around his mouth. He didn't look good. The girl called for her again. "He says to hurry, my lady."

"Go, then," Jamie ordered. "Stay in yer chamber; do ye ken?"

His amber eyes dared her to disobey. "I understand," she agreed.

They turned out toward the stables, and Galiana rushed to the back of the ovens. The heat hit her like a wave, but after being so cold, she didn't mind at all.

Gregor wasn't alone. Will slowly met her gaze.

"Will? Will! Jamie and Franz were looking for you." She stepped away to call for the knights, but Will jumped up and grabbed her arm.

"Nay, my lady. I've a message for your ears alone."

"Oh. Will—" Galiana sighed, hoping the squire wasn't going to profess his love for her. She'd hate to break his heart, but she'd be gentle. If anything, this experience of lusting after Rourke had given her compassion toward those who felt they loved her for her beauty alone.

She wasn't vain; it was a simple fact of life that she was beautiful. At times it was difficult, and at other times it made things simpler. She was just now beginning to recognize its potential power.

She gestured for Gregor to give them privacy.

"From the most beauteous woman in the world," Will sighed, his heart shining from his eyes.

"From the most beautiful?" Galiana reiterated, remembering the same phrase falling from Rourke's lips. "Who?"

"Queen Eleanor," he placed his hand over his heart.

"Oh." Once again, she couldn't compare to a queen. "Well—what does she say?"

"She wishes to meet with you and Lord Rourke tomorrow morning, just before the sun rises," Will said in a hushed tone.

"Where?" Galiana joined him in a whispered conversation. Mayhap intrigue was easier to learn than she'd thought. "Why can't she speak to us here?"

"Nobody knows the queen is near. She does that sometimes, to keep her hand in, she says." His voice was filled with admiration.

"I'll get lost, for certes." Galiana panicked.

"Lord Rourke knows the way—tell him to take ye to the old manor lodge; he'll know."

She was sure he would, damn him.

Pausing, Galiana asked quietly, "Does Rourke know you are in league with the queen?"

Will shook his head, his expression a mixture of regret and pride. "Not yet, my lady, but I will tell him this day."

"You have until dinner, Will, else I will say something. He believes you to be loyal."

"I am loyal! 'Tis lucky for me that my lord Rourke does nothing against the queen, aye?"

Galiana almost asked if Will, and the queen, knew about Rourke's first allegiance to Scotland, but then her brow scrunched with confusion and she kept her mouth closed. What if she asked and gave Rourke away?

"If you go now, Rourke is alone in his room," she suggested. "I don't suppose you know where I am staying?"

Will laughed and pointed her to the correct hall. "Up those stairs, my lady. Stay left. Ye're at the very end of the hallway."

When she reached her chamber, it was occupied. Her things were laid out on her bed for all to see, and the two ladies in the room were sorting through her jewels.

"What are you doing?" Galiana demanded, her spine stiff. "Those are mine."

The two ladies, both pale but one blond and the other brunette, immediately dropped the baubles with a clang.

"I was searching for . . ." The blond glanced at the brunette, who simpered, giggled, and shrugged.

"You caught us being nosy."

"My apologies," the blond said, her cheeks pink. "I'm Lucinda." She started putting things back in the jewelry bag.

"I'm Rohan," the brunette said, still not one whit sorry, Galiana noticed. "You've got much nicer jewelry than the normal downtrodden second cousin to a lady that usually gets the end of the hall chamber."

"Is it true ye're married to Rourke Wallis?" Lucinda's smile was angelic. Galiana didn't trust it, especially since the lady was now uncorking and sniffing each of Galiana's scents. In her opinion, angels would have better manners.

"Why aren't ye makin' the knights sleep in the barn or something, so that ye can have that gorgeous man to yourself?" Rohan ran her hands down her hips. "Or does he prefer the company of his men to yours?"

"Don't be mean," Lucinda tittered nervously.

Galiana, so glad she'd not kept the magic ring with the rest of her jewelry, went to the bag and dumped it again, deliberately sorting and counting the contents. She arched her brow, and held out her hand to Rohan.

"My falcon brooch?"

Annoyance crept across the lady's face as she shook the ornament from her sleeve. "I was going to borrow it."

"Most people ask first."

"Come on, Lucinda. Let's not stay here with her 'highness.' Don't ye just hate people who think they're better than everyone else? I'd wager Lord Rourke doesn't want to stay with his wife. It makes dallying easier, eh?"

Lucinda, cheeks flaming, followed her friend from the room, her wrists smelling suspiciously like violets.

"'Tis true I'd not turn him down, if he were to glance my way." Rohan turned and gave Galiana an evil wink.

Gali's vision turned red. "You're not his kind." Rohan's comments cut, whether she wanted to admit to bleeding or not. "Too cheap." She shut the door in the woman's face.

Was the wench right? Did Rourke not want her around? Did she put a crimp in his spying style? Did he actually have to pleasure each woman he pried information from? Which made her wonder what he'd wanted from her.

She knelt by the side of her bed, her stomach sick. This was the man she loved, and, aye, she loved him. She couldn't stay married to him, because he would tear her heart out and stomp on it without a second thought. She couldn't survive such a brutal onslaught.

Too numb to cry, Galiana rose, choosing the green silk dress for her first court appearance. She was a

Montehue—descended on her mother's side from Queen Boadicea. She was a warrior, fighting with the gifts she had: her beauty, her charm, and her grace. If Rourke wanted the Breath of Merlin, then as her last gift to him, she would make sure he had it.

By the time she went downstairs for dinner, she was armed from her small feet encased in delicate heeled slippers to her sparkling white teeth. She was hunting for a prince.

Rourke sat next to Jamie, Godfrey, and Franz. Will served them, as was his job as squire. The boy had been acting strange, but Rourke hadn't had time alone to question him. Will claimed to have gotten lost and somehow ended up in the dog kennels.

The boy lied, albeit smoothly. Rourke recognized the signs.

"Where is the lady?" Impatience and concern for Galiana wore at his frazzled temper. What if she was being mocked for not having the current fashions? Galiana was a disaster, and all he'd seen were pieces of drab tunics and cloaks; she had plenty of heavy cloaks. Women's tongues were deadly and sharp as an arrow point. Sometimes as poisonous.

"For the hundredth time"—Jamie drank from his mug, wiping the foam from his upper lip—"I don't know."

"Should we have Will go searching for her?" Franz

asked. Worry was evident in the question, along with something else Rourke couldn't put his finger on. Did the knight have feelings for Galiana, beyond mere flirtation?

He'd kill the little Frenchman before he ever got the chance.

"Nay, here she is," Will said in an awed voice. "My lady!" he shouted above the din—so loudly it got the entire hall's attention. Rourke was amazed when everyone stopped talking.

Poor Galiana. What had she worn? He would not have her treated with scorn, nor humiliation. He stood so quickly the bench skidded back, even with Jamie and Franz's weight on it. "My lady! I've saved a seat by me. I've not touched a morsel, waiting for your hands to feed me."

Jamie snickered. "Too late to be charming; the lass has seen your true colors." He cleared his throat, holding up his hand to his mouth, and then said, "She's lookin' this way."

Will sighed. "She's coming toward us, a vision in green."

"Green?" Rourke didn't care for green, but he kept his welcoming smile in place until he felt her hand on his arm.

"Thank you, my lord Rourke. 'Twill be my great"— she paused for effect—"pleasure to tempt you with the most succulent pieces."

Laughing applause sounded throughout the hall as the court approved the newcomer.

Rourke swallowed. His prim, country lady sounded

like a skilled seductress. His body throbbed to life, re-membering the feel of her lips and the scent of her skin. The unkept promises of pleasure between them.

If he saw her dress as a shade of brown, and yet it was green, then what color, in truth, was her hair?

The length of it brushed the floor as she sat on the bench betwixt him and Jamie. The color mattered not one bit as he easily imagined himself and Galiana naked except for the covering of her soft curls.

He bit the inside of his cheek to stay focused on the here and now.

"Thank you, good sirs," she said in greeting to all of the knights and lords at the table. Jamie had been careful to seat him with men they knew.

"Greetings, my lady."

"Well met, my lady."

"Would ye care for some wine, my lady?"

Rourke heard the sincere desire to please in each of the men's voices, and he didn't like it.

"Will you not choose something for me, my lady?" He put his hand out on the table, hoping to cover hers. Instead, he knocked over a goblet.

"Ah!" Galiana quickly righted the mess with a laugh. "How clumsy of me," she said, moving her napkin around the damp puddle while calling for Will to get more napkins.

"It was my fault," he growled.

"Nay, although you are most kind to take the blame,

my lord."

"Will it stain?" he whispered.

"'Tis water, my lord," she answered back. She leaned over, her lavender and lemon scent encompassing him. "Open your mouth, sir, and have a bite of this. Game hen. The thigh is the best part."

"I prefer the breast," he said, accepting the meat and chewing. He wanted her as ruffled as he was. He liked it better when he was in control.

Will rushed back, coming to a halt behind Rourke. "Here are some towels. My lady, the prince wants an audience with ye."

Rourke stiffened. He was in no position to tell the prince nay, and he was in no shape to protect his wife from the royal upstart.

He detected the faintest of tremors in her voice, and yet she answered graciously, "For certes! I am most eager to meet Prince John and thank him for his hospitality."

"And yer husband thanks him, too," Jamie suggested with a jab to Rourke's ribs.

"I'll go with you," Rourke said, praying he could play the part of loyal follower without giving his hand away.

"Do ye think that's wise?" Galiana asked. "I will go alone."

"The prince didn't invite ye, Rourke. But ye'll have me, my lady," Will answered gallantly. The squire was coming along, Rourke thought. Eleanor would be proud.

If he squinted, Rourke could make out the raised

royal table on the dais. Jamie had said Constance and Magdalene were both sitting with the prince, as was William Marshall, who'd been traveling through and was staying just for the night.

Rourke would bet the man was gathering information on the barons present, and that the wily William Marshall, loyal to whatever man was in power at the time, was quite interested in who sat closest to the prince.

Jamie had set them two tables down—close enough to be seen, but not so close that the prince could overhear their conversation. Jamie excelled at reading people's lips, so he sat where he had full view of the royal table.

Rourke would owe his foster brother once this mission was over, for taking on the lion's share of the work. Mayhap he'd gift him his property in Wales? Far away from Scotland and King William's wrath, should Jamie decide to make a life with his Margaret.

"I'll be back, my lords. Save me a bite?" Galiana's voice poured over him like sunshine. She lifted the goblet of wine and drank before getting to her feet.

"For courage?" he jested softly.

She leaned down to kiss his cheek and said, "Aye, pray for me that I don't faint. 'Tis overdone here at court, methinks," she laughed.

He grabbed her by the hand. "You will be fine. He's a man, like any other."

She left, and he groaned. She'd been wearing the

magic ring on her hand. God help them if the prince recognized it . . .

They were all going to be drawn and quartered.

Chapter Eighteen

A man like any other? She couldn't have disagreed more. Prince John sat back at the royal table as if he'd stuffed himself and could no longer move. His hands were weighted down by jewels, and she quickly turned the ancient ring on her finger around so that a simple band of silver was all that showed.

Could she flirt with a prince without getting burned? Or should she act the modest lady, awed by his power? Men liked that.

She didn't hesitate to follow her instincts.

Smiling with but a small corner of her mouth lifted so that her cheek dimpled, she glided toward the dais. Galiana stopped at the bottom stair and dipped her head, inhaling the underlying scent of sandalwood and ash. Prince John's cologne.

The women at the dais giggled, but Galiana kept her composure. The lady Magdalene whispered something unintelligible to the pretty blond next to her, who laughed.

"Ye needn't bow to me, my lady," the prince intoned. "Come, join me."

She slowly lifted her long neck, knowing his eyes were taking in her entire form. Her slender fingers, her narrow feet. Her pale, slim neck. She saw him catalogue her assets and knew by his parted lips that he was captivated.

Galiana didn't bother glancing at the women, who understood they'd met a rival and laughter wouldn't be tolerated. She took the seat next to the prince's, folding her hands in her lap and gazing at him with wide open, interested eyes.

"Your name?" He reached for her hand and kissed each fingertip.

Galiana hid the coil of revulsion his full, greasy lips brought to her sensitive skin. He was a snake, hiding and biding his time. She lowered her eyes demurely.

"Lady Galiana Montehue."

He lowered her hand and laughed in surprise. "Really? And tell me, lovely lady, are you married?"

"Aye." She made a show of gesturing to where Rourke sat, tension in the breadth of his shoulders. She prayed nobody else would notice. Mayhap it was caused by his feelings for her.

"To Lord Rourke Wallace?"

Gali chuckled, deep and throatily. "Aye, my prince. He won me in a wager."

Prince John choked on his wine and hastily set the goblet down. "Aha, so you know about that?"

"I was surprised to find that my prince thought I was a worthy prize." She laughed softly as his eyes grazed her figure. "How would you have heard about me, a simple country girl?"

"Simple?" He reached over to caress her knee. "If all country girls were like you, I'd take up the plow."

Galiana giggled appreciatively.

"Your father was here over the summer, and I admit I overheard him speaking with my mother. His older daughter had just wed, which left you, and an even younger daughter, aye?"

Careful to stifle her fear as she thought of lovely Ela as a pawn in this prince's hands, Galiana sighed. "'Tis true; he was here."

"He was asking a boon of the king—something about a special dispensation?"

Gali bowed her head, knowing she had to hide her anger. The prince had known about it all along and had deliberately chosen to disregard the matter. Rourke had been right. She lifted her face and smiled. "That's hardly important now. Wouldn't you agree, my prince? Thanks to you, I've met a man I'm proud to call husband."

"My lady, you've charmed me." Prince John rubbed his hands together, lackadaisically meeting his squire's eyes as he motioned for him. "Perhaps I was too hasty. I have a gift for you. A second chance, if you will."

Confused, Galiana kept nothing but rapt interest on her face. The ring burned into her palm, and she knew to be on her guard. An ominous feeling pervaded her being, and she allowed a wrinkle of concern to settle on her face. "My prince?"

"It's been brought to my attention that I may have been"—he paused—"rash in my choice of husbands for you. Your good servant—" Prince John gestured for his squire to come forward, and Galiana couldn't contain her shock at seeing a bent, dirty old man being escorted onto the dais.

"Father Jonah?" Galiana rose to her feet, her stomach revolting against the harm done to the priest. "What is the meaning of this?"

"Whoa, ho," Prince John laughed. "There's the fire I was looking for behind the pretty mask. So you claim this man as one of yours?"

"Aye." Galiana wouldn't cater to the prince's sick humor, nor would she allow herself to be the butt of his joke. "What has he done? Pray tell all of us"— she gestured to the rapt faces watching the prince's sick show—"what this old man has done to offend you. I will see to it myself that he makes amends."

She saw William Marshall purse his lips in thought, but she knew she had to battle the prince alone. For her family's honor, she would win. Thanks be to Boadicea, she had her own armory.

Using her cat-shaped eyes to enthrall, she tilted her lips in an inviting smile. She sat back down in the chair, letting her hair cascade over the prince's bare forearm. "Of course, he shall be punished again for whatever misstep he's taken."

"He claims I've made a mistake. I, the prince of England. And that this dispensation allows you, a mere woman"—his eyes raked her with lust and the perverse need to subdue that which threatened him—"to choose your husband for yourself."

Galiana moistened her lips and let her lids lower before widening again. Accepting his challenge.

"'Tis the truth he speaks, but as I said earlier, the point is moot. You've chosen my husband quite wisely, my prince." This time she leaned over to rest her hand appealingly on the prince's hand. "My thanks." There. Acknowledgement that I bow before his power . . . Fool.

He stared at her without blinking, and she kept her teasing smile in place.

William Marshall started a slow clap. "Well done, my lady. For certes, I'm not clear why you have such a thing as the dispensation, but if the king signed it, then it would hold in court."

"'Tis the queen mother's signature, on our king's behalf," Galiana replied modestly.

"However, if ye're happy with Lord Rourke"— William Marshall gestured at her furious but gorgeous husband—"and I don't see why ye wouldn't be"—he paused while the crowd laughed aloud—"then Prince John did indeed do you a great service."

Galiana vowed to say a thousand novenas for William Marshall's soul. He'd saved her from an impossible position by joining her game. She knew the prince had been ready to nullify her marriage to Rourke—for whom? And why?

He'd been the one to marry her off in the first place!

She didn't miss the daggers the golden-haired woman to John's right was sending her. It was clear to her that the blond and the prince were romantically linked. Magdalene glared at her as well. How to extricate herself from the snake pit?

"I have no gifts to give such a man as you, my prince." Galiana dimpled innocently. "But if you like, I can sing and play a tune for you."

His brows rose, and she covered her unintentional innuendo by standing and gesturing to Will. "Now, if you'd like. Will, can you fetch my lute? I'd like to play a song for the prince, and all of his court."

The golden-haired lady made a mew of distress, and Galiana couldn't help but look at her. Beautiful, as a royal bride should be, yet she wore too much rice powder to try and cover the circles under her eyes. A silver chain dangled down her slender bosom, and at the end of the chain was an enamel pendant. It was shaped like a shield, with red trim and blue and yellow checks, with a rose centered on it.

Brittany.

She frowned, something about the design sparking her memory.

"What is it, Constance?" the prince asked. "Are you not in the mood for music?"

The golden beauty whispered something in the prince's ear that made him chuckle before he looked at Galiana with a shrug. "She's worried you'll ruin her dessert."

Accepting the sting of the public insult, Galiana dipped a graceful curtsy. "Mayhap another time then." She'd made the offer, been rebuffed, and now she was free to go. With her priest, of course. Constance was a bitch, and there was no other word for it.

"I'll make certain Father Jonah remembers his proper place, my prince. May I take him now, afore he offends you further?"

Prince John waved his hand, acting bored with the game of cat and mouse. He allowed Constance to feed him bits of apple while Magdalene chattered like a magpie, jealousy over Constance evident on her stealthy expression. Who had the woman been arguing with in her chamber? The prince?

Nay, the voice had been deeper.

She met William Marshall's gaze, sent a silent thank you, and walked as stately down the stairs as if she were being squired by a king, and not a broken priest.

A brute of a knight who smelled like latrine water

tried to catch her attention, but she ignored all, keeping her eyes straight ahead. She didn't even stop at her own table, but kept going until they were out of the great hall before slowing to a shuffling walk that was easier on Father Jonah.

"I thought to save ye, my lady. Instead, he kept me locked away. I'm sorry. The boys?"

"On their way to Celestia's."

"Priest!" Rourke thundered as he caught up to them. Had he run from the hall? Ruining her graceful exit?

Jamie, by Rourke's side, shouted, "You deserve to be flogged, and worse, for what ye did to the manor!"

The priest lifted his head, his lip swollen and stained with dried blood. "I did nothing, asides get Ned out of there before either of ye killed him."

"Layla poisoned the stew," Galiana said sternly. "Not Father Jonah."

"We know about Ed," Rourke informed the priest coldly. "What do you know of Sir Robert?"

"Sir Robert? Your knight? Why would I know something about one of your men?"

"He's dead, Father. Murdered, after paying Layla to add buckthorn bark to the food." Galiana patted the priest's shaking arm to calm him.

He made the sign of the cross with trembling fingers. "I know nothing about that."

"You know a lot about nothing," Jamie scorned.

"Where are Franz and Godfrey?" Galiana searched,

but didn't see the two men.

"Godfrey took Franz to our chamber. The meal was burning his guts," Jamie rubbed his belly.

Rourke exhaled, allowing his frustration to be seen very clearly. It was unusual for the man to show any honest emotion, and Galiana realized he must be more shaken than she thought. If only he would let her soothe him.

However, his voice was smooth as he said, "Let's go to the stables; we must talk. Galiana, well done, indeed. William Marshall had the right of it there. Prince John was going to set our marriage aside and give ye to Lord Harold."

Rourke wanted to see Galiana—not just the shadows of her. He knew her with his fingertips; he knew her with his lips; he knew her with his heart.

He couldn't tell her he'd been ordered by King William to set her aside and wed Constance—especially not after she'd just told the entire court how happy she was being married to him.

And he couldn't kill her.

Sweet Jesu, how his life of lies was catching up to him.

"Prince John—" he started to say.

"Are he and Constance having an affair?" Galiana's question pierced another hole in his mental blindfold, and Rourke grabbed Jamie's arm at the realization. She added, "The woman glared daggers at me."

"Christ's bones," Rourke breathed. "What if they—"

"We need to save our talk for the outdoors," Jamie warned.

Will came running, Galiana's lute in his hands. He skidded to a stop. "What happened?" He breathed heavily. "I thought ye were going to play for the prince."

"Outside!" Rourke thundered, not willing to waste another minute on lying.

Jamie led the way, with Rourke right behind him. He kept his hand on his sword, his expression stern. He didn't want any interference. It was time to clear the air.

The stables were familiar, and Rourke felt his tension subside as the smell of hay, apples, and horseflesh wafted toward him. He and Jamie had convinced more than one pretty maid to roll with them in the straw, he reminisced with a smile. Although now the only "pretty" maid he wanted was a prim, sarcasm-prone lady who had compassion and grace.

He had to break her spirit, or her neck.

He didn't like either option.

Rourke could make out the horses hanging their chins over the stalls as he walked down the center of the stables. The wooden structures, while not clear, were boundaries he could see and not walk into. Jamie searched each stall to make certain they were alone.

At the end were vacant stalls, and the instant they were inside one of them Will broke out into a frenzied string of explanations that Rourke couldn't make sense of.

"Stop!" he said, sitting on a bale of hay, and remembering Galiana's courage on their wedding night. "What say you? Slowly, Will."

Jamie said, "Hold. Father Jonah, ye can be the lookout."

The old priest's voice trembled as he asked, "What do I do?"

"Go back down a couple of stalls, and sit back against one of them. If someone's comin', let us know. Sing or something. And don't listen too close to our conversation, else we'll have to kill ye."

"Jamie!" Galiana exploded.

"Jamie." Rourke shook his head.

The priest left the stall and walked a ways before Jamie told him to halt and take a seat. "Act like yer nappin', without nappin'." Jamie peered over the edge of the stall door to watch until seemingly satisfied Father Jonah could follow simple directions.

"Are you ready, Jamie?" Galiana asked in a toosweet tone.

"Lass, don't start! What if we're talkin', and someone comes up ta kill us all?"

"Kill us? Please, sir, you have an obsession with murder."

Rourke whistled. "Truce, the two of you. Will wants to speak his piece, and then we can combine what we know, and mayhap get out of this with our lives."

"You mean we really are in danger?"

"Galiana, later," Rourke said with what he felt was infinite patience.

"Pox on that!" she exclaimed.

Jamie burst into laughter, breaking the tension between him and the lady. Rourke nodded to his foster brother before gesturing to his squire.

"Will?"

"I tried to tell ya, I did, and then ye were never alone. Why is that, my lord? Even if it were just Jamie, I would have said something, but no, ye've got more guards than the bloody king. Fat lot of good it did him, too. Bugger."

Rourke grinned. "Tried to tell me what, Will?"

"I work, sometimes, for the queen."

Rourke somehow kept his temper from exploding, though he ground his back teeth so hard something cracked.

"Which queen, boy?" He'd welcomed Will into his home, and had considered him a younger version of himself. And what queen had he always served? "Eleanor."

"Aye," Will answered miserably.

Jamie gave a sardonic snort of laughter. "Old bird."

"You aren't mad?" Galiana asked with obvious surprise. "Either of you?"

Rourke nodded, clasping his hands together, his two index fingers making a point. "I'm mad, all right. At myself. Should've seen it."

"Aye," Jamie agreed. "It's plain as day, now that the rascal admits it."

"You're all insane," Galiana huffed. "Anybody else you would have hung by their toenails! I thought—"

Rourke cut her off before she asked more of the wrong questions. "Will, why did you admit it?"

"I thought ye knew, and that ye were takin' me back here to beat me, or worse."

"I take it ye were missin' earlier 'cause ye were meetin' the queen?" Jamie scratched his scalp.

"But she's not here," Rourke said, certain he would have known if she was. Unless he'd fallen from grace somehow; but he couldn't imagine it. The queen rewarded loyalty with staunch support, and he'd always been true to her. King William understood.

"Not here, no," Will said. "But close enough by. She wants to meet you and the lady Galiana at the old manor lodge. She said ye'd know the one."

"Of course!" Rourke stood, ready to leave immediately.

"In the morn," Galiana said, censure in her tone. "Before the sun rises."

"What ails ye?" Rourke demanded, his own head pulsating with ache.

"She says jump, and you all, three men, ask how high?" Galiana stood, her hands on her hips.

"Aye," Rourke said in unison with Will and Jamie.

Galiana crossed her arms.

"She's our queen. Raised us from nothing, to the men we are today—whether you approve or no, my lady, we are alive because of her." Rourke hoped Galiana could understand, because any woman he loved would have to.

And if she, the greatest schemer of all time, were here, then mayhap he'd get to keep his lady.

"An orphan, I was," Jamie said. "She saw to it that I was trained, squired, and knighted."

"I love her," Will said simply and best.

"Oh . . ." Galiana sighed. "That's lovely."

"Enough of that, now." Rourke rubbed his temples, but nothing eased the dull, persistent pain behind his eye. "We must find a way out of this trap before we become a part of it. Jamie, you noticed all of the barons here? And Lord Harold—he's wearing Prince John's insignia now, out in the open. If the prince can gather as many men as all of that, then who says he can't be king?"

"We do," Will said. "By finding that thing the prince stole."

"Well, lad, tell us what ye know about that?" Jamie kicked at the straw.

"Nothin', Jamie! Only that sometimes, nay, mayhap just the once, I heard talk of it. I don't know what it is, only that King Richard once had it then returned it to King William, and now the prince has it. And ye're worried that if he has it, he can be king, so we need ta get it back."

"None of you are loyal to Prince John?" Galiana seemed to be pulling her hair out, so Rourke put his hand on her arm.

"I told you—I'm a spy for King William."

"You are?" Will plopped to his knees.

"Now we'll have to kill the little sod," Jamie growled.

"I won't say nothin'!"

"You can't kill him, Jamie. He would have figured it out eventually." Galiana's reasonable tone irritated Rourke, so he dropped his hand. "Does Eleanor know you have split loyalties?"

"Before this"—he gestured to the stable roof—"I was a damn good spy. Not that you'd know."

"I believe you," Galiana said, a hint of laughter coloring her words.

"Hail Mary, full of grace," Father Jonah said suddenly, and loudly. "Our Father, who art in heaven . . ."

They all quieted as a man with a loud voice questioned what Father Jonah was doing in the stable. His stench overpowered the earthy scents of the stables, and Rourke gripped the hilt of his sword.

Harold.

Jamie grunted a question of whether or not they should attack Lord Harold before the knight caused any more trouble.

Rourke shook his head. It was time to gather information, not create more trouble.

Father Jonah and Lord Harold left the stables together and, as soon as it was clear, Rourke told everyone it was best to split up. "I will know more by tomorrow. We must all be on guard!"

Galiana hadn't been able to sleep, and she was far from her best this early in the morning. The crisp winter air roused her from sleep as she made her way to the rear of the castle, where Rourke and Will were waiting with the horses.

What did one wear to a secret assignation with the queen? The queen who, even after years of being a royal dowager, at an age when she should be missing her teeth and sipping porridge, was so beautiful she could enthrall men as young as Will?

A woman like that had to hold the secret of power in the palm of her hand.

She took extra care with her ablutions, proudly wearing the ring from King William but covering it beneath a leather glove. It was cold, after all, and in some cases beauty had to make way for comfort.

Galiana was rewarded for her care by Will's uplifted brow of appreciation.

Rourke barked, "What took you so long?"

"Me lord is crabby this morn. Clumsy and still asleep is my guess, eh? Ran smack into a servin' wench carryin' her lady's bathing water." Will chuckled, thinking it a fine jest.

Immediately concerned, Galiana glided to where Rourke was sitting stiffly atop his mount. "I'm here now, my lord. In my desire to make a good impression on the queen, I took too long."

His expression softened, and she knew he was just worried about making a slip—which could be deadly; she understood that now.

"Let's ride, before my arse freezes to the saddle."

"You speak so sweet," Galiana said drolly. "Will, thank you, and please make certain Jamie knows to look for us in a few hours?"

"Aye," his brow furrowed in consternation, but then he dipped his head, waved, and ran for the inside of the castle where it was warm.

"I can get us back, just as I can get us there," Rourke grunted.

"Are you not a morning person, my lord?" Galiana nudged her horse toward the path through the park leading to the forest. "I asked Will to look for us—on the off chance we're attacked. We still don't know who killed Robbie, aye? And I'm simply not handy with a sword." She added extra sarcasm to make the point very clear.

"Aye, but you're deadly with your mouth," he said, moving his horse ahead to the tree line.

Galiana grinned at his back. "Mayhap you should let me lead," she suggested, racing in front of him.

"My stallion will follow on the trail, Galiana."

"So will mine, my lord."

"You're very full of yourself, my lady."

"I didn't sleep." She glanced over at him, gifting him with a shy smile she knew he couldn't see very well. "I was worried for you."

"Me?" His golden brown brows drew together in an aggravated vee. "I don't need anyone to worry for me."

"Now that I know you constantly court danger, I can do nothing but worry. And worry causes—"

"Wrinkles. I remember." He laughed in spite of his bad mood.

"Besides"—Galiana found that she liked flirting with her husband—"you were right, and I wouldn't want to be married to Lord Harold. He seemed quite, er, aromatic, in the hall yesterday."

Rourke grinned, and Gali's heart leapt with unadulterated want. How could a man be so gorgeous?

"When we get to the trees, take the path to the left. You know which way that is?" He lifted his left hand.

"One little mistake, under duress, and now I have to listen to this?" She sighed heavily.

"You could have gotten killed."

"Or worse, kidnapped." She shuddered, remembering quite well the way Lord Christien had pinched her breast.

"I'll protect you, Gali," Rourke promised.

"I feel completely safe with you, my lord. 'Tis the enemy I can't see that sends me fits of apprehension. But let's not talk of that. Did you beat Will last night?"

"Beat him? Why would I do that?"

"Because he is a spy for Queen Eleanor." Galiana wasn't sure how the spy business worked. "It seems everyone is a spy."

He shook his head, his body at ease as the horse

cantered. His arm was relaxed at his side, his forearm resting on his thigh. But she'd seen how fast he could draw his sword from the scabbard at his waist.

Intriguing.

"He guarded the door, as always. 'Tis good to love the queen."

Was it so wrong of her to want that kind of love for herself? To desire his strength? His mouth? His essence? She would make him a scent, and it would be summer woods and mayhap just the smallest hint of oak. Or . . . She closed her eyes and breathed in, regretting the impulse as she coughed on the cold air.

"Are you all right?"

"Aye." She ducked her head.

"Franz is still sick. He was sleeping when we came in last night. You could feel the fever coming off of his skin like the heat from a fire."

"Did you ask for a physician? A healer?"

"It's his arm, where Christien—damn him—struck Franz with the arrow during the chase."

"Nay!" She accepted guilt. "If I'd made the right turn, then we never would have come out where they were."

"You didn't do it on purpose. No matter how much I joke, it isn't your fault." Rourke looked over at her and said in the direction of her horse's head, "We should have redressed the wound, but with everything so chaotic, I forgot. He's my man, Galiana. I will take the blame. You won't."

Love for him warmed her through.

"Thank you."

He stared straight ahead, and she could feel his frustration. "You are handling this situation with great skill, my lord."

"What choice do I have?"

"Well—" She paused, considering how it would be to have one of her senses taken away. "I would cry."

"You think I should cry?" His voice mocked her, and she jerked her chin in the air.

"Nay. I said that is what I would do. You just get bossier by the minute."

"I don't."

"Ha."

After half an hour of riding in silence, she said, "I was trying to compliment you, and, instead, we argued. I wanted you to know I admire you. Can you accept that without growling at me?"

She watched his jaw clench, and his hands fisted in the reins. "I don't growl."

Rolling her eyes toward the canopy of trees, she said, "We've reached a crossroads."

"We go right."

Galiana eyed the trail. "There's not even a squirrel's footprints," she said doubtfully.

"We go right." He started to push his horse forward.

"Let me," she said, not wanting him to ride into a tree. "Your horse is so well trained he'd let you brain him with a pine if you told him to go forward."

"At least the beast knows not to question me."

"I'm no beast." She went ahead, her horse lifting her hooves as delicately as if she were walking on ice instead of a foot or more of snow.

"I didn't say that."

Galiana shrugged off his ill humor, knowing that if she had to switch places with Rourke her mood would be a hundred times more foul. "Stay as close as you can."

He snorted at her order, but did as she said.

It was difficult going, but eventually Galiana spied a long wooden building. "It looks abandoned, my lord Rourke."

"Is it the old lodge?"

"I don't know," she answered, looking around the winter wonderland. "I don't see the queen. I don't see anybody." But she felt something malevolent, and she wished she was back at the castle.

She could identify the danger there and protect her man.

Chapter Nineteen

"Is someone there?" Rourke asked, turning his mount in a semicircle.

"You feel it, too?"

"You don't see anyone . . ."

"Nay. I'm sorry to disappoint you, but I'm frightened. I'm going to knock on the door of the lodge and see if anyone is inside."

He heard the shaking courage in her voice, and he couldn't have been prouder.

"Wait for me. We'll stay together."

Mayhap she'd been right, and they should have had Jamie follow them. However, the queen had wanted a secret meeting. What if he'd just signed the death warrant for him and Galiana both?

Fool.

He squinted past the sharp pain in his head, making out the low wooden building and the posts in front. "Let's tether the horses."

"You think we should wait outside for the queen?"

"Part of my job," he said through gritted teeth, "is to assimilate my surroundings. I learn what I can, give away as little as possible, and protect the royal family. I used to be very good."

Now he couldn't find his way out of his own chamber without tripping over the pot.

Using logic, he told himself it had been barely a fortnight since the—he glared at Galiana—the veritable root of his current problem: the accident.

"You're still very good. You saved my life," she added.

"Imagine how much better I would be"—he cringed, recalling the fiasco of their wedding night—"if I had use of all my faculties?"

She was silent.

Another chill whistled across his neck and down his spine. "Let's go inside." He jumped off the horse, deciding that tethering the beast might be cruel if someone wanted him dead. His stallion was trained to come when called and had saved Rourke's sorry neck more than once. If need be, he could carry Galiana, too.

She didn't argue, for once, and when she saw that he didn't tie his stallion, she left her horse free as well.

"There's a step," she said. "Just one. Can you see it?"

"Aye." He could see outlines and gray shapes, and

he prayed he would not be stuck in this purgatory for the rest of his life. He knew color, damn it.

"Should I knock?" she whispered.

The urgent sense of being watched intensified. "One tap; then open the door." He should have remembered the queen had wiles he'd never understand. "She's already inside."

"But Rourke, it looks deserted! There are no horses, no footprints . . ."

"Galiana—knock."

She did, and opened the door. She even waited for him so they could enter side by side, and he took her elbow with unspoken gratitude.

His queen could not find him less than adequate.

Relying on his other senses, since sight afforded him nothing but a graying mass perched on a bench before an empty fireplace, he discreetly inhaled. The signature scent of his foster mother clogged his throat, and he was overcome by emotion.

Galiana dipped her head and, using her elbow as a guide, led him across the room.

"Rourke, my boy," his queen said. "You look tired. Is that a scar on your angel's face? Lady Galiana, you are lovely."

His queen was all things gracious.

Galiana subtly let him know he should stay still so she could curtsy. Which she did, with all the aplomb of a lady, according to the queen's low murmur of approval.

407

Rourke's blood warmed.

He narrowed his gaze, seeing the broad forehead of his queen. Her eyes—he remembered the spark in them, though he couldn't see it now. Her oval face. Her haughty chin . . .

"You're staring at me as if you've never seen me before," she chuckled self-consciously. "Time has visited me." She put her hand to her cheek.

"Nay, my queen," he said roughly. "You are all things beautiful. It's been so long since we've met that I am but searching for the affection you once you held for me."

She stood and opened her arms, inviting his embrace. "You rascal of a boy, you always were my favorite. And your lady will think you mad, talking in such a manner."

"Nay," Galiana said. "'Tis a miracle to see Rourke's heart is warmer than he shows. His love for you has given me hope. Although now that we've met, I can see why you command the affection and respect of so many. I am deeply humbled."

Rourke stepped back, taken in by Galiana's speech.

"She's a pretty tongue, Rourke. You should keep her."

Rourke stilled. His queen rarely said anything for the sake of it. This double entendre meant she knew of King William's decree.

"Aye? So many vie for the lady's hand that even though the vows have been said."

"And consummated?"

Galiana gasped.

"Aye," Rourke nodded, refusing to dwell on his less than stellar performance.

"Blessed by a priest?"

"Nay, there wasn't time."

"Father Jonah could do it as soon as we get back to the castle," Galiana said.

"Good. I will it to be so. Tell me, Rourke, did you find the bauble you were looking for?"

Rourke could feel Gali's distress and reached out to touch her arm. She lifted her hand, grasping his and hanging on.

"The queen knows of the Breath of Merlin, Galiana."

"And Will told me you are wearing the ring? Do you have it?"

"Aye," Galiana answered in a hushed tone, releasing Rourke's hand.

"And do you see the past with it?"

Rourke tilted his head, not even bothering to wonder how the queen knew such things. She was the font of information.

"Aye," Galiana said.

"That makes you the guardian of the stone, my girl, whether you want the chore or not."

"I don't understand."

"Let me see the thing . . ."

Galiana took off her glove and removed the ring

from her finger, placing it without hesitation in the queen's palm.

"'Tis beautiful. Old as time, but it never worked for me. It leaves me cold, and yet for you?" The queen handed the ring back, and Galiana put it on her finger.

"I walk through lush greenery, as if I am truly there."

Rourke was astounded by the far-away quality in his wife's voice.

"Over a rambling stream. Trees are everywhere, alive and new. Raindrops that taste as sweet as honey fall on my tongue. Lions sleep beneath huge mountainous ledges, and men have small encampments—very primitive, but powerful.

"There is a central bonfire, where the lions and men come to talk. But the lions are dying. Merlin says the time has come. The biggest lion—he is not ready to give up the land, and man isn't ready to take it on by himself. Wolves nip at their heels, as do bears and dragons. All want to rule the British Isles, but it is not to be. Man, together with the majestic lion, beg Merlin to let them rule together. There is but one way, and each male makes the sacrifice."

She stopped to catch her breath, and Rourke inched closer, offering her comfort if she chose to accept it. She seemed to calm as soon as their shoulders touched.

His sensual lady.

Rourke was as captivated as the queen, having never heard the story before. Never from a true witness. Who would have believed a woman could travel back into time? It was eerie and magical.

"What is the sacrifice?" His queen leaned forward, offering her support as well.

"Their first male babe." Galiana's breath quickened. "It is night, and there is a terrible storm that keeps the intruders away. Lightning flashes across the sky, and thunder shakes the ground, which waves beneath my feet. On the end of a rocky ledge, so thin it doesn't seem like it can take the weight, the man kneels, offering his babe. The infant isn't crying, even though rain pelts his face. The lion brings his cub, carrying it by the scruff of the neck before laying it down next to the male. The man and the lion walk away, and Merlin appears.

"Tall, foreboding in his dark power, he points his staff at the two males and invokes the spells of magic older than any can remember, and he blows a stream of air that is so frigid it traps the two souls of the male offspring, cub and man, inside his frozen breath."

"Sweet Christ," his queen said, bringing her hand to her heart.

"Merlin said that so long as the lion and the man ruled Britain for Britain's sake, they would keep the throne. Whoever dares to hold the Breath of Merlin risks permanent blindness and possible madness. But if the stone deems you worthy, you can see who will be king. It is possible that the bearer of the stone can be deemed worthier than whoever holds the crown."

"God's blood. And John has done it?" The queen fell back onto her bench.

"If he hasn't yet, he will," Rourke said sadly. Her boys were not always good to her, yet she loved them all.

"Richard is being held for ransom, even though John ordered him killed. Praise be that the emperor is a greedy man who needs Britain's cooperation, else— never mind that."

"I'm sorry, my queen," Galiana said.

Compassion radiated from Galiana's skin, stronger than her lavender and lemon perfume. He cared more for her than was wise.

But if there was a chance to keep her? Aye, he would listen to the plan. If it didn't hurt Scotland, or England, then he would listen. And hope.

"Sorry? Don't be. Constance carries John's babe, and she's chosen Rourke to be the 'father,' whilst John marries Alice for France. Constance is too smart, and John's too sly. William wants you to do this thing; I don't. Find the stone, and take it away. I charge you, Rourke, and you Galiana, to be its guardians. Take the cursed thing back to Scotland. I will talk to your fa— your liege."

Rourke heard the slip and understood it was intentional, just as he understood he wasn't supposed to question it. He reached down and squeezed Galiana's fingers so she wouldn't say anything either.

The answering press of her fingers relieved his mind.

"I must go. You two stay here another hour or so, so that nobody grows suspicious."

"An hour? My queen, we must get back and fulfill your mission," Rourke said.

"You have a comely wife, and an empty lodge—methinks you can find some way to pass the time." She chuckled, then reached her hand out to cup his face. "You are a good man, Rourke Wallis. I've always known you could be a danger to my throne, but I've trusted you despite it. Go to Scotland."

And with that, she was gone in a flurry of gray skirts.

"Oh my," Galiana said with awe.

"Aye." His heart ached. What if he never saw her again?

"She is used to ruling, with her beauty and with her will. I think I love her, too, Rourke."

"She liked you; that was certain."

"Will we really hide in Scotland?"

"I must think." He made his way to the bench and carefully sat down. "I don't know what to do, Galiana. I've been raised to be a spy. It is in my blood. What happens if I can't find the Breath of Merlin? What if I fail?"

He felt the caress of her hand as she smoothed back his hair. "You will find it. I will help you. We will save King Richard, and God can help Prince John. I quite like William Marshall, but the other barons and lords left me unimpressed. They all seem angry, and ambitious for more land and power."

"That's what all royals want. As you've witnessed in the vision, they've always been willing to sacrifice their own to make sure they keep it."

He thought of all the different things he'd been charged to do. This latest went against all of them. If he honored the queen, he could keep his bride, but he'd have to give up the power gained from his years of playing the court.

He'd have to give up the adrenaline rush of being a master spy.

Did it compare to the rush of love?

He didn't know.

If he followed his liege's . . . his father's—his heart cramped—directive, then he'd have to put Galiana to the side, which he couldn't do since they'd consummated their vows. Or kill her—but he would rather plunge a blade into his own breast before harming one dull, brown hair on his lady's head.

He was caught, but good. Prince John's wishes no longer mattered to him, especially if he was dallying with Constance. Rourke had no desire to have a royal's bastard foisted on him. And a male born of John and Constance would be dangerous.

His blood didn't jump at the thrill, as it might have a month before.

But . . . if he stayed with Galiana, he'd be putting

414

her life in danger. He knew secrets that were with killing for.

Galiana's tender touch moved from his hair to his nape. Her voice was husky as she asked, "Should I start a fire?"

"I can do it," he said.

"Let me." She pressed her hand down on his shoulder. "I want to. You have much to think about, as you said. Your forehead scrunches"—she traced the pad of her index finger down the center of his brow—"here." She dropped a kiss to the top of his head.

He wanted her.

He couldn't kill her, and he couldn't set her aside.

He'd take her.

And this time there would be no doubt in her mind that loving equaled great pleasure.

Galiana coaxed the meager flames into life, prodding the logs until they cooperated. "There." She sat back on her haunches, quite proud of her accomplishment.

Her mother was not the kind of woman who thought maids should do every little thing, so she'd made sure her daughters were self-sufficient—in theory. Building a fire had never been something Gali excelled at.

Too smoky, too puny . . . Someone always had to come and fix it.

At least with Rourke's limited vision, he couldn't be

too picky.

"Sit back," Rourke charged. "You'll die of lung disease from the smoke."

She sighed with exasperation. "You have plenty of skills besides sight to keep you in your line of work, my lord."

"Sarcasm is not an attractive quality in a lady."

"Pox on it, then. If I am to be the guardian of the stone, what do I care about being a lady? I'll need to learn to hunt and make my perfumes from nettles and berries or something."

"You sound happy," he said, a question in his tone.

"I might be."

"If I take you to Scotland and hide the stone, I can't stay with you."

"What?" Her heart broke.

"It would be for your safety."

"I am good with a rock, my lord." She folded her hands together in her lap, knowing he was going to set her aside, despite the queen's approval.

How could she let him know she would care for him, despite his blurred sight, despite his moral flaws, despite his arrogance. Saint Agnes help her, she loved him.

He needn't be perfect for her. His imperfections endeared him to her even more. They showed a moral man who did his duty at great cost to his own soul. He'd been taught by the people he loved that spying and gathering information for their power was important, and he showed admirable loyalty to their cause.

But what about his personal happiness?

Aye, her heart was shattering. He knew about sacrifice.

"Galiana," he said, his voice rough.

"Yes?" She turned to look at him, to study him for what might be the last time. If they were caught searching for the Breath of Merlin, they'd be killed.

The ring heated on her finger, and she stared down. The blue gem shone clear, and tears sprang to her eyes.

She would love her husband, with her heart, her soul, and her body, and let him make the choice to be who he would. But he had to know what he would be giving away.

"I—you know that King William is my sworn liege," he said, raking his fingers through his thick, golden brown hair. The light sprang off of golden strands, and it took all of her willpower to keep from stroking him.

"You heard . . ."

That his father was his liege . . . "Aye," she said. She'd heard.

"He wants me to wed Constance. He sent word that she's already agreed to set her husband aside."

"And what of Magdalene? Betrayed by you and her best friend?" Galiana couldn't help put feel sorry for the woman who was nothing but a royal pawn.

"Don't pity her; she always knew the score."

"I think she loves you."

"She knows better than that," he scoffed dismissively. "I'm to set you aside, to save your life, Galiana—you won't be penniless, nor starve. I have a small tract of land and a fortress in the highlands; you can live there in peace. I'll not bother you, and I'll send you funds."

"You think to pay me off?" Her temper built, and it was becoming increasingly difficult to remember she was a lady.

"It is that or kill you." His voice was so stark that she knew he meant every single word.

She clutched at her throat, unable to breathe. Sucking in air, she felt tears leak from her eyes as she realized he couldn't possibly care for her if those were the two options he was considering for their future. "You could do that?"

He slammed his fist into the wooden chair. "Nay." He sounded tortured. "I can't."

His conscience was ripping. She could feel his torment as if it were her own. She rushed forward, on her knees, tears falling from her eyes at his vulnerability, that he would trust her enough to let her see his pain. She clutched him to her breast.

"You can't kill me; you can't," she put her mouth to his.

His mouth was brutal, his muscled shoulders hard and clenched beneath her fingers. She wished she could swallow his anguish as she swallowed his warm breath. Their tongues clashed, battling as they fought each other and themselves.

They were fated to be together, and equally fated to be apart. She would take the stone and protect the Breath of Merlin and the future of Britain. Rourke would leave her and marry Constance of Brittany, so that he could raise Arthur, or John's bastard, to be loyal to Scotland, too. King Richard partnered with King William against King Philippe—the lion and the man against the rest of the world.

"Why are you crying?" He crushed her beneath him, kissing her tears as they trailed down her cheeks and neck. "You can't care for me. You don't approve of me. God's bones, Gali, I am not worthy of your tears, let alone your heart."

She reached up, grasping his face tenderly. "I never said I gave you my heart—'tis cold, and you wouldn't want it."

His eyes dimmed until they were a smoky gray. "I can't take it."

Shrugging as if it didn't matter, this cruel rejection of her feelings, she traced the shape of his brows, the light pink scar on his temple, the dimple in his left cheek, his strong jaw—his lips.

He didn't move, as if he knew she needed to remember him by touch, as well as scent and taste. She closed her eyes, trusting her senses to show her his essence— that noble part of him that he hid so well.

"I want you," she whispered, feeling his pulse accelerate. "You promised me an experience that I would remember with pleasure. You owe me this." She nipped his lush lower lip, knowing his face by memory alone. "Don't you dare start thinking—just feel. Show me what your heart is saying. No lies between us. No words."

419

His voice was strangled with emotion as he dropped his forehead to hers. "For once I need to speak the truth. You shower me with compassion, you share your vulnerability, and it slays me. Your caring is deadlier than a sword to the gut, and yet I can't push you away."

"I don't want to be pushed, Rourke," Galiana said between deep kisses that joined them at the mouth.

His body pinned her to the rough planks of the dusty lodge floor. She brought her arms up around his back and hugged him tightly. If she could spend her last hours on earth feeling like this, then she would gladly shuffle her mortal coil and meet God with a satisfied smile on her face.

Rourke's hands were everywhere: tangled in her hair, smoothing her waist, barely skimming her breasts, resting at her hips—

Her body was on fire from the inside out. Her legs were restless, and she needed to feel Rourke's skin against hers. Flesh to flesh, spirit to spirit—that was the only way she'd be satiated.

She unclasped the brooch holding her cloak together and shrugged out of it. Her tunic was too restricting. Clothing felt too heavy against her body; it was suffocating her.

Rourke's hands bumped into hers as they each sought to remove articles of clothing that were in the way. "Here—stay still," he said, his hands caught between her hair and the tie of her undergown.

Gali relaxed and allowed him total control. She trusted him. His agile fingers quickly righted the knot, smoothing the tendrils of hair as if they were strands of silk.

For certes, he was holding her as if she were precious glass from the shores of Normandy. She didn't want to be held as if she'd break.

She desired him, as a woman desired her soul mate. Her body trembled with anticipation, toes curling against his hose-covered calf.

With strength Boadicea would have admired, she flipped her warrior to his back. "You're wearing over-much, my lord."

"I agree, my lady."

His eyes stared up into hers, and she quickly asked, "What do you see, when you stare at me?"

She brought her face low, so that their noses touched.

"I see you, my lady, with your smooth, broad brow. Your oval eyes and your noble nose. Your pointed chin, that chin I've grown to admire in its haughtiness."

Giggling, Galiana said, "I am not haughty."

His warm palm lightly smacked her bare bum. "Not now," he agreed before kissing her again and again.

When she could think again, she told him to stay still. "I'll have you as naked as me, my lord."

"You're lovely," he said, his hands smoothing over the flat expanse of flesh betwixt her ribcage and mound.

"Even gray and drab?" she joked, unconcerned about her looks as she reveled in Rourke's worshipping touch.

421

His index finger poised over the edge of her curls and she shifted teasingly.

With a groan, he grabbed her hips and rolled her beneath him, while she yanked his shirt off over his head. "Mayhap I'd not survive looking upon you, my lady, in color."

"You are a charmer, Rourke," she said, running her hands over his muscled chest. Golden brown swirls of hair led the way to below his hose, and her fingers followed the path.

He grabbed her wrist. "Let me. You would have me reach my peak too soon. Patience, my lady."

"I'm tired of having patience, and I'm most tired of being a lady."

He nuzzled her neck, his warm breath tickling her skin, and her nipples peaked with anticipation.

"What would you be?"

She arched her neck backward. "Wanton. I would be a slave to your touch."

Rourke's thick, hard penis thrust against her belly. "This touch?"

Whirls of pleasure seared through her bloodstream, spiking her sensitivity to new heights. "Hmm," she answered, trying to widen her thighs to allow him access to her woman's core.

She'd known it would be heavenly, when they had time to do it right.

"Stop."

Her body did as directed, but the pulse in her neck

beat rapidly.

"I will brand you with my tongue, my hands. You will never have another lover who knows your body as well as I."

His masterly touch matched the demanding cadence of his words as his mouth, tongue, lips, and fingers caressed her spine, her neck, her breasts, her belly. She could barely breathe at such a heightened state of need. "I'm ready, my lord. I couldn't be more ready."

Her legs quivered, her skin ached, and if she didn't find release soon, she'd go mad. And then he spread her thighs with his knee and plunged into her welcoming moistness. Her inner muscles clenched around his hard length and convulsed with repeated quakes of pure pleasure.

He held her close, until her trembling ceased, then whispered in her ear.

"We're not done, my lady." His pelvis thrust forward again and new spirals started at the base of her spine.

"I promised you pleasure, and you will have it."

Chapter Twenty

Rourke had visited heaven, and it smelled like lavender and lemon. Heaven tasted like honey, and mint, and felt as soft as mink. He'd visited, and now he had to spend the rest of his dreary days on earth, a place that would forever be dark and murky without Galiana to light his way.

She was quiet as they left their lodge. He'd never be able to come back without thinking of her, in all of her generous glory. She was the best lover he'd ever had, because she gave her heart in every touch. She'd said she hadn't given him her love, but he was branded by it, just as he'd branded her with his.

What was he to do?

Disobey his liege and risk being beheaded for a chance at happiness? Did he deserve such a thing? His prim miss . . . Nay, she wasn't prim, and he could never again think of her as plain; to him, she was as vibrant and beautiful as any woman could be—and then more. She made him think he could be a better person.

"Do you regret what happened?" He had to ask. Her silence unmanned him. He'd never meant to hurt her—but he had. And he would again.

"No regrets."

They rode along, and finally she said, "This is it—the path back to the castle." She reached for his arm. "I am glad that we made love, Rourke. It was beautiful, and I will never regret it. If that's the only memory I have of you to keep me warm while I am in Scotland, I will make it be enough. But you need to promise me that when you retire from this life, you will come to me."

"You'd wait?" Rourke couldn't imagine such an offer. Then remembered Margaret's promise to Jamie. Mayhap love was that overwhelming. That strong. Nay.

"I'm your wife."

"You won't be," he said harshly. "I'll divorce you."

She sighed. "In my heart, then, we'll belong to one another still."

"I'll not make you any such promises, other than the ones I already vowed. You'll never go hungry, and you'll have a place to live."

"I have my own property."

"In Scotland?"

"Well. No. But I could buy some."

"Let me do that much."

He heard the oath she muttered and laughed bitterly. "I am trying to soothe my own pride, for it feels like I'm abandoning you."

"Fate is forcing our hands, mayhap."

"I must put the country first. I pledged, and I swear it's the only honorable thing I've ever managed to maintain."

She protested.

The insight to his own character was not wanted, nor did he appreciate seeing himself in such a dismal light. "I need to finish it."

Her horse came next to his, and Galiana blew him a kiss. "All right. We need not talk of love, my lord. Let us discuss our strategy."

Rourke's admiration for his wife grew. "Constance of Brittany wants power. At the scene of his murder, Robbie had Brittany's device, a small token. Like a shield."

"A token from a lover, mayhap?"

"Galiana, how many lovers do you think Constance has?"

She sniffed. "How many does she need to see her son on the throne?"

Rourke closed his eyes, letting the wind play over his face. Galiana had an excellent point. When it came to matters of court intrigue, some noble members felt no price was too high.

He used to agree.

"Mayhap Robert deliberately left the token in sight

426

so you would have a clue to follow."

Rourke opened his eyes to the drab gray world around him. "Or what if the murderer left it as a false trail?"

"'Tis no wonder your head aches all the time. Intrigue around every corner. When you find one answer, another questions pops up like a weasel in a garden. I will be your eyes, Rourke."

"I need you to use the ring. It should give off some sort of signal when it nears the Breath of Merlin."

"So what? We will wander the halls until we get a sign? Do you not realize how large Windsor is, my lord?"

"It might not be the best plan, but we are in a hurry. Besides, I grew up with the royals, and I know a trick or two."

"All right. And I can ask—subtly, of course—if Robert had any high-born lovers."

Rourke groaned. "We can't invite any suspicion."

They reached the stables, where Jamie was waiting with Will. "Well, lass, how did it go?" Jamie helped Galiana dismount while Will took her horse. Rourke felt he should be doing more, but now was the time to pull away, both emotionally and physically.

He had a country to save for a king.

Galiana could feel Rourke leave her as if he had sliced her from his body. She supposed this was a handy skill for a spy, but as his lover, it hurt.

She answered Jamie's question. "It went as well as could be expected. The queen is lovely. My lord Rourke is stubborn, and honorable, and I might just hate him."

Stalking past Rourke and Jamie, she tapped Will on the arm. "Serve me, if you please. I must get to my room and bathe before meeting Rourke for a private lunch. If I go on my own, I'll no doubt get lost, and I'm starving, so we mustn't have that. When I don't eat, I frown and frowning causes—"

"Wrinkles," they all answered in unison.

Embarrassed, she lifted her chin and hoped the tears she was trying so hard to hold back wouldn't fall.

"It would be my honor to help you, my lady," Will hedged.

Jamie cleared his throat. "But somethin's happened whilst ye were gone."

"What?" Rourke's question was sharp.

"Yes, Jamie, what? I see now that you're pale. Is it Franz? Has he worsened?" Galiana made for the entrance to the stable to help the ill knight, but Jamie caught her arm.

"Franz is missing," Jamie paused. "Godfrey is dead; jumped from the top of the ramparts, with a note saying he killed Robbie."

Galiana brought her knuckles to her mouth to stifle a gasp. Godfrey had seemed such a decent man.

"Too neat." Rourke kicked the mix of straw and dirt at his boot.

"Aye," Jamie agreed. "Will and I both thought so, too."

Oh yes, she reminded herself. In a spy's world, nothing was ever as it seemed at first glance. "Franz left the chamber this morn? Obviously." She waved the question away. "He hasn't returned. Robert dead; Godfrey admitted to it—Magdalene!" She snapped her fingers.

"What?" Rourke stared in her direction.

"I got lost yesterday after we arrived, and I overheard a conversation." She blushed as she recalled her attempts at eavesdropping, "A man—I believe now it must have been Godfrey—was arguing with the lady, and she asked if he'd killed Robert. He said nay, that it hadn't been him. But he was going to blackmail her with whatever he knew."

"Franz." Rourke's jaw clenched, and Galiana wished she had the right to soothe his anger over the betrayal.

"He's sick, man. We saw it. No way could he have pushed Godfrey." Jamie shook his head, not believing it.

"I cleaned his wound that first night, and it was but a scratch compared to some of the other wounds ye've all had." Will sighed. "But I assumed it got infected. I never imagined he would be pretending."

Galiana remembered seeing Franz's banked fury back at Montehue Manor and wondered if he'd been hiding his true nature all along. "How did he come to join your party?" Her mind was spinning around like a top.

"King Richard, actually," Rourke said. "He and Franz were friends, and he'd lost his lands to King

Philippe while on crusade. I was doing my queen a service." Rourke pounded the wooden stall with his fist. "I was watching him, and he never made a misstep."

"Let's wait and see, Rourke, before we accuse him unjustly." Galiana spoke more for Rourke's benefit, and not because she believed in Franz's innocence, although in truth, she'd have pegged Godfrey for the stronger man if it came to a shoving match.

"The castle's in an uproar, and Prince John was calling for ye," Jamie said. "I told him that you and yer wife were on a tryst."

Galiana felt the heat rise to her cheeks and looked longingly toward the stable door and escape.

"He believed it?" Rourke asked.

"Your reputation precedes ye, Rourke." Jamie laughed, as did Will, but Galiana felt sick at the thought of Rourke with anybody but her.

"Enough." He pinched the bridge of his nose and closed his eyes. "Damn this ache. Will it never stop?"

"Rest," Galiana said, knowing that once they found the stone, she'd have no right to tell him what to do.

"When do I have time for that, my lady? For certes, not since I met you."

"What?" She stepped back, stung. "Even before then, I'm sure. When was the last time you napped, or slept the night through?"

"My work doesn't allow a deep sleep."

"Aye," Galiana said, the tears spilling free at last.

"Ye'd hate to wake your companion."

"I'd hate to have a dagger plunged into my throat."

"'Tis the company you choose." Galiana turned, unable to stay a moment longer.

"Wait for me, lady," Will called as he raced after her. "Wait."

She paused, relying on her training as a lady to blink away the tears before she turned toward the squire. "If you could just help me find my room."

"For certes, me lady."

"I don't wish to speak of anything."

"Of course not," he said, keeping in step with her.

"Your lord is a difficult man," she said.

"Aye."

"And he doesn't understand how full of honor he really is."

"Nay?"

"He should let himself believe in . . ."

"In what?"

"Nothing. I told you I didn't want to talk about it."

He opened the door to the castle, showing her which stairs to go up. "Should I wait for ye?"

"Nay. I've decided that if Rourke wants to meet me for lunch, or anything else," she added with a grim look, "then he can find me."

She reached her room after a few wrong turns and thanked the saints it was empty. Later, after having washed her face and put on fresh clothes, she regretted her impulsive decision to make Rourke come to her.

The regret was compounded by the return of Lucinda and Rohan. Galiana quickly folded her hands together so that the magical ring was covered.

The brunette asked slyly, "What's that upon your neck? A love bite? The entire castle is talking about you and your husband both being gone whilst your husband's knight committed suicide."

Lucinda giggled, not hiding her curiosity. "Is Rourke as wonderful a lover as they say?"

Galiana pursed her lips, not even thinking about wrinkles. "'Tis none of your business." She lifted her chin. "Why would anyone care what my husband and I were doing?"

"I thought it was very convenient for you both to be 'gone,' as did Prince John. But show him your neck; then he'll know your man—Jamie, was it—spoke the truth." Rohan laughed with spite. "Better to be branded a whore than a murderess."

"Whore? We're married." Galiana narrowed her eyes, her fist curling at her side.

"All know that the prince wants you wed to Lord Harold." She pinched her nose and waved the air beneath it.

"Why would he want that?" Galiana's insides were one tight knot as she kept her outside as calm as possible.

Lucinda tilted her head. "He was going to sever your handfasted marriage last eve, but you held the better hand, playing the prince's ego. I thought it was nicely done."

"Magdalene is not happy," Rohan added, sending Lucinda a dark look. "And when she's not happy, the lady Constance isn't happy, and when she's not happy . . ."

Galiana breathed out. "Prince John isn't happy." Nodding, she said, "Lady Magdalene really loves Rourke?"

"So she claims, the cold snake." Rohan shivered. "Besides, Prince John promised a reward to Lord Harold—which could be you. Ye've lands, and money."

Betraying nothing, Galiana asked, "What service did Lord Harold perform to deserve an heiress?"

Both the girls shrugged. Galiana wondered if Lord Harold had muscle enough to wrestle with Godfrey and win—possibly pushing the knight over the ramparts. If Rourke didn't believe Godfrey committed suicide, then neither would she.

It was imperative that she find Rourke before Lord Harold did. If what she suspected was true, then Lord Harold would stop at nothing, including murder, to gain his prize. Who pulled the lord's strings? Prince John, on behalf of Constance? Or Magdalene? Lady Magdalene had said Constance wouldn't be happy to hear of the blackmail.

A loud pounding sounded on the flimsy door, and all three of them jumped back as it broke in the frame. Rourke stood there like an avenging archangel, righteous fury etched on every gorgeous angle of his face.

Lucinda sighed, and Rohan smoothed her hair.

Galiana stayed outwardly cool. "My lord, now I will have to find another chamber, and this one was difficult to come by."

He glared, and she wondered what he saw. She glided toward him, putting her left hand on his bulging bicep. "Rourke, these are my roommates, Lucinda and Rohan. They were just telling me that we are the laughingstock of the castle and that all know we were out making lo—, er, engaging in a tryst," she informed him.

He made a forbidding noise in the back of his throat, and Lucinda seated herself on the edge of the bed in a rush.

"I explained that we are wed, but it seems that Lord Harold—"

Rohan interjected, "Gossip, my lady—that's all! No need to bore Lord Rourke with it."

Galiana turned on her heel and put her hands together, centered at her waist. "For certes? Mayhap we should go to Prince John?"

Rohan's face flushed a violent red.

"Aye, that might be best. Although in truth the prince seemed very, very angry. It could be best to go on another tryst—ah—not that I think," Rohan stammered.

Taking pity on the wench, Galiana lifted one hand. "Thank you, thank you. We'll just head down to the great hall and see if we can find him."

Urging Rourke to turn around before Lucinda started drooling, Galiana gave him a slight nudge to the hall.

He lifted a hand, giving the women a general salute.

"My ladies," he said before turning and taking three steps forward. Galiana held tight to his forearm.

"That went well," she said.

"Don't play your games with me. I found you."

"You can't possibly be angry."

"When you tell a blind man to search for you in a castle with more rooms than a rabbit warren, that man has the right to be bloody pissed off," he groused.

"My apologies. You aren't blind, not really, and I was going to find you once my temper cooled."

"Temper. Am I the only one to bear the brunt of your ill humor? All I hear about from my men is your sweetness."

Galiana sniffed, but turned her head to hide a smile. "I never have an ill humor. Now. I have a theory . . ." She swiftly changed the subject by whispering what Rohan had said regarding Lord Harold. "What do you think?"

Rourke paused, clasping his hand over where hers rested on his arm. "I'd rather believe ill of my enemy than of my friend."

Galiana nodded, feeling his anguish. She knew he would have cut Franz from his life if the betrayal were true, no matter how much the wound bled.

"Let's find Franz, shall we?"

"I have this itching at my nape that tells me time is short. I think we must find the Breath of Merlin first."

She gasped, holding up her right hand to show him the ring. "Mayhap you're right."

"Is it . . . glowing?"

"Aye." Galiana twisted her hand lightly back and forth so that the torchlight from the wall sconces made the stone a brightly colored prism. "It's changed. We have to hurry. The stone is in danger—or else we are."

"You're practically running. How do you feel?"

She bit her lip. Her nerves were taut, and her muscles clenched as if awaiting the signal to fight. Laughing, she said, "Like a warrior."

"You are the strangest woman I've ever met."

"Lucky you," she quipped. She gave in to impulse and danced a few steps, which made Rourke laugh, too. Gali adored the sound of it. It seemed Rourke rarely found something genuinely amusing.

"Be serious, now, lest you end up as Lord Harold's bride."

"That is serious," Galiana stopped dancing. "As serious as getting hanged for thievery, or just plain killed because I've become expedient. Lady Magdalene wants you, my lord, and I am in the way of her heart."

"She didn't mean anything to me."

Galiana shivered. "Don't tell me such things. It makes me sad for you. To share something as beautiful as what we've shared and not have it mean something? I couldn't make love in such a calculated way."

"What I've shared with you I've never felt before." He coughed uncomfortably. "How's the ring, now? Is it brighter? Are we getting closer?"

"'Tis the same as it was—a sparkling sapphire blue."

Now was not the time for an emotional debate. She'd be smart and capable so that he'd come to need her.

Rourke stopped before the staircase, then took two paces back. A large oil painting in an ornate frame hung on the wall, almost from floor to ceiling.

He asked, "Is anyone coming?"

Gali looked around the hall and down the stairs. "Nay."

He pulled on the frame, and the picture opened like a door. "Careful," he cautioned. "There's a step up. Stay to the right."

"Where will this lead?" Galiana could hardly suppress her excitement. Secret halls! She'd never been so daring in her life.

"The treasury in the prince's apartments."

Her excitement turned to trepidation. "Oh, dear."

"We will be all right. Prince John went out riding, to relieve his temper, so I was told. The Plantagenets are more than half mad, I think."

Galiana climbed up into the secret hallway. It smelled old and dry. Musty. It was as dark as the armoire she'd hidden in as a girl.

She almost asked for a candle, but then remembered Rourke had come to her without a light. She'd trust him to lead the way. He was quite familiar with the dark.

He closed the painting behind them and Galiana shut her eyes tightly so that when she opened them again, they'd adjust to the black interior.

Rourke held out his hand and grabbed hers. "Don't

be afraid. Jamie and I used to live in these."

"Ed and Ned would love it here," she whispered, embracing the adventure.

"Did I meet them both?"

"Aye."

"When I moved into your parents' chamber—that was a different twin than the one we caught writing the letter to King Philippe."

"True." Was he angry?

"I always wanted a twin. You could never be lonely."

Galiana's heart lurched to her throat at the admission. "For certes, my lord, the good queen couldn't have survived two of you," she said softly.

His laugh was her reward.

He stopped suddenly, and she collided into his back. "Want to see what kept Jamie and me enthralled for hours at a time?"

He opened a peephole in the wall. "Look."

Galiana peered through the tiny hole and spied a lady applying fresh powder to her bosom. She tapped his arm. "Pervert."

They walked a few more lengths when Gali had a thought. She pulled on Rourke's belt. "Which one belongs to the lady Magdalene?"

He smacked his forehead. "We'll have to cross over to the other tower."

"Can we do that from here?"

"We'll find the Breath of Merlin first."

"Aye," Galiana agreed. "It was just a thought."

"A good thought. One I wished I would've had. I was so determined to avoid the lady that I didn't think to peek at her. You've the makings of a master spy, Gali."

Hearing her pet name fall so easily from his lips did strange things to her already battered heart. "I think I'll make a better guardian," she said. "Hidden away in the wilds of Scotland, where nobody wants my head on a platter."

"You are afraid, my lady?"

"Naturally," she admitted without shame.

"I could love you."

She put her hand to her breast and teased rather than answer seriously, "But you won't."

He stopped. "This is the royal tower. The prince has his apartments here, as does Queen Eleanor—when she's in residence. King Richard, too."

"Prince John's got the tower to himself now? Ample places to hide something precious." She lifted her hand and the ring, which hadn't so much as twinkled for the past few moments, suddenly flashed to life.

"Oh!" She jumped. "We must be close."

"Shh." Rourke held his index finger to his lips. "Someone's passing."

"How can you tell?" Galiana gently pushed him aside and peered through the hole. The royal hallway was stunning.

Gold paint shimmered from the ceiling, and frescoes

TRACI E. HALL

decorated the wall. Flowering plants, in winter—
Galiana shook her head with amazement—blossomed in
ceramic vases. Marble statues of Venus and her cherubs
were clustered in the corner. A door was closing, and she
couldn't see who had just entered the chamber.

"Is the prince's chamber at the end of the hall?" she
whispered.

"Nay, 'tis King Richard's room."

"Someone just went inside. Is there a peephole?"

"Nay. I made the mistake of telling Richard about
the passageways, and he had the hole to his chamber
blocked."

"Smart man," she sighed. "Since I hardly think the
king is secretly staying in his own room, I wonder why
Prince John would violate his brother's privacy."

"He's trying to steal his brother's throne. What is a
bed compared to that?"

"Now who's being sarcastic?" She took a deep
breath. "Which door leads to the treasury?"

"It isn't a real treasury, but Jamie and I called it that
because of all the private jewels the family kept there.
The real treasury is in London."

She put her hand to her throat. "Hardly convenient
when choosing a necklace."

"The life of a royal isn't simple," Rourke said with a
straight face.

Gali giggled before getting back to the subject at
hand. "So what do you propose? Dashing across the

hall and barreling down the door of a locked room?"

"Too noisy." He unhooked a length of tightly coiled rope from his belt and handed it to Galiana.

She took it. "What is this for?" The ring flashed with mystical blue fire. It looked like trapped lightning, and she could almost smell the rain from her vision. "We must hurry."

"I feel the urgency, too."

They stared at one another before Rourke asked, "Are you sure you want to do this? I've bullied you into it. You can walk away right now, and I won't hold it against you. My fight is not your fight."

She curled her upper lip in a deliberate mean face and shook the rope. "I'm tough," she growled. "'Tis my king we're saving. And what kind of guardian will I be if I'm not willing to die to keep the stone safe?"

Rourke stepped back from her mock fierceness. She was wonderful, and he could feel the power radiate from her being. Her eyes glowed, and he saw a bright, un-earthly light flash within them.

He frowned. "Are your eyes green?"

She sniffed in answer. "Rourke. The rope? Am I supposed to wear it? Toss it? Hang myself from it?"

Disconcerted, he grabbed the coil back. "You'll drop into the room from above."

"What?" She rubbed her hands together. "I'm not fond of heights. And I definitely don't care for broken bones."

"You won't break any bones." He waved her complaints

to the side, remembering how he and Jamie had crawled between the floors to find a way inside the room. If the queen had found them out then, they wouldn't have survived till their next birthdays.

By memory alone, he showed Galiana where to climb.

"You won't fit, Rourke," she said.

"Aye, that's why you're going. Keep the rope in your left hand, Gali. You can do it. Quiet, though, so John won't hear you."

He heard her crawl along the ceiling, then find the loose panel leading down into the treasure room. She put it to the side with barely a peep, and then he could do nothing but listen helplessly as she tied the rope around a stud in the wall.

"Must I tie it round my wrist?" she whispered. "What if I fall?"

Taking a calming breath, he answered, "Can you climb down it without slipping?"

"I wish I had my gloves," she said. "You should have told me to—"

"Shh!"

"Sorry," she answered in a hushed tone.

Rourke tugged at the hair falling over his eye. It would be a bleedin' miracle if they got out of this alive.

Every tiny inch she moved tore at his gut, and now he worried she'd skin her palms. He should have suggested gloves. A master spy thought of every possibility. He'd never worked with a novice before.

He waited, holding his breath, wondering if she was sitting on the edge of the ceiling too afraid to grab the rope and descend into the room below. Rourke started to climb up after her, when he heard an impossible sound.

The door across the hall was open, and she was waving to him to come across if he could.

Rourke grinned. She was damn good for a novice. He peeked out the hole as far down as he could, when he saw the door to King Richard's chamber open.

John was coming. His belly clenched tight, and he waved his hands in front of the peephole even though he knew she couldn't see him. Damn, damn—he'd put her in danger.

Was it the prince? He couldn't tell since a heavy cloak with a fur-lined hood blocked his already shadowy view. The blurry person walked with masculine strides, and Rourke put all of his energy into sending Gali a message to shut the door before she got caught.

Miracle of all miracles, she slowly closed the door to the treasury just as the man walked by. As if sensing something out of place, the hooded figure straightened, glancing at the treasury door. Had he heard something? Galiana hadn't made a sound.

Two heartbeats away from jumping out of his hiding spot and slaying the man, royal or no, Rourke watched the man continue on and walk down the stairs, leaving the private apartments.

He'd seemed so familiar. The way he'd held his arm, as if it were sore . . .

Franz.

Rourke let out the breath he'd been holding. Why would Franz be in Richard's room?

Chapter Twenty-One

Rourke searched the hall again.

Empty.

He slowly opened the painting, and stepped out on the carpeted floor. Gali silently opened the door, and he raced on ghostlike feet across the expanse of wood and carpet to where his wife awaited.

"That was too close," he said, grabbing her to him and planting a kiss on her full mouth.

"Aye," she agreed, kissing him back.

"It wasn't the prince in King Richard's chamber; it was Franz."

"I thought I smelled his cologne. 'Tis sweet, for a man."

"Sweet?" Rourke stilled. "You don't think . . ."

Galiana lifted a shoulder. "I don't know. Mayhap they met on crusade."

"But I've seen Franz with women," Rourke protested.

"Some people like both," Galiana said in a pragmatic tone. "Look at King Philippe."

Rourke snapped, "I don't. 'Tis women only for me."

"Women?" There was no mistaking the frosty nip in her tone.

"Never mind." He moved across the room, which was more crowded than he remembered. Or perhaps he'd gotten bigger, or his vision was playing with his memories. "'Tis different," he said, careful to keep his eyes down so he didn't trip on anything.

"I don't see anything that could be the Breath of Merlin."

"Let me look." If it wasn't here . . .

"Richard's room," she said as if reading his mind. "The dust here hasn't been disturbed in a while. All of this seems to have been forgotten."

"How will we get in? The rafters aren't open above the other chambers."

She held out a group of keys. "I found a whole ring in the lock on this side of the door."

"I'll do it," he said, taking the keys. Dread whispered across his shoulders at being in the open hall and not at his stealthy best.

"We go together. We must be together. I feel it." She lifted her hand again, and Rourke could see the eerie glow coming from the ring.

He couldn't argue with old magic.

He opened the door and peered out into the hall. Becoming a shadow, he stayed close to the wall as he ran swiftly toward the kidnapped king's chamber. Galiana copied his every move. Stopping at the very last door, Rourke let the calm that he always felt as he did a job take over. He closed his eyes and let his fingers trace each key until he touched one that felt right.

Opening his eyes, squinting against the pain in his forehead that even dim light brought, he put the key into the lock and turned until he heard a satisfying click.

"How'd you do that?" Galiana's warm, minty breath fanned his face. He almost kissed her again.

"'Tis luck, my lady."

"Nay, some sort of skill. Mayhap a touch of magic. You have beautiful hands, Rourke."

He opened the door and leaned inside, hoping Franz hadn't been having an assignation in the king's chambers.

"A man doesn't have beautiful hands."

She sniffed and followed him inside.

"It's rather gold," she said with awe laced through her tone. "I thought it would be—"

"Plainer?"

"Well, he's never here. It seems a waste to keep a chamber in perfect readiness for someone who might not ever use it." Galiana closed the door and locked it.

"A king is not just 'someone,'" Rourke said, somewhat defensively. His entire life had been about pleasing the royal family. "Well-trained servants dust the room

447

on a monthly basis."

"This would be the perfect place to hide what everybody is searching for," she said, seemingly mesmerized by the frantically flashing ring on her hand. "You would think this would burn, it glows so bright."

"If it hurts, take it off," he ordered with alarm.

She wore a smile as she shook her head. "It doesn't. Besides, I've never felt so close to my sisters before."

"Your sisters?" He looked around as if they'd materialized somewhere in the room.

"They have magic; I told you. Boadicea's magic."

"That." He hadn't believed her at the time. Considering she was wielding a magic ring, and they were in search of a magic stone created from a sacrificial lion cub and a male infant, whose souls were trapped in Merlin's breath . . . He never should have doubted her.

"And now I have it, too."

He heard the pride in her voice. "Magic. Does it change who you are?"

"I don't know, yet. I felt something similar to this while creating my perfumes, and when we . . ."

He followed her as she turned the corner, waiting for what she would say next. Had she felt the power, the magic, when they'd made love?

"Sweet Mary! Ah, Rourke, good heavens—you see this, don't you?"

He shook his head to clear the images of Galiana with her back arched in passion. The point of her index finger glowed with blue magic. A strand of lightning went from the tip of her finger to the murky opaque object in the center of the king's canopied bed.

His knees locked together, and he had the insane urge to kneel before the sacred globe. Now that he knew the history behind the orb, it held a malevolent feel. Were the two innocent babes trapped forever? What would happen if the large orb broke?

Shivers dotted his skin with goose bumps.

Were their infant souls restless? Did the babes choose who would be blinded forever and who was worthy? Fear coated his tongue. Even the gray and brown vision he had now was better than nothing. Dare he risk losing everything?

"Come here, Rourke," Galiana said without a trace of fear. "Look at the way the light shimmers and jumps from one side to the next. The opaque part is clearing; it's like it is welcoming us. You."

"Me?"

"Mayhap it remembers you, from . . ." She frowned. "From before. But that can't be right, can it?"

"Let's grab it and get out of here."

"What's wrong?"

His head pounded, and the blue light from both the ball and the ring seared into his brain. He walked forward, unable to stop himself. He wanted to destroy the orb, to make the agony go away.

"This hurts, damn it." He scrubbed at his eyes, but

the pain worsened until he finally dropped unwillingly to his knees.

He knew without looking that he was at the edge of the bed. The damn orb wanted him kneeling in supplication, and God's nails, he was doing it.

"Rourke?" Concern pitched Gali's voice higher than normal. "What are you doing? Nay—don't touch it!"

"I can't help it. It's drawing me to it. My head . . ." He leaned forward, his forehead on the mattress, his fingers inching toward the Breath of Merlin, though his muscles strained to keep his hands at his sides.

"It could blind you," she breathed, her words thick with fear.

"Aye."

A calming sense descended over him for a second, and no more—but it offered respite from the pain in which he could think clearly. "I have to know if John would be king, or if William should have it all. This is a chance in a lifetime. My father would want me to do it." He thought of all the things he'd taken for granted. All the times he'd worked and sacrificed for the crown, for the royals in his life. It seemed fitting that they drive him mad, in the end.

"I want to do it. Protect yourself, Galiana! Get out of here." He fought to keep his hands on the cover of the bed, his muscles burning as sweat popped out along his brow. Mayhap madness would be a relief from the constant pain in his head.

"I'll not leave you!" she cried.

"Knowledge is power," he breathed out like a tourney horse at the end of a joust. "I would save you if I could." Then it was too late for speech as his hands clasped the globe. It was cold. So cold his teeth chattered hard enough to crack. He was going to die, he thought clearly, and what legacy had he left for his kin? He had no family, he'd not shared his heart with another, and he realized he'd neglected life's true gift. Not power, but love.

His soul leeched from his body into the glowing blue circle of light. The mocking laugh of Merlin echoed in his ears. How had he ever considered himself worthy?

And then Galiana's hands covered his.

Warmth, fiery red and passionate, battled the cold blue for his spiritual essence. Lush greens, so deep and rich he'd never seen them before, wrapped leafy tendrils around his feet. He stood against the wind, and he felt rain, cool rain, not ice any longer, dash his cheeks. He was in the orb, but he wasn't alone.

Galiana stood next to him, and he saw her. She was so beautiful; tears slipped from his eyes. Tall, stately, elegant. She shone with an inner light. Her heart was pure. In the vision, inside the orb, they held hands and walked side by side.

Her hair, a red that glimmered with burnished gold, fell to below her hips. And her eyes were as green as the forest around him. There was no need for words as he told her how beautiful she was. She smiled shyly and

451

urged him to hurry on.

They were to be the witnesses.

The British Isles had sacrificed much for power, and the current kings had forgotten their allegiance to the land. First and foremost, to the land.

Rourke felt a kinship with the lions they passed on the way. He wasn't afraid as they gathered around him and Galiana. Walking among them was right, and he wondered what it meant.

They stopped before a large bonfire, and the flames parted. Merlin, a wizard who was already old at the beginning of the British Isles, said, "You could be one of them."

Galiana's sharp intake of air was the only clue she'd understood.

Rourke gripped her hand, thinking if he let go, he'd be lost in the orb forever.

"I could be king?" The idea was preposterous, and yet . . . tempting.

"Your sire is king," the wizard said impatiently.

"My mother?"

"A king's sister—an abbess, now. You met her in Shaftesbury. She'll be known one day, but not known. She chose to hide her name. But for your sake, she'd come forward."

Rourke's brow furrowed, but his head, praise God, didn't ache.

"By what right of secession?" Rourke asked.

"Secession? Ye have the blood of kings in your veins!

You are a warrior! Ye'd take the bloody throne, starting with Scotland, and moving north, until ye hold the entire isle."

Rourke felt the weight of the crown pressing down on his head, and the pain allowed him to think clearly. He'd never wanted that power for himself—had only gone after it for the love of his father.

"Nay. I don't want it." The words set him free, and Galiana squeezed his hand.

"I knew ye'd say that." The wizard spat three times. "Richard was careless, and, aye, William, too, although he's my favorite. John? Pox on him, eh? But he'll get the crown—eventually," Merlin cackled.

"Eventually?" Galiana asked. "Not now."

"Nay. That fool being held for ransom will get another chance at England. But beware—France cannot take British lands. If that happens, the stone will break and the isle will fall into the sea. That was the bargain that was made, and so it shall be!"

Rourke pulled Galiana to him as the ground beneath his feet shook and rumbled.

"Eleanor." The wizard gestured for Rourke and Galiana to follow him into the fire. "Now there's a lady that was born to power. She's a ruler, that one. If only she'd had a penis, I wouldn't be worried now."

Rourke choked, and tried to blame it on the smoke.

Galiana giggled and elbowed him.

"You're strong like that, Galiana—never forget who

you share blood with! Magic comes in all forms." He flicked his wrist, and a bouquet of lavender filled his hands. He turned, handed one stalk to Galiana, and tossed the rest aside.

"You'll make a fine guardian—if ye don't get killed leavin' the castle. John's furious, now, and he's lookin' to see who stole what he'd stolen. Rourke, yer certain ye don't want the throne? If not by the sword, then by subterfuge. Ye could claim Constance's brat as yer own."

"No." He'd never been more certain of anything.

"Watch your back, then. John is not your only enemy. Ye've heard of a woman scorned?"

Galiana inhaled sharply.

Rourke waved his hand against the mist. "How do we return?"

Merlin threw back his head and laughed, slapping his knee and then bending forward to hold his belly.

Rourke shifted from one foot to the next. "What's so funny?"

"You—worried about how to escape from a magical orb. Magic, boy, magic. I've still got it—though it wanes." His mirth disappeared, and he stomped toward a rocky ledge. He snapped his fingers, and a staff appeared.

"Watch, and witness. King or no, Rourke Wallis, you and all of your seed are charged with protecting Scotland, England, and Wales."

Rourke watched the scene unfold, just as Galiana had told it to Eleanor. The man, offering his infant son for power, and the lion, knowing his time was over. Rourke didn't want the power. He never had. He'd sacrificed enough.

The Breath of Merlin glowed eerie and mystical as it perched on the rock ledge. Merlin waved his staff around, causing more lightning to streak across the storming sky.

"Blessings on you both. Take care, and guard the stone! You must leave the castle immediately. Send Will to Eleanor—she meets with your father even now."

Merlin's voice faded, as did his image, and Rourke felt the loss of power as his body cooled.

When he dared to open his eyes, afraid he'd be blind forever, he saw . . . nothing.

Blinking, he focused on Galiana's voice.

"Rourke? Rourke, you are scaring me! Wake up, wake up!" She shook his shoulder.

He counted each beat of his heart and opened his eyes but a fraction at a time. When he was at thirty, his eyes were half-slit, and he could see shadows. As before. He made himself go slowly, to savor each line as Galiana's face became clear for the first time since they'd met.

Her mouth dropped open in surprise; then she snapped it shut, but she couldn't hold back her happy grin. "You can see!"

He said a prayer of thanks to Merlin for truly opening his eyes. He and Galiana would leave, and love, together.

Reaching out to touch the softest pale rose of her

cheek, he knew he'd never seen a more beautiful woman. "You weren't joking," he said in awe.

She leaned into his touch, her pleasure evident. "Hmm?"

"You. Passably pretty. Beauty being the bane of your existence? I thought you were being sarcastic."

Her eyes widened before she burst out laughing. Rourke knew, as she rose elegantly to her feet, he'd never get tired of watching her. Her chin— "I thought you had a pointy chin, but it's not so bad," he said.

"Not so bad?" She put her hands to her hips. Shapely hips that had welcomed him in love.

God, he thought humbly, was this what love felt like? He wanted to hold Galiana close, to protect her, to worship her . . .

"Ow!" She shook her hand. "The ring stung me!"

"Merlin did say we had to hurry." He could examine his newfound feelings later. When they were safe.

"You'll leave me in Scotland for certes, now. I don't want you to, but you can see again. You are wonderful at what you do; you said so."

"My father wanted me to be a spy. I want to be with you. You've reached inside my cold heart and thawed feelings I thought were dead to me." This time he went ahead and grabbed her, kissing her with all of the passion growing in his soul.

"Rourke," she whispered, her green eyes filled with love. He swore he could see the lush green forest of time in them. "I love you."

She saw the hope sparkle in his golden gray eyes and vowed to tell him ten times a day how much she cared for him. He'd never had anybody to protect his heart from the world.

The ring gave her another sharp sting, longer than the last one.

"We have to go," she said, shaking her injured hand. Rourke reached out for the dull quartz-like stone. No sign of its glowing brightness remained, but Galiana quickly pulled him back from the bed.

"What?"

"Don't touch the orb again." She shivered. "'Tis dangerous to you, now. Are you sure you wouldn't be king?"

"Aye. It must remain our secret, this . . ." Rourke gestured toward the orb."

Galiana couldn't detect any regret in his tone, just relief. She exhaled slowly. "I will guard that secret as closely as I do the Breath of Merlin. Shall we return to the treasury? Our things are there."

"We don't need them. It would be easier to escape the castle through the painting."

She lifted her hand with the ring, which was spitting blue fire. "The Breath of Merlin may be quiet, but this thing won't shut up. We must hurry."

Rourke grabbed the coverlet from the bed. Its rich cloth of red and gold was decorated with prancing lions. "What better royal shroud?"

"'Tis perfect." She wrapped the orb in the cloth and knotted it tight. "Danger is coming." She could feel it in her bones. She ran to the door, pulling Rourke by the hand. Racing down the hall at a speed she'd never dared go in her heels before, she stopped in the center. To the left was the treasury; to the right, the painting with its secret hallways. Rourke turned to the painting, but Galiana's instincts urged her to hide elsewhere.

Her heart pounded with fear, and her mouth was so dry she couldn't swallow. Tugging Rourke closer than a shadow, she chose the treasury. The knob turned magically beneath her fingers, and they went inside. She slowly, slowly, shut the door behind them. Gesturing for Rourke to get behind a trunk, which he refused to do—stubborn man—she pressed her ear to the door.

Someone was on the other side.

If whoever was out there turned the knob, she and Rourke wouldn't be guardians of anything. They'd be dead.

The keys!

Rourke pressed them into her hand. She slipped the key into the lock without a sound, praise all the angels, and held her breath.

The knob jiggled. It turned.

The key held as the ring on her finger warmed to an uncomfortable degree. She was the guardian now, and it was up to her and Rourke to see that the Breath of Merlin saved Britain from falling into the deep sea.

It was a simple chore, aye? She lifted her chin and

felt, rather than heard, Rourke's chuckle.

The door handle stopped moving. The sweet scent of nasturtium assaulted her senses.

Franz.

The ring remained warm, so she stayed very quiet.

"Merde."

She heard the word, and then rushed footsteps ran down the stairs just as the painting across the hall creaked the tiniest bit.

For a deserted hallway, the place was busy.

John's cologne, that awful sandalwood and ash, announced his arrival.

She was too afraid to breathe.

Her pulse battered against her neck like a trapped butterfly.

Rourke's tension was tangible, and she could feel him brace his body for battle.

Whistling, John made his way down the hall toward what Gali hoped would be his own chamber . . . What if he entered Richard's rooms and noticed the mess she and Rourke had made? Or worse, the missing orb?

Gali's mind whirled with possibilities. What if Franz worked for John and was even now telling the prince his suspicions of her and Rourke . . . They had to leave. Immediately.

The door to Prince John's bedroom opened, then closed, and Galiana carefully expelled her pent-up breath as the ring on her finger cooled.

She turned, pointing to the coil of rope in the ceiling.

Rourke shook his head, and she easily read his expression. We aren't coming back here.

Closing her eyes, trusting the ring with her and Rourke's lives, she opened the door and darted across the hall to the painting. She felt Rourke behind her as she ran blindly through the secret hallways. "My chamber?"

Rourke whispered, "No time to pack. I'll buy you whatever you want. Let's just get to the horses."

"We'll need Will," she said.

"I have a feeling he'll be in the stables."

Not only was the faithful squire there, but their horses were already saddled. Galiana noted her cask and bags tied to the leather seat and leaned in to kiss Will's cheek. "How did you know?"

Will shrugged, discomfited. "I had a dream. Weird old man with a beard. Bossy, he was. I was half afraid ye wouldn't come, and more afraid ye would."

Galiana laughed, accepting and believing in the strange turn of events. "You know, then, that you must ride to Queen Eleanor. Tell her all is well. And ask her to speak to King William; she'll know what about."

They mounted, and Galiana's ring warmed. She squirmed with urgency.

"I know—we must hurry," Rourke said.

"What is the great rush?" a mocking voice asked.

Galiana wished she'd walked away from the castle and never come to the stables for their horses. How had the prince found them out so quickly? Franz. Poor Rourke, to be betrayed by a friend after all.

Prince John stepped forward into the light and raked Galiana with a sharp, powerful gaze. "You didn't shut the painting in your hurry to leave the royal apartments. Where are you off to now?" He clucked his teeth and rubbed his manicured beard. The jewels on his rings glittered with the malice of their owner. Galiana hated the smell of sandalwood.

Rourke brought his horse next to hers. "Painting? I don't know what you are talking about." Rourke shrugged. "It wasn't us in the royal apartments, my prince," he lied as smooth as glass. "There are guards posted at either side of the stairs preventing anyone going up."

Prince John arched both his brows and gestured to the man standing behind him in the shadows. "You've skill at outing a liar," the prince said. Galiana's dismay heightened when she recognized William Marshall.

Was he one of the prince's loyal minions, turning his back on his king in favor of immediate power? She'd thought better of him. Relying on her training as a lady to see her through whatever happened next, she lifted her chin and refused to lower her gaze.

"Do you deny the prince's accusation?" William Marshall asked.

Galiana held her tongue. Rourke, glib liar that he could be, spoke for them both. "Aye. We've been enjoying our time together," he reached over to put his hand possessively on her neck, his thumb caressing the love bite she'd forgotten about.

This time she did lower her gaze.

William Marshall chuckled. "Ah, well, and where was it that you trysted, then? For certes, I'd not risk my health being where I knew it would get me hanged if I had such a lovely lady at my side."

Prince John huffed. "Where then did ye go?"

William Marshall walked forward, his power that of a caged mastiff. Gali shivered as he tapped her leg. "Tell us, lady, where you went for your lover's kiss."

Was he deliberately giving her an order she didn't have to lie to? Without any acting at all, her cheeks flamed as she recalled her wanton behavior before the fire. She swallowed. "The manor lodge, kind sir."

William Marshall gave her a smile and a pat on the knee. "She's tellin' the truth, my prince. Besides, you remember the stories Richard told of playin' in those secret halls as a boy. It was probably a young page takin' his turn at 'bravin' the halls; they're supposed to be haunted, aye?"

He laughed, and the prince was forced to laugh with him.

Galiana realized then that William Marshall knew it very well could have been Rourke in the halls, but he was playing his own game, and it coincided with theirs. Hope rose like the sun at dawn.

"I'll see what's in those bags," the prince demanded. "Why are ye leaving the castle in such a rush, if you have nothing to hide?"

Just then, Jamie and Father Jonah walked into the crowded stables.

"Well, there ye are, my lady!" The priest waved as if he hadn't seen her in years.

Scowling, Jamie bellowed, "Where have ye been? I pay for the last three rooms in Runnymeade, and you're nowhere to be found. Being married has ye whipped like a dog, Rourke."

Rourke scowled back. "Watch your tongue, man."

Galiana clapped. "Rooms!"

"Rooms? Why do you need other rooms?" The prince crossed his arms. "There is plenty of space here at the castle."

"Well," the priest said in hushed voice. "After Godfrey committed suicide, my lady Galiana felt like she and my lord Rourke had overstayed their wlecome. You were so angry." The old man shuddered.

"And if they had a room ta share," Jamie added belligerently, "they wouldn't have ta sneak off to an old lodge, now would they?"

Galiana sucked in a breath at Jamie's daring.

A loud trumpeting horn blew, and a liveried page stood at the stable entrance.

"In God's name, now what?" Prince John said, throwing his hands upward with disgust.

"'Tis the dowager Queen Eleanor and King William of Scotland, requesting everyone to come outside, where there is more room."

The young boy blew on the horn again for good measure before ducking out of sight.

Galiana felt the loss of warmth as Rourke removed his hand from her neck and quickly reached over to clasp his hand in hers, or at least as much of it as would fit.

"I love you," she said, wanting him to feel her support for what was to come.

He squeezed her fingers once and nodded. "And I you, my fair lady."

"That's sweet," Prince John drolled sarcastically, turning on his heel. "What could my mother possibly want now?"

William Marshall chuckled and led the way. "Let's go find out, my prince."

Gali and Rourke dismounted so they were on foot with the others. Will led their horses out and stood back, next to Jamie and Father Jonah. Rourke handed Will the satchel he'd purloined on their way out of the castle. The squire had no idea the satchel he carried so carelessly held the Breath of Merlin, a stone that could make a king.

A magical orb that could foretell Britain's future.

Stepping out into the grayish day, Galiana stood proudly next to her husband as they faced the king and queen, who were seated on horseback. She was very aware that Rourke was meeting his father for the first time knowing the king was truly his sire.

He remained stoic, of course. Rourke had many dark

wells of emotion, and she planned on delving them all.

A delicious shiver raced up her spine, and she kept her fingers entwined with his. She wondered if her palm would fit around—

"Behave," he said from the corner of his mouth.

"I don't have to," she whispered back, thrilled with her newfound power. "You've broken the curse, my lord."

"What bloody curse?" Rourke turned and grabbed her shoulders, concern in his gorgeous eyes.

"Beauty's curse. You never saw my beauty, and you love me without it. I was trapped by fear that nobody would ever see me, and yet—you loved me when you thought I had a pointy chin. And you gave me magic."

He grinned, bringing his mouth a hair's breadth away from hers. His teeth shone white behind his plush lips, and she sighed with contentment.

"You're sure I love you?"

Unable to contain her emotions for one heartbeat longer, she launched herself at her warrior and held on tight. "I would wager my life on it."

A screech sounded from the castle steps as a stunning woman ran down the stairs with a dagger in her hand. "He's mine! Mine, mine, mine!"

Rourke dropped Galiana behind his large body, and she was forced to peek between his ribcage and his raised arm to see her enemy.

Lady Magdalene was lovely, if a man was attracted to crazed women with murderous tendencies.

"Kill her! Harold, damn your eyes, kill her—the thieving bitch stole my man."

Jamie chuckled, unconcerned, and shared a jest about Rourke's animal attraction to the female species with King William, who, Galiana, noticed, preened proudly before clearing his throat.

"Who is Harold?" the king asked.

The crowd all turned toward the large knight, who was even more wild-eyed and unkempt than usual. He glared across the small expanse of yard at Rourke; then his gaze landed upon Galiana. She winced.

He wanted her—dead or otherwise.

Rourke grasped the hilt of his sword, challenging his enemy, once and for all.

The queen leaned across their horses to whisper something in the king's ear.

"Dead, eh? Sir Godfrey killed Sir Robert, then jumped from the ramparts? A knight doesn't commit suicide. Bollocks." He listened and nodded some more, then scratched his brow.

"Lord Rourke, two of your men are dead," the king pronounced.

"True. And Franz is missing," Rourke said.

"This woman"—King William gestured toward Magdalene—"has ordered Lord Harold to kill your"—he stumbled over the word—"er, wife. What do you say to this?"

Rourke kept his gaze steady upon his father's as he said, "My liege, I see that the lady Magdalene wears the colors of Brittany on her belt. A pin with the device was found next to my murdered knight, Robert. At first I thought it was his, but now I wonder if this order to murder is not the first one the lady has given to Harold."

Oh, Galiana thought. He is good.

Harold lunged forward, his sword half-drawn.

Galiana snapped her fingers. She remembered where she'd seen that design before. She eyed the line of people watching the scene unfold. Constance.

The duchess of Brittany proudly stated, "Aye, these are my colors, but I gave no orders to have anyone killed."

Magdalene screeched before Constance quelled her with a royal glare.

"Lord Harold is leaving," Gali said in an aside to Rourke. "He runs with a limp. An injury from when you felled him from his horse, mayhap?"

King William overheard her and ordered Lord Harold to be stopped. The royal knights captured the man immediately.

Magdalene held a hand to her forehead but waited to hear what was said next before actually fainting.

Rourke replaced his sword in its scabbard and purposefully marched before Harold, who strained against the knights' hold. "Did you kill Robert and Godfrey on the duchess's orders?"

Harold spat at Rourke's feet, and Galiana wished she could slay the rogue herself.

Her husband turned to Magdalene and held out his

hand. "I never promised you love," he said. "I was as honest with you as I could be. Why would you want me dead?"

"Never you," she cried, clasping his hand to her breast. "When Robbie sent word of your marriage, I—I couldn't think straight." The woman had tears trailing from both beautiful eyes. "Prince John wanted ye married as a test of your loyalty, but it could've been to me! I begged Constance for you, but she said nay."

Galiana looked at Constance, whose lovely face seemed carved from marble.

Magdalene kissed Rourke's fingertips. "I love you. I could help ye. I'd be a better wife than her, or Co— I just would be," she cried.

"Why did Robert die?" Rourke tugged his fingers from Magdalene's grasp and faced Harold.

"I don't know what ye're talking about." Harold strained against the knights' hold.

Rourke reached inside his tunic. "You're saying this isn't yours?" He tossed the enameled brooch at the vanquished knight's feet. Harold cursed.

Magdalene cried, "It was all Harold's idea; it was his fault."

The gruff knight tensed. "Lady Magdalene ordered Lady Galiana dead. Robert wouldn't follow my instructions, saying he wanted a directive from Constance. He challenged me, and I had to kill him. It was self-defense, Rourke."

Galiana could see her husband didn't believe that,

not exactly, but he nodded sagely and said, "Well, Godfrey must have witnessed the foul deed and decided to take advantage of an opportunity for blackmail. He has a wife and bairns, and not a lot of extra to provide for them." He looked back at her and winked.

Her belly flipped with lust. Rourke was in his element as he put the pieces together. Pointing at Magdalene, he said, "Rather than pay the blackmail and let Constance know what you'd ordered done behind her back, and in her name, you thought it would be an easy matter to kill Godfrey instead."

Caught out, Magdalene burst into true sobs.

Rourke turned back to Harold and shrugged. "You killed because you love Magdalene."

"Nay!" Magdalene said through her tears. "That can't be."

Harold scratched his nose. "I admit to nothing."

"My liege"—Rourke faced the king and queen—"if I may offer a solution? Sir Robert had no family, and it seems his loyalty was not to me but to Brittany."

Constance dipped her head slightly.

"Godfrey's crime was wanting to provide for his family. I will send a gift to Godfrey's widow on behalf of his service to me."

Galiana sighed at her husband's attempt to right a wrong, and protect the innocent. He had honor, indeed.

"Might I suggest that you wed Magdalene to Harold, and banish them from England? I want no more blood on my hands."

"No!" Magdalene yelled, running to Constance and falling at her best friend's feet.

The royals exchanged a quick glance before Queen Eleanor nodded regally. Prince John agreed, relief on his brow. Galiana didn't want to know what secrets John kept. Constance turned her back on Magdalene and accepted Prince John's arm.

Gali closed her eyes in empathy, knowing that the passion she felt for her husband would be enough to make her consider murdering another who might stand in their way. But the difference was, she wouldn't do it. Magdalene would have to make her peace with God.

Lord Harold, and his stench, would be earthly punishment enough.

John's malicious glare, coupled with the furious stare from Constance, sent warning vibes from her scalp to her feet. She and Rourke had made enemies this day, and they were best away from court. She wouldn't miss it—but would Rourke? It had been his entire life.

Rourke came to her, wrapping his arm possessively around her shoulders.

"I'm married to a woman I love. I am not going to set her aside. I request permission to man a fortress in Scotland. The place"—he gave his sire a steady look—"calls to my blood."

The queen tightened her lips, but the king shrugged, as if he'd never had designs for putting Rourke on the throne. Galiana was tempted to punch him in the nose, but Rourke grabbed her hand and kissed her fingers.

Queen Eleanor casually looked over the saddlebags on their mounts, her gaze sliding over Galiana as if they'd never met, though their meeting had just been that morn. She was good, Gali thought. Rourke had learned how to keep secrets from a master. Franz suddenly pushed through the crowd, his face sickly and drawn. He walked directly to Queen Eleanor.

The queen bent down as he whispered up into her ear, and she smiled.

The Frenchman wouldn't look at either Galiana or Rourke as he mounted a horse to follow the queen, who lifted an unconcerned shoulder. "I've asked Franz to rejoin my service, on behalf of King Richard. Do you mind, Rourke?"

Her husband stiffened next to her as he lied, "Not at all, my queen. My thanks for the use of him."

"Scotland, Rourke, is cold as a witch's teat," the queen announced with a cheeky grin. "Dress warm, and keep your wife"—Galiana curtsied as the queen finally smiled at her—"safe. Guard her well."

The king dismounted before Rourke, and Galiana felt her husband tense, though his expression remained the same.

William was as handsome as sin, his hair auburn instead of Rourke's rich brown, but with the same golden highlights. His eyes flashed with the same golden depths.

Gali could see why this man would have been Merlin's favorite to lead, but Fate was whimsical, and none could tell the future for certain.

"You are quite beautiful, my lady," King William said.

"I fear my chin is rather pointy, my liege." She accepted his offered hand, making sure he saw the ring on her finger.

Rourke snorted.

King William's brow arched as he asked, "You're willing to rot away in the damp mist of Scotland?"

She pressed as close to Rourke as she dared. "Aye. Well, I'd rather not rot, actually."

The king looked from her to Rourke and shrugged. "'Tis obviously a love match, and who am I to stand in the way of love? Stay at your post, and serve me well."

The king got back on his horse and waved to the crowd, which continued to grow. They broke into applause, and without thinking, Galiana turned and bowed, urging Rourke to do the same

"This is where we exit the stage, my lord."

He was laughing, and that unholy glint in his eye made her wish they were alone. "I agree; it would be a good time to leave"—he inched them closer to their mounts—"before Prince John remembers to go through our bags."

472

Two days later, Will raced back from where he'd been scouting ahead for a village to stay the night. "There's travelers coming, bearing a green and white banner. Do we fight?"

Galiana perked up from her doze. She and Rourke were taking full advantage of their private sleeping quarters, and sleep was the last thing on her mind in the cozy evenings, when the two of them were learning everything they could about one another.

Her body ached deliciously, she thought with a slight stretch.

"Green and white? Those are the Montehue colors, Rourke."

Rourke groaned. "Your family would storm Windsor?"

"Of course they would come to save me."

"You don't need to be saved."

"That's true, but they don't know that."

"How would they know to find you here?"

Did he sound guilty? For taking her away? Galiana sniffed daintily and looked up at the sky. "Well, uh, Mam sometimes has these . . . well, they're intuitions . . . and she's occasionally right, so . . ." She exhaled.

"I thought you said you and your mother didn't get any magic."

"I didn't lie, my lord, so stop looking at me like that. 'Tis just a bit of a hunch, and not always accurate. One time she made my father drain the pond for treasure, but there was nothing."

"Treasure." He scoffed.

Galiana took the glove from her hand and waved her ring. "You can't tell me you don't believe in treasure."

"You are the only treasure I need." He leaned over and kissed her on the mouth.

She smiled. "You'll like my family."

He looked uncertain. "Your father is a big man, you said?"

"Aye. Viking ancestors."

Rourke pinched the bridge of his nose as Jamie and Will looked to him for direction. "Just . . . wait," he said.

Father Jonah wore a large grin as her brothers galloped toward them, twin blond hellions on matching chestnut steeds.

Galiana reached over to grab each one into a hug, the horses jostling for space. "Brats!" she said over her laughter.

"We're here to rescue ye," Ed announced, glaring at Rourke. Her husband kept his expression distant.

"Aye, come on, Gali, and see Mam, afore our father tears the lord's head from his shoulders."

"Ned." Galiana lightly punched her brother on the arm. "Lord Rourke is my husband."

"We were too late," Ed cried, racing back to her parents.

"I love him!" Galiana yelled at the top of her lungs so her father wouldn't pierce Rourke through.

Her father lowered his drawn sword, and her mother

started clapping.

"You do?" Dierdre cried, cantering to her daughter with an arm outstretched for a hug. "You love him, my beautiful darling?"

"Aye, Mam." Galiana kissed her mother's cheek, then reached out her hand for her husband's. He smiled, that slow uplifting of lips that made fools of women everywhere. "This is Rourke Wallis."

"Oh, my," her mother simpered.

Rourke pulled a rolled letter from his tunic and handed it to her mother.

"Rourke?" Galiana raised her voice. "Why do you have my letter to my family? Did you read it?"

"Before you lose your temper, Gali, I never broke the seal. I thought you were possibly sending a note to King Richard . . . but I couldn't betray your privacy."

"Galiana, don't yell," her mother reprimanded as she read.

"You thought I was a spy?" Galiana hefted her chin, letting the anger fade as she remembered his job for the royals. It had been his duty to ensure she could be trusted. "You didn't break the seal? Really, my lord?"

"I was beginning to love you, even then," he said.

"Oh!" Her mother waved the missive. "She loved you, too. See here? It was fate. Welcome to the family, Rourke Wallis." Lady Deirdre turned to the twins. "You didn't tell me your sister's rapist was so good-looking, nor titled . . ."

The boys snorted, and her father bellowed, "Deirdre! Stand back. Let me meet this man who thinks to steal my daughter away from the bosom of her family."

Galiana pushed her horse forward, but Rourke wouldn't let her take the sting of her father's wrath.

"Lord Montehue," Rourke said smoothly. "I'm Lord Rourke Wallis, and these are my men, Jamie Fitzhugh and Will Montgomery. 'Tis true, your daughter was a prize. But in the weeks since we've met, I've come to realize the true treasure is in her love."

Galiana and her mother both sighed with pleasure.

"God's bones, I've ridden these past days with bloodshed on me mind, and, and, what in the hell are ye doin'?"

Rourke handed over his sword, hilt first, to her father, and Galiana knew there would be peace.

"Damn it, man." Her father accepted the sword, then searched his daughter's face. "Ye're sure?"

"Aye, Daddy, I love him."

Her father handed the sword back. "Welcome to the family, son. Come on—we're but a day's ride from Falcon Keep. Ye might as well meet the rest of our growing clan."

Rourke nodded sagely, Jamie and Will on his heels. Her brothers galloped circles around Father Jonah, and her mother chattered about Celestia and the baby, a boy named James, and Nicholas, and Ela, who adored the baby and wouldn't let the infant out of her sight, and . . .

Galiana listened to her mother's voice as she watched

her normally smooth husband try and figure out his place in their family. The smile teasing the corners of his mouth made her happy, because he was happy. The ring warmed against her finger.

The year began with a new beginning and a prayer for an adventure, and now she was the queen-appointed guardian of the mystical Breath of Merlin. Her beauty hadn't gained her happiness; her hair and her eyes hadn't won her Rourke's love. Her warrior's spirit had captured her knight, and she vowed to forever be the guardian of his heart.

Epilogue

April 1194

Rourke rode next to his liege as they left Winchester. "How do you think it went?"

King William, a born horseman, adjusted his seat. "Almost three weeks with Richard. 'Twas good he was crowned again. Britain needs him to be king."

Rourke agreed. "Naming Arthur as heir helped, too. The lines are clear. Do you think Richard will stay and rule?"

"The man is restless, a Plantagenet." King William spat into the dirt, as if that explained everything. "Who knows?"

Rourke sighed. The ways of the royals were not his ways, though he understood the lure of power. He'd not missed his spying days; being able to act as his liege's guard occasionally let him keep his hand in . . .

In the event that balance of power should shift again, and Britain should need a king.

"How's your lady?"

"Excellent. I miss her, and the twins."

"Girls." His liege shook his head.

"I like my girls," Rourke defended.

"Aye, I suppose," King William's eyes shimmered with mirth. "Ye're too easy, son. Do you mind if I ride home with you? I'd like to see the babes."

"You have your own daughter," Rourke said, secretly happy his father cared.

"She's attached to her mother; that's the pity. I'll be able to forge an alliance with Germany, or France, mayhap next year."

Rourke nodded, glad his daughters didn't need to be pawns. Red-haired beauties with magic in their tiny fingertips, they had a royal dispensation, too. They'd be raised to guard the Breath of Merlin and the future of Britain.

He sort of felt sorry for the men who thought to conquer them.

"Race you?" He didn't wait for his father to answer, but dug his heels into his horse's flanks. For the first time in his life, Rourke was a whole man. Above all royal ties, he valued the woman who, with beauty and honor, shared his life.

Galiana, I'm coming home.

TRACI E. HALL

Traci E. Hall began her love affair with words long before being able to spell. Rhyming led to creative thinking because no matter how hard you try, there is no word that rhymes with orange. Combining imagination with her flair for vocabulary eventually segued into bad poetry, and finally, story telling. Creating ghosts and things that go bump in the night, adding a happy ending and true love, all make Traci thrilled that floral design didn't really work out.

Traci is the current president of Florida Romance Writers, a chapter of Romance Writers of America, and a member of Spacecoast Authors of Romance. She has been interviewed in both radio and newspaper medias. Traci credits volunteering and networking for helping her reach her goals, and her blog Babes for making the journey so fun.

Traci is fascinated with history. She's been known to spend more time than allotted on research because she gets caught up in old diaries or papers that are as compelling as *People* magazine.

Married for almost twenty years, Traci believes in the power of love and happily-ever-afters. She has two teenagers, who have hungry friends, and she's learned to whip up cheese quesadillas for twenty in ten minutes or less. In her down time, Traci likes to read, or go walking on the beach, or maybe play triple yahtzee with her hubby while listening to Bowling For Soup. S he is addicted to cheesy B horror films, and her collection includes: *Shawn Of The Dead, Dead And Breakfast*, and of course, *The Lost Boys*.

www.traciehall.com

TRACI E. HALL

Love's Magic

It is 1192. Celestia Montehue is the odd-eyed misfit in a family of flame-haired goddesses descended from notorious Queen Boadicea. While her sisters are tall and beautiful, she, the eldest, is blond and petite, with one green and one blue eye. The only thing she has in common with the family legend is her magical healing ability. Constantly fighting for her place among her siblings, she refuses to settle for less than her due. Coming to accept no one will ever be able to love her for who she is, she vows never to marry.

Nicholas Le Blanc is a haunted man. Though trained as a knight under the Baron Peregrine's name, his childhood in a monastery has convinced him he is a bastard. Then, on crusade, his caravan is ambushed; all men are lost and the sacred relic they carried is stolen. Nicholas is captured and suffers a year of torture, ultimately escaping . . . but only after being forced to kill a woman to win his freedom. Guilt poisons him as surely as the hidden wounds in his soul.

An arranged marriage does not bode happiness for the two tortured souls. Nor does Celestia's new home, a broken down keep—haunted by the ghost of Nicholas' mother, a suicide—and a stagnant green moat. Then a maid is murdered and a curse revealed. Worse, Celestia has fallen in love with her tormented husband. Will they both be doomed? Or is there healing, indeed, in *Love's Magic*?

ISBN# 978-193383627-0
Mass Market Paperback/Paranormal Romance
US $7.95 / CDN $9.95
AVAILABLE NOW
www.traciehall.com

TRACI E. HALL

Boadicea's Legacy

Ela Montahue is a talented sorceress with the ability to heal, but distressed over a complicated ancestral legacy. Long ago, a mystical woman known as Boadicea, the famed queen of the Iceni tribe, issued a difficult decree.

As her descendant, Ela must wed for love, not practicality, or she will forfeit her supernatural power. In medieval England this is not a socially acceptable order to follow. For her family's sake, she should marry Lord Thomas de Havel, a vile landholder with a cruel streak and a desire to see slavery reinstated—a man with good connections to King John's court. This arrangement would put the Montehues in a safe position in the new regime. The stakes are high—her dignity, her pride, and possibly her life in childbirth.

When Ela refuses this repulsive marital transaction, Thomas de Havel abducts her and wages battle against her father in retaliation. Only Osbert Edyvean, a knight with the highest creed—honor, faith, and logic—can save her and preserve her gift. A businessman for the Earl of Norfolk, Osbert has been paid to find Boadicea's spear. Rather than bring back this obscure artifact, he rescues Ela, intending to take her to the earl and obtain his parcel of land.

Wary of the supernatural aura surrounding this woman, the admirable knight fights his overwhelming passion for a beautiful lady he wants to protect . . . and love. This is Boadicea's true legacy.

ISBN# 978-160542078-3

Mass Market Paperback/Paranormal Romance

US $7.95 / CDN $8.95

JUNE 2010

www.traciehall.com

Garden of the Moon
Elizabeth Sinclair

In the year 1850, Sara Wade is a single woman living with her parents.

But Sara isn't just any woman. Sara has an extraordinary gift: She speaks with ghosts.

Ashamed of her daughter's "affliction," Patricia Wade sends Sara away to live alone at Harrogate Plantation, bequeathed to Sara by her adored grandmother. Set among towering, ancient oak trees and a garden so lush and beautiful it rivals Eden itself, Harrogate represents a haven for Sara—a place to escape where she won't be scrutinized and reprimanded for every move she makes.

But Harrogate holds more than Sara's freedom. Within Harrogate's borders abide two ghosts: one who is determined to win her heart, and another who will stop at nothing to ensure that never happens.

Destiny awaits in the *Garden of the Moon*.

ISBN# 978-193383698-0
Mass Market Paperback/Paranormal Romance
US $7.95 / CDN $8.95
DECEMBER 2009
www.elizabethsinclair.com

A Lost Touch of Magic

Amy Tolnitch

Veiled by the mists of the highlands are tales of beautiful, magical, and sometimes dangerous worlds. One such realm, Paroseea, dwells hidden within the stone walls of a medieval fortress, Castle MacCoinneach. Yet danger has escaped paradise and stalks the halls of Castle MacCoinneach seeking vengeance, patiently waiting for the return of the fallen laird.

You must return.

Those words, uttered by the ghost of Padruig MacCoinneach's beloved sister, send him back to the highlands and a life he forswore. To save his remaining sister and aid his clan, Padruig will do anything. He never expected that he would have to marry his ally's daughter, whom he deems both a reckless child and a potent temptation.

You are the price.

With these callous words, Padruig destroys a fantasy Aimili de Grantham has long nurtured, created from her memories of Padruig himself. A cool, dismissive stranger has replaced the golden man of her dreams, a stranger she must wed. Worse, the fey part of her senses that evil lurks in the shadows of Castle MacCoinneach, and she has nowhere to turn.

One true laird and one of fey blood.

Strangers they may be, but Padruig and Aimili are destined to join together to defeat a force beyond their imaginings. It will take trust, faith, and most of all, love to save themselves, their clan, and discover . . . A Lost Touch of Magic.

ISBN# 978-193475551-8

Mass Market Paperback/Paranormal Romance

US $7.95 / CDN $8.95

AVAILABLE NOW

www.amytolnitch.com

THE DREAM THIEF

HELEN A. ROSBURG

Someone is murdering young, beautiful women in mid-sixteenth century Venice. Even the most formidable walls of the grandest villas cannot keep him out, for he steals into his victims' dreams. Holding his chosen prey captive in the night, he seduces them … to death.

Now Pina's cousin, Valeria, is found dead, her lovely body ravished. It is the final straw for Pina's overbearing fiance', Antonio, and he orders her confined within the walls of her mother's opulent villa on Venice's Grand Canal. It is a blow not only to Pina, but to the poor and downtrodden in the city's ghettos, to whom Pina has been an angel of charity and mercy. But Pina does not chafe long in her lavish prison, for soon she too begins to show symptoms of the midnight visitations; a waxen pallor and overwhelming lethargy.

Fearing for her daughter's life, Pina's mother removes her from the city to their estate in the country. Still, Pina is not safe. For Antonio's wealth and his family's power enable him to hide a deadly secret. And the murderer manages to find his intended victim. Not to steal into her dreams and steal away her life, however, but to save her. And to find his own salvation in the arms of the only woman who has ever shown him love.

ISBN# 978-193281520-7

Mass Market Paperback/Paranormal

US $6.99 / CDN $9.99

AVAILABLE NOW

www.helenrosburg.com

KILL ZONE

VICKI HINZE

Psychologist Morgan Cabot commands a special military support team that provides a unique service. While they are highly trained for military combat, their special abilities don't require training—they are gifts. Dr. Cabot and her teammates, Taylor Lee and Jazie Craig, are "highly intuitive": they hear, feel, and see things that others can't. They are the Special Abilities Team, and they function outside of normal protocol—and the American public can never know of their existence.

The Secretary of Defense of the United States has called upon Cabot's team to stop Thomas Kunz, a sadistic terrorist who specializes in black market arms sales and intelligence brokering.

Kunz's brand of terrorism threatens the United States on multiple levels—his funding is infinite and his reach is global. His modus operandi, using doubles to infiltrate and gather classified information, puts him in a unique position to make the fears of every American citizen a reality.

Colonel Jackson Stern and his brother, Bruce, a biological warfare expert, have become Kunz's lastest targets. When Bruce's wife is found stabbed to death, Jackson dedicates himself to a quest for the truth.

Will Morgan's team help Jackson uncover Kunz's secret plans before it is too late? Or will the most secretive terrorist organization in the world transform America into a terrifying and deadly *Kill Zone*?

ISBN# 978-193475561-7

Mass Market Paperback/Suspense

US $7.95 / CDN $8.95

AVAILABLE NOW

www.vickihinze.net

DO YOU BELIEVE IN MAGIC?

ANN MACELA

According to lore, an ancient force called the soulmate imperative brings together magic practitioners and their mates. They always nearly fall into each other's arms at first sight. Always . . . or so the story goes.

But what happens if they don't? What happens when one mate rejects the other—in fact won't have anything to do with him? Who doesn't even believe in magic to begin with?

Computer wizard Clay Morgan is in just such a position. Francie Stevens has been badly hurt by a charming and good looking man and has decided to avoid any further involvements. Although the hacker plaguing her company's system forces her into an investigation led by the handsome practitioner, she vows to keep her distance from Clay.

The imperative has other ideas, however, and so does Clay. He must convince Francie that magic exists and he can wield it. It's a prickly problem. Especially when Francie uses the imperative itself against him in ways neither it, nor Clay, ever anticipated.

ISBN# 978-193383616-4

Mass Market Paperback/Paranormal Romance

US $7.95 / CDN $9.95

AVAILABLE NOW

www.annmacela.com

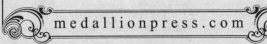

Want to know what's going on with
your favorite author or what new releases
are coming from Medallion Press?

Now you can receive breaking news,
updates, and more from Medallion Press
straight to your cell phone, e-mail, instant
messenger, or Facebook!

For more information
about other great titles from
Medallion Press, visit